THE
PRICE OF
PARADISE

THE PRICE OF PARADISE

SUSANA LÓPEZ RUBIO

TRANSLATED BY ACHY OBEJAS

amazon crossing

Previously published as *El Encanto* by Espasa in Spain in 2017. Translated from Spanish by Achy Obejas. First published in English by AmazonCrossing in 2019.

Published by AmazonCrossing, Seattle

www.apub.com

Amazon, the Amazon logo, and AmazonCrossing are trademarks of Amazon.com, Inc., or its affiliates.

ISBN-13: 9781542093620 (hardcover)
ISBN-10: 1542093627 (hardcover)
ISBN-13: 9781542043571 (paperback)
ISBN-10: 1542043573 (paperback)

Cover design by Shasti O'Leary Soudant

Printed in the United States of America

First edition

For my grandfather, for giving his name to the protagonist.
And for Alberto, always.

PART I

CHAPTER 1

PATRICIO

1947

The first thing I realized when I stepped onto the pier in Havana was that I wasn't dressed right for Cuban weather. None of us who got off the ship were wearing the right clothes. My wool pants and jacket made my skin itch, and the hat that had so many times protected me from snow in Asturias now threatened to boil my brains under the tropical sun. In contrast to the Cubans—men in linen suits and women in print dresses—we were like a sweaty flock of sheep. I looked with envy at the customs agent. His short-sleeved white shirt was the living image of comfort. As we waited, our documents in hand, a mulata secretary, with bare legs and a dress that showed off her naked shoulders, provoked hoots and whistles from the men in line. That was a considerable achievement, given how exhausted and hungry we were after more than forty days squeezed into tiny bunk beds with mush as our only nourishment.

"If you don't stop with the wolf whistles, I'm gonna have to smash a piano on your heads!" she said.

A Galician gentleman at my side read my mind. "Ay, carallo! The women here have more temper than God has talent."

The customs agent waved me over. "Name?"

"Patricio."

"Surnames?"

"Rubio Gamella."

"Age?"

"Nineteen."

"Spanish?"

"Yes."

"Reason for your journey?"

I was tempted to tell him the truth: "See here, sir, the reason is there's so much misery in Spain that we have to dunk our bread in puddles, there are no cats left in my town because we've eaten all the rats, the Republicans killed my mother because she had a cousin who was a nun hiding in our house, and then the Nationalists killed my father because he refused to bend his knee before a portrait of the caudillo. I have no family left, but I don't wanna spend the rest of my life breaking my back in the mines, devoured by lice, and I sold my grandmother's wedding ring—may she rest in peace—so I could buy a third-class ticket on a ship and start from zero, with just the clothes on my back, on the other side of the world. The reason is I wanna survive."

Yes. That's what I should've said. But on the boat, people had been talking about how Cuba had begun to turn away Spanish immigrants and how we shouldn't give them an excuse to deport us.

"Reason for your trip?" the customs agent repeated, getting impatient.

I swallowed my misery, and with a wide smile, I responded the same way as the rest of the passengers. "Vacation. I'm on vacation."

I left the customs office and looked around. The seaside esplanade opened before me, jammed with people, cars, noise, and life. Against a brilliant blue sky, the Morro Castle lighthouse seemed to watch over the city and its inhabitants.

I got dizzy from the heat and had to sit down. The trip had been so torturous, and the possibility of reaching Cuba so remote, I hadn't even stopped to think about what I would do once I got to Havana. The only certain thing was that this wouldn't be easy. My belongings consisted of five things: a wool suit, a hat, shoes, a photograph of my parents, and a can of pickled sardines a Portuguese couple had given me on the ship.

I could, however, count on five other secret weapons. The first: my self-confidence. Ever since I was a child, I'd been immune to shame, and my motto has always been to ask for forgiveness instead of permission. The second: my blue eyes, inherited from my mother and accompanied by my father's good looks. The third: my imagination. The same imagination that, instead of helping me memorize a long line of Goth kings, generated excuses so I could play hooky from school. The fourth: my youth. I had just turned nineteen, and this annulled my fears, turning me into a cub eager for adventure. And, lastly, the fifth and most important: hunger. Hunger for life, for a future, for color—a hunger grown not in a matter of months but years. They say faith moves mountains, but hunger is never far behind. Hunger had propelled a boy from a small Asturian village across the ocean all the way to the Pearl of the Antilles.

Feeling a little better, I got up and started walking again. I dedicated my first few hours as an expatriate to just walking, my eyes wide at all the marvels before me. The Paseo del Prado, the cathedral plaza, the Malecón . . . the city was a beehive of families, tourists, quacks, shoe shiners, peddlers selling erotic photos, and even fortune-tellers who'd read your future using seashells.

The city was a feast for the eyes and ears. Music pervaded every corner of Havana. It came streaming out the doors of the cantinas, from the transistors resting on the window ledge of every house, and from the trumpets of the street musicians and bands that used the corners and plazas as their stages.

When I got to Chinatown, at the corner of Zanja and Galiano, I was so awestruck by a poster advertising the Tropicana Club—with its dancers and their ostrich-feather headdresses—that I didn't notice the streetcar barreling toward me.

"Get out of the way, comemierda!" screamed the conductor.

Even though the streetcar managed to brake just before it crashed into me, I couldn't keep from falling on my ass. A man in a suit stopped to help me.

"Are you okay?"

I nodded; it was my dignity that hurt.

"Didn't you see this gentleman was busy drooling over the legs of those beautiful dancers?" the man scolded the conductor. "And you almost sent him straight to Colón Cemetery! Goddamn it, man."

It was a fact: Cubans were capable of speaking with the utmost refinement and, simultaneously, cursing like poor devils.

"I'm really sorry, my man," the conductor said. "Next time he can be just a little bit more careful, and everything will be aaall riiight."

My tour ended at the beach. Sitting on the sand, I devoured the can of pickled sardines as the sea caressed my tired feet. The sun was a crimson marble surrounded by an orange halo in a sky sprinkled with seagulls in flight, like black dots on the horizon. Before the sun had sunk to the sea, I'd fallen asleep, right there on the beach.

The next day, I was awakened by the barking of a peddler.

"Coconut, lemon, and pineapple popsicles, sir! Delicious shaved ice, ladies!"

I opened my eyes, disoriented, and discovered I was surrounded by families enjoying their day at the beach. They gazed at me with embarrassment and curiosity. A little brown girl dropped her ball and came up to me.

"Hi, are you a castaway?"

I didn't know what to say. I simply smiled, happy to know that in Havana, my life, like that of a castaway washed up by the ocean waves, was about to start again.

CHAPTER 2

After I left the beach, I washed my face in a fountain and walked over to the San Isidro neighborhood. The owner of the dairy in my town had a friend, who had another friend, who had a cousin in Havana who told him weeks before that recently arrived Asturians got together at a place called El Popular, a bar on Porvenir owned by a widow from Avilés. I wasn't too optimistic about actually finding it: the bar could have closed by then, or it could have been on a different street, or the dairy owner or his friend or his friend's friend or his friend's friend's cousin might have been lying. But, against all odds, it turned out to be quite easy to find the place. It was small and charmless.

Inside, a half dozen tables and six shabby chairs lined a dirty bar. The place was a hole-in-the-wall, but the bottles of cider on the shelves made me smile.

The owner must have been fifty-something. She had flabby cheeks and wore her hair up in a gray bun; she looked at me with a furrowed brow.

"Bonos dies?" I said, greeting her with my Asturian dialect in an attempt to win favor. "Que bona manana fai."

But the woman needed just one glance at me to guess my situation. She snorted angrily. "It's gonna be terrible! Don't even talk to me," she grumbled as she dried her hands on a rag. "Just arrived? Probably on the ship from Lisbon yesterday. Well, you can get out of here. This isn't the Red Cross."

She must've been sick of all the hungry people looking for help. I realized I had to make her laugh so she wouldn't throw me out.

"No," I responded.

Surprised, the woman arched her brows. "No?"

"I came by plane," I said as seriously as I could, "in first class." I whispered, "But you'll need to keep my secret."

It was clear she didn't believe a word, but my impertinence intrigued her, and she decided to play along. "And just what is this secret I'm keeping?"

"That I'm a marquis."

The woman took a quick look at my clothes, which were still sandy from the beach, and choked on her own spit.

"'To be or not to be,' said the Marquis of Foolish Misfortune!" she said, and guffawed.

Her laughter seemed like a good sign. "No, the Marquis of Belvedere."

"Never heard of it."

"It's a beautiful land in the Naredo Valley. My name is Patricio, and it is my great honor to meet you."

"So what are you doing here looking like a nobody, Patricio?"

"I've come in secret, trying to find a woman," I said, improvising. "She is the love of my life, but her parents don't want her to marry me."

"Why not? Aren't you supposed to be a marquis?"

"Yes, but my title means little to her family, for she is the princess of Nueva Celemina."

"And where's that?"

"Uff. Far. Very far."

The woman laughed again.

"May I ask your name?" I said with my best smile.

"Constantina—Tina," she said, correcting herself instantly.

Another good sign.

"Tina, please, you must keep my secret. Disguised as a beggar, I've managed to evade the princess's guards. Now I have to convince her to run away with me. But until then, no one can know I'm not poor."

"No problem. You certainly look the part."

"I also need a favor."

"And what's that?"

"A plate of food."

"Really?" she said, sounding more sarcastic than angry.

"You have to understand that, since I'm trying to pass for poor, I can't carry money with me. But I promise on my title I shall return and pay my debt with interest."

Tina sighed with disdain. But that didn't keep her from cutting a good slice of just-made Spanish tortilla and plopping it down in front of me, to the delight of my stomach. I immediately began to drool.

"Go on, go on . . . before I regret this."

I devoured the delicious egg-and-potato cake in a flash. And I tried to make the most of the situation by asking her a thousand questions.

"Do you know a place where I might be able to sleep?"

"Other than the Hotel Nacional, of course."

"Of course. You know I have to pretend to be poor."

Tina pushed back a loose strand of hair and pointed to a young man seated at a table in back. "Talk to El Grescas. But don't go telling him any stories about being a marquis, or he'll punch your lights out."

That seemed like good advice, given that his name meant "brawl," so I decided to just tell him the truth.

"Bonos dies."

The guy didn't respond. He was more interested in chewing his toothpick than he was in talking to me. I just watched him for a minute. He couldn't have been more than twenty-five, but he already possessed the threatening air of a gorilla: tall, considerable corpulence, and arms and legs as thick as trunks. One of his front teeth was chipped.

I tried to hide my nerves. "I'm Patricio."

El Grescas rolled the toothpick between his teeth and maintained a hostile silence. It was clear as day he did not give a royal damn about talking to me. Fortunately, my eyes happened to land on the tiny shield on his old T-shirt. The shield was sky blue with an anchor intertwined with a white cable, and it gave me the strength to open my mouth again.

"Alza el rabu, marinín!" I exclaimed. "Alabí, alabá, alabí, bon, ban! Nobody can beat the Luanco Marines, and if that should happen . . ."

I left the phrase unfinished in the air, the way a fisherman launches his bait and waits for the fish to bite.

"This would be quite a coincidence!" he growled, unable to resist.

Now I let the line out. "Where are you from? I'm from Santa Benxamina."

El Grescas scratched his head with a simian gesture and spat on the bar floor. "Don't get confused. Just because we're from the same place doesn't mean I'm gonna help you. There are more Asturians in Havana than flies."

"All I asked is where you're from."

He spat again. "That's how you all start. And as soon as I tell you, we'll find a mutual acquaintance or a friend. Maybe we'll even realize we're cousins, and then, of course, you'll say: 'Cousin, are you gonna abandon me?' Then you'll ask to borrow money, or for help finding a job, or a place to sleep. So you can just get out of here and go play your shitty little games somewhere else."

"I don't plan to leave until you tell me where you're from."

The gorilla got up from his chair, and I tried to control my fear. He was a whole head taller than me. Well aware of the impact of his full stature, he began to crack his knuckles threateningly.

"I'll make you a deal. If I tell you and it turns out we have somebody in common, I get to punch you in the stomach. Still wanna know?"

A punch in the stomach was never a good thing, but what else could I do? I had no one else to turn to, and I couldn't sleep on the beach again.

"I'll take my chances," I said, but my voice trembled.

"I'm from Carabanzo."

A town just a few hours from mine. "I only know one person from there."

El Grescas grabbed me by the back of the neck like a newborn kitten. "You asked for it."

With my heart beating so fast it echoed in my ears, I just talked without thinking. "Begoña García de Ron. Beautiful like no one else, but she's had more boyfriends than I've got fleas."

El Grescas loosened the pressure on my neck. Given the expression on his face, it was obvious he knew her. Suddenly, a very disturbing thought came to mind.

"She's not your wife, is she?"

He shook his head, and I sighed with relief.

"Good, because she was the easiest woman in the whole town."

But my relief lasted only until he spoke the following four words. "Begoña is my sister."

Shit. There was no way to fix this, so I closed my eyes as tightly as I could and prepared myself for the punch. And it came, so hard it made me double over. El Grescas followed it with a big laugh.

"Fucking Christ, you're Patricio?" His bad mood had vanished. "The same Patricio my sister hooked up with at the open-air dance a couple of years back?" I nodded as I fell into a chair in order to hold my aching stomach. "The punch was for losing the bet," said El Grescas.

I was still trying to get over the blow to my belly when El Grescas hit me with a sudden slap that caught me right in the neck.

"And that's for calling her a whore," he added.

"I didn't call her a whore. I just said—"

"Though that she is," he said, interrupting me. "A bigger whore than a hen, but she's still my little sister, you understand?"

I said yes once more as I struggled to stop the tortilla I'd just eaten from coming back up.

"Begoña told me you made her very happy that summer. And that on your day off from the mines, you'd walk three hours each way just to see her."

It was true. Begoña and I had been a couple of lovebirds until—

"She left you for El Tiburcio?" El Grescas voiced my thoughts. "Or was it Manuel?"

I took a deep breath so I could get enough strength to answer. "I think she left me for both."

"That's my sister!" exclaimed the gorilla, laughing it up. "The García de Rons don't fuck around."

"Clearly. Your sister broke my heart, and you just broke my rib."

El Grescas rewarded my response with a slap on the back, something between camaraderie and violence.

"While we're on the subject of Begoña, how is she?" I asked. "How are things going for her?"

"Not bad. She got married and everything."

"To El Tiburcio? Or Manuel?"

"Neither! To a photographer from Madrid, a guy named Paco. He has a photo studio on the Gran Vía. They're on their second kid already."

"So she finally got her head on straight—"

"Well, if I were Paco, I wouldn't get too comfortable. Wasn't El Tiburcio a redhead? And wasn't Manuel blond?"

"Just like copper and hay."

El Grescas pulled a color photograph from his wallet and showed it to me. In the picture, Begoña posed with her husband, who had black hair, and their two kids—really beautiful kids, but one was blond and the other a redhead.

I laughed. I couldn't help it.

"I'm glad things are going well for her," I said sincerely.

He put the toothpick behind his ear. "Oh man . . . look, I didn't wanna talk to you. But I also can't let an ex-brother-in-law of mine sleep on the street, right?"

That was the moment I realized El Grescas was as noble as he was brutish.

His story was very similar to mine: He'd been born in an Asturian ghetto in the bosom of a family so poor that it was a rare day when they could find a piece of meat to put in the pot. The fact that Grescas had grown to such proportions was something of a miracle, considering that during his entire childhood he'd never taken more than one bite of anything. There was a family rumor that one of his great-grandmothers had had an affair with the Giant of Extremadura, well known in the last century, but the truth was the thickness of El Grescas's bones came from his eagerness to survive, which had led him to eat anything he could hunt with his slingshot: sparrows, squirrels, even lizards. Anything at all so he could be strong enough to work in the mines and take care of his family.

El Grescas kept trying to make something of his decrepit life until his parents—both of whom had ruined their lungs with coal dust—gave him their blessing to start a new life far from all that misery. That's when he decided to emigrate. He'd chosen Cuba for the same reasons as I had: because we shared a language and in the neighborhood bars back home there were rumors about Spaniards who had gotten as rich in Havana as the conquistadores in El Dorado.

What the stories didn't say, El Grescas found out at the ports in Lisbon: the Cuban government was up to its ears in ships loaded with starving Spaniards. Given that he was neither dumb nor lazy, before he left, he filled a suitcase with rocks to pretend he actually owned something. After fooling customs, he threw his rock-filled suitcase into the sea off the port of Havana and, just like me, never looked back. The first days were tough until Tina, who owned El Popular, let him sleep in the warehouse in exchange for carrying barrels of wine, olives, and other merchandise. A few weeks later, he'd saved enough to trade the warehouse floor for a mattress in a guesthouse. When we met, El Grescas had been in Havana for three months, surviving on odd jobs. He was the very incarnation of a go-getter. He was afraid of nothing if it meant earning money.

Although I didn't even know his real name (and it would take years to find out), I had just met one of the two best friends I would ever have in this life. That very afternoon, I ran into the other one.

CHAPTER 3

The Trocadero guesthouse was on the street of the same name, right in the middle of Old Havana. It was also known as the Bedbug Boardinghouse. The narrow three-story building from the nineteenth century was painted sky blue and had once housed a medical clinic for venereal diseases. A sign reading "Secret Ailments Cured Here" still hung from one of its balconies.

It didn't get its nickname by being a breeding ground for those happy little bugs—although its mattresses were plenty full of them— but for the two sisters who ran the place: Patria and Norma, twins about seventy years old and as wrinkled and tiny as bedbugs themselves. The two women were always short on money, so much so that they had only one pair of dentures they took turns using. On Mondays, Wednesdays, and Fridays, Patria ate first, and on Tuesdays, Thursdays, and Saturdays, it was Norma who first sank her teeth into their lunch. On Sundays they ate mashed-up beans, and the dentures rested in a glass of water.

Inside, the guesthouse was quite picturesque, for want of a better word. It was a cross between a china shop and a galleon, and its hallways and rooms were filled to bursting with knickknacks and plants, making it seem like a haunted house. The Bedbug Boardinghouse was a sort of headquarters for shabby immigrants like me, but we weren't the only guests. There were also Cuban peasants, guajiros, who had come from the countryside to try their luck in the capital. Among them was Guzmán.

Guzmán shared a room with El Grescas and me, and it didn't take long for him to become our compay. Skinny and short, he had grown up on a farm with eight brothers until his parents, drowning in debt, placed him under the wing of a spinster aunt who lived in Cienfuegos. What began as a forced separation ended up being a blessing. His aunt was a teacher, and besides providing him with food and shelter, she gave him an education. Guzmán was very clever, and he could have managed to graduate from school, but after his aunt's death, he had to move to the capital and start working. Fate led him to the Bedbug Boardinghouse and, after that, he became my bunkmate.

I still remember when he first shook my hand. He didn't look me in the eyes but instead looked at my feet.

"Nice boots, man. Leather with heavy-duty thread and a suede tongue?"

As it turned out, my new friend had a peculiar trait: he was obsessed with shoes. He claimed it was because he was always barefoot on the farm and didn't have his first shoes until he went to live with his aunt. They were just cheap moccasins, but they made Guzmán feel like king of the world. On top of that, he earned his living as a shoe shiner. It was a tough job. He was bent over cleaning shoes from dawn to dusk, but he would always say, "A gig with no boss and no clock to punch, and you get to meet people . . . what's not to like!"

In fact, once he saw that neither El Grescas nor I had a penny to our names, Guzmán convinced us to become shoe shiners like him. He even put us in touch with two retired shiners who were willing to lend us their chairs, brushes, and polish in exchange for a commission.

Those were good times. Every day, we woke up before dawn and set out. We usually started in the Parque de la Fraternidad to catch the workers who wanted to walk into their offices with newly shined shoes. At midday, when it was so hot that women's high heels left holes in the softened asphalt, we sought refuge in El Popular for a couple of hours. After that, we spent the afternoon in the lobbies of the hotels that were full of American tourists or on the patios of the cantinas, which were also jam-packed with foreigners enjoying their piña coladas in the shade of banana trees. We ended the day at the bars: at Sloppy Joe's or El Floridita, there was always a good reserve of elegant men willing to spend a few coins to spruce up their expensive shoes. We always did the last few shines at Complaciente because El Grescas had his heart set on La Tacones, a black girl with the voice of an angel who sang boleros there and ignored him with sovereign disdain.

Our regular clients nicknamed us the Three Musketeers because we always worked together, making a memorable trio. El Grescas, the size of a gorilla; Guzmán, short as a pygmy; and me, neither one nor the other. All three of us had our weak and strong points. El Grescas was boneheaded as could be, but he could make friends from here to hell. His shoe-shining style wasn't the greatest, but his clients—normally Spaniards—were mostly paying for the conversation.

"Hey, Grescas, you wouldn't happen to know anyone who'd like a case of Black Label?"

"Ask Pedro, from Santander; he's a good guy. He works at a cantina in El Cerro. Tell him I sent you, and hey, if he buys it off you, you owe me two pesos for my time."

Guzmán was the only one of the trio who was a good shoe shiner. It was a pleasure to look at a pair of shoes when he was done with them, and he also worked as a street guide for the tourists.

"If the wooden sole is giving you grief, I'll change it out for a rubber one right away. By the way, have you been to our capitol building yet? It's just like the one the Americans have."

Lastly, I had no talent whatsoever for suede or polish. But my contagious smile and my cheeky attitude earned me quite a few clients.

"How can I put it, sir? I once shined Errol Flynn's shoes; the poor guy had bunions like you wouldn't believe. And Clark Gable, his feet stank even through his shoes, but they weren't really shoes, more like hooves . . ."

In the end, the life of a shoe shiner was tiring, but it was worth it. Or that's what I thought. But what I didn't know then was that it could also be very dangerous: if you give a bad shine to the wrong person, you could end up with a bullet in your head.

CHAPTER 4

That night began like any other. We decided to set up shop in the doorway of the Calypso, one of the city's stylish nightclubs. It took up a whole block, and its facade was painted emerald green. In fact, that was its nickname: the Emerald of Havana. The clientele was very exclusive, and there was a strict dress code: tuxedos for men and evening gowns for ladies. Since it was Havana, the colors of the tuxedos ranged from the classic black foreigners usually wore to the boldest possible options, with some guests daring to wear white, blue, and even green jackets that matched the club. If the men were dressed to the nines, the ladies were never far behind. Seeing them in their silk dresses and their long sheer skirts with their shoulders high and their hair adorned with feathers or flowers was a show in itself.

The Calypso was a paradise for music lovers. It featured a septet playing sones, a French charanga band for danzón, and even a jazz band playing foxtrots that would have inspired Fred Astaire himself to get out on the floor. On really special nights, all the orchestras got together to double up on trumpets, add a piano, and form the Conjunto Calypso, which also included the voices of the most in-demand soloists and even special international stars, thrilling the chosen few who made it through the club's doors.

Since it was rumored the Calypso's dancers were better-looking than the dancers at the Tropicana and the Sans Souci put together, the line to get in stretched around the block, which was wonderful for us when it was time to pick up clients.

Between shines, the three of us shot the breeze.

"So what's that weird fruit called?" I asked Guzmán.

"Guayaba."

"And the other one?"

"Guanabana."

"And you're sure they're not the same thing?" I repeated.

"No, dammit! They're nothing alike!" exclaimed Guzmán.

"Well, I think they're the same thing too, like cacahuetes and alcahueses," interrupted El Grescas.

"What's a cacahuete?" asked Guzmán.

"It's what you throw at monkeys and parrots," he answered.

"Oh, peanuts."

"You never had a parrot, Guzmán?" El Grescas wanted to know.

"Not me. But a neighbor of mine had a parakeet. She talked better than all three of us put together—she even knew a tongue twister."

"You have tongue twisters in Cuba?"

"Hard ones! 'Cómpreme coco, compadre, compadre, cómpreme coco. No compro coco, compadre, porque como poco coco como poco coco compro.'"

"The parakeet said that?"

"Knew it by heart. And she also knew this one: 'Camarón, caramelo, caramelo, camarón, camarón, caramelo . . .'"

"If I say it fast twenty times, will you both give me a peso?" I challenged them.

"Try it."

"Camarón, caramelo, caramelo, caram . . ." I messed up, and all three of us laughed. "Camarón, caramelo, caramelo, camarón, came—shit!"

We were so immersed in the game that I didn't even realize a man had sat down in my chair. The first thing I saw were his shoes: white leather oxfords that must have cost a small fortune.

"Good evening." I greeted him in good spirits, without raising my eyes. "I'd like to propose a wager. If you can say 'camarón, caramelo, caramelo, camarón' twenty times in a row, I'll shine your shoes for free. And if you mess it up, you leave me a tip. What do you say?"

My wisecracks usually made my clients laugh, but not this time. That man wasn't just any client.

"Shut up and shine," he spat at me.

His voice, as hoarse as the growl of an animal about to attack, sent a chill down my spine. I had a bad premonition, and I raised my eyes. The man was wearing a gray suit and a silk tie decorated with an ivory pin. His face was hidden in the shadow of his hat's brim until he puffed on his puro habano, and the cigar's fire illuminated a pair of cruel green eyes.

Anyone with sense would have obeyed him and kept quiet, but I've always had a big mouth.

"Don't be a spoilsport, man," I insisted. "Camarón, caramelo, caramelo, camarón . . ."

I was concentrating so hard on the tongue twister that, without realizing it, I grabbed the wrong rag and stained one of his white shoes with brown polish. Truth be told, it wasn't the first or the second time it had happened to me. I was a terrible shoe shiner.

"Oh no! I'm sorry," I said. "Guzmán, can I use your stain remover?"

When I turned around, I saw my friends had gone pale and were looking at my client as if he were the devil himself. Something was wrong, very wrong. This was confirmed when I felt the cold touch of a pistol on the back of my neck.

"Do you know how much these shoes are worth, cabrón?"

I didn't answer. My tongue was frozen in place with fear.

"I'll tell you. They're worth more than your whole filthy life."

The man took off the safety with a click that sounded as terrifying as a hammer striking the last nail in my coffin.

El Grescas took a step forward, prepared to jump on him and snatch his weapon. But the guy, with all the calm in the world and without taking the cigar out of his mouth, snapped the fingers of his free hand, and just like that, two huge men in suits appeared, flanking their boss.

"You. Don't move. You think I wouldn't kill two pieces of shit instead of just one?"

I closed my eyes and felt time slowing down. An obsessive thought began to flutter inside my head, like a butterfly trapped inside a glass jar: *I can't die because of a tongue twister. I can't die because of a tongue twister.* But then I remembered my parents. Both dead, both murdered for stupid reasons. It was only logical I should follow the family tradition.

"I c-can get rid of the s-s-stain," stuttered Guzmán. Silence. A bead of sweat rolled down my forehead and fell to the ground. "Let me fix it, p-please, sir. I know for s-s-sure you wouldn't be able to get out the b-b-blood," he insisted, his voice trembling.

After a few agonizing seconds, the man lowered his gun and gestured to his bodyguards to step back.

Then I received a forceful kick that left me lying on the ground. The man, pistol still in his hand, ordered Guzmán to approach.

"Fix it!" he said once Guzmán knelt before him.

Guzmán's hands trembled as if he were having a spasm. Even with all that pressure on his shoulders, his skill was such that he managed to clean off the stain in a flash.

"There you g-g-go . . ."

The man thoroughly inspected his shoes, and after a long silence, he smiled with satisfaction.

"Your friend has saved you this time, loudmouth," he told me. Looking at all three of us, he continued, saying, "I don't wanna see any of you lowlifes here again. If you cross my path, I'll gut you. Understood?"

With a final puff on his cigar, the man stepped into the darkness of the street, and he and his men disappeared into the shadows. Our sighs of relief were so heartfelt, you could've heard them on the other side of the island.

As soon as he left, Guzmán and El Grescas ran to my side and helped me stand up. My legs had turned to rubber, and it took a couple of tries to get me on my feet.

"Are you all right?" El Grescas spat on the ground, furious. "I'll be damned; he was gonna blow our heads off!"

"We have to get to La Tercera and report that madman," I gasped.

La Tercera was Havana's police station.

"No, no, no!" Guzmán's eyes almost popped out of their sockets. "No police! Don't you know who that guy was? César Valdés!"

I'd never heard the name, but El Grescas's face dissolved into a mix of disbelief and terror.

"César Valdés?" he repeated. "César Valdés!"

"The same."

"Who the hell is César Valdés?" I interrupted.

"He's a don. You know, like Al Capone or Lucky Luciano. A gangster."

"A mafioso?"

"They say he started as an opium and marijuana smuggler, and it didn't take long for him to make it big. Now he's the owner of the Calypso and one of the most powerful men in all of Cuba."

"But as rich and powerful as he may be, he can't go around murdering people whenever he wants," I protested.

El Grescas gave me a slap on the back. "You're an idiot! It's the mafia! If he felt like it, he could make a wallet by skinning your balls, and nobody would lift a finger. Get it?"

"Aren't the government and the police supposed to fight against the mafia?"

"Ha!" snorted Guzmán. "César Valdés went to Batista's house for lunch, and now he's having drinks with Grau. The politicians live off the mafiosos' money. Not only do they never throw them in jail, they even protect the sons of bitches."

Bang! Suddenly, an explosion behind us made us throw ourselves on the ground like three marionettes whose cords had just been cut. With great care, we lifted our heads and discovered it was nothing more than a group of friends who had uncorked a bottle of champagne in the middle of the street.

"We should g-g-go," I stuttered, my nerves shot. "I don't know about you two, but I could sleep for a week."

That episode marked the end of my brief career as a shoe shiner. To shine shoes, you had to be able to set up shop in the doorways of the nightclubs, and I valued my own skin too much to cross paths with César Valdés ever again.

CHAPTER 5

Guzmán and El Grescas used to say you could divide Havana into high and low, the Havana of the rich and the Havana of the poor. And both sections were nose to nose. On Sundays after Mass, the millionaires who dropped their money at the casinos and the criollos who broke their backs at the coffee plantations so their patrons' wives could have tea at La Casa del Café con Leche on Obispo mingled on the benches outside the cathedral. While Marlon Brando bought a diamond watch inside Cuervo y Sobrinos, the beggar at the door would wet her child's pacifier in chicory because she didn't have any powdered milk. These two worlds were right smack next to each other, separated by invisible barriers.

Back then, there was only one way a poor person could go from sleeping on an empty sack to a feather mattress: the lottery. Those five numbers were a magical portal from one world to the other. Because of its ability to perform miracles, the lottery in Cuba provoked authentic devotion—one to which I would soon subscribe as well.

One afternoon, El Grescas came back to the guesthouse with several lottery tickets.

"Do you wanna earn a few dimes? The black guy who sells the lottery tickets at El Popular is in the hospital with appendicitis. He says if we sell these tickets for him, we can keep half the profits."

It was a fantastic opportunity . . . until I saw the first five of the ten numbers: 8-5-9-4-3. That number was bad luck times three. Most people chose their number through the charada, and the number eight was death; fifty-nine was the number for insanity, and forty-three was the scorpion.

"Grescas, you realize this is gonna be like selling a black cat and a broken mirror from under a ladder?"

"That's the challenge, asshole. There must be somebody in Cuba who isn't superstitious."

But El Grescas was wrong. We began our adventure at the market at Cuatro Caminos. We're talking about the most important food market in the whole city, a gift to the senses.

It was a giant building, as noisy as a beehive, with the market spread out around a central courtyard divided into three floors full of stalls and storage. Inside, there were thousands of vendors with every type of produce imaginable: cassava, sweet potato, taro, avocados, California apples, mangoes and bananas of all sizes, whole pigs and whole lambs, and live lobsters still scrambling around. The marble staircases gave the place an aristocratic air, which the customers filled with their caterwauling and screeching.

"Chickens, turkeys, and rabbits! These pigs' feet are finger-lickin' good, man!" the vendors would bark.

But when we tried to sell the lottery tickets, the customers and clerks crossed themselves upon seeing the number.

"Get that away from me, you vultures," they would clamor.

We tried the cart drivers and fishermen who brought in their hauls, but they laughed in our faces.

"Holy Virgin of Charity! That number isn't even good enough to make a bonfire to warm our asses!"

Just a few hours before the number was to be called, we hadn't sold a single ticket, and everything looked pretty bleak. Not even the nuisance nuns (as we called our landladies) who played the lottery religiously every day wanted to buy a ticket from me.

"This is a winning number. I have a good feeling about it! Just think: you could buy dentures for each of you," I said, trying to butter them up.

"If you're so sure about the number, you play it. And I hope it's one heck of a prize, young man, because you already owe us two months' rent," said Patria. Or Norma. I could never tell them apart.

We were in the little front room of the guesthouse when the doorbell interrupted our chat. Norma—or Patria—told me to stop bugging her and went to the door. But because she was so short, she couldn't reach the peephole. She took the telephone book, threw it down, and climbed on top, using it as an improvised footstool. The whole scene gave me an idea, and I went running back to my room.

"Hey, Grescas! What if we call all the telephone numbers that begin or end in 8-5-9-4-3?"

"What for?"

"Because they won't think it's an unlucky number! In fact, they might find the coincidence amusing and buy."

Excited, El Grescas jumped up from the bed and squeezed me against his gorilla chest. "You're so clever, ex-brother-in-law!"

And so, we began to call all the numbers in the phone book that contained the infamous 8-5-9-4-3. The first call was a fiasco: a grouchy old man screamed at us for having woken him from his nap and hung up. But on the second call, we sold a ticket. And on the third one, another ticket. On the fourth, a pair of tickets . . . the system worked so well we had to recruit Guzmán to help so that between the three of us, we could write down the buyers' addresses and take their tickets over to their houses.

After we finished with the telephone book, we decided to go for license plate numbers. The plan was simple and consisted of us basically running around the city looking at license plates, and if we found one with the same numbers as our tickets, then we would tackle the owner and overwhelm him with the miraculous coincidence.

I didn't have to look very long. At the Malecón, I saw a Chevrolet with license plate 859, the first three of our ten numbers. The car was parked in front of a cantina, and I figured the owner was probably inside having a drink. I decided it was worth it to wait and try to persuade him to buy a few tickets.

To pass the time, I sat down on the piece of rock that separated the sidewalk from the sand and entertained myself by looking out at the beach. There was a very good-looking girl wearing a bathing suit just this side of scandalous as she read a magazine by the sea and sunbathed. When she finished reading, she got up off the towel and, to the delight of the other beachgoers, stretched like a cat and started doing pirouettes. There was no doubt she was a dancer, and I bet myself she worked at the Shanghai, a club where the girls performed nude on stage. The fact that she was alone at the beach was a point in favor of my theory. The more conservative young women never stepped away from their herd of friends for fear of what people might say. Among the spectators, there was a young man who seemed particularly spellbound. Dark and handsome, he had a gloss about him that suggested he was well nourished, which meant that even though he was only wearing a bathing suit, it was immediately obvious he came from a well-off family. It was also noticeable, even if I'd been a mile away—because of the anxious way he kept pulling at his hair—that he was trying to gather enough courage to go talk to the dancer.

My beach soap opera was interrupted when the car's owner showed up. He was graying at the temples and wore a white linen suit. He seemed like a nice guy, so I launched myself straight at him.

"Good day, sir! Today is your lucky day because I'm about to change your life." I took out my roll of tickets and showed him. "Look at the license plate on your car. Isn't that an extraordinary coincidence? I was just walking by here, selling this lottery ticket. You can't deny that this feels like fate."

The man could hardly contain his laughter. His eyes were bright and alert, and it was clear he wasn't somebody who was taken easily.

"Just walking by, huh? I was having a cup of coffee on that terrace, and I noticed you sitting here for a good while," he said.

His accent had a slight Asturian cadence, and I felt a bolt of joy.

"Well, sometimes you have to give fate a little push. Are you from Asturias?"

"Yes, but I'm also a little Caribbean," he said. "I've been here for decades."

"Paisanu, this is indeed fate, so now you really have to buy a ticket from me."

The Asturian shook his head gently. "I'm sorry, but I think the only way to get rich is to work. It's not about luck."

"Me too, me too! But wouldn't you like to become a millionaire from one day to the next?"

"There's only a one-in-a-million chance that's the chosen number."

"You said it. There's a chance! Just think what would happen if it was picked, and you hadn't bought a ticket. I'm telling you"—my imagination took control, and I began to fantasize—"you'll feel so bad, you'll regret it for the rest of your life. You'll grow bitter, and you'll have to turn to drink to feel better. You'll wind up a drunk, you'll lose your job, and your wife will leave you and go as far away as possible, even to China. Then you're gonna have to sell your house and your car just so you can get a plane ticket to get her back, but it'll be too late because she'll have fallen in love with a Chinese guy. And it won't end there because on the way back to the airport, you'll get lost in the jungle and be devoured by a tiger. I'm saying . . . wouldn't it be better to spend five lousy cents now on a lottery ticket and sleep peacefully tonight?"

The guy laughed heartily at the drama I had just unfurled for him. "So you're saying if I don't buy a lottery ticket from you, I'm gonna end up devoured by a tiger?"

"Or by a lion. In the jungle, you never know."

"You're not gonna stop, are you?" he said, still laughing.

"I've got no other choice. If I don't sell these tickets, I won't be able to eat tonight."

The Asturian gestured for me to follow him, opened the trunk of his car, and pulled out a suitcase. "I'm gonna propose something. Have you heard of El Encanto?"

I nodded. Of course I'd heard of that store. It was a Havana institution, the most elegant place to buy high couture, French perfumes, and other luxury items. I'd always been curious about going inside, but for a poor person like me, shopping at El Encanto would have been as impossible as going to the moon.

"We're opening a new branch this week. The biggest store in all the Americas. If you can sell clothes as well as you sell lotto tickets, we could find a position for somebody like you."

A job! Like a street dog who's just been offered a pork chop, I felt all the muscles in my body tense. But not only that . . . a job at the most famous store in Cuba? It had to be mine!

"What do I have to do?"

"Show me you're as good as our salespeople."

The Asturian opened the suitcase, and he pulled out a thick woolen scarf. "I just got back from Paris. The job is yours if you can manage to sell this scarf in the next ten minutes."

I had to sell a scarf in Havana? With the temperature at 40 degrees in the shade? He couldn't be serious. "Here? Now?"

"If you don't think you can—"

"I can, I can!" I said. "How much do I sell it for?"

"Five pesos."

The man gave me the scarf and leaned on his car.

"You have ten minutes," he reminded me.

I looked around. It was noon and the street was deserted. What could I do? I thought about going into one of the cantinas to look for clients or coming up with something crazy. Maybe I could say it gave the wearer magic powers? But five pesos was too much money to waste on such nonsense. I took a deep breath to organize my thoughts: *People buy things they need, and no one in their right mind needs a scarf when it's 40 degrees in the shade. Unless . . .* My eyes fell on the well-off young man and the dancer. I came up with a truly crazy plan. Lacking a real need, I had to make one up. I ran toward the girl.

"Good afternoon, young lady. Would you be interested in earning a few pesos?"

The girl furrowed her brow but smiled slightly. I could see interest and distrust wrestling in her.

"How much?"

No doubt, she was a dancer. A more respectable girl would have never heard me out. "Five."

"What for?"

"For one of your kisses."

The girl's brows arched in surprise, but she wasn't scandalized, and she didn't slap my face. "Just one? On the lips or on the cheek?"

"On the lips."

"Just a peck?"

"It'd be better if it was like in the movies, but a peck will do."

"The kiss is for you?"

"No, the kiss is for the first man who comes up to you wearing a wool scarf."

I immediately rushed over to the shy guy. "I come with a message from that girl. She says she would like to give you a kiss. But on one condition . . ."

With less than a minute left to complete my task, the young man paid me ten pesos for the scarf, and I gave five to the dancer. Both of them were well aware I was playing Cupid for my own benefit, but they decided to play along anyway. I was giving them the perfect excuse to meet and get to know each other.

I went back to the Asturian, and we watched the results of my scheming. To the amazement of everyone on the beach, a young man wearing swim trunks and a winter scarf approached this young woman, and she rewarded him with a kiss just like in the movies. I was delighted to see that, after they kissed, they stayed together, talking. The young man from the well-off family had found an in with the dancer. In fact, he looked for me and gave me a thumbs-up.

The Asturian laughed with satisfaction and slapped me on the shoulder.

"I've never seen two more satisfied clients in my whole life! The job is yours. Come to the store tomorrow at eight in the morning. Here's my card."

The Asturian took off in his car, and I looked down at the card: Aquilino Entrialgo. Founding partner of El Encanto.

That afternoon, El Grescas and I followed the lottery with special interest. As might be expected, our ugly and unlucky number didn't win so much as a dime. But with Mr. Entrialgo's card in my pocket, I'd already won the lottery.

CHAPTER 6

The intersection of Galiano and San Rafael Streets was known as Sin Corner. It got that name for its irresistible stores and how they attracted the most elegant ladies, just like honey draws flies. It was common knowledge that the favorite pastime of the women in Havana was to go shopping, and for the gentlemen, it was to admire them and sing their praises. So the much-talked-about Sin Corner was, in fact, really a corner of misdemeanors: the women looked at the displays, the men looked at the women, and everyone was happy. The most enchanting stores were Woolworth's—also called El Ten Cents in Havana—La Moda shoe store, and La Isla Café, where shoppers could have an ice cream to regain their strength and go on with their day. But the crown jewel was undoubtedly El Encanto.

The building took up an entire block, and the facades were decorated with huge marble pillars. Up front, there was an enormous portico reinforced by columns so people could look at the displays even when it was raining. A giant sign crowned the main entrance.

The morning of my first day at work, the street was buzzing. The store was inaugurating its new headquarters, and expectations for the new building had been the city's main gossip of late. An hour before opening, there was already a great throng of customers and curious onlookers crowded around the door.

Just as the Asturian had instructed me, I headed for a side door at eight in the morning. A kind clerk opened it for me.

"Good morning," I said in greeting. "I was told to come here. I'm supposed to start work today."

The clerk gestured for me to follow her. "Come with me, please."

I crossed the threshold, and my mouth dropped open. This was more than a store; it seemed I had entered a palace. The walls and floors were so shiny, it was a pleasure to look at them. There were mannequins and tropical plants everywhere. The signs hanging from the ceiling announced all kinds of products, each one more desirable than the last and all accompanied by the store's logo: a lady and a gentleman from the early twentieth century. "Distinguish Your Gifts with a Label from El Encanto," proclaimed the signs. But what impressed me most were the counters. In that sea of dazzling tiles, the counters were small islands jam-packed with marvels. The construction itself was art: they were made of noble wood underneath and glass on top to show off the merchandise. Although I couldn't stop staring like a fool, I managed to follow the clerk to an elevator.

"Go up to the fifth floor. You'll find the office there. Ask for the personnel department."

The elevator operator closed the door and pushed the button for number five. She was wearing a truly beautiful uniform consisting of a black dress with long stockings. She was roughly my age, with bangs, a turned-up nose, and a squirrel-like demeanor.

"We take off in three, two, one . . . now!" she said, joking around.

As we were going up, I noticed the elevator operator looking me over.

"You borrowed that suit, didn't you?" she asked me.

I nodded. I had sold my Asturian wool suit weeks before so I could pay rent at the guesthouse, and with what little money I had left, I'd bought a floral shirt and a pair of short pants, neither of which was appropriate for a serious job. Guzmán had told me, "The first step to not being poor anymore is to stop looking poor." Luckily for me, both El Grescas and Guzmán had suits they could lend me. But, of course, Grescas's was gigantic on me, and Guzmán's was tight. In the end, I had no choice but to combine them and wear Grescas's shirt, which looked like a bedsheet on me, underneath Guzmán's coat, which I could barely button. And I'd also had to roll up the pants so they wouldn't drag. The worst were the shoes, a pair of loafers two sizes too small.

"Is it that obvious?"

"Yes," she said, honestly but without malice. "You look like a scarecrow. It's a shame because you have the bearing of a movie star. Those blue eyes of yours are beautiful."

The compliment surprised me and made me feel good. I didn't know what to say. The elevator operator giggled, as if she had a little bell in her throat, and it was truly enchanting.

"Don't worry too much, they'll give you a uniform. You just smile, say yes to everything, and then come and ask me about anything you're not sure about. You have an ally here."

"Wow, thank you."

"Nothing to thank me for yet. You can pay me back by inviting me to the movies or buying me a piece of chocolate cake with your first wages."

I was utterly speechless. Was she flirting with me? Ever since I'd arrived in Havana, the last thing on my mind was having a girlfriend. My needs were much too acute. It was survival, basically. But in that moment, the idea of going to the movies with the elevator operator who laughed so pleasantly seemed like the most tempting thing in the world.

"I see you get right to the point."

"What choice do I have? I spend the entire day in the elevator, and I can only talk for a minute. If we start off with pleasantries, we won't have time to say anything." The door beeped when it opened, indicating we'd reached the fifth floor. "See? We're already here."

Before getting out, I tried to scratch out a few more seconds of conversation. "What's your name?"

"Nely, and you?"

"Patricio."

"Remember, I'm in the left-hand elevator," she said, winking at me.

Unfortunately, not everyone at El Encanto was as charming as Nely. When I got to the personnel department, I was welcomed by a man in his fifties. He had eyes that popped out and a long and fine catlike mustache over very thin lips that were permanently pursed, giving him a kind of rictus.

"May I help you?"

"This is my first day of work."

"That's impossible. We're not hiring anybody."

I showed him the card Aquilino Entrialgo had given me. His mouth twisted into disgust, and his mustache twitched. I found him so unpleasant that, in my head, I called him Don Gato.

"Mr. Entrialgo told me to come today."

"That can't be. Where did you get this card?"

A secretary heard us and interrupted. "Excuse me, Mr. Duarte. Mr. Entrialgo left a message just in case a new employee . . ."

The woman handed him a scrap of paper. It must have legitimized my story because, after he read it, Don Gato glared at the secretary.

"Thank you, Dulce. You can go now."

The man did not apologize for his mistake. Later, I learned his name was Carlos Duarte, he was the chief of the English Room in the gentleman's section, and I wasn't the only one who'd given him a nickname. Among the employees, he was known as Little Dracula, Mr. Bones, and, the most precise, Two-Face, because he was charming as all hell with the bosses but an ogre with the employees below his rank.

"You'll start as a cannonball."

"Excuse me?"

"A cannonball, an errand boy. You'll do everything," he said, brusquely. "You'll run errands as fast as a cannonball, understood?"

"Understood."

"Go ask for a uniform and get dressed."

By the time I'd put on my new uniform, which was a black blazer, belt, and matching pants—and the best part was that it was all my size—it was only a few minutes before the doors were to open. All the employees were at their posts behind the counters. It was an emotional moment, like the seconds just before a referee whistles the start of the game, the instant before a kiss, or that moment before it rains when you can already smell the wet earth.

Five minutes before nine, the store owners—the brothers José and Bernardo Solís Fernández, along with Aquilino Entrialgo and César Rodríguez, who was their cousin—made their appearance and greeted their employees with affection.

"I'm so happy to see you, Indalecio! How are you, Julita? And your kids? Catalina, you look so beautiful! Juan Andrés! Tell me, how is your mother getting on with her rheumatism?"

I was impressed those men had learned their workers' names. Of course, since they were bosses, it's possible they were getting it all wrong, and nobody dared to correct them.

"Patricio!" Aquilino Entrialgo's use of my name did away with my theory. "Don't tell me you finally won with your lottery number!"

"Not at all. You were right not to buy that number," I answered.

"Then I'm not going to get eaten by a Chinese tiger anymore?" he said.

"Rest easy."

Aquilino gave my shoulder a pat and gestured for the others to come closer.

"Friends, this is Patricio. From the old country, Asturias. He could sell snow to an Eskimo."

"You know the saying," I said, trying to downplay the compliment. "'Need will teach you more than school.'"

They all reached out to shake my hand. I was so nervous and afraid my hand was too sweaty, but if it was, they were kind and pretended not to notice.

"Wonderful to meet you, Patricio. I'm José, but everyone calls me Pepín. Let me introduce my brother, Bernardo, and my cousin, César, whom we call Don Cesáreo."

"Thanks for having faith in me."

"No need to thank me. What makes this company great isn't us, but the sum of all the small efforts by each honest worker."

"I promise I won't let you down."

Aquilino Entrialgo glanced at his wristwatch and gestured for one of his employees to move toward the main entrance.

"It's time! Eduardo, if you could be so kind as to do the honors."

The man opened the doors; without realizing it, I was holding my breath. A flood of customers came rushing in. The store got going like a well-oiled machine. The women's heels echoed on the floor with a happy clatter that blended with the sounds of the keys as the clerks unlocked the displays.

To make the opening even livelier, there was a small orchestra with a velvet-voiced singer playing a most relaxing song.

A part of me—the part that had suffered the most hunger and need—warned me not to get too dazzled by this frivolous world, this Encanto. No matter how beautiful, it was just a store where bored rich people bought things they didn't need. Yes, the majority of the customers were very well off, but there were also plain and ordinary people who came in to pass the time. That's when I realized it didn't matter if they were rich, poor, men, women, young, or old. As soon as they crossed the threshold into El Encanto, they all shared one thing in common: the sparkle in their eyes like kids on Christmas morning. El Encanto didn't need electricity because the way their customers smiled could have lit up the entire store. This was dreaming in its purest state.

That's when I really got it.

Everyone goes through difficulties in life. Health problems, money troubles, struggles with love—all of them more or less serious. Not even royalty is immune to misfortune. For example, the woman in the green dress, the one standing, hypnotized, in front of the Revlon lipstick display, could very well have been taking care of her old, infirm mother. The gentleman trying on the Italian Borsalinos might have worked at a job that made his life miserable. Every customer who walked through the door was carrying his or her personal torments: from a chipped nail or an incurable disease to a love betrayed or any other kind of heartbreak. But as long as they were at El Encanto—whether they were buying a suit priced at thousands of pesos or a little trinket or simply strolling through the store—they'd forget their cares, if even just for a while. That was the magic of El Encanto.

I was brought out of my trance by a screech from Don Gato.

"Hello? Cannonball! Run to the storeroom and bring us a wedge to steady this counter."

I immediately obeyed. Luckily, I remembered to take the elevator on the left, and Nely helped orient me.

"Listen. The first floor has the most departments. Jewelry, perfume, cosmetics, books, shoes, and photography. The second floor has the gift department, record players, radios, the tailor, and the English Room for the gentlemen's most current fashions. And on the third floor, there's the French Room for the ladies and the teenage department for the youngsters. On the fourth floor: toys, kids' clothes, and kids' shoes. On the fifth: appliances, housewares, mattresses, and offices; the storeroom's also on the fifth floor. It's the third door. Will you remember?"

"I'll manage."

Somehow, I completed my mission. I found the wedge and steadied the furniture. I had no sooner stood back up when another clerk called me over.

"Cannonball!"

In the next few hours, I confirmed that "doing everything" couldn't have been more on target. Here were a few of my errands: searching for merchandise in the storeroom, sweeping the floors, cleaning the windows, alphabetizing the books, and minding a pack of poodles and other lapdogs while their owners tried on various hats and hair ornaments.

While I was brushing the dog hair and drool off my pants, another clerk made some kind of sound so I'd look her way.

"Boy! Take this box over to the gifts department. Then take ten and get something to eat."

I obeyed and took off with the box. The idea of having a cup of coffee with a pastry made my guts gurgle. In fact, I was so busy fantasizing about sinking my teeth into a guava-and-cream-cheese sandwich that the collision took me by surprise. In less than one tenth of a second, as I turned the corner, someone was coming along without looking and crashed right into me. The box flew from my hands and crashed on the floor with the sound of shattered glass.

Oh please let it be metal pieces or rubber toys or something very, very resistant, I thought. But it didn't turn out that way. My worst fears came true when I opened the box and saw it contained little animal figures made of porcelain. I raised my eyes, ready to say a thing or two to the idiot who had run me over.

That's when I saw her for the first time.

CHAPTER 7

Her eyes were brown, like hazelnuts, and so pretty they looked like honey. She had lustrous jet-black hair gathered in a ponytail. Her blushing cheeks were sprinkled with freckles. She was wearing a red dress that showed off a lovely figure and matching high-heeled sandals. You could tell from a long way off that she had money. Her diamond earrings alone probably cost more than the houses back in my village in Asturias. I figured she was about twenty-five. She was, without a doubt, the most handsome woman I'd ever seen in my life.

Alarmed, the young woman in the red dress knelt on the floor by my side, and we examined the box together. All the little figures had survived intact except one: a zebra whose legs were broken. I gulped. My first day could not have gone any worse. If they charged me for the broken figurine and took it out of my salary, I'd be working for free for a month. That is, assuming they didn't fire me.

Then the girl took the initiative.

"I'll buy them," she said confidently. "It was my fault."

"My bosses won't let you," I responded as I thought about Don Gato and the problem I'd just taken on. "We always have to side with the customer."

"As well you should," she answered with a complicit smile. "I want to buy that zebra. I want to buy the whole lot."

"I appreciate the gesture, ma'am, but I'm afraid my bosses won't let you buy a zebra with broken legs."

My forehead was now drenched with sweat as I played out the consequences of the broken zebra in my head. In an instant, my future had turned black, very black.

As if she'd read my mind, the girl's soft voice interrupted my lament. "You're not the sort who gives up easily, are you?"

She offered me her hand with the innocence of a child saving their accomplice in mischief.

"It's okay. Come with me," she said.

What could I do? I took her hand and let her lead.

A little later, after going up various staircases, we arrived at a little maintenance room. We went through a door painted the same pearl-gray color as the wall that led to another small room full of brooms and tools. Once there, the girl sat down on a wicker chair and started looking through some old boxes until she found a tube of glue. Leaning on a little wooden table, she put the zebra's tiny legs back together. Her cheeks were flushed with concentration.

I watched her in silence, not believing everything that had just happened.

It was as if I'd been unmasked, as if that girl had gone right past my facade and reached the real Patricio. No, I was certainly not the sort who gave up the first time. Her assessment made me feel more alive than ever. And that we were huddled in that little room seemed to suggest rules were made to be broken.

I needed to know more about this very special girl who, by this point, I could address more informally.

"How did you know how to get up here?" I asked her.

"The store was open yesterday for a little while exclusively for a group of privileged customers. I broke my heel, and one of the clerks came here for some glue," she said, not lifting her gaze from the little zebra figure.

"Are you a privileged customer?"

"Yes," she chirped like a little bird.

The girl looked at me with sad eyes, and my heart trembled. Those eyes seemed like quicksand: easy to fall into and impossible to climb out of.

"What's your name?"

"Gloria."

"I'm Patricio."

We shared a complicit silence. Gloria began to blow on the little zebra's legs to dry the glue.

"Do you think zebras are black with white stripes or white with black stripes?" I asked with my usual impudence.

To my surprise, she answered without any doubt or hesitancy.

"They're white with black stripes," she affirmed.

Seeing my astonishment, Gloria began to laugh and had to cover her mouth with her hand.

"It's to confuse the lions," she explained in a low voice. "The lion's eye can't distinguish the stripes; what they do is create an optical illusion that allows them to camouflage."

"How do you know that?"

I was increasingly fascinated by Gloria by the minute.

"I read it in a science book," she said.

"Do you like science?"

Gloria nodded.

"I've always thought science was for people more clever than me," I said.

"Oh please! Science is everywhere," she said, the tone of her voice rising. "Einstein said that science is nothing more than curiosity in everyday thinking, so we can all be scientists."

"Einstein is the genius with the crazy white hair?"

"Yes, the one who invented the theory of relativity."

"What's that?"

"It means space and time are variables, and both depend, in a newly discovered space-time continuum, on speed."

We were performing for each other in that little room. And, apparently, we were both doing very well. With all the back-and-forth, I was still asking myself about her sad look. Gloria was enchanting, but she was a mystery as well.

"I didn't understand a word you just said," I replied.

"I'm sorry. I don't get a lot of opportunities to talk. And much less with people my age."

I was surprised by her response. What was Gloria's story? Overprotective parents, perhaps? Whether in Spain, Cuba, or China, it was well known that the daughters of well-off families lived in ivory towers.

"Tell me more about that theory of relativity," I said.

"I'm going to give you an example. An hour with a pretty girl feels like a minute, but a minute under a hot light seems like an hour, right? That's relativity."

"I couldn't agree more," I said, and I couldn't have meant it more.

Just like in the theory of relativity, I could have stayed in that room with Gloria my whole life, and it would have seemed like a second. The revelation hit me like a lightning bolt: I was in love. Lost, crazy, and irremediably in love with this woman.

Without any notion of my feelings, she looked at her wristwatch and jumped with surprise.

"I have to get back. My husband will be looking for me," she whispered sadly.

Husband.

The word was like a dagger in my soul. I wanted to die, but I tried to keep it together. I thought maybe there'd be an overprotective father, but a husband made sense too. How could she not have a husband? And even if she'd been single, somebody like me had no chance with somebody like her. That was very sensible reasoning, but it didn't keep my heart from feeling as if it had just gotten kicked.

"Shall we go?"

Somehow, I managed to nod. We put the now-repaired zebra back in the box with its porcelain buddies and returned to the store.

In the gift department, nobody noticed the defect, and, true to her word, Gloria bought all the figures in the box.

As we were saying goodbye and I was handing her the now gift-wrapped package, she leaned over and whispered in my ear. "I love talking to you."

But before I had a chance to take in the violet scent on her skin and the embrace of her warm breath, a screech coming from behind us made us jump.

"Gloria! Where the fuck have you been?"

That voice made my hair stand on end. It was raspy and animalistic. Even though my head had not yet recognized whose it was, my muscles tensed and my entire body went on alert.

"I was looking at dresses," said Gloria in a thin voice.

As I tried to slip away with my head lowered, I saw something that made my blood run cold: a pair of very familiar white oxfords. *No, no, no, please, Lord God, no!* I thought as I raised my eyes and confirmed the worst of my nightmares.

Gloria's husband was César Valdés.

CHAPTER 8

GLORIA

My name is Gloria, and the day I turned seven years old, Albert Einstein gave me a hat. It was my last good memory, and it happened December 22, 1930, when I was still a happy, carefree little girl. Before my life took a turn for the worse.

The famed scientist had arrived in Havana the day before, when his ship came into port before departing for San Diego, in the States. The hours he spent in Cuba were well documented by the press. His morning began with an official visit to the secretary of state. Then he had lunch at the Hotel Plaza with members of the Academy of Sciences. He took a stroll in the bucolic local countryside and visited Rancho-Boyeros Airport, the Mercado Único, and the gardens of the Acueducto de Vento. Even though it was December, the scientist was bothered by our city's piercing sunlight, and his hosts decided to take him to El Encanto, where José (Pepín) Solís gave him a Panama hat: a moment immortalized by Gonzalo Lobo, also known as Van Dyck, the best photographer in Havana.

But what the news reporters didn't know was that, before returning to his ship, Einstein made a final stop at La Golosa, my family's sweet shop.

La Golosa was the cutest store in central Havana—as pretty as a candy box. It was on Galiano Street, squeezed between the two most renowned department stores: Fin de Siglo and El Encanto. At the entrance, shop windows full of treats enticed customers. Panetelas, puddings, merengues, molded sugar, sweet potato tarts, pumpkin flans, cakes, coconut cookies, and candied grapefruits were just some of the delights available to take home or enjoy right there in the shop. If the customers wanted to complement their sweets with a cup of coffee, they were welcome to do so in a grand tearoom with chandeliers and red velvet seats. That room was the apple of my mother's eye, and she decorated it with such loving care that it could have been a second daughter.

Inspired by the tearooms of nineteenth-century Paris, a bookcase held a collection of tiny, hand-painted porcelain teapots, rivaling in preciousness the little paintings of the streets of Montmartre that hung on the walls. Bougainvilleas in flowerpots contributed their fragrance to the sweet shop's magic. It was a little palace in central Havana where the customers could feel like princes and princesses.

Though French-inspired, La Golosa was a Cuban sweet shop, and proud of it. On one of its shelves sat an old transistor radio my parents tuned to music programs: the melodies of the Sonora Matancera, the Conjunto Saratoga, and Antonio Arcaño's orchestra were the perfect accompaniment to our sweets. To contrast with the French finery, my father had also brought in a piano and several wooden cages with exotic birds that squawked as if they were still in the jungle. Of all the birds, my father's favorite was Raimundo the parrot, whose cage was strategically placed at the entrance so he could welcome the clientele.

"Give us a sweet!" and "Give us a kiss on the beak!" were Raimundo's favorite things to say.

My folks owned the store, and their marriage was as sweet as their cakes. Gregorio—the son of Galician immigrants—and Dorita—a Cuban woman from Vertientes, a little town in Camagüey province—came from middle-class families and had grown up without luxuries but also without hardship. Ever since they were kids, my mom and dad had felt a passion for cooking. Fate brought them together at a hospitality school when they tied for first place with their delicious rice pudding recipes. In less time than it takes for a soufflé to rise, they fell in love, got married, opened their candy shop, and had me, their only daughter. They baptized me Gloria because my mother was making a sweet bread known in Cuba as pan de gloria when she went into labor.

As I grew, so did our business. From its humble beginnings to more than a dozen employees, our candy shop became the street's proudest success story.

The Galician Sisto brothers and the Asturian Solís brothers, owners of the Fin de Siglo and El Encanto, respectively, were loyal customers. If anything confirmed the human touch of the Sistos and the Solíses, it was that, despite the fact that their huge department stores were direct competitors, those gentlemen considered themselves professional peers and always treated each other with great respect. My parents made friends with all four of them, and when I was just a kid, Galiano Street was my little kingdom. When I wasn't in the sweet shop, I was running back and forth between Uncle Joaquín's shop and Uncle Pepín's.

The sweet shop's earnings allowed my parents to enroll me in an American school and to buy a new house. It was a beautiful place a few blocks from my school, but it hid a secret: a monster lived in the walls of my bedroom.

I discovered it the first night, when I was awakened by noises in the wee hours. Creaks and cracks came from the partition walls. Based on my grandmother's teachings, I immediately deduced it was a chicherecú, a demonic imp with red eyes and sharp fingernails. My maternal grandmother, Lala, practiced Santeria and knew all the different varieties of güijes living on the island, from the most inoffensive, like the babujales who only sought to scare and mock their victims, to the Living Death, the terrible lady who rode through dark nights in her funeral carriage, searching for fresh souls.

Lala was my favorite grandmother because it was impossible to be bored with her. She wore her gray hair wrapped in a turban, like the black women, and she liked to put on colorful dresses. Like the good witch she was, she was always mixing potions, salves, or spells. Besides, I had no other grandparents to compare her to, because my dad's parents had died of illness when he was still young, and my Lala's husband had also died of fever.

When I told her about the chicherecú, Lala immediately placed a red candle under my bed to scare it away, but the imp was persistent and came back to torment me every night. And so there we were, grandmother and granddaughter, wrapped up in our witchery, when the solution appeared in the most unexpected way.

Mr. Einstein's visit came totally by chance. The chauffeur driving his car stopped at a red light, and Elsa, his wife, was enchanted by our window display and convinced her husband to stop for coffee and dessert. My mother waited on them, having no idea she was in the presence of one of the most important men in the world, and convinced them to order an atropellado matancero with egg yolk, coconut shavings, and pineapple bits. While Elsa bought the cakes, Albert Einstein sat down in the tearoom and was surprised to discover a little girl beneath his table: me. Thanks to the monster in the walls of our new house, I had picked up the habit of taking shelter under furniture.

"Hi, there, little girl," the gentleman with wild white hair greeted me in English.

"Good afternoon, sir," I replied with the English I'd learned at school.

"What are you doing down there?" he asked.

"I'm hiding from the monster. I turn seven today, and since I'm big now, it'll eat me tonight."

"A monster!" he repeated, fascinated. "What kind of creature is this?"

"It's a chicherecú, an evil güije, with vampire teeth and bear claws. It lives in the walls of my house."

"How do you know it lives there?"

"Because I hear its creaks and thumps in the night."

The white-haired gentleman burst out laughing. "And you say you only hear it at night?"

"Yes, in the daytime the lousy thing must be asleep because it's very quiet."

"There's no monster in your house. What you're hearing is called expansion and contraction."

Expansion and contraction. In my child's brain, those sounded like the names of ferocious demons.

"What kind of monsters are they?" I asked.

"They're not monsters; they're laws of physics. All the materials they use to make houses, like wood and metal, expand in the heat of day and contract in the cool of night. They grow when it's hot, and they shrink when it's cold."

That sounded so extraordinary that I figured this gentleman, so wise and with such a mustache, must be a witch doctor, like my Lala.

"The expansion and contraction is magic?" I asked.

"Even better, it's science."

In the front of the shop, my mother finished serving the cakes out of the refrigerator, and Elsa called to her husband to get back in the car.

"Meine liebe, siehe . . ."

Einstein got up from the chair and gestured to her to wait a moment. Before he left, he took off his Panama hat and put it on my head.

"When you're afraid, put my hat on and remember that the best way to beat monsters is to read science books."

From then on, I followed Mr. Einstein's advice, and science books became my inseparable companions. Thanks to my reading, I discovered a person ages faster when they are up a staircase than when they're on the ground floor, due to the force of gravity; that there are more stars in the universe than grains of sand on all the beaches in the world; that an octopus has three hearts; and that our universe will die in about five billion years.

Science gave me answers that a superstitious Cuba, obsessed with saints, couldn't offer. And, for me, there was more magic in my mathematics, physics, and astronomy books than in all the dens of the old fortune-tellers to whom Havana's residents turned. Science became my way of understanding the world, and my fear of the chicherecú in the walls of my house disappeared.

"Abuela Lala, did you know the center of the earth is as hot as the sun?"

"Mijita, that must be because of Oyá, the queen of the dead, mistress of the flame and patron of the cemetery, who is one of Changó's most beloved favorites. When she gets mad, she turns into fire."

Since I had begun to consider myself a woman of science—or a little girl of science, rather—my grandmother's superstitions made me furrow my brow.

"That's all backward, Abuela."

"Backward? Not at all. I'll ask your grandpa's ghost and see what he thinks."

"Ghosts don't exist," I insisted, exasperated.

My grandma laughed and looked at me with doglike simplicity. "Who says?"

"Science. You can't believe in science and ghosts at the same time!"

"Of course you can, mijita. Of course you can."

Sadly, not all the monsters of my childhood were made-up. A few years later, I would meet another, much more dangerous monster. One that would change my life forever.

CHAPTER 9

The monster wore a stone-colored tropical suit and an expensive tie. He smelled like cigar smoke and Moroccan leather. His shiny black hair, with a white streak on one side, and his attractive smile made him look like Gary Cooper. The danger with this monster was that, as handsome as he was, he didn't seem like a monster. Any woman would have felt lucky to have a man like him pay attention to her. Any woman who wasn't twelve years old, that is.

He approached me on the corner of Zanja and Galiano, at the intersection where the buses and electric streetcars started their routes. Like many girls my age, I collected Susini postcards, little stickers gathered in an album and attached with fish glue to one of three hundred slots. The local kids would meet up under the porticos on that corner to trade our stickers. I normally went with my mom or dad, but that Sunday I had gone alone because the candy shop was bustling, and I had sworn on La Milagrosa I would be back by lunchtime. But all my plans went to hell when that man interrupted me.

"Hey, sweetheart. I like your freckles. Can I have them?"

I didn't answer. In school they'd told us we should never talk to strangers.

"I'm César. What's your name?" he insisted.

I kept ignoring him, hoping he would go away and leave me in peace.

"Are you mute? Cat got your tongue?"

In the years since, I have often remembered that cursed moment and imagined myself running away. Because that's what I should have done: turn my back on that man-monster and run, run, and run without looking back.

Instead, I stayed there, like the unwary child I was.

"Maybe you're not dumb, just stupid." The guy looked at me with no shame. "And an asshole to boot."

My next words sealed my fate and my family's. I simply couldn't keep quiet.

"I'm not an asshole! I just don't want to talk to you," I responded defiantly.

The man smiled, amused by my bad temper and, I suppose, excited like a cruel lion upon learning the gazelle plans to make a stand before being devoured.

"So can you tell me why you don't wanna talk to me? What could I have done to you, poor girl?"

"I don't know you," I told him directly.

"That's a lie. We just met right now. Just so you know I'm a friend, would you like me to buy you some candy?"

"No. I already told you I don't talk to grown-ups I don't know."

"Grown-ups? But I'm only twenty-six! Not so long ago I was going to school myself, you know? I bet you don't have any teachers as young as me."

I kept quiet, not knowing what to say. I just wanted to get away from there as quickly as possible. But he persisted. "Don't play hard to get, girl. Come on, tell me your name."

"I don't want to."

When he saw I wasn't going to say anything else to him, the man changed his tactics.

"I don't need you to tell me. I already know. Your name is Bonifacia, and your parents are the scrap dealers on San Rafael Street."

"I don't have an ugly name like that!" I shouted, furious. "My name is Gloria!"

"But your parents are scrap dealers from out in the country, isn't that right?"

"No! They have a sweet shop, La Golosa." I corrected him with pride.

"Well, then of course you don't want candy," he said, smiling. "You should have said so before! But don't worry. I'll buy you something else. Whatever you want, in exchange for your freckles. Because it might not be today," he added, looking at his watch, "but someday your freckles will be mine."

And then he left, as triumphant as Gary Cooper walking down the main street of a town in the Wild West. The lion had the name and address of the gazelle.

The next week, on Tuesday, when I came home from school and walked into the sweet shop, I almost fainted from fright when I saw César sitting at one of the tables. As soon as he saw me, he gave me a knowing wink. He finished his cup of coffee, and making sure no employee saw, he placed a gift-wrapped package in my hands before he left. It was an album of Susini postcards, the entire collection already glued in place.

"Give us a kiss on the beak!" squawked Raimundo the parrot, almost scaring me to death.

That was the first of many gifts. Every Tuesday, the wolf showed up at our candy shop for a snack. And he did so disguised in sheep's clothing. Because César always knew how to take advantage of his Gary Cooper looks to hide his true intentions.

Several months went by, and my parents awaited him every Tuesday with a table prepared just for him. A cup of coffee with donuts for the elegant gentleman. César was a good customer: gracious, good-natured, and generous. Especially with me, of course. He always brought me some kind of present: rag dolls, pearl earrings, caramel sticks, and silk stockings . . . a strange mix of gifts for a little girl and gifts for a woman; these never disguised his interest in me.

I still had so much to learn about life. My first impression—that intense, unpleasant sensation of my body tensing up every time he came near me—was gradually diluted by the gifts; he slowly won my trust by showing up, week after week. He'd wink at me behind my parents' backs, and his words to me sounded like they came from a love letter. It was a crazy thing: I was still a little girl, more interested in playing with dolls than in trading kisses with older men.

One day, when I was still around thirteen, he made me sit on his lap, and after he pushed the hair out of my face, we just looked at each other, our faces a few centimeters apart. He was seducing me, and I was allowing myself to get caught up. He came a little closer and whispered that the time had come for him to claim those freckles. My entire body was on guard in an unwholesome combination of fear and excitement, of attraction and anger with myself because I, poor thing, had now surrendered.

A few months later, César formally asked my father for my hand in marriage. My parents were flabbergasted, and they asked for some time to think it over. By that time, they had heard the rumors. César wasn't just any guy; he had accumulated a fortune thanks to his murky business dealings. My suitor was a member of the mafia, and you can't say no to a mafioso.

"Gloria is still very young. Although if you keep getting to know each other and love comes up sooner than expected, who knows?" my dad argued, playing for time.

But after his investment, César was determined to claim his earnings. And he decided to leave no doubt as to how far he was willing to go for anything—or anyone—he thought of as rightfully his.

That was the last night I ever slept without nightmares. The last night of my childhood.

On the third day after he asked for my hand, when my parents went to open the sweet shop, they found an incredible surprise. Someone had smashed the glass door, and shards that shone and looked like snowflakes covered the paving stones on the sidewalk. The lock was broken and the door was open. But the worst was inside. While the employees consoled my mom, my dad came face-to-face with the end of the world: Raimundo the parrot and all the other birds had been slaughtered. It was brutal. The twisted heads and torn wings were a terrible sight. In the tearoom, the chandeliers were shattered, just like the collection of teapots, and all the red velvet chairs were slashed to ribbons.

When my father went to report the incident to the police, an officer told him these things happened, and there was nothing they could do.

"These things happen? Are you crazy?"

"I'm sorry, sir. We can't help you here," the police officer answered, not looking him in the eye.

"I want to talk to your superior immediately."

"My superior will tell you the same thing. If you shake a hornet's nest, you have to deal with the stings."

My dad came home in a rage. He was faced with an impossible decision: to give his blessing to the union of his young daughter with a mafioso or to let us all suffer the consequences. The decision would have broken anyone's heart but, in his case, it was literal. I didn't know it, but my dad had suffered from heart problems since he was very young. He was born with a beautiful heart but also with a defective valve. It was one of those things he had never told me so as not to worry me, until I found out in the worst possible way. That night, my father had a heart attack in his bed. Don Gregorio Beiro Moreira, the kindest and sweetest man in the world, died in a car on the way to the hospital.

When they notified us of his death, my mom collapsed on the floor. In an instant, she stopped moving, speaking, or eating. The doctors said she had suffered a massive stroke due to the shock. My mother became a living ghost. I had to feed her sugarcane foam and morsels of bread soaked in milk. I changed her underwear as if she were a baby. She needed someone by her side at all times, day and night.

That was when I gave up. I sacrificed myself. I couldn't let the lion eat the whole flock.

What would have become of my life, of our lives, if I hadn't given up so soon? Peace always has a price . . .

Two weeks after my father's death, I turned fourteen, and César Valdés took me as his bride. On December 22, 1937, we celebrated the wedding at the cathedral in Havana. No detail was overlooked: the long white dress to symbolize my purity, the veil to ward off evil spirits, and the cake adorned with little dolls. Since tradition dictated that the more layers the cake had, the more years of happiness the newlyweds would enjoy, César bought one taller than Morro Castle.

When he put the ring on my finger, I realized that, more than a bond, it was a trap. I couldn't smile in my wedding pictures, as much as the poor photographer tried to catch me not looking panicked.

"Come on, darling, say queso in English. Cheeeese!"

We had the reception at the Calypso, and it went on for so long that I fell asleep in a chair, defeated by my aching feet—it was the first time I had ever worn high heels—and by my disgust. Without waking me up, my new husband took me in his arms, carried me to the car, and drove us to our new house: a three-story palace surrounded by a huge estate in Miramar, the most expensive neighborhood in the city.

The most painful part of my wedding night was not losing my virginity in his arms, but the words he whispered in my ear while he ripped off my dress, snapped off my brassiere—which was too big for me because I didn't yet have breasts to push up—and pulled down my panties.

"See, dummy? I told you your freckles would be mine."

CHAPTER 10

I'm not a woman who complains, and I would be lying if I said my married life was an inferno. At the very least, it's a most comfortable inferno. César kept his word, and the first thing he did to make me happy was to buy a pretty house in the Vedado neighborhood for my mother and my Lala, with a nurse and a maid to take care of all their needs.

And if the house he bought for my family was pretty, our own home in Miramar was a palace fit for a princess. We had three floors equipped with the most modern appliances—an oven, a refrigerator, a washing machine—and a ton of staff to deal with them. César was proud that I never had to wash a dish and that my closet, which was the same size as many an apartment in Old Havana, was lovelier than many boutiques. My dressers were so stunning, they would have made any woman cry. My dressing room, wallpapered with drawings of royal palms, was filled with floor-to-ceiling dressers made of mahogany and a type of Cuban cedar that insects won't attack. The floor was made from planks of yellow-pink cuajani, and they creaked deliciously when you stepped on them. There were two velvet armchairs for when I got tired of changing clothes and a mannequin on which I could try out my ensembles first.

In the drawers, my clothes were organized by color: dozens of skirts, blouses, and dresses painstakingly ironed and perfumed by my black maids. I had an entire dresser dedicated to accessories, another just for evening dresses, two for bags, and an entire wall just for shoes. I could see myself from head to toe in two huge mirrors, and there was a beautiful French dressing table for my jewelry with a little matching chair so I could sit and comb my hair and put on my makeup.

Swearing by his sainted mother, my husband was not about to allow me a career or a job because God wouldn't want my pretty little head to burn out from so much thinking. Therefore, my life's only mission was to please him and look pretty whenever we went out, me hanging off his arm. Without obligations, my life was just one eternal weekend. It was all appearances, one long runway.

So I wouldn't get bored in my golden cage, César would give me a roll of pesos and another of dollars every day so I'd get excited about going shopping at El Encanto accompanied by sly Marita, his snitch of a little sister.

Only eighteen, Marita was Havana's golden virgin and one of the most envied women on the entire island. She was dark-haired and handsome and had green eyes as cruel as her brother's. Marita was beautiful, yes, but she was also a viper and one hell of a gossip. Spoiled and conceited, she counted on a whole squad of suitors whom she treated badly, like a mean cat playing with poor little mice before sending them off to hell.

Marita was considered the queen of Sin Corner, and her favorite entertainment was to take my arm while we strolled past the display windows at El Encanto looking absolutely dazzling. The difference between us was that while Marita delighted in provoking envy, I detested it. I understood it was inevitable that my life seemed like paradise. I had a handsome and powerful husband who adored me. That César was a gangster was also exciting, not something ugly. The romantic idea of the mafiosos had taken hold in Cuba. No one ever seemed to stop and realize that not everything shiny was gold.

Whenever I got nostalgic, I'd remember how I'd been a rebellious and curious child. It was that rebelliousness that had made César notice me. After my marriage, my joy disappeared, and I lost the habit of talking to people. Marita was my only friend, although that wasn't my decision. César had taken care of it. Since he was so macho, he got jealous of any male who came near me, and he didn't stop until he managed to make sure I had no life outside our marriage. He could have friends and a good time out of the house, but woe to me if I dared do the same!

There were times I thought the best way to make him happy would be to transform myself into one of those many appliances he'd bought. I could get a button that my husband could use to turn me off when he left the house, and then he could press it to turn me on when he came back. An automated woman, without feelings or desires of her own and who didn't function outside his presence.

But the worst part of my life with César was having to sleep by his side every night. Like Gary Cooper, César could be quite enchanting, but at the same time, behind that mask he hid the face he'd shown me the very day we met: that of a domineering bully.

The mask had slipped before, and now it was getting worse. César's gifts weren't holding my attention; the life César offered made me feel trapped. What I mean is, I had made a pact with the king of the jungle; during the day, I could enjoy a life of luxury and comfort as long as I forgot about myself.

In bed, César was selfish and always put his pleasure before mine. But having surrendered already—once you gave in to his blackmail, there was no going back—he had a free hand to do and undo whatever he wanted at will. My body warned me things weren't the way they should be. My skin never got used to his skin. When my husband made love to me, I wanted to turn into the living dead, like my mother, to leave my body and let the ugly and disagreeable moment pass. In the first years, as soon as it was over, I'd run to the kitchen with the lie that I needed a glass of water—it made César mad if I hid in the bathroom—and I would rub myself all over with a little Chinese sponge in the sink until I could wash away his pig smell.

Those first months were the worst. Every night, as I gritted my teeth in rage under the weight of César's sweaty body, I would dream about hiding a machete under the pillow, splitting his head open, and cutting his dick off, but to do so would be to sign my own death warrant. My husband was not only twice my age but also twice as strong. As time went by, I not only built up a heap of hatred toward him but above all—and even though it may seem strange to say it like this—toward myself too: that resignation, that acceptance, made it so that every day there was an ever-increasing distance between me and the girl I had once been.

Heaven may have finally wanted me to get some relief when I turned sixteen years old. When I became a young woman—a real woman, with tremendous hips and breasts that finally filled my bras—César calmed down. Instead of wanting to fuck me every night, he would leave me alone for entire weeks. My new curves never interested him as much as my old scrawny body.

I remember one morning when I went with Marita to the church at Regla and just stood in the chapel of the fishermen's Virgin, the doors open wide to the sea. A really ugly thought came to me: *Jump. Now. If you do it, you won't have to put up with one more kiss or any more of his drooling.* The idea gave me such solace that I walked all the way to the waterline. But just as I was gathering my courage to jump, I got such a stomachache. And instead of leaping, I vomited right into the waves. The doctor who examined me later told me something that sent my plans to end my life to hell.

"Congratulations. You're going to be a mother."

Months later, I brought a little girl into the world, Daniela. She was born a few days before I turned seventeen. I was terrified I would hate my daughter at first sight. I wasn't lacking reasons: half of that creature came from César's seed. But as soon as they put her warm, pink body on my breast, I fell in love with my little girl. César never got tired of telling me he would have preferred a boy so he could someday inherit his business, but his disappointment only made me love Daniela even more.

Daniela was the most beautiful girl in the world. Unlike her father, who bought loyalty with money and threats, Daniela won everyone over with her wonderful personality. I stopped feeling guilty because I realized I now had a mission to complete in this life. I swore to myself that all the happiness I'd been denied would be my daughter's inheritance. Daniela was my only reason to keep going.

That is, until that cannonball from El Encanto showed up to offer me a second chance.

Ours was quite a collision. I was running through El Encanto without looking, delighted because I'd managed to lose César and Marita and was finally enjoying a minute to myself. My plan had been to run to the book department and buy the new edition of Charles Darwin's *On the Origin of Species*—César had thrown my old copy in the trash—when, all of a sudden, I crashed into Patricio.

Thanks to a porcelain zebra, we met. A broken zebra, but because of the miracle of good glue, no visible marks gave away the damage. Like me.

I liked his demeanor: those blue eyes, that straight nose, a lush mouth, and a firm chin. A svelte body and curly hair. Of course, being used to not looking at boys out of respect for and fear of my husband, it took me quite a while to realize the young man was so handsome. God knows I would never have talked to him, but he was so anxious about losing his job over the broken zebra that my instinct led me to help him. And wouldn't you know it, I gave him advice I should have followed myself: you don't have to give up so easily.

In the maintenance room, while I glued the zebra's legs back on, the cannonball and I talked about the theory of relativity. I had never spent so much time alone with a man who was not my father or my husband. Men frighten me, that's the simple truth. But this cannonball was so young and so sweet, he didn't strike me as a threat. And besides, this young man listened when I talked, which was a real novelty for me.

To have disappeared for that little while earned me a real scolding from César, but I didn't care. I'd had a good time with the cannonball. And in some way, all that hassle had allowed me to see myself, even if for just half an hour, as the rebel I used to be. And yet, in spite of all the good feelings, it never crossed my mind we would ever see each other again.

I was no fool. I was used to provoking interest in men. A lot of men used to catcall me and make all sorts of amorous proposals on the street until they realized my husband was César Valdés, and then they'd scram. But with Patricio, everything would be different.

I realized it the day after the dog died.

CHAPTER 11

The dog was named Canelo, and he was butt ugly. The size of a big rat and bald, he had rheumy eyes, a prominent underbite, and a flimsy tongue he wrapped around his snout all the time. His owner, Ernesto, had worked for us as a gardener until he died of a stroke, and the little dog stayed on. When Daniela saw how lonely he was, she adopted him. To the dismay of her father, Daniela let him in the house whenever she could. That little animal was her weakness, and she shared her bread-and-cream-cheese snack with him every afternoon. César would go ballistic every time he saw the ugly thing lying on one of the rugs. He thought our daughter would get sick of the dog, but Daniela's devotion was sincere. For his part, Canelo adored her right back, was extremely loyal, and spent all day tangled around her feet.

"Canelo, Canelito, wag your little tail!" Daniela would sing to him with all the innocence of her eight years.

Since nothing truly ugly doesn't also have its charm, even I grew to love the little dog. Canelo ended up winning me over and officially came to live with us. That's pretty much what guaranteed that things would not end well.

It happened one night after dinner. As if it wasn't enough that he was so ugly, Canelo was also older than Methuselah and farted like crazy. That night, his intestines must have been particularly riled up because Daniela had given him her leftovers. We were all in the living room when we got a whiff of the first fart. Daniela and I glanced at each other, trying to contain our laughter. That dog's farts were stealthy, treacherous, and very stinky. César wrinkled his nose, but he was distracted reading the newspaper, and he let it go. But then Canelo committed the greatest mistake of his life when he curled up on César's feet and let loose with a second fart. The poisonous cloud reached my husband's nose, and in a fit of rage, he leapt up and grabbed the animal by the neck.

"Goddamn it, this dog is rotten inside! What a disgusting fart bomb!"

Canelo didn't even get a chance to bark before César kicked him, and the dog smashed against the wall.

Whether from cracking his skull, the kick in the guts, or a stroke from sheer fear, Canelo died instantly.

Daniela and I froze with terror. When Daniela saw that the unlucky little animal wasn't moving, she broke into sobs.

"Daniela!" César scolded her. "It's just a mutt. Don't throw a tantrum now."

"He was not just a mutt; he was my dog! And you killed him!" Daniela sobbed.

I immediately got between them, trying to protect my cub, hiding her in my skirts. I would have much preferred César kick me than do any harm to Daniela.

"What the fuck did you say?" growled César.

"She didn't say anything," I answered.

Daniela bit her lip, but her tears kept coming. I put my arms around her to console her. Furious, César stormed out and slammed the door.

"You're as spoiled as your mother!" he yelled from the other room.

The next day, Daniela was still inconsolable, so César ordered me to take her shopping.

"Just grab a good wad of pesos and buy her a toy. Or two. Or two dozen! But get her to stop crying, for the love of blessed Saint Barbara, or my head is gonna explode."

As soon as we got to El Encanto, we went up to the toy department. The entire section was marvelous. Even though it had been designed for toddlers, and all the shelves were at their height, the dolls were so pretty and the stuffed animals so soft that more than one grown man or woman had fallen into temptation and taken one home.

The department's big attraction was a miniature, a great landscape made on a divine scale. Several electric trains circled an alpine mountain with little towns, little sheep, and even rivers made with real water, not just silver paper. The other good thing about that department was that things were priced for everyone's pocketbook, from dollhouses that cost thousands of pesos to blind bags that went for only two cents. No kid left El Encanto without a toy. And to make the visits even more fun, the employees would wear costumes to entertain the little ones.

That day, Patricio was dressed up as a pirate and was showing a group of kids and their moms how to work a car made out of Meccano pieces. As soon as we approached, I saw his face light up.

"Ladies and gentlemen! Boys and girls! El Encanto, the most fabulous store in the world, presents the most fun toy for young and old! With the Meccano pieces, you'll be able to make absolutely anything you can imagine. Come on over, see for yourselves."

As everyone went to investigate the new invention, Patricio came over to say hello.

"Good morning, young lady." He extended his hand to Daniela with great ceremony. "What's your name?"

Daniela shook his hand firmly.

"Daniela."

"Can I tell you a secret, Daniela? I'm not a real pirate."

"I already know that."

"How did you find me out?"

"You don't have a peg leg."

Patricio couldn't help but laugh. "So besides being as beautiful, you're also as clever as your mother. Did you come to buy a toy?"

Daniela sighed so sadly that Patricio could clearly see something was wrong.

"What's the matter?"

"I wanna cry, but I shouldn't," the girl answered, her lower lip trembling.

"Why not? Crying is good. I cry a whole lot," he said tenderly.

"It's just that my dad gets upset when I cry, and I shouldn't upset him."

When she mentioned César, Patricio made a face as if he'd drunk something painfully cold.

"Why are you sad?" he asked her.

"It's because of Canelo."

"That's her dog. Was. Yesterday, he died," I tried to clarify without too much explanation.

"And you miss him?"

Daniela nodded, and two big tears rolled from her eyes.

"I don't wanna forget about him," she said, and hiccupped.

Patricio thought about Daniela's words for a moment. "I promise you're never gonna forget Canelo. Do you know why?"

"Why?"

"Here, give me your hands."

He took her little hands and moved her fingers carefully until just her thumbs pointed upward. Then he put his own hands against the light so they were projecting a shadow on the wall.

"It's a little dog!" she exclaimed, delighted.

"That's how you'll always have Canelo with you."

For the first time since the death of her dog, Daniela smiled at me. I'd come in with the intention of lifting my daughter's spirits by buying her something. But I realized that man was offering me an honest chance for the first time in a long time. You can't buy the important things, as he'd amply demonstrated. Deep down, I still knew that too. It's astounding what a simple gesture can reveal. That afternoon, I went back to being myself.

CHAPTER 12

PATRICIO

As soon as night fell, Havana was jammed with people who wanted to dance. Music came from everywhere: open windows, the lips of office workers who whistled songs by Celeste Mendoza on the bus on their way home, the melodies in the drumming of women's heels as they walked to the beat of the cha-cha. At the beaches and in parks, friends would form improvised jazz bands, and even if all they had were trumpets, a trombone, and some bongos, they'd play mambo, son, afro, rumba, and bolero.

In a city with so much music, it would have been a sin to not take advantage of it, so going out dancing was like an obligation for all good Cubans. And like Sunday churchgoers, music lovers had many temples from which to choose. As much because of their prices as their variety, the cantinas were some of our favorites, especially at that twilight hour when the swallows give way to bats. A Havana cantina could count on several ingredients: rum, music, and people who wanted to have a good time. Among the nocturnal fauna, there were always the "women of the night," girls who dressed scandalously, and "birds of paradise," who used the dance floor to get everyone's attention. The "women of the night" weren't exactly prostitutes, but a mix of gifts, cocktails, and flattery could buy their love for a few hours.

For a country boy like me—who had grown up with the cold of Asturias deep in my bones and whose idea of fun was a pint of bitter wine after a backbreaking day in the mines—those nights of salsa dancing in the tropics, with my back bathed in sweat, a mojito in hand, and a beautiful girl against my waist, were an earthly paradise. I'd come to Havana so hungry that I took huge bites of the city every night.

My first year working at El Encanto went by very quickly. They were very intense months, but I wouldn't change them for the world. Thanks to my position as a cannonball, I darted around like a fish in water through the insides of that great store. There wasn't a single employee who didn't use the informal "tú" or a department I didn't know like the back of my hand. I could have found my way through El Encanto with my eyes closed.

I thought my fascination would go away—or at least cool off—as the months went by, but it didn't turn out that way. Every time I strolled through the front door, I felt the same as I had the first day. How could I not? Entering El Encanto was like being invited to a high-society party. With fresh flowers on the counters, the uniformed clerks, and the mannequins wearing radiant silk taffeta dresses, it was a festival for the senses.

With my first check, I was able to pay my debt at the Bedbug Boardinghouse and ask Nely, the elevator operator, out for something to eat. But I wasn't the only one who prospered. El Encanto also brought good luck to my buddies. A few weeks after I got the job, Guzmán got a position as a clerk at the Garbo shoe store on Rayo Street, and El Grescas was hired as a waiter at King Kong in Regla.

With our three salaries, we decided it was time to become emancipated, and we rented a three-bedroom apartment in San Isidro. We were in an old attic, and the rafters creaked every time we opened and closed the door, but for us, it seemed like a palace. We were all used to sharing bunk beds, so having our own rooms was a major luxury. The attic had plenty wrong with it—water stains on the ceiling, broken tiles in the bathroom, and a prehistoric kitchen—but it was all worth it for the terrace. It was our secret oasis among the rooftops, offering excellent views of the noisy merchants below, other terraces jammed with clothes drying on the line, and a window through which we could see a mulata woman—we nicknamed her Cachita—who had the wonderful habit of walking around her house with barely any clothes on. That terrace was our special observation tower, and at the end of each workday, we would sit in our wicker chairs and enjoy stunning sunsets over the sea.

To thank the bedbug sisters for their patience with us, we bought them a second pair of dentures and treated them to a small banquet of fried steak, crispy green plantains, and other crunchy foods so they could try them out. Norma and Patria were so happy, they bid us farewell with tears and waving handkerchiefs.

After a year with the company, I was promoted from cannonball to intern: in this position, I had more responsibility and sometimes worked as a clerk. The best part was Don Gato's face when he told me.

"The owners are very satisfied with you," he mumbled through gritted teeth with his characteristic mustache tic, "but don't get overconfident because I've got my eye on you."

Life was good to me, as much at work as in my personal life. From the first time we went out, Nely made it very clear she was interested in me. I remember the afternoon we went to see *Gilda* at the Candilejas Theater. We were surprised by rain when we exited. It was one of those Havana downpours that seeps right through to your bones in a matter of seconds and makes the old women pray: "San Isidro, water carrier, take the rain and bring back the sun . . ." Luckily, we were able to take refuge in a small church. While we waited for the rain to stop, Nely noticed a statue of Saint Anthony.

"Did you know that, here in Cuba, we believe if a young woman stands Saint Anthony upside down, she'll surely find love?"

"You believe in that stuff?"

Nely shook her head.

"All that witchcraft can drive you nuts. I prefer to be direct, as you well know," she whispered as she brought her lips to mine.

That was our first kiss. A kiss that ended with a great and mutual start when we heard the priest barking from the altar, "Dammit! Stop that dirty business and wait until after you're married! You scoundrels! Communists!"

"We're going!" Nely yelled back. "May God make you a saint, Father!"

Laughing, we left the church, running through the rain. With her bangs soaked, her arms bare, and her body shivering, Nely was more enchanting than ever. We kissed again, and the taste of her lips blended with the raindrops streaming down my face.

"When are you gonna ask me to be your girlfriend?"

"First, we have to fall in love."

"I don't think it's gonna take much more for me to fall in love with you."

"Really?"

Nely looked around. She realized, like somebody who suddenly understands the answer is right in front of them, that the downpour had flooded the street and completely drenched our clothes.

"It's as clear as this water," she answered with ringing laughter.

Nely was stupendous; there was no doubt about that. But, unfortunately, you don't get to choose when it comes to love. With Nely, I enjoyed the moment, life as it was, all laughter and bells. Gloria, on the other hand, was like a bolt of lightning that ran through me from the top of my head to the tip of my toes. With Nely, I lived the present intensely, but Gloria invited me to discover who I could be in the future, something that produced a dazzling vertigo. And all of us, especially survivors, know that life doesn't make sense. As much as I didn't want to see it, from the day I met both of them, my fate was sealed.

Of course, Nely was the obvious choice, but Gloria owned my heart. And it was also obvious Nely had several advantages over Gloria. The two main ones: she loved me, and she wasn't married to a mafia capo.

The logical thing to do would have been to give up my obsession with Gloria and concentrate on Nely, but I could never make up my mind. To gain some time, I made up a story about having a girlfriend back in Spain with whom I still corresponded and whom I had not yet forgotten. Nely was understanding and agreed to be patient with me. We both signed up for the employee English classes, where we would pass the time translating song lyrics into our pathetic English and then sing them at the top of our lungs out in the streets.

> *Kiss me,*
> *Kiss me a lot,*
> *As if this was the last time, the last night . . .*

Besides having a childlike humor that mirrored mine, Nely was also politically restless.

"The state is so corrupt, and our politicians are such blockheads that if they got down on all fours, they'd eat grass," she would tell me. "They should have a bit more shame and try to steal our money a little less."

Since I'd lived through and left behind the foolishness of our tremendous civil war in Spain, I had never been passionate about politics, but back then I'd pick Nely up from her meetings and delight in her excitement when she talked about the up-and-coming Orthodox Party. "Cuba for Cubans!" was its motto, and its leader was Eduardo Chibás.

Between English classes, snacks, meetings, and movies, Nely and I would kiss like we laughed, that is, whenever we were happy and felt like it. But our thing never went anywhere, never got serious. Yes, we were good friends, very good friends, but for me, that was all. Realizing

Nely's feelings for me were deeper than mine for her, I always tried not to make her suffer unnecessarily. And even though we were friends, we never went to bed together because she was a virgin, and that, I told myself, was a gift she should only share with someone who was truly in love with her.

The situation provoked a lot of teasing from Guzmán and Grescas. Especially when, one night on the terrace after too many daiquiris, I confessed I hadn't slept with her.

"You still haven't done it with Nely?" Grescas looked at me with astonishment. "But you've been to the movies I don't know how many times! How long did it take you to bed my sister?"

"An hour," I confessed. "But that's because she led me into the woods and took off her slip!"

Guzmán started laughing, and Grescas pinched him so hard on the arm that he doubled over from the pain.

"Are you laughing at my sister?"

"Damn!" Guzmán protested. "You started it!"

"Only I get to criticize Begoña, understand? That's why she's my sister."

Because they were my best friends, they both knew about my love for Gloria, and their opinions were always the same.

"Forget about that dame and keep the elevator operator. Nely is great, much better than a nobody like you deserves."

"Grescas is right, buddy. As they say here in Cuba, that Gloria farts higher than her ass. She's so far out of your league, she's completely impossible to reach."

With my friends' sensible advice in mind, I would start off to work every day with the intention of making Nely my girlfriend. I'd go into El Encanto, get on the elevator, listen to her jingly laugh, and think: *Today. Today is the day I ask her.*

But then Gloria would come by the gift section to buy a little porcelain figure and tell me things from her science books, and my heart would leap. With Gloria, everyday things were left behind; our conversations took us to distant galaxies, to skies so wide they didn't even have a horizon. It may have seemed like insanity, but my instincts were never wrong: she, and no one else, was the woman for me.

"Patricio, did you know there's no sound on the moon? So it would be impossible to whistle. Isn't that amazing?"

"That's marvelous. And speaking of the moon, do you think freckles come from the moon?"

"We can only hope! I have a bunch."

"Your freckles would be out of this world."

Unfortunately, most of our chats were cut off by Marita, Gloria's sister-in-law.

"Gloria, I'm bored. Can you just pay so we can go look at makeup?"

"Yes, yes, of course . . . I'm taking this little porcelain bear."

"You bought one exactly like that last week!"

"Oh yeah? Then I'll take the polar bear."

"Mother of God, you've got a little zoo going in that cupboard at the house."

Needless to say, I would wrap the little porcelain figures with the speed of a limping turtle, just so I could enjoy a few more moments of her company.

"Gloria, I had the book department reserve a book with drawings of the solar system for Daniela."

Once more, Marita stuck her nose in.

"You!" she scolded me. "What are you, a clerk, doing getting cozy with a customer?"

"Excuse me, miss."

Marita took Gloria's arm and led her away. "Gloria, my dear, you're sweet as honey. But you can't be so trusting with the employees," she said, making sure I heard everything. "Besides, the quality of the clerks at El Encanto has really fallen lately. They're losing their luster."

Marita felt a special antipathy toward me. It may have been because I was immune to her beauty and knew that behind her pretty face lurked an evil bitch. Or maybe it was because, like those dogs who hear sounds humans can't perceive, she had somehow picked up on the complicity between her brother's wife and me, and she did not like it one bit. Never mind that, next to her, my social status was akin to that of a cockroach.

I was not the only employee she intimidated. Marita Valdés was a nightmare for all the workers at El Encanto. The reasons? A tongue like a viper; her bad, spoiled-girl manners; and her mafia brother's support. Every time she walked through the door, the employees would swallow hard and try desperately to keep the fear off their faces—until there finally came a day when destiny taught her a lesson for us.

CHAPTER 13

It was an open secret that El Encanto was the favorite department store for music and film stars. It didn't take long for me to experience it myself. One day, when I was still a cannonball, they sent me to organize the shirts in the tailor's shop. The English Room was a men's clothing section par excellence. It was a very selective department, decorated like the English gentlemen's clubs of the past century. Its walls were covered in oak, and shirt-making tools were built into the panels. To complete the atmosphere, the room was lit by green gas lamps, and the armchairs were soft brown leather, Chester-style. The Union Jack was framed above the cash register, almost giving you the impression you were buying a suit on British soil. That afternoon, I was engrossed in my work when a client interrupted me, speaking in English.

"Excuse me. Where's the restroom, please?"

I was astonished. Before me stood John Wayne, the unrivaled big-screen tough guy. It was strange to see him dressed in a white cotton shirt instead of a cowboy vest, but that face was unmistakable. After gasping like a fish out of water, I managed to pull myself together. *Restroom? What the hell is a restroom? Shit, he means el baño!* I thought, thanking God for my English classes. With my terrible accent, I managed to point the way.

"Gracias, amigo," he said.

The rest of the day, I couldn't wipe the stupid smile from my face. One of the most famous actors of all time had called me a friend. I remembered the theory of relativity Gloria had talked about so much. For Mr. Wayne, it must have been unimportant, but without knowing it, he had participated in one of the crowning moments of my life. How many people could claim to have pointed out the bathroom to the Ringo Kid, the legendary gunfighter from *Stagecoach*?

John Wayne wasn't the only illustrious customer at our tailor shop. The list was long. Maurice Chevalier and Lucho Gatica were frequent buyers of our sporting attire. Lana Turner, Nat King Cole, Cesar Romero, María Félix, Ernest Hemingway, and Tyrone Power had our credit card. The latter left us a legendary anecdote.

As a regular client, Marita knew—and terrorized—the store's employees every day. There was only one floor where she rarely set foot: the men's section, which she only visited when she had to buy a gift for her brother.

That day was César's birthday, and she had decided to give him an Italian tie. With her typical aplomb, Marita entered the English Room and saw a man with a black suit and regal poise examining the silk ties. Marita snapped her fingers to get his attention, but the guy paid her no mind.

"Hey! Sir!"

The man continued to ignore her, engrossed in his work. Furious, Marita pushed in front of him.

"Are you deaf?" she spat at him with scorn. "I demand you attend to me this instant."

"Sorry, ma'am, but I'm afraid I don't speak Spanish."

That was the straw that broke the camel's back.

"You don't speak Spanish? Comemierda! How can a shop clerk not speak Spanish? I wanna speak to your supervisor immediately!"

By then, Marita's tantrum had gotten so intense that a good number of curious customers and employees had gathered around, including Gloria and me.

When we saw the face of the "shop clerk" who was being told off, Gloria and I shared a look of astonishment, and we almost couldn't contain our laughter. I understood Marita's mistake: the man was wearing a dark suit almost identical to our uniforms.

"I think you should tell her," I whispered to Gloria.

Gloria approached her sister-in-law and took her hands to calm her down.

"Marita, this gentleman isn't an employee. This is Mr. Tyrone Power. The movie star."

Marita was speechless, but it was too late. By then, Tyrone Power was fed up with the crazy shrieking that had interrupted his choosing a tie for the premiere of his latest picture. To make things worse, Mr. Power barely knew a half dozen Cuban words but, as it turned out, "comemierda" was one of them.

"Comemierda? Did that woman just call me an asshole?"

I had to nod my head.

"Can someone please tell this lady she's a rude mule?"

His words were met with laughter from the crowd. *Rude mule* would be "mula maleducada" in Spanish, a serious insult for one of the best-known women in the city. Faced with an avalanche of laughs, Marita gathered up what little dignity she had left and beat a hasty retreat with her head held high. Gloria's sister-in-law thought the incident would fade away with the passage of time, but she couldn't have been more wrong.

The story of how Tyrone Power had called Marita Valdés a rude mule spread like wildfire through all of Havana. Even her brother César found it hilarious when the story reached his ears.

Sadly, the lesson in humility from Mr. Power didn't work any miracles. Marita continued torturing the employees of El Encanto, but now we had a secret weapon. Every time she mistreated us, as soon as she turned around we brayed like mules behind her back.

The episode had another unexpected consequence. Gloria told me Marita (who had never been made to blush before in her life) could never again watch a Tyrone Power film without turning burgundy.

CHAPTER 14

But not everything that happened in those years was so amusing. One episode also became sadly renowned and helped César's dark legend grow even more in the city. It happened on my day off from El Encanto, and I only heard about it. In truth, I don't know what I would have done if I'd been there.

The protagonist was a poor boy, eighteen years old, named León. The boy had a dream of opening his own store to sell guayaberas, traditional Cuban shirts, and in order to learn the business, he started working at El Encanto as a cannonball at around the same time I did.

León was from Curtidos, a small town on the other side of the island, where many of the residents were Haitians who had sailed up the Windward Passage to seek their fortune in Cuba. León's mother was a widow from Port-au-Prince whose husband had drowned while fishing for snapper and yellowtail on the high seas.

Before setting foot in the capital, León had grown up surrounded by cotton on the plantation where his mother worked. The poor woman was sorely displeased when her son decided to pack his bags and set out for Havana, but she had no option but to give her blessing and let him go.

León's only sin was that he was a nice guy and as awkward and clumsy as an overgrown puppy. I was fond of him because we had both been raised in small villages. The only difference was that I had spent many months at sea between Santa Benxamina and Havana in order to move on with my life, while León still hadn't left his shell. Like me, the boy had a big mouth. And, also like me, he had the misfortune of crossing paths with César with no idea how dangerous he was.

His fate was cut short one afternoon when Gloria and Marita were shopping in the French Room.

If the English Room was gentlemen's territory, the ladies reigned in the French Room. It was simply a little piece of Paris in Cuba. The place was an attraction in itself, decorated as the spitting image of the palace at Versailles, with golden clocks, marble tables, statues of cherubs covered in gold leaf, crystal lamps, and mirrors everywhere.

Its elegance drew gasps from the ladies, but there were few who could actually shop there. The French Room was the high-end section, where they created exclusive pieces made to order. Unlike clothing manufactured on sewing machines, the clothing in the French Room was made by hand with extreme care, using only the most special fabrics.

The star designer and the soul of the workshop was Alberto Suárez. The man had begun his career at El Encanto as a poster artist, but he had so much talent, the bosses didn't take long to nickname him Manet, like the famous French painter. After that, he made the jump to designer, and in short order, he became the king of hearts in a high society that craved sophistication. Among his most frequent customers were Ernest Hemingway's wife and Wallis Simpson, the Duchess of Windsor, but the waiting list for his pieces was longer than a phone book. His dresses were works of art that could transform a woman into a goddess. And, like all works of art, they were priceless.

On that fateful afternoon, César was going to buy a new dress for his sister and another for his wife. He needed Marita and Gloria to be ravishing so he could show them off. The occasion deserved it: María Luisa Gómez Mena, Countess of Revilla de Camargo, had organized a party in her art gallery on the Prado to bring together the crème de la crème of Havana's aristocracy. César was already an important man in the city, but rubbing elbows with the great families represented a final step in his path to power.

With a flash of his checkbook, César reserved the French Room and closed it down for a whole afternoon so they could be at ease and Manet could put his finishing touches on the dresses. In case they needed anything, he also ordered that half the personnel of El Encanto be at his disposal.

When they had been there awhile, Marita began to get hungry and fancied a snack. Just like that, Manet called for the closest cannonball, who happened to be León, and gave him the task of going out for coffee and buns. The boy obeyed with enthusiasm.

Minutes later, León came back with the snack laid out on a silver tray. And that was when he committed his fatal error. While he placed the coffee, glasses of sugarcane juice, and sweet buns on an end table, Gloria emerged from a changing room in her new dress: an exquisite number made from cherry-colored silk, with a boat neckline that revealed her delicate collarbones and a bow around her waist. It was sensational on her. She looked so good, León couldn't help but pay her a compliment.

"Girl, if Saint Lazarus saw you, he'd drop his crutch and start running!"

My colleagues told me a sepulchral silence followed the comment. It had been an innocent compliment; anyone who knew León would have sworn with their hand on the Bible that the kid didn't have a shred of malice in him and that he didn't mean to be disrespectful. The flattery wouldn't have mattered if not for one key detail: he had just flirted with the wife of a well-known mafioso, right under her husband's nose.

Everyone sat there, flabbergasted, waiting for César's reaction. The employees were paralyzed. Manet himself stood stock-still, the pins he used to fix dresses still hanging from his lips.

Gloria turned white, and César remained silent, incredulous at the young man's impertinence. His face took on the look of a bull mastiff staring down a chihuahua that had just tried to steal his dinner. León recognized his mistake and, looking down at the floor, apologized. But it didn't do him any good. César couldn't tolerate such overconfidence, especially not in public. He cared less about the compliment than about having his deliberately excessive reaction serve as a warning to anyone who might try something similar in the future. I had witnessed his contained rage when his authority was questioned, but that day, he released it with unexpected brutality.

"I'll make sure you regret that, little fucker," said César, walking toward León.

"Please, no!" Gloria tried to intercede.

"It's only fair to give him what he deserves, my dear," her husband answered. "And you always ask me to be fair, don't you?"

His fury could be discerned in the little details. An unwholesome glimmer in his green eyes, the white knuckles as he clenched his fists, and the slight furrowing of his lips like those of a beast about to attack.

"César—"

But there was no time. Moving at lightning speed, César punched León like a serpent strikes, hitting him in the gut. The young man collapsed on the floor, his eyes rolling back in his head and a look of confusion on his face. That wasn't enough for César. Even knowing his enemy was nothing to him, just a poor kid unable to defend himself, César wanted a fight, and he took his anger out on the boy. He rained kicks on León until he lost consciousness. The gangster finished the beating with a huge kick to the head. According to witnesses, the sound of León's skull cracking into pieces echoed through the floor.

No more proof was needed to show that César was an evil man. If the boy's behavior had displeased him, a word would have been enough to put an end to it, but instead, he tore his body apart like León was a rag doll. And he relished it.

After that last kick, the manager rushed in, alerted by the employees' screams, and discovered the gruesome scene.

Calmer, César fixed his hair, rolled down his shirtsleeves, and sat back down as if nothing had happened.

"Get him out of my sight. Let's keep going."

From that point on, there were different versions of the story. Some say León didn't make it to the hospital, that they didn't even call an ambulance. But it didn't matter much, because the ending was always the same. León died from the brutal beating, and no one, absolutely no one, did a thing to stop it. It goes without saying that his murderer was never accused of anything. The mafia had the police in its pocket and eating out of its hand, just as Guzmán and El Grescas had told me.

César Valdés had always been a special customer, but that day he practically became a god. The employees attended to Gloria without even daring to look her in the eyes or graze her hair. In the end, a simple compliment directed her way could mean death.

CHAPTER 15
GLORIA

I always knew my husband was a killer. Otherwise, you don't get to be a gangster. As early as our honeymoon, I tried to find out a little bit about his activities. César couldn't travel very far from Cuba because his business demanded his presence, so to celebrate our marriage, we spent a few days in Santo Domingo. We stayed at the Majestic Hotel in Boca Chica, in a pretty suite very close to the beach. The Dominican Republic had an advantage over Paris, New York, or any other place where newlyweds might spend their honeymoons: people there tended to ask fewer questions when they saw a man traveling with a fourteen-year-old girl.

I still remember the looks from the bellhop, a young mulato boy with sallow cheeks, who took our luggage to the room as César pinched my butt. I'm sure he had previously assumed we were father and daughter, but my husband's generous tip made sure he didn't ask any questions. He waited until César had turned his back before he gave me a sympathetic look and insulted my husband.

"Son of a bitch cradle-robber," he silently mouthed.

The first time I mustered the courage to ask César about his work was the afternoon of the first day of our honeymoon, as we were sunbathing on the beach. This was back in the days when César had not yet managed to quiet the rebel girl inside me.

"Those things are not of interest to young women," he answered, giving me a kiss on the tip of my nose. "You just worry about being pretty and telling the cook to have dinner on the table when I get home."

I gathered a fistful of sand and let it slip through my fingers.

"But I'd like to know," I insisted.

My brow furrowed, and César pressed his finger on my forehead to smooth it out.

"Baby girl, don't be such a gossip," he scolded me. "If you worry, you're gonna get wrinkles on your face, and I'll have to stop loving you. Is that what you want?"

Nothing would have made me happier than for my slimy new husband to forget about me and leave me alone, but out of caution, I swallowed my pride and shook my head.

"That's what I like: as they say in Cuba, a closed mouth attracts no flies." César got up to signal the conversation was over. "Let's go back to the suite. It's hot as fuck out here!"

After that, all my questions about his business were ignored with growls or angry looks.

I didn't have another opportunity to ask again until years later. It was New Year's Eve, and my husband had had roast pork and drunk wine like a beast. It was near dawn, and we were still in bed, having just had sex. César was so drunk, he couldn't stop talking, and I decided to take advantage of the situation.

"I just want to know one thing. Have you ever killed a man?" I asked suddenly.

César laughed so hard, it made my blood freeze. He tried to grab a cigarette from the cabinet, but he was so drunk, it took him four tries. He lit it and took a long drag.

"Are we back to your questions, you gossipy little rat? You have to go sticking your nose in everything," he snarled.

César kept smoking. His cigarette was a red light in the dim bedroom.

"There are many ways to kill somebody," he whispered after a while. "You can do it with a pistol. Or with a knife. Or with a cord. You can also do it with your own hands. Although that's just at the beginning."

"At the beginning?"

"When you don't have any money, and you live in a shitty town, you're willing to do anything to get to that place in the world where you know you belong. When you're rich, you don't have to kill anybody yourself. You can pay some poor sucker to do it for you."

"Is that what you do?" I asked in a low voice.

"No, not me."

César leaned in to whisper in my ear. I was scared, but I didn't let it show. His breath smelled of wine, of the spicy pepper from the roast pork, and of tobacco. In spite of his movie-star good looks, my husband was rotten inside.

"I'm still killing with my own hands," he murmured, his voice thick with pleasure. "There's no reason to lose the habit. If you get too comfortable, there's always someone a little hungrier than you ready to steal your crown."

A few minutes later, he was fast asleep. The following morning, he got up with a hell of a headache and no memory of our conversation. But I never forgot it. Every time César touched my skin, or worse, took Daniela in his arms, I was tortured by imagining what savage things he had done with those same hands.

That was the only time I ever caught César off guard. I never had another opportunity. From that moment on, my husband clammed up and never again said a word to me about his business.

But I didn't give up and decided to try and talk to Marita. My relationship with my sister-in-law was pretty difficult. I knew César had had Marita brought in from a tiny town in the countryside on the pretext that the girl would have better opportunities to find a husband among the moneyed single men of Havana. But my husband's decision was not a big brother's selfless gesture. What he wanted was to recruit Marita as his trusted spy so she'd spend all day on my heels. Another woman, young like me, was the perfect choice to be my chaperone and give him a report of my day-to-day activities. In exchange for her being my shadow, my husband paid all her expenses and took care of all of her wants.

And Marita could hardly believe her luck: she'd gone from the narrow confines of her small town to a life with endless comforts, all for the modest price of being my nanny. She accepted the deal without hesitation. Marita was transformed from a peasant from the provinces into a young lady from Havana who looked at the world over her shoulder so no one would realize she could barely read and write.

God knows I always treated her with affection, but Marita was too much like César for us to ever be real friends. My sister-in-law was selfish and abusive, a bad seed, but what I could never forgive her for is that she never once put herself in my place as a woman. She never questioned her brother's marriage to me, a girl just a few years younger than she was. With Marita, I learned women who don't raise their voices when men behave badly are as bad as they are.

The only time I ever saw her contradict her brother was when she was seventeen, and it was because of a young love. Everything happened shortly after Marita arrived in Havana. César set her up in the guest room. My sister-in-law was full of herself and always said God had not yet made a man who could tame her. Well, maybe he couldn't tame her, but the man next door could always make her laugh. His name was Rubén Collins, and his parents were an old American couple who had come to Cuba to import chewing gum. The Collinses were absolutely certain that the mint-flavored confection, rubbery as the green caimito fruit, was the future.

Marita and Rubén would hang out together at night in our garden—next to a low wall that was very easy to leap over—and on at least one occasion, I caught them kissing. After stealing a few more kisses, young Rubén had the very bad idea of coming over to our house and asking César for permission to visit his sister. César not only refused but also told him to go to hell and threatened his family so that they moved out of our neighborhood and sent their son to study at a boarding school in the United States.

"Listen up, little sister," César told Marita as soon as the Collins family had fled from Miramar. "If you let another hooligan start coming around, that'll be the end of life on easy street. I'm sending you back to the country with a swift kick in the ass."

"Rubén is no hooligan," Marita insisted. "Someday he'll inherit the family business."

"He's a nobody—an oaf," roared César. "You're not gonna marry a comemierda. Someday, I'll find you a husband who's got a good business, like a coffee plantation or a tobacco farm and not that chewing gum bullshit."

"But I want him."

"You'll do what I say. You're still just a stupid girl."

Lovesick, Marita said the most hurtful thing that popped into her mind. "When you married Gloria, she was a little kid."

I couldn't see what happened next because my husband leapt up, grabbed Marita by the arm, and locked himself and her in the other room. The next morning, when Marita got up to get her café con leche, she had a black eye and was no longer interested in arguing.

One afternoon I heard her crying in the garden, by the low wall where she and Rubén used to see each other. Without a word, I walked toward her, hugged her, and let her cry on my shoulder. We stayed like that, holding each other for a little while, until my sister-in-law brusquely pushed me away.

"If you tell César you saw me crying, I'll cut you," she threatened, drying her tears with the sleeve of her dress.

"My husband's a monster."

"Don't talk crazy. He'll smash your head open."

"He's a monster and a killer."

"Where do you get such ideas?"

"Do you know where he goes every night? His business at the Calypso? Do you really think we'd live in a house this beautiful and have so much money if he were an honest man?"

I could see my words had hit their mark. Marita knew. She knew, deep down, that her brother was a gangster. But that knowledge threatened her lifestyle, so she had adopted a more cowardly attitude: denial. Out of sight, out of mind.

"I don't know or wanna know anything about that. César loves us very much, and that's the truth."

"You're right," I said sarcastically. "César loves us so much, he practically stole me from my family, and now he's separated you from Rubén."

As soon as I mentioned Rubén, my sister-in-law's eyes got watery, but she pulled herself together immediately.

"Rubén wasn't good enough for me. I deserve a better husband, and someday I'll find him. And you should thank God for yours instead of talking behind his back," she hissed at me before going into the house.

Without my sister-in-law's support, I had no choice but to eavesdrop through cracks in the doors when César was gossiping with his buddies in the living room late at night or giving orders to his men. But my husband was very careful not to discuss important subjects at home, and the only real information I managed to learn about his activities was what I could get out of the household staff.

Mirta was different from the other maids, and not just because she was the oldest. César was very guarded about his privacy and usually only hired women who were very discreet and performed their tasks as quiet as mice. According to my husband, the best quality in a maid—or in any female, for that matter—was that she obey without complaint.

But not Mirta. She would sing while she ran errands, which César detested.

She was also not a woman who liked to go unnoticed. Mulata and playful, she had a huge birthmark on her face that took up all her cheek and part of her forehead. It was pink, in the shape of a boot, and stood in strong contrast to her black skin. She liked to joke around about how the birthmark was her mother's fault.

"My mother, may she rest in peace, was crazy about Italy. Her dream was to go to Venice, so she spent her pregnancy eating spaghetti and polenta, and this is how I came out, with Italy's boot on my beautiful face," she said, laughing.

I adored her and thought she was beautiful, but César always ordered her to stay in the kitchen so no guest would see her. If he didn't fire her, it was for two reasons. One, Mirta was an absolute animal when it came to household chores. She made the bed and washed at lightning speed, and she was as strong as two mules. The other reason was that she made an amazing spicy oxtail stew that my husband loved. Mirta's magic hand with the hot peppers saved her job.

Certainly, the antipathy between César and Mirta was mutual, no matter how much she, as the household help, had to respect her boss. The animosity also extended toward Marita, who made no effort to hide her disgust every time Mirta and her birthmark went by.

But Mirta knew she could be herself with me. She was fond of me and became my accomplice in the house. It was she who would tell me the gossip about my husband circulating in the city.

"They say at the boss's club, they sell opium and cocaine."

"They say your supermacho husband has prostitutes working in his club, and all the dancers are for sale."

"They say he makes so much money, he keeps it in golden ingots and buries them in coffins in Colón Cemetery."

"They say he killed a man because he beat him at dominoes."

"They say he killed another man because he parked his car wrong."

"They say he killed a waiter because he brought him a canchanchara toddy made with cheap rum."

"They say every Monday at noon, one of César's collectors goes in a side door at the Presidential Palace and hands over briefcases filled with millions of dollars."

They say, they say, they say . . . all of Havana knew more about my husband than I did. Unfortunately, it was very hard, if not impossible, to tell the difference between what was real and what was not.

Even though I was frustrated by wanting to know and never knowing, my curiosity diminished and eventually disappeared once the bright light of Daniela appeared in my life. I resigned myself to the idea that my husband was a mystery, and I tried not to think about what he did when he wasn't at home. I was fine with him being far from me and my daughter. Like most spouses of dishonest men, I adopted a defense mechanism that was cowardly but efficient: I would look the other way.

Until everything went to hell because of a dress.

When César beat that poor cannonball from El Encanto to a pulp, I was so blown away, I didn't know what to do. Patricio wasn't at the store that day. And it was better that way because what happened turned my stomach, and I was ashamed of myself. The worst part of the entire episode was that after my husband cracked the boy's head open, everything went on as if nothing had happened. They rushed the boy to the hospital, and César, Marita, and I continued with our shopping in the French Room. After a few adjustments to my new dress, we went back home and had beef with cassava puree at our usual dinnertime.

The police did not come with their squad cars to detain César or even question him. Our routine went on so undisturbed, I began to wonder if I had imagined the whole thing.

Until the party at the art gallery. The invitation said it was an exhibition of new paintings, but all the guests knew it was just an excuse to drink, chat, and be seen. María Luisa Gómez Mena, the Countess of Revilla de Camargo, had invited all of Havana's aristocracy. For my husband, who was always looking for new business contacts, that soiree was as enticing as a honey pot to a wasp.

We arrived when the party was at its peak. The host had contracted Benny Moré—el Bárbaro del Ritmo—to perform in person, and our arrival coincided with the moment when he was singing his soul out on the refrain from "Desgraciado." He sang of suffering, of his life being a puzzle he couldn't solve, and the words cut right through me.

The waiters in dinner suits crisscrossed the room with trays full of champagne flutes while the food was laid out in a buffet, savory on the left side of the room and sweet on the right. The women were wearing so much jewelry, they twinkled under the light of a very beautiful spider lamp hanging from the ceiling.

I, too, looked like some gorgeous rosebud. I was wearing the red dress designed for me by Manet at El Encanto, along with teardrop diamond earrings and a matching choker. Marita also looked very pretty wearing an aquamarine dress and matching jade pins in her black hair.

César got together with the rest of the gentlemen and ordered Marita and me to go gossip with the women. I served myself some fritters from the buffet and sat down to talk with our host. As soon as I crossed my legs, I noticed a bloodstain on my skirt, as small as a bean. It must have been the cannonball's, splattered when César kicked him in the head.

Since the dress itself was red, nobody had noticed. But that tiny little stain stirred something in me. It was proof that savagery had indeed occurred, that my husband had kicked a man's brains in for having the audacity to say something nice to me. The sight of that little bloodstain affected me so much that I spent the rest of the party absent, almost like a spirit. Marita asked over and over if the fritters had upset my stomach. If my husband was a killer, what did this say about my behavior? I was the only person who could've saved that poor man, which made me César's accomplice.

I spent a dreadful night eaten up by guilt and impotence. The next day, I decided I needed to do something. I waited until nap time to escape. César was out of the house and Marita had lain down after lunch. With Mirta's help—she didn't mind lying to cover for me—I climbed out the window, found the driver, and went to the hospital where they had taken the poor young man to find out how he was doing. I asked doctors and nurses where he was, but no one wanted to tell me. They all said they didn't want to violate the patient's confidentiality, but it was clear they didn't want to talk out of fear. Finally, with the help of a little roll of pesos, I managed to get a nurse to tell me what had happened.

"The boy who got beat up? He died a few hours after he was brought here. They've sent the remains to his family."

When I heard about his terrible fate, I was so shaken, I had to sit down. With a few more bills, I got the nurse to show me his file. The poor boy, may he rest in peace, was named León, and next to his name there was an address for his mother in the town of Curtidos, which I wrote down on a piece of paper.

When I got back home, I was so racked with guilt, I wanted to throw up. A man had died, and I had done nothing to stop it. It wasn't my fault my husband was a bastard, yet I felt equally responsible.

I opened a jar on my dresser and took out a bracelet of linked emeralds. César had given it to me for my fifteenth birthday, and because of the size and weight of the rocks, I knew it had to be worth a ton. I stuck it in an envelope without a return address and sent it to León's mother. I included a note along with it: "My most sincere condolences. Nothing can return your son to you, but I hope this will at least help alleviate some of your material needs." I immediately gave the envelope to Mirta so she could send it discreetly from a post office.

As soon as I handed over the letter, I hung up the dress, without washing it, on a mannequin in my dressing room. The little bloodstain on the skirt had become a reminder that César was a dangerous beast. And that I had to change. I had to get out of that golden rat cage, I told myself, for myself and for my daughter.

CHAPTER 16

PATRICIO

At El Encanto we prided ourselves on making life easier for our customers with gift certificates, credit cards, and anything else to facilitate their shopping. But the one advance that really caused a furor among our clients was when we put in the escalators. These were stairs that took people up and down without having to take a step; it was one of the marvels that justified a visit to the store. Many Cubans visiting the capital came to the store just to go on the escalators, as if they were an attraction at a fair.

The escalators were a marvel of engineering with wooden handrails and metal steps. They were made by the same company that manufactured the escalators for Macy's in New York, and when they were imported, many Havana residents followed the process of their installation with great curiosity. It was written about in the newspapers, under the headline, "At El Encanto, Escalators Give Your Legs a Vacation."

There was only one person in all of Cuba not happy about the arrival of this new invention: Nely.

"If everybody in the world uses those dirty escalators," she said, pouting, "who's gonna ride the elevator?"

I would console her with a kiss on the cheek while trying to contain my laughter, given her helpless expression.

"This is just a novelty, nothing more, Nely. The elevators will always be here."

"And what if they're not? What if they fire me?"

"People will ride the elevator, if for no other reason than to see how pretty you are."

"Will you?"

"Of course."

"Then I'll be fine," she responded, as warm as ever.

The day the escalators debuted was one of the most exciting I can recall. People, including kids, got in line just to go up and come down again. Every now and again, the escalators would cause a little whiplash or make a loud sound, which only caused greater excitement for kids and seniors. There was a festive atmosphere, as if the circus had come to town.

But all the joy abruptly ceased when César came in the store. That beast was violently dragging Gloria behind him by the wrist. I was so worried about her, I decided to follow them without being seen.

César yanked her all the way to the jewelry department and pushed her up against the counter. Poor Gloria's eyes were swollen from crying, and she moaned in pain when her body hit the counter.

The jewelry department was small and tidy, located in a small room to give it an air of exclusivity. The display cases used a thicker glass than in the rest of the store and were locked with not one but two keys. Inside the cases, the precious stones rested on velvet trays, as fresh and appetizing as exotic fruits.

The manager of the jewelry section—Diego, a man with graying temples who looked like a lovable grandfather—approached them, trembling like a leaf. I grabbed a broom and pretended to sweep the floor.

"Good morning, can I help you?" asked the manager with a voice that cracked from fear.

"Yes," snarled César. "We want a bracelet with an emerald."

"I don't need another bracelet," muttered Gloria.

César slammed his hand down on the counter, which made Gloria start, not to mention the manager and even me, though I was quite a distance away.

"Yes, you do need it!" roared César. "Do you know why? So you'll learn to be more careful."

The manager quickly checked the display cases, but I could see him going pale.

"I'm afraid we . . . we don't have emerald bracelets right now," he said.

César stared at him so fiercely, it looked like poor Diego was about to faint.

"Then what the fuck do you have with emeralds?" barked César.

"We . . . we have some necklaces."

"So give me a necklace."

The manager opened a drawer and brought out a purple velvet bag. From it he pulled an exquisite gold chain from which hung an emerald the size of a hazelnut. A rock of that kind would cost more than a car or a house. Without even asking the price, César took the necklace and threw the velvet bag into a trash can, like a gluttonous child taking the wrapper off a piece of candy. Then he grabbed Gloria and put the chain around her neck with all the arrogance of an owner putting a collar on a dog. The whole scene made me sick.

To the amazement of the manager, César pulled out several rolls of bills from his jacket and dropped them on the counter.

"If that's not enough, I have more."

"It's . . . it's more than enough, Mr. Valdés," stammered Diego as he gathered the money.

There was more money in those rolls of pesos than any honest worker could earn in his whole life. As soon as payment was settled, César turned his attention back to Gloria.

"I'll remind you that bracelet you lost was my gift to you for your fifteenth birthday," he said.

"I didn't do it on purpose."

"That's not an excuse! You can't just go losing my gifts." César was becoming more livid by the moment. "And it's not about money! I could give three monkey shits about the money!"

To make his point, he pulled out another roll of bills and threw it at the manager's face, almost giving him a stroke.

"What infuriates me is you not taking care of my gifts. Your lack of care is a lack of respect toward me. Do you understand?"

Gloria nodded and lowered her eyes in submission.

"Do you like your new necklace?" demanded César.

"It's very pretty. Thank you," said Gloria, trying to calm him down.

"I'm glad you like it. This necklace is a gift from your husband, and you're gonna take care of it until they bury you in it. And woe to you if you lose it. If you do, you'll be going to the grave sooner than expected!"

As he was screaming at his wife, César's fist had been going up and up until it was at the same height as Gloria's face. When I saw he seemed ready to hit her, all the muscles in my body tensed in anticipation of a fight. If he'd touched a hair on her head, I would have launched myself at him without concern about the consequences. Fortunately, a timely intervention saved us both.

"Excuse me, sir." His driver came running in. "It's quarter of, and I need to remind you they're waiting for you at the casino."

Gloria let out a sob, and César dropped his fist.

"I have to go. Don't wait up, I'll be home late tonight."

As soon as César left, Gloria covered her face with her hands in a gesture that was part relief and part despair. Diego looked at her sympathetically.

"Are you okay, Mrs. Valdés?"

Gloria shook her head because she couldn't talk. It took only one look to see there was a knot in her throat, and if she tried to speak, she'd break down. To spare her from crying in public, I went up to her and offered my hand.

"It's okay. Come with me," I whispered.

They were the same words from our first meeting. But this time, our roles were reversed. Now it was I who had to protect her.

Our small storeroom was too stuffed with paper and stationery, so I had to find someplace else where Gloria could cry freely without interruption.

And then I had an idea. Since everybody was fascinated with the escalators—even the elevator operators—the elevators were abandoned. I took Gloria to the one on the far left. It was break time, and Nely wasn't there. Once inside, I pushed the button for the top floor. Between the third and fourth, I pushed the emergency stop. With a squeak, the elevator paused between floors. There was an alarm system for situations like this, but I was careful not to touch it. That way, we would have a little more time before we were interrupted.

I turned to Gloria and shrugged.

"That's it. We're completely alone now."

With a sigh of relief, Gloria let herself fall apart. The last of her armor fell away, and she began to weep like a baby. I held her against my chest and let her cry all she needed. She held me with all her might, staining the front of my shirt with her tears. I rested my chin on her hair, taking in the smell of her shampoo. I could feel her heart beating like a sparrow trapped in her chest.

Gloria cried and cried until she couldn't cry anymore, and then she dropped, exhausted, on the floor of the elevator. Without letting go of her hand, I sat by her side and handed her my handkerchief so she could blow her nose. The necklace with the emerald was dazzling, a shiny and sinister green on her chest. I looked away, disturbed by the sight of her neckline.

"Feeling better?" I asked.

"A little. Thank you."

"Your husband shouldn't make you cry," I said, and I meant it. "To the contrary, he should make you smile."

"It's not the first time he's hurt me. And it isn't going to stop."

"He doesn't deserve someone as special as you," I added. It was more than I needed to say, but I couldn't help myself.

"I didn't marry him of my own free will," she whispered.

Gloria seemed uncomfortable talking about her husband, so I decided not to pry. Her voice had a sadness and resignation more appropriate to an old woman than a twentysomething girl. It broke my heart to see someone so young so defeated by life. To cheer her up, I tried to change the subject and did what I do best: I became a clown.

"Back in my village, we have a special technique to get people to stop crying."

"I don't think it's going to work with me," Gloria warned me. "My tears are endless. I'm a bottomless well."

"You have to lift your head and look up, so the tears will go back inside your eyes."

"They'll overflow."

"No, they won't, you'll see. Look up."

Gloria did as I said and raised her head. Slyly, I caught her off guard while she was looking at the elevator ceiling and kissed her outstretched neck. My little trick surprised her so much that she did, in fact, stop crying.

"You've got some nerve!" she said, scolding me but not at all angry.

We both chuckled. I was happy to see her go from crying to laughing. But the moment didn't last long, and Gloria's eyes clouded over again in a matter of seconds.

"Don't do that again. My husband would kill you for less," she said, darkly.

"It would be a happy death."

Gloria smiled and noticed my shirt was wet and stained.

"I got snot all over your shirt."

"It doesn't matter. Angel snot," I said, half joking, half not.

Suddenly, Gloria furrowed her brow and brought a finger to her lips. "What's that? I hear footsteps on the roof."

Surprised, I looked up, like a fool, and Gloria slyly took advantage of the moment to give me a nibble on my unprotected neck.

"Now we're even!" she exclaimed, satisfied.

Her brown eyes linked with my blue ones, and the two of us stared at each other as if we were connected by some kind of invisible force. Just like at the beginning of a storm, the air in the elevator seemed charged with electricity. It was precisely the moment in which you'd strike a match to light a flare. Or the second when the car you're riding on the roller coaster hits the peak before dropping. It was an intoxicating mix of adventure and danger. We were two young people breaking the rules, excited to know we were braver together and could reach the stars if we decided to do so.

Someone shouting outside the elevator broke the spell. "Hello? Is anybody there?"

I recognized Nely's voice.

"Yes, we're here! The elevator just stopped all of a sudden," I lied.

"Do you want me to get maintenance?" she asked.

"Just a sec. I'm gonna try one more time."

I sighed, annoyed, and pressed the button for the third floor. The elevator started back down.

When the doors opened, Nely was waiting expectantly. Her worry was transformed into surprise when she saw Gloria with me in the elevator, and that she had been crying.

"Are you okay, ma'am?" Nely asked. Our clients' comfort came first.

"Yes, yes. I almost had a heart attack when we got stuck in there, and I started crying, but I'm okay now."

"Do you want me to call the nurse?"

"That's very kind of you, but it's not necessary. I'm absolutely fine." Gloria pulled herself together and said goodbye. "Have a good afternoon."

Gloria walked away, blowing her nose, while I just stood there, stupefied, watching her back as she disappeared into the crowds.

"That is really bad luck. That's César Valdés's wife, the last person you wanna be stuck with in an elevator."

"Why's that?"

"Just imagine if something serious had happened!" said Nely, not the least bit suspicious that our time in the elevator had been deliberate. "Her husband would have had you cooked and served. Don't you remember what happened to that poor cannonball, León? Listen to me; if you run into her again, run like the devil."

"If she comes to shop, somebody has to deal with her."

"Let someone else do it. You're too pretty to end up as a punching bag for some mafioso pig."

It was good advice, and anyone with half a brain would have followed it. But it was too late for me. Gloria Valdés had completely rattled my senses.

CHAPTER 17

In 1950, if someone had asked me to name the most beautiful creature in the world, I would have said Gloria Valdés, without a doubt. But there was another woman who occupied an honorable second place: Ava Gardner. With her perfect face and her femme fatale ways, Ava Gardner had already starred in several movies and was destined to be a movie goddess.

Thanks to the many gossip columns in newspapers and magazines, even the most common of us mortals knew Ava Gardner had already been married twice and was known as a heartbreaker. There were tongues wagging that Frank Sinatra—despite being a married man and a father—had been circling her and had invited her to come to Cuba. And, of course, no Hollywood star could set foot in Havana without coming by El Encanto. For this reason, her visit became a very big deal among the employees. And who could deny that it was particularly exciting for the boys.

The day before her visit, the bosses raffled off the honor of being her escort, the person in charge of accompanying her through the store and taking care of her needs. The winner was Don Gato, who debuted a needle-thin tie and curled mustache for the occasion.

Expectations were high, but Ava Gardner pulverized them. Her arrival at the store was breathtaking. She wore a print dress with tropical fruits and flowers that clung to her curves and left her shoulders and legs bare, a little matching hat, and enormous sunglasses. She was simply spectacular. So much so that people began to open a path before her, like the Red Sea parting before Moses. The customers gazed at her with pure adoration, the women jealously guarding their husbands. It felt as if a panther had been let loose in the store. Next to such a feline, Don Gato was sweating up a storm, and his mustache tic was out of control. Every time Miss Gardner said something to him, he'd nod, looking like he was either about to have an orgasm or a heart attack.

The rumor spread like wildfire among the employees: Ava Gardner was looking for lipstick. Don Gato showed her samples by Max Factor, Cutex, Revlon, Myrurgia, and L'Oréal, but none seemed to please her. Before long, the situation had gotten desperate. Ava Gardner had tried more than a dozen lipsticks and had not yet found what she was looking for. When management heard what was going on, Aquilino Entrialgo came to the store and asked for me.

"Patricio, this is an emergency. Miss Gardner cannot leave the store without her lipstick. What would that do to our reputation?"

He was right. El Encanto prided itself on meeting the needs of even the most demanding customers. If a star like Ava Gardner left without finding what she was looking for, it would be a public relations disaster. We couldn't let that happen.

The company's prestige depended on one lipstick, and I was determined to find it.

With as much aplomb as I could muster, I went up to Ava.

"Good afternoon, miss. Perhaps I can help," I said in English.

Ava Gardner lowered her sunglasses so she could give me a good look. I noted she liked my youth and my demeanor. Don Gato, on the other hand, did not care one whit for this interruption, and his eyes burned with anger. Luckily, Mr. Entrialgo was with me because, if he hadn't been, the twitching man would've tossed me out of there with a swift kick in the ass.

"Let's see, Blue Eyes," Ava Gardner said in English with a smile that revealed a marvelous dimple on her cheek. "I'm looking for lipstick, but no one's shown me anything I like."

"Maybe we're not going about it the right way. What, exactly, do you want the lipstick for?"

"I don't understand your question."

"Most salespersons will ask you what color you want, or they'll advise you according to your skin tone or your clothes," I explained. "But I always like to ask what you need it for."

"Oh yeah?"

"Yes. In my experience, pink lipstick is best to sing boleros or eat oranges. On the other hand, more brownish tones are better for telling secrets or making declarations of love. Red lipstick is perfect for whistling at the strong man at the fair, for sticking your tongue out at catcallers, or blowing a kiss at a sailor."

Ava Gardner laughed when she heard this. I took a quick glance at my companions. Aquilino Entrialgo was smiling, and Carlos Duarte—Don Gato—looked so full of hate that it seemed like smoke was about to pump out his ears.

"Very well. I'll tell you what I need it for. Do you promise this will stay between us?" whispered Ava.

"Of course."

"It's for a kiss," she confessed. "It's for a gentleman who interests me, and I need our kiss to be unforgettable."

My first thought was that this guy was very lucky. Then I put it together. Frank Sinatra! Could she be talking about Frank Sinatra? Confirmation came swiftly.

"You know," she said, "your blue eyes are almost as pretty as his."

"Does the gentleman in question have the best voice in the entire world?"

"Maybe," she responded playfully.

With great pomp and ostentation, I opened a drawer and brought out a lipstick of the most intense crimson. "For a special kiss, I recommend this Chanel lipstick without the slightest hesitation. It is the lipstick of first kisses par excellence."

Ava gave me a smile that could have melted the North Pole. "You don't say . . ."

I nodded with complete confidence. "If the gentleman does not fall in love with you after this kiss, come back to El Encanto, and we'll refund your money."

"You don't say," she said again between laughs. "I'll take it."

By her express request, I stayed by Miss Gardner's side the rest of the afternoon. Our next stop was the French Room. She was very impressed with our haute couture, which rivaled the most select Parisian fashion houses. Because it couldn't be any other way, Alberto Suárez—Manet—came to personally attend to us. Ava was captivated by his creations, and while she tried on a half dozen evening dresses, I waited for her, leaning against the dressing room door.

I was more than surprised when, after a bit, a woman's voice came from inside, asking me to come in and help button her dress. I obeyed immediately, wondering at that familiar voice. Then I looked at the woman's back: a creamy, nude back, sprinkled with little freckles like a sky full of stars. It was Gloria's back, and I couldn't take my eyes off this constellation of freckles.

Without her realizing it was me, I delicately buttoned her dress. She looked in the mirror and spun around.

"Patricio!" she said, surprised but grinning. "It seems fate likes to bring us together in tight spaces."

"It seems that way, yes."

The sight of her back had left me dazed. I felt completely lost. I thought I was going to burst if I didn't say something.

"You are . . . you are . . ."

What could I say? That she was perfect? Marvelous? Both at once? Perfelous? Marfect? Nothing seemed right.

"You are Gloria among the angels," I whispered.

Gloria went quiet, impressed by the seriousness in my voice. Suddenly, I noticed her hand was near mine. Our fingers intertwined for an instant . . .

That's when Ava Gardner's sexy rasp interrupted the moment. If Gloria and I were the king and queen of coincidental meetings, we were also royalty when it came to inopportune interruptions.

"Hey, Blue Eyes, where are you?" Ava called.

I stepped out of the dressing room, trying to keep up appearances.

"Good boy," she said, laying eyes on me. "I need somebody to take my new dresses to my hotel."

"Of course. I'll have one of our cannonballs deliver them to you."

"I would prefer you bring them yourself."

I was completely baffled. By now, Gloria had also stepped out of the dressing room and was standing at my side, her eyes wide with surprise.

"Bring them to my room. At nine," she ordered with a purr.

She gave me a goodbye kiss on the cheek and then one right on the lips. She walked away, her hips swaying so beautifully that more than one clerk from El Encanto suffered a stiff neck that night from having turned his head too fast to look at her.

After Ava Gardner's farewell, Gloria and I stayed behind in a tense silence. It had nothing to do with the complicity we had enjoyed just moments before. Now it was clear Gloria didn't like any of this.

"I hope you have a fun time at the hotel. Tomorrow you'll have a story to tell your grandchildren," she said before walking away with a firm step.

I didn't know what to say. My head was spinning like a washing machine. Ava Gardner had just made an insinuation, and Gloria was jealous? It was too much. My reflexes collapsed, and I just stood there, stiff and still like a fool.

I spent the rest of my shift keeping my distance from everyone and working like an automaton. I needed the advice and comfort of my compays, so I called Grescas at the cantina and Guzmán at the shoe store and asked them to meet me for dinner at Los Aires Libres restaurant over on the Prado. When I arrived, my friends were already enjoying several bottles of Hatuey beer under an enormous fan hanging from the wooden ceiling. It was dusk, that magic moment when the offices empty out and the cantinas fill up, that shift change in the city when the day laborers—office workers in linen shirts and uniformed clerks—give way to the denizens of the night—singers in colorful dinner jackets and women in sequined dresses.

"Alza el rabu, marinín!" Grescas said in greeting. "What do you need to tell us that can possibly be so urgent?"

I sat down, loosened the knot on my tie, and let the air from the fan dry the sweat on my forehead.

By the time I finished relating all the details of what had happened, I still had one hour before my meeting with Ava. Needless to say, the looks on my friends' faces were priceless. They went from incredulity to astonishment and then to envy, and then from envy again to astonishment and ended up with a mix of admiration and teasing.

"You're gonna spend the night with Ava Gardner!" barked Grescas. "Do you realize how legendary that is?"

"You're a tiger, my man!" confirmed Guzmán.

The folks at the table next to us, a middle-aged couple who seemed a bit uptight, looked at us kind of stupefied, and I asked Grescas and Guzmán to please shut up.

"I don't think I'm gonna go," I muttered.

My friends looked at me as if I had just said I'd come in from Mars on a flying saucer.

"Are you a fag? Is that it? Don't worry, you can tell us." Grescas put his arm around my shoulder.

"No."

"Are you castrated, then? Did they cut your dick off when you worked in the mines?"

"No!"

"Well, if you're not a fag and you're not castrated . . . then you're a fool! A total fucking fool!"

El Grescas tried to slap me around a little bit, but luckily, Guzmán got between us.

"Explain yourself, Patricio, because it seems you've lost your mind," exclaimed Guzmán.

"It's Gloria. I'm so in love with her that the idea of being with another woman, no matter how big a movie star she is, just doesn't feel right."

"But you make out with Nely," said El Grescas.

"I know, but that's different."

"Well, what do you want me to tell you? I don't see the difference," insisted my friend.

"But there is a difference," I responded.

"And Nely's so cute," said El Grescas. "And now this thing with Ava Gardner . . . you're a fucking fuckhead. That's what you are!" He gestured like he was going to smack me again.

The couple at the table next to us got up, making noises like they were offended. "Oh, youth, what a pity," I heard the woman say through gritted teeth as they left. Guzmán got between me and El Grescas to shield me again and spoke with all the calm he could muster.

"Listen, Patricio: Gloria is married. Married to a guy who almost blew our brains out, as I recall. Are you really gonna skip this chance at happiness for a woman you'll never, ever be able to so much as touch? You're not a man, my friend; you're a nineteenth-century damsel."

My friends were right. Of course they were right. I didn't owe Gloria anything. In fact, if I had to worry about hurting anyone's feelings, it was Nely, and I hadn't stopped to think about her even once all day. I decided to do a little experiment and asked myself: Would I blow the opportunity to sleep with Ava Gardner in order not to hurt Nely? The answer was an absolute no. So why was I willing to do it for Gloria? And what's more, I thought, what if I got run over by a trolley tomorrow, like what almost happened on my first day in Havana? How sad to die having missed a chance to bed Ava Gardner. Ava Gardner! I would be the most unfortunate corpse in the cemetery.

"So," El Grescas said, "what are you gonna do, Miss Nineteenth Century?"

CHAPTER 18

A distant church bell struck nine in the evening when I knocked on the door. She was wearing a simple cotton dress and slippers. Her dark hair was messy, and her face was clean, with no makeup. She was the most beautiful creature on earth. When she saw me, she gave me a smile so bright that I knew, without the slightest doubt, I had made the right decision.

Gloria was worth more than ten Ava Gardners put together.

"Hello, Gloria."

"Patricio! What are you doing here?"

"I brought a book for Daniela."

At the moment, I was so worked up over my decision to turn down Gardner and my desire to see Gloria that I didn't even think about it, but I had just committed a monumental gaffe. César himself, or that snake Marita, could just as easily have opened the door. Thank heavens, a cosmic coincidence—the kind Einstein liked so much—had ensured all the housekeepers were otherwise engaged so it was Gloria herself who answered the door.

"You came just to bring a book?" Her smile grew ever brighter.

"It's a scientific book, so she can be as clever as you."

In reality, we both knew I had come to show her I had stood up Ava Gardner. But my excuse made her laugh.

"I've also brought a tortoise." I showed her the little porcelain figure. "For your collection."

Gloria burst out laughing, and her eyes sparkled like two newly reignited embers.

"You're crazy. Come in, come in; don't stand in the doorway."

The house where she lived was majestic: a mansion with three floors and massive picture windows. It was covered in vines and ivy, and it had a huge shaded terrace. The place was surrounded by gardens with fruit trees and plants bursting with flowers. Compared to Santa Benxamina, with its sparse daisies and poppies, the wildflowers in Cuba were a riot of shapes, colors, and sizes. The fruits were overwhelming: for the life of me, I couldn't remember their names, but I enjoyed their exoticism. Out of the dozens of plants, I only recognized a couple: the pot of golden flowers with glossy yellow petals the size of a wineglass, and the flowering pine with bunches of intensely purple, bell-shaped flowers. The paradisiacal scene was completed by a huge oval swimming pool—an alberca or pilota, as the Cubans would say—ringed by statues of dolphins that spurted streams of water from their mouths.

The place was so impressive, my first thought was that Gloria lived in Scarlett O'Hara's mansion from *Gone with the Wind*.

"César is at the Calypso, and Marita's gone to bed early. Come on. Daniela's already in bed, but she might not be asleep yet."

We went up a marble staircase to the second floor. In the hallway, we passed a middle-aged maid with a striking birthmark on her face. She looked nice, and I smiled at her. The woman seemed grateful for the gesture and returned the smile.

"Go to bed, Mirta," Gloria told her fondly. "This gentleman is a friend of the family. You don't need to say anything to him, or to Marita."

The maid nodded at Gloria knowingly.

Daniela's room was everything a little girl could ask for. Located in a corner of the house, it was like its own mini apartment, with an en suite dressing room and bath. It had a wooden bed shaped like a pirate ship and shelves full of toys. I noticed there were lots of drawings stuck to the closet doors—of her mother and their deceased dog, Canelo—but not a single drawing of her father.

We approached her galleon bed. The little girl was somewhere between awake and asleep, and she opened her eyes halfway to peek at us.

"Hello, Daniela," I whispered softly. "I brought you a book so you can learn about the stars and the planets."

"Patricio," she said with a smile, "what are you doing here? Am I dreaming?"

"Yes, you're dreaming," I joked.

"If you're in my dream, it must be a good dream. I have nightmares most nights."

"Don't worry," I assured her. "I'll protect you. Tonight, you're gonna dream about all your adventures on your pirate ship. And you'll find a treasure chest full of gold doubloons on a mysterious island where the trees are made of candy."

"I like that. Will you come with me on the ship?"

"Sure."

"And Mamita?"

"Of course. And your dad too, if you'd like."

The little girl pursed her lips and curled into a ball on the bed. "No, Daddy can't. He always has a lot of work. And Canelo?"

"Canelo's at the prow of the ship, barking at the moon."

Daniela was fading back to sleep, so I left the book on her pillow. The little girl gave me a drowsy hug. I hugged her back and tucked her in.

"Canelo, Canelito, wag your little tail," Daniela sang softly as she drifted off.

When Gloria and I went back down to the sitting room, the door to the main terrace was open, and a wonderful aroma of flowers and nighttime came in from the garden. The murmur of the water in the swimming pool was also quite lovely.

I wasn't sure where to sit. It all looked like a museum. The furniture was made of solid dark wood, and it looked like it cost a kidney. The touches of color came from a few little palm trees in pots and some glass tables with traditional handmade figurines. There was a huge mahogany bar inlaid with mother-of-pearl and arrayed with more bottles than most cantinas. Even the ashtrays in that house must have been worth a fortune.

In the end, I decided to settle into a leather sofa, feeling as out of place as a street mutt in a palace.

"What are those flowers that smell so good?" I asked.

"They're mariposas. Aren't you familiar with them?"

I shook my head. Gloria stepped out to the garden for a moment and returned with a flower she'd plucked so I could see it. It was immaculately white with three long petals that looked cold as ice.

"They're also called 'fragrance of snow' or 'cane of amber.'"

"Well, I just decided mariposas are my new favorite flowers," I declared.

"I'm glad."

Gloria placed the flower in her hair and held out her hand, palm up, a playful look on her face.

"Will you give me the tortoise?"

With great ceremony, I handed over the tortoise figurine I had brought from El Encanto. Gloria opened a hardwood cupboard with glass doors and placed it beside the rest of her collection. There was a whole porcelain zoo in there. Animals from every continent mixed together with no rhyme or reason. My eyes settled on the broken zebra that had started our friendship. I decided to confess something to her.

"Can I tell you a secret?"

"Tell me."

"Every figurine is a symbol of a conversation, and now seeing them in front of me, I realize I remember them all."

Gloria's cheeks lit up with a mixture of embarrassment and delight. She was so aglow, it was a pleasure to look at her. I realized then she was still holding the tortoise figure.

"The day you bought that deer, Daniela had lost a tooth," I said. "The day of the rhinoceros, you were really happy because you'd just finished reading *Twenty Thousand Leagues Under the Sea*. But you were in a bad mood when you bought the kangaroo because you had a toothache," I recalled.

Gloria sat down beside me on the sofa. Our knees were very close, almost brushing each other.

"Why did you decide to come and see me instead of spending the night with Ava Gardner?" she asked.

I decided to be sincere and take a leap with no safety net. That was what I liked most about Gloria: when we were together, she always made me braver.

"Do you remember the day we met, with the zebra, and you explained the theory of relativity?" I asked her. I took a deep breath and emptied my heart: "Well, that theory's right. A second with you is better than an entire lifetime with someone else."

By then, we were talking so close together, I could see the little craters in the irises of her brown eyes. Our breaths pulsed with the same rhythm. Our lips were nearly meeting, but I was in no hurry to consummate the kiss. Her warm breath on my face was already like heaven. If I could, I would have paused the universe at that instant.

I closed my eyes; I don't remember who took the final step to make our mouths come together. Gloria's lips were warm and sweet. Her tongue was like velvet. After a shy start, the kiss became more passionate. From brushing our lips to intertwining our tongues. We were breathing heavily.

The moment was so intense, I didn't hear the front door slam. The kiss was suddenly interrupted. When I stopped feeling Gloria's lips, I felt helpless. It was like getting out of a hot bath and stepping into the cold of Antarctica.

"What's wr—?" I tried to ask.

Gloria covered my mouth with her hand and signaled me to stay quiet. César was home. Like two startled cats, Gloria and I shot in opposite directions until we were sitting at the far ends of the sofa.

Without noticing my presence, César took off his hat and jacket and started talking to Gloria while serving himself a drink at the bar.

"Hey, baby. I'm back from the club. I got Josephine Baker to agree to come to the Calypso! Can you believe that?"

I could tell he was in excellent spirits . . . until he turned around.

"And who are you?" he growled.

Gloria answered for me, trying to hide the tremble in her voice.

"He's a clerk at El Encanto. He came to bring me some shopping."

César furrowed his brow and scrutinized my face. I felt cold sweat running down my back, making my shirt stick to my skin. Would he remember when I was a shoeshine boy and he almost blew my head off?

"Do I know you from somewhere?" he asked.

"From El Encanto, Mr. Valdés," I managed to answer without my voice shaking too much. "I've attended to you a few times in the English Room."

His cruel green eyes continued to look me over for a few more seconds, but luckily, he quickly lost interest. I wasn't important enough for him to waste time on. César turned his attention to his wife.

"What was so urgent they had to bring it from the store? You couldn't wait until tomorrow morning?"

"Heels," Gloria said, improvising.

"Don't bullshit me."

I could tell she was dying of fear, but the need to protect me gave her enough courage to come up with an earful of lies.

"Tomorrow, Marita and I are going to breakfast with Luisi, Guillermina, Patty, and Bárbara. Last week, Luisi wore a divine pair of red heels, so I needed some new kidskin ones. Or don't you want them to be jealous of me?"

Gloria put on a face of such feigned helplessness that César burst out laughing.

"Forgive me. Sometimes I forget how crazy women can get about those things."

César kissed Gloria, and I had to look away, disgusted. My powerlessness made my stomach turn. I would have preferred César point a pistol at my head again instead of having to see him kiss Gloria.

Unable to bear the sight a second longer, I stood up and made for the door. "If there are no further instructions, I'll be going."

I know it was imprudent, but I couldn't resist turning around to look back at Gloria. Before I walked out the door, she locked her eyes on mine, picked up the tortoise figurine, and pressed it against her lips.

That night, I couldn't close my eyes. I stayed awake remembering Gloria's kiss, again and again. By the time daylight came, Gloria and I had kissed a million times in my imagination, in every possible way.

I got up with bags under my eyes, but I was so full of happiness, I almost skipped down the hall. I had so much energy I could've swum to Asturias to eat sobaos with sidriña for breakfast and made it back to Havana in time for lunch.

When I walked into the kitchen, Guzmán was making coffee. He burst out laughing when he saw my face.

"Well, well! From that smile on your face, I'd say Gardner made a man out of you."

"I didn't end up going to the Nacional," I said, shrugging.

Guzmán's jaw dropped. "What?!"

"You heard me. I came home, I got ready . . . but at the last minute, I changed my mind."

"You stood up Ava Gardner?"

"Not exactly. I sent her the dresses with a cannonball and wrote her a note in English to apologize. In fact, I sent El Grescas to the hotel to leave it at reception."

"Well, El Grescas didn't sleep here last night."

This time, it was my turn to gape. "What?!"

"See for yourself. His bed's still made."

We heard the sound of the key in the door, and El Grescas strolled into the apartment as if he were the king of Rome. If I was in a good mood that morning, El Grescas wasn't far behind. For starters, he came in singing, "Salud, dinero, y amor." His hair was a tangled mess, his tie was undone, his huge gorilla chest was exposed, and his shoelaces were untied.

Guzmán and I looked at each other, incredulous. It was absurd. It was madness. It was impossible. And yet . . .

"Yup, it's exactly what it looks like," confirmed El Grescas.

"But how?" gasped Guzmán.

"Yesterday, when this dummy sent me to El Nacional with the apology note, I went to take it to reception, but the bellhop told me Miss Gardner was at the bar. So I decided to give it to her in person."

El Grescas interrupted his story to light a cigarette. Guzmán and I were about to faint from curiosity.

"And?" we demanded in unison.

"When she first read your note, she looked annoyed, to tell you the truth. But then we got to talking—"

"Talking?" I interrupted. "How? At best you know four phrases in English, and she doesn't speak Spanish!"

El Grescas puffed up his chest with pride.

"That's exactly why she thought it was so funny when I said, 'Morenaza, you have stolen my heart. Ay, jamona! You are tocino de cielo.' The fact is, after a few cocktails, we understood each other perfectly. And pretty soon, no more words were needed, because when we went up to her room . . ."

El Grescas went quiet to better delight in our shocked expressions.

"Don't stop now. You were just getting to the good part!" protested Guzmán.

"I'm a gentleman," said El Grescas, and to show it, he spat in the sink instead of on the floor. "All I'll say is that my backside's so sore, I won't be able to sit down for a week. The rest is between Lavinia and me."

"Lavinia?"

"That's her middle name. Ava Lavinia." He sighed, spellbound. "By the way, I need a favor. This morning when I woke up, my lady had already left, but she left me this note. It's in English. Could you translate it for me?"

El Grescas took a piece of paper out of his shirt pocket. It was marked with the crest of the Hotel Nacional.

"'Dear Agapito. Thank you for giving me such a wonderful night. Ever yours,'" I translated. "The best part is, it's signed! This is the greatest autograph of all time."

"There's something I don't understand," commented Guzmán. "Who's Agapito?"

"Who else?" growled El Grescas. "Me."

"We've known each other for years, and you've never told us your name."

"You guys don't have an ass like Ava's."

And that was how, after three years of friendship, we finally found out El Grescas's real name was Agapito. He just had to sleep with a Hollywood star to reveal it.

PART II

CHAPTER 19

GLORIA

The night Patricio rejected Ava Gardner to bring me the porcelain tortoise, I realized I had fallen in love with him.

With his sweetness, he had shown me kisses can work miracles, like making my blood boil, turning my legs to water, and transforming my heart from a stone into a drum. After that, every kiss from César was torture. My husband's kisses tasted sour, but Patricio's spit was sweet.

The morning after our furtive kiss, I went with Daniela to visit my mother and my Lala. Daniela adored visiting her great-grandmother Lala, who made pumpkin flan and taught her magic spells every week. Her grandmother, on the other hand, immobile in a wheelchair with a blank expression on her face, scared her a little, but she was such an affectionate little girl that she always went up and gave her a kiss. My grandmother and my mother still lived in the house César had bought them in the Vedado neighborhood.

The house was small but very pretty: a one-story villa with arched doorways and a whitewashed facade with light-blue embellishments that gave it a lovely seaside feel. Lala had turned it into a happy home thanks to her particular gift for decoration. My grandmother had the soul of a magpie and accumulated all kinds of shiny knickknacks. The place was a combination of a good witch's cave and a metalworker's shop, and there were always seashells on the side tables, quartz rocks to ward off evil spirits, and the rag dolls she used for her Santeria.

The most special part was the patio. It was in the back of the house, and it was an enchanting place from which to enjoy the garden. Lala used to say that little piece of Havana was her lair and her refuge.

While Daniela played and looked for crickets, Lala led me to a love seat on the patio and served us lemonade. It was early, but it was already so hot the sweetness of the drink mixed with the salty taste of sweat gathered on my top lip.

"The garden is lovely, Lala," I said to please her.

The garden was my grandmother's pride and joy. She spent hours planting and tending to it. And since her spells required all sorts of herbs and sprouts, her garden looked like a little jungle in which the weeds grew alongside the most delicate flowers. If ever an enchanted garden existed, without a doubt, it was my Lala's.

"You like it? I've planted tamarind, nightshade, doradilla, wormseed, and piñuela. I hope the agrimony takes as well; it's wonderful for fevers. And the malambo, which cures cramps. I'm gonna make infusions for your mother to see if we can get her out of her state."

Lala still believed in her superstitions, and she was sure that, thanks to the gods of Santeria, someday she would manage to cure my mother and teach César a lesson. When she'd first met him after my father's death, she immediately realized what kind of person he was. Even at the wedding, she knew the cause of my unhappiness was my husband, but what could a poor old lady do against one of the most powerful gangsters in Cuba? Every week she plotted a different curse in hopes of doing him harm.

"The next time you come," she said, "bring me a lock of your husband's hair."

"And where am I going to get that, Lala?"

"From the bathtub or the basin."

"Why do you want it?"

"If you burn a lock of someone's hair with the flame of a red candle under a waning moon, it'll make them lose their mind, quick as can be."

"That's not true, Lala."

"Your science tells you that?"

Lala and I still debated our different ways of seeing the world.

"Anyone with a little bit of common sense in their head would tell you that," I answered.

"But mija, haven't you always told me scientists themselves know science can't reach real truths?"

"Yes," I admitted, "but only because every answer brings a thousand more questions."

"I know you like to analyze things, Gloria, much more than I do. But as scientific as you are, you're also Cuban, girl. We Cubans carry magic in our veins."

"Not me, Lala."

"Shut your mouth. And if you can get me one of his fingernails when that asshole husband of yours cuts them, that'd be perfect," she added. "You're also gonna take this fish, which was caught by a blind fisherman during a full moon, so the cook can make soup and make him sick with ciguatera. Do you promise?"

"I'll try," I said to stop her scolding me.

Suddenly, Lala fixed her wide eyes on me and sniffed my face as if she were a hutia, one of those rodents from the countryside.

"Mijita, something's happened to you. You're different. You even smell different."

Maybe her spells weren't very effective, but my grandmother was a great witch when it came to reading my mind.

"Nothing happened, Lala," I said, not sounding very convincing. "What on earth could have happened to me?"

"Your poor mother may have almost lost her mind, but you can't fool me."

A grandmother wasn't necessarily the best confidante for talk about infidelity, but I had no friends, and I'd never been one for confessing my sins to the priest. I interlaced my young, sinful hand with her old, veiny one.

"Oh, Lala, you have to keep my secret . . ."

The words left my mouth with no restraint. I told her everything. My first meeting with Patricio, the months and months of seeing each other at El Encanto when Marita and I went shopping, our falling in love, and our kiss.

"I'm so afraid, Lala," I said in conclusion.

Lala stayed quiet for a few seconds. I was ready to be severely reprimanded for being a loose woman, but instead she laughed and kissed me on the forehead.

"Don't be afraid! Just think, every kiss you give your Patricio is a kiss you steal from your husband. It was time, mijita, for you to find true love."

"I don't even want to think about what César would do if he found out."

"Girl, you better cheat on that asshole every chance you get."

"Lala!"

"I know you got married against your will, Gloria. That degenerate stole you from your parents, he stole your innocence, he stole your life . . . but he hasn't been able to spoil the miracle of falling in love for the first time."

My grandmother snorted with excitement before continuing. Two tears fell from her eyes and lost themselves among the wrinkles on her cheeks.

"Because you love Patricio, mijita. I can see it in your eyes."

"Yes, I love him."

I spat out those three words with the same pleasure a little girl spits out papaya seeds. My grandmother hugged me, and I breathed in her talcum and soap. She stroked my hair like she'd stroked it when I was a little girl and took shelter in her lap because I was afraid of the monster in the walls.

"Everything will be fine, mija. I'll pray for you to the Anima Sola every noon and midnight. 'Sad, lonely Anima. No one calls you, but I call you. No one loves you, but I love you. I know you cannot enter heaven, being in hell. Protect my granddaughter and the man her heart has chosen, amen.'"

I returned home with my soul cured, feeling joyful after my Lala's blessing. But my happiness didn't last long. César and Marita were waiting for me in the main room. It was very strange for them to be home at midday. César never got up before lunchtime, and Marita was normally with the hairdresser or at the beauty salon at that time. The two siblings looked disgusted.

"Pack your bags," my husband told me. "Tomorrow we're leaving for Villa Valiente."

I turned as white as a corpse. Villa Valiente was the little town on the other side of the island where César and Marita had been born.

"Our uncle Aurelio is badly hurt," added Marita. "A mule kicked him and split his head open."

I had no relationship with my in-laws. I knew César's parents were from around Las Tunas, but that was about it. My husband and my sister-in-law barely talked about them, and I knew the two siblings were estranged from their parents, although I never bothered to find out why. I remembered Uncle Aurelio from our wedding day: an old man with lip sores who drooled when he talked and who pinched my bottom the first time we met.

"Will we be away from Havana for long?" I asked, unable to conceal my annoyance.

"You and Marita will be there as long as Uncle Aurelio needs you. I'll go for two days and then come back to Havana," answered César, as if the issue were settled.

I cursed Uncle Aurelio, the mule, the bitch of a mother who gave birth to the mule, and myself for cursing so brutishly. I could think up all the vulgarities I liked, but the truth was I had no say in the decision. I could only pack my bags.

That afternoon, I got ready with special care. If we had to be apart, I wanted Patricio to remember me as the prettiest girl in Havana. I chose one of my brightest dresses, white with a pineapple pattern and a full skirt. The two straps tied behind my neck to leave the back open. I gathered my hair in a high ponytail that I decorated with an orange bow. My manicure was also orange, matching the pineapples on my dress. I completed the outfit with some exquisite sandals that had low heels and buckles fastened over my ankles. In spite of my colorful outfit, I felt as if I were getting dressed for my own funeral.

When Marita and I arrived at El Encanto, I spotted Patricio in the book department, so I pretended I needed to buy a novel to read on the car ride—and, of course, I needed the shop clerk's wise counsel. Marita was bored by books so she went to look at makeup and left me alone. While we flipped through the pages of Jules Verne novels, Patricio and I had a chance to talk.

"I have to leave Havana. To go to the countryside."

Patricio's blue eyes lost their shine.

"When?" he whispered.

"Early tomorrow."

We fell silent, inconsolable. I cleared my throat to get up the nerve to keep talking.

"And I don't know when I'll be back."

I feared Patricio's reaction, but it was clear he was different from César.

"The time doesn't matter. You'll find me here," he said, calming me down.

"It could be days, or it could be months."

"I would wait a century for you."

My heart rose when I heard him.

"Every second I'm not by your side feels like an eternity," I told him, fighting to hold back my tears. "But when you miss me, there's one thing you can do."

"I'll do anything."

"Buy a bunch of mariposas. If we both smell the flowers, it'll be as if we were kissing again."

"I'll do it, I promise."

Before I could stop myself, I took Patricio's hand, placed it on my chest, and let him feel my heart.

"I love you," I whispered.

"I love you more," I heard Patricio answer as I drew away from him.

As soon as I left El Encanto, I burst into tears.

CHAPTER 20

Villa Valiente was full of flies. At all hours, everywhere. Black with a flicker of green on the wings and fat like the marbles the kids played with on the streets. That town had more flies than the devil's tail. They would clump together around the cows' tearing eyes and along the rims of glasses, and get tangled in Daniela's hair. She would scream in disgust every time she heard their humming. The staff at Uncle Aurelio's house didn't have the proper supplies to kill them, so they handed out fly swatters so we could defend ourselves as best we could.

I never told anybody, but I suspected I was the cause of this plague. Without Patricio, I was the living dead. It made sense that flies would come to devour me.

Used to the comforts of Havana, we got sick of the flies, of the countryside, and of Uncle Aurelio's laments in just one day. But César had promised to be with the old man in his last hours, and promises to family were sacred. So there we were, Marita, Daniela, and I, even when his last hours turned into months.

The old man got worse, then better, then worse, then better . . . the head injury he suffered from getting kicked by that mule wouldn't heal. The constant changes in his state of health brought out my most petty side, and I began to think the old man refused to heal and refused to die just to mess with us.

I would later regret these ugly thoughts and remember that the old man was single with no children and that we couldn't just abandon him to the mercy of his staff. Because Uncle Aurelio was ill-humored, the staff would frequently "forget" to give him the medicine that would make him stop screaming. It was our duty to take care of Aurelio. But the flies. Those dirty flies made it really tough.

To top it all off, the dirt in Villa Valiente was a muddy red in which it was impossible to plant mariposas.

There wasn't much to do at Uncle Aurelio's farm. Marita would usually spend the day at the stores in Manatí, a nearby city that could be reached by bus. I preferred to stay home, reading the few astronomy books I'd been able to cram in my luggage, while I made sure Daniela studied and did her homework. God knows that, every now and again, I'd feel guilty when I saw Uncle Aurelio in bed. Doing everything to dodge his roving hands, I'd comb his white hair, dipping the comb in cologne. The mule had left him with an ugly head wound that had to be constantly disinfected and bandaged. One day, I gave him a little sip of a liquor made from herbs dedicated to Yemayá to help him deal with the pain, and he just began to yak. That's how I found out my husband's family history.

"Listen, pretty girl . . . my brother, Cristóbal Valdés, César's old man, was a traveling photographer who went from town to town taking pictures. One day, he stopped in Villa Valiente, and the town's mayor asked him to take a picture of his favorite hen."

"Excuse me? Did you say *hen*, Uncle Aurelio?"

"Hen, yes! A Cubalaya hen, cinnamon-colored. She laid so many eggs, they could make bread every single day. The mayor held that hen in very high esteem. The problem was that Cubalaya hen was a very fierce character and wouldn't let anyone treat her like some tadpole. They needed somebody to hold her for the photograph, and they chose a very pretty little girl who had the sweetest hands in town and the kind of tough personality necessary to put up with the scratches and the pecking: Rosina Ocariz. Cristóbal fell so hard for Rosina that, after he took the photograph, he asked her out. That night, Cristóbal and Rosina had a tumble, and nine months later, César was born."

"Didn't they get married first, Uncle?"

"No way! They never so much as strolled by a church. By the time that fucker of a husband of yours was in diapers, Cristóbal and Rosina couldn't stand the sight of each other. In fact, they separated with their backs up like screeching cats and immediately married other people."

"Other people?" I was astounded. Having a child out of wedlock was the most scandalous thing I'd ever heard. Especially considering it had happened forty years ago and in an itty-bitty town.

"Cristóbal met a beautician, Guadalupe, and married her. They had four more brats. Marita, your sister-in-law, is the oldest of that bunch."

I was very surprised to hear this. I didn't know Marita was just César's half sister on his father's side.

"For her part, Rosina put a spell on a sugarcane factory owner named Amador, who got her pregnant quicker than a rooster. Or a hen." Aurelio choked on spit from laughing at his own bad joke. "They had five little peeps."

"So who did César live with? His mom or his dad?"

"Ah, that's the thing. Both and neither. Both Cristóbal and Rosina had remade their lives, and César was a living reminder of that mistake from their past. They took turns with him, but that little snot-nosed brat never fit in. He was like some sticky mess in both families, and they never got tired of telling him how much easier it would have been if he'd never been born."

I thought about this for a long time before speaking again.

"I suppose it's because of that, that César is—"

A man obsessed with power? A dictator who always had to have his way? A tyrant who married little girls he could dominate? A broken boy who grew up to be a heartless adult?

That's what I should have said, but I opted for something less brutish.

"How he is."

Aurelio pinched my butt and continued his story.

"I remember one Christmas when Cristóbal and Rosina couldn't come to an agreement about who the kid was gonna spend it with. César got out of school, and neither his father nor his mother went to pick him up. He spent Christmas Eve with a shepherd and his wolflike dogs, horrible beasts who terrified him with little bites. After that, he was so scared of dogs, he'd dream about them and wet the bed. If only people knew that one of the most powerful men in Cuba wet his bed until he was ten years old!"

The old man laughed so cruelly that I defended my husband just to get back at him.

"It must have been very hard not to feel loved."

"Oh please." Aurelio pinched me again. "There are worse stories. When my grandfather's brother, Rafael, was a baby, his bastard of a father threw him down a well to save himself from having to feed one more mouth. And my grandmother Pepita? She lost a leg in a train accident."

The old man went on telling me terrible stories until I couldn't take any more, and I stopped listening. After he exhausted himself relating these miseries, he fell asleep with his mouth open, drooling.

But his stories had awakened my curiosity, so I went around the house, looking at all the framed photos in search of an image of César as a boy. I finally saw something in an old family portrait hung on the wall.

In the picture, two couples—I figured they were Rosina and her husband, Amador, and Cristóbal and his wife, Guadalupe—were posing with a young Uncle Aurelio and their respective litters of babies. I didn't have any trouble recognizing Marita, a little girl with a haughty expression who posed proudly in a dress with an embroidered bee's nest. The one I had trouble identifying at first was César. For starters, my husband was cut off in a corner of the photo. He was standing apart from the group, and nobody had bothered to make sure he was in the frame, in spite of the fact that his gaze was unquestionable—the eyes on that emaciated boy didn't reflect fury or malice but rather a deep sadness and loneliness. I wondered then, as I smiled sadly to myself, what Gary Cooper had looked like in photographs at that same age.

CHAPTER 21

PATRICIO

Without Gloria, Havana lost its joy; although at first sight, it was hard to tell. Sunlight still bathed the Malecón while passersby sat on the wall and bought peeled coconuts from the street vendors. The cantinas' shady patios continued to provide relief to thirsty citizens, who ordered cold beer under the fans. In hotels and clubs, orchestras still stirred foreigners to dance until dawn. Yes, perhaps for the rest of the world, the city was still radiant, but I knew the truth. Without Gloria, Havana was a lesser Havana.

To the puzzlement of my two closest friends, who had no idea what the hell was happening to me, I became a full-blown grouch. One night, during one of our typical conversations out on the terrace, they got on my nerves so much, I had to confess the reason for my wretchedness.

"You got cocky, huh, screwing around with your spoiled brat!" El Grescas scolded me.

"Don't be so bitchy," I replied. "It was thanks to me going to see Gloria that night that Ava Gardner invited you to her room."

When I mentioned Gardner, El Grescas changed his already dumb expression to that of a dopey lamb, goofy smile included.

"Oh, my Lavinia! They say she's been seen out with that Frank Sinatra guy . . . I don't understand it. I'm way better-looking," he lamented.

Sick of our ramblings, Guzmán interrupted.

"Both of you are forgetting the most important part of this!" Guzmán looked at me with deep concern on his face. "Don't you realize you're risking your life, that César Valdés will make mincemeat out of you if he finds out you kissed his wife?"

Of course I'd thought about it, but my obsession with Gloria was stronger than any concern for my own skin. My infatuation was like an invisible shield protecting me from the sinister side of the world. Being with her was like taking flight, reaching the impossible. Nonetheless, distance is the worst possible torment for lovers.

"The truth is, I don't care," I sighed sadly. "Gloria's gone, and who knows when she'll be back. And if she does come back, who says she won't regret everything that happened between us?"

"That would be best," Guzmán let fly, with his typical good judgment. "Best for her to forget you and not put you in danger."

El Grescas put out his cigarette and opened three bottles of beer.

"Whatever happens, you can't go on like this, a soul in torment," he told me. "What's up with Nely? She's crazy about you, and you're running around after spoiled rich girls."

"It's true. Nely always looks at you like she wants it," confirmed Guzmán.

But I'd been avoiding the elevator operator. After I kissed Gloria, my feelings had become clearer than ever. I felt incapable of kissing any lips but hers. But I couldn't tell Nely I had fallen in love with a married woman, much less that it was Gloria Valdés. So I opted to avoid her until I could get up the nerve to clarify things.

El Grescas offered one of his life lessons, along with a slap on the back.

"A roll in the hay with Nely would do you a world of good. I'm telling you, it'd make the hurting stop, just like that. In the meantime, drink that beer while I make you a cocktail."

Living up to its name as the Pearl of the Antilles, Cuba was the mecca of cocktails. In all the bars and cantinas, the baristas mixed liquors and fruit juices like witches brewing their potions. Havana was full of these wizards, their concoctions working magic on thirsty palates. In fact, cocktail hour was such an institution that the fashion designer Christian Dior renamed his evening dresses as "cocktail dresses." The name began to appear in fashion magazines, and it didn't take long for the female customers at El Encanto to show up en masse, searching for the new item.

"Patricio, dear, do you have this 'cocktail dress' they're talking about in all the magazines?" a different woman would ask every few minutes.

I always repeated what I'd heard from Manet, our designer.

"A cocktail dress isn't a specific dress, but an elegant dress with a knee-length skirt. It's normally decorated with lace or jewels, and we carry a variety of models . . ."

Just like with the dresses, there were also cocktails for every taste. On the menus at the most prestigious hotels, they numbered in the hundreds. There were the most classic, like the martini, the alexander, the old-fashioned, the screwdriver, and the manhattan; the sophisticated, like the Applejack Rabbit and the frangipani; and the tropical, like the piña colada, the mai tai, caipirinhas, margaritas.

But, of course, the crown jewels, the Holy Trinity of cocktails, were the three Cuban classics: the daiquiri, the Cuba libre, and the mojito.

The Cuba libre was invented during the war with Spain, when soldiers drank rum and cola and toasted with their battle cry: *"Por Cuba libre!"* The legend of the daiquiri was that it was first blended at El Floridita, when the place was still known as La Piña de Plata. As far as the mojito, it was conceived by a corsair so his crew could hold off scurvy thanks to the vitamins in the mint leaves, but it was popularized by the famous Bodeguita del Medio.

Hemingway, who knew a little about writing and drinking, said it best: "My mojito at La Bodeguita, my daiquiri at El Floridita."

Besides their taste, cocktails were objects of desire because they were embellished like little works of art: olives, maraschino cherries, miniature parasols, slices of fruit, paper parrots, and even sparklers were part of their typical decoration.

Guzmán and I liked them a lot, but if there was a true cocktail fan among us, it was El Grescas. He had tried them all. His refrigerator-like build provided him with an astonishing tolerance for alcohol. In Asturias, he could only drink the sour, homemade apple cider made in the lone bar in the village, and the first time he tried a daiquiri in Cuba, with its sugar and white rum, he died a little out of pure pleasure.

Then El Grescas discovered an unexpected gift, thanks to his job at the King Kong cantina. He had gone from being a regular to working on the other side of the bar, so instead of drinking, he had to learn to make drinks. And, to the surprise of the owner, the other employees, and himself, he wasn't half bad. On the contrary, despite his brutish manners, his big mitts had a knack for mixing and preparing the most sophisticated drinks. His mojitos were to die for or, in his own words, "They were the nun's tits."

Following his success as a bartender, Guzmán and I encouraged him to come up with his own cocktail. But none of his experiments got off the ground, until the morning after his night with Ava Gardner, when inspiration slapped him in the face. El Grescas shut himself up in the cantina, and with an arsenal of bottles at his disposal, he invented a cocktail that would make history. Guzmán and I were his guinea pigs, and as soon as our lips touched that mix, our hearts stopped. The taste was sweet but refreshing. Intense but delicate. Sophisticated and familiar all at once. We emptied the glasses in two swigs.

"Damn, compay, what's in this beauty?" asked Guzmán.

"Ha! As if I'd tell some riffraff like you! A good bartender never shares his secrets," answered El Grescas, trying to seem refined.

Guzmán tipped back his glass to get at the last drops.

"You have to baptize your concoction," he said.

"What if I called it El Grescas, after me?"

"You could call it the Agapito," I joked, risking a slap.

Just like that, my ass of a friend knocked the back of my neck so hard that I saw stars.

"A good cocktail should have a name that's exciting, suggestive, mysterious . . . ," mused Guzmán, paying no attention to us.

"The Ava Gardner!" exclaimed El Grescas. "My Lavinia is everything you said and more."

"There's already a cocktail called the Ava Gardner."

"What if I called it Lavinia?"

"That sounds like *ladilla*, and no one wants a drink named after crabs," I teased.

"You're headed right for a smack in the face, and I'm good for it," threatened El Grescas.

Suppressing his laughter, Guzmán lifted his hands, indicating that we should stop.

"Let's think of something else. What's your favorite Ava Gardner movie?" he asked El Grescas.

"The one where she wears that black dress that gives her an ass like a twenty-dollar mule. *Forajidos*."

Guzmán's face lit up. "A forajido! See? That's a killer name for a cocktail."

"It really doesn't sound half bad," admitted El Grescas, satisfied.

"Say no more," I concluded. "Why don't you make us three forajidos, and we'll toast to the forajido?"

"Done and done," said El Grescas with a laugh.

El Grescas started serving his cocktail to the cantina's regular customers, and it was an immediate hit. Soon, word got around, and people started showing up just to try a forajido. There were nights when the line stretched out of the little establishment, and people waited in the street. El Grescas's boss was thrilled with the sudden success and declared him his star bartender, with a raise thrown in for good measure. As the drink's inventor, El Grescas also demanded a percentage of each forajido served, and every night he left with a solid bonus. He was the only one who knew the formula, so he concentrated his efforts on preparing one after another, as many forajidos as needed. Not even his best friends knew the recipe. You could make out the taste of rum and grenadine, but those were only two of an infinite number of flavors.

"There's rum, right?" I tried to get it out of him again and again. "It tastes like Bacardi to me."

"Don't know, could be . . ." Grescas would answer with a mysterious air that drove me up the wall.

"It also tastes like lime . . . no, wait! Pineapple?"

"Don't know; could be," he repeated again and again, giving nothing away.

It was useless. When the forajido became popular, rival cantinas and hotels took an interest in the miracle. Faced with El Grescas's refusal to reveal the secret, they hired tasters who managed to identify many of the ingredients. But when they tried to blend them, it tasted nothing like the original. In order to make an authentic forajido, they'd have to figure out the exact proportion of each ingredient, and that recipe existed only in my friend's stubborn noggin.

Everything went to hell when César caught wind of the forajido's success. El Grescas was a fly who had disturbed his spiderweb, and soon he would get what he deserved.

CHAPTER 22

César's first attempts at getting hold of the forajido recipe were disguised as attempts at friendship. The first was especially devious.

One night, a gorgeous black girl named Rita turned up at the cantina. As soon as she set foot in King Kong, all eyes were on her. She was made up like an artist, with a white sequined dress that glittered with every swing of her hips, pink shoes, and her dark curls pulled back into a braid adorned with a flower. The beautiful Rita sat at the bar and ordered a forajido. El Grescas served it with pleasure.

"She was so fine, I even gave her an extra umbrella in her drink," El Grescas confessed afterward.

Rita flirted blatantly with El Grescas, and a few forajidos later, they were swapping spit in the back room. They left the cantina together and, at her suggestion, came back to the house.

Guzmán and I were eating mashed plantain for dinner in the main room, and we were stunned when we saw Rita. Her black hair was shiny with sweat, and the sequins on her dress shimmered with every step she took. Her eyelashes were so long, it was a miracle she didn't cause a cyclone with every blink. Her thick lips, in red lipstick, looked juicier than a ripe piece of fruit. We were so taken aback by our friend's new conquest, we barely managed to stutter a "good evening." Rita waved at us, and El Grescas pulled her into his room.

According to El Grescas's story, once they were alone, they started kissing, and soon they were getting down to business. But when my friend began to undo the snaps on her dress, Rita said something that threw him off.

"That tasty cocktail you make at the cantina, what's in it?"

"A little of everything," answered El Grescas, who was more interested in getting her clothes off than in talking about cocktails.

Rita moved his hands off her dress.

"Come on, big man. Don't be mean. Tell me how you make it, I'll keep your secret," she insisted.

"What for, brown sugar? I'll make you all the cocktails you want."

Rita gave him a mischievous look.

"Let's make a deal," the girl proposed. "For every ingredient you tell me, I undo a snap."

El Grescas was in a jam. On the one hand, he was starting to feel funny about her taking so much interest in the recipe. On the other, the temptation to see more of her ebony skin was too much.

"Bacardi . . . ," confessed El Grescas.

Keeping her word, Rita turned around and undid the top snap of the dress, revealing her tempting shoulders.

"Grenadine . . . ," my friend whispered.

Another snap, and there was a naked back that took his breath away. With the next snap, her dress would slip to the floor, and her whole body would be revealed. El Grescas was about to tell her another ingredient but, before it left his mouth, his head got the better of his manhood, and he asked Rita a couple of questions.

"Why are you so interested?"

Rita answered with another question. "What's it matter? Don't you like me?"

"I like you a lot. More than a fat kid likes candy," admitted El Grescas.

"So . . . if you give me the whole recipe, I'd be very grateful," purred Rita.

"And if I don't?"

Rita moved closer to Grescas until her lips were almost touching his. But, just before they came together, she paused.

"Maybe I have a headache, and I should get going. That'd be a shame, don't you think?" she threatened.

El Grescas brushed his lips against Rita's neck. His hands moved toward the dress's snaps . . . and did them up again. To Rita's confusion, my friend got up from the bed, opened the bedroom door, and gestured for her to leave.

"Thanks for everything, babe. But I don't pay to go to bed with anyone."

"I didn't say anything about money!" she exclaimed.

"If I have to pay you with the forajido recipe, it's kind of the same thing."

"You do me a favor, and I do you a favor."

"If you think that way, I think you're a little too whorish for me. With all due respect."

Rita stood up and walked toward him. El Grescas was afraid he had offended her, and she was going to slap him in the face. But instead, Rita burst into tears. Perplexed, El Grescas tried to console her with a pat on the shoulder.

"Are you all right? I'm sorry, I still talk like a country boy. I didn't mean to offend you."

"No, you're right," sobbed Rita. "You're exactly right."

Rita went into such a fit of tears that we heard her whimpering from the main room. Unsure of what to do, we peeked into the bedroom. El Grescas looked at us with absolute confusion.

"I don't know what happened," our friend said. "Did I do something wrong?"

We sat Rita down on the terrace. Guzmán made her a cup of aniseed tea while El Grescas gave her handkerchiefs to dry her tears, and I clowned around to make her laugh. Thanks to our teamwork, we managed to stop her crying.

"Brains have never been my strong suit, but you can nail me to the wall if I have the slightest idea what just happened," said El Grescas, scratching his head.

More composed now, Rita decided to confess the truth. "I work for César Valdés. I'm a dancer at the Calypso, his club."

When she mentioned César, the three of us tensed up like cats who'd just heard barking.

"César ordered me to go to the cantina and sleep with you in exchange for the recipe," said Rita. "Please, keep your mouths shut! If he finds out I told you, he'll kill me."

The terror in her voice made it clear it wasn't a figure of speech.

"César can do that?" I asked her. "Make you go to bed with men?"

"César does whatever he wants with us. All the dancers at his club are in debt to him. In my case, my sister needed an operation, and he fronted me the money. I owe him thousands of dollars. All the girls at the Calypso are his property."

El Grescas, Guzmán, and I looked at each other with a mix of rage and powerlessness.

"That son of a bitch! You don't deserve to be under his thumb. Haven't you thought of running away?" asked Guzmán.

Rita sighed and shrugged.

"It'd be useless. If I ran away, my family would pay for it," she murmured, defeated.

"And you had to seduce this idiot?" I asked, pointing at El Grescas.

Rita nodded. "The forajido is the most requested drink in all Havana. And in this city, nobody can get ahead without César taking his cut. He wants that cocktail, and he won't stop until he gets it."

Guzmán and I glanced over at El Grescas to see his reaction. We all knew it was a war he couldn't win. Even so, my friend let loose an admirable but quixotic outburst.

"Well, if he's so brave, let him come and ask me for it! He shouldn't send a woman to do his dirty work, let alone one as fine as you."

Flattered by his gallantry, Rita gave him a kiss on the cheek. "You're a sweetheart. Are you sure you don't wanna tell me the recipe? It wouldn't be such a sacrifice to go to bed with you."

Guzmán let out a snort of envy. "Who would've thought! First Ava Gardner and now you . . . what the hell do beautiful women see in this gorilla?"

"Oh, Guzmancito, you've got a lot to learn," El Grescas teased.

"But won't César be angry if you go back without the recipe?" I asked Rita.

A shadow fell over the dancer's face, and she sank back into sadness. "Well, of course. If he finds out I didn't get you to sleep with me, he'll call me an ugly cow and give me a beating."

"And if you tell him we spent the night together and I still wouldn't give you the recipe?" proposed El Grescas.

Rita shook her head. "That's worse. He'll beat me even harder for spreading my legs for free."

The four of us fell silent. Rita was stuck in a tough situation. It didn't look good until suddenly I came up with a possible solution for her dilemma.

"I have an idea," I announced. "Tell him El Grescas turned you down because he's in love with someone else."

"He'll wanna know who the woman is and how she's prettier than me."

"I wasn't thinking of a woman," I said with a smile heavy with implication.

It took El Grescas, Guzmán, and Rita a few seconds to catch on. When they understood what I was getting at, El Grescas bellowed so loud I was afraid fire was going to come out his nostrils.

"Queer? Me?" he howled.

"Think about it. It's the only way Rita can avoid paying the consequences."

"A pillow-biter? A fairy? Don't even think about it! I have a reputation. What are my people gonna think?"

"What people?" I asked.

"I don't know—people! My friends."

"We're your friends, and we don't care if you're a fairy," said Guzmán.

"But I'm not!" shouted El Grescas, exasperated.

Rita ended our stupid conversation.

"Do something, or I'll die like Chacumbele, who didn't even have time to say goodbye," she begged.

Rita looked at him with her big eyes, and with a bat of her lashes, El Grescas's prejudices were lost in the wind.

"Oh, what the hell. If I have to pretend to be queer, so be it," he said.

And so ended César's first effort to get at El Grescas, but it wasn't the last.

In fact, a few days after the episode with Rita, a good-looking and well-mannered man showed up at the bar to order a forajido. When El Grescas served him, the young man brushed his hand against El Grescas and winked at him.

"When do you get off, handsome?" the guy asked without the slightest subtlety.

There's no doubt El Grescas thought about murdering me just then.

One way or another, El Grescas fended them off and continued dodging César's pawns. The matter became more sinister when the mafioso got tired of asking for the cocktail recipe the nice way. One night, a guy who introduced himself as the headwaiter at the Calypso came to the house.

He wore a scar across his cheek and had a back almost as wide as my friend's. I thought, *If that guy's a waiter, I'm a dancer at the Tropicana.* There was no doubt he was one of the thugs who did César's dirty work, one of his attack dogs. El Grescas and the goon disappeared into the kitchen with some beers while Guzmán and I waited with our ears pressed against the door in case our friend needed reinforcements.

The guy started out very polite, offering El Grescas a job at the Calypso in exchange for the forajido recipe. When he rejected the offer, the thug added a juicy sum of money to the offer "as a show of good-will." Again, El Grescas told him no, and the guy doubled his offer, reaching a sum with which my friend would have been able to buy a small apartment. His best option would have been to accept, but the Asturian was never known for his good judgment.

"Well, the thing is, the recipe's not for sale. Tell your boss that if he wants to drink a forajido, he'll have to line up at the cantina like everybody else," he said, all cocky.

"You're making a mistake. I can't see the future, but this I do know: soon you'll wish you had given me the recipe the easy way."

Our friend sighed with the arrogance of a prisoner who knows he's heading to the gallows but is too proud to beg for mercy.

"There's nothing to discuss," he answered. "In any case, I've never been much good at knowing what's good for me."

The next night, the thug's threats came true when they ambushed El Grescas as he was leaving King Kong. The poor guy came home with a black eye and had been beaten to a pulp. While we rubbed alcohol on his cuts, he told us how it had happened.

"The bastards were in the alley, hiding behind the dumpsters. At least they had to sniff up those stinky fishbones while they were waiting for me. Then they jumped me and punched the hell out of me. But you better believe they got theirs," he concluded with pride.

"You have the hardest head in the world," scolded Guzmán. "You should've accepted the offer. Then at least you would've gotten some good money instead of getting your ass kicked. You're up to your neck in a war you can't win."

El Grescas shrugged his shoulders, which provoked a groan.

"I can't help it! It's irritating when someone tries to make me do something. My sister's the same way, isn't she?" he asked me.

"Well, sure," I said. "No one has more pride than her."

"That's how we are in the García de Ron family. I'll tell you a story about us. In the village, after the war, the new mayor came to our house one day and told my father he had to hand over all his cows. Just because this goddamn snob was on the winning side, and my father was with the losers."

"And what happened?" I asked.

"My father refused to give him the cows, of course."

"And it turned out well? Your old man got to keep his cows?" asked Guzmán.

"No way." El Grescas spat a bloodstained gob on the floor. "When the mayor and his friends walked into the stable, they went flying into the air. There was a bomb waiting for them instead of cows. But my dad ran out of dynamite and couldn't finish the lousy sons of bitches off and just roughed them up a little. When they recovered, they went after him, broke his legs, and took every last inch of our land. You understand the lesson of the story?"

"Not really," I confessed.

"The moral is that the powerful win. They always win. But it cost them, goddamn it. It cost them! The only thing poor bastards like us have left is the comfort of knowing we stood up to them."

El Grescas's story turned out to be prophetic, because things were about to get worse.

CHAPTER 23
GLORIA

During our long stay in Villa Valiente, César came by once to see if his uncle was finally going to die. When he saw that wasn't the case, he decided to return to Havana.

As he was getting his luggage together again, Marita and I shot glances at each other. It wasn't fair that César got to go back to the city while we had to stay in seclusion with Uncle Aurelio. The sky was threatening a storm.

"All three of us could go back," suggested Marita, who was unable to hide her desire to return to her life of luxury in the capital. "I think Uncle is feeling much better."

"Don't give me that nonsense," snarled César. "Can't you see his head is cracked open like a coconut?"

"Please, let me go with you," his sister begged. "Even if just for a few hours. I'll just swing by a few stores and come back right away."

But César wasn't convinced.

"Shut your mouth! Family is sacred; we always have to be present when we're needed."

I was dying to go back to Havana too. My skin burned just from thinking about spending time with Patricio again. But my husband was so angry at Marita's insistence, I didn't dare ask.

"Your obligation is to take care of our uncle, goddamn it, because that's what women do," César barked before going out the door.

As soon as he was gone, Marita gave a chair a tremendous kick and sent it flying to the other end of the room.

"Dear God, take this hex off me and let that old man kick the bucket!" she said, adding curses. Then she locked herself in her room.

In keeping with Marita's bad mood, dusk brought a tremendous storm. The sky turned gray, and the smell of wet dirt rose from the earth. The wind was blowing so hard that the old man's employees had to herd the cattle and lock them in the barns. The palm trees were so agitated, the trunks looked like they were about to snap, and the leaves broke off and flew in every direction. When rain started to hit the windows, it was like a giant's fist pounding and little streams formed on the glass. Lightning illuminated the sky with a flash and was followed by a terrible thunder.

When I went to Uncle Aurelio's room to say good night, the old man was delirious and tossing and turning in bed. I touched his wet forehead with my hand. His fever was getting worse.

"Are you okay? Are you afraid of the storm?"

He looked at me with disdain. "Please! There are many things that make me more scared than a little bit of thunder. The pests hiding and scurrying in the pillows and sneaking in my ears and stirring up my brains. The lizards laying their eggs in my nostrils. And the rats running around in the dark. As soon as you let your guard down, they'll come and steal your eyelashes so they can make fans for themselves."

"Don't say such crazy things, Aurelio. There are no pests like that here. And why would the rats need fans?"

"To fan themselves, girl. Don't be such a dummy."

The poor man was really out of it, and I left the light on so he wouldn't have to worry about the eyelash-thieving rats.

After we made do with provisions that included sour orange juice and a box of ginger crackers, Daniela, Marita, and I took refuge in a bedroom, planning to spend the night all together. My daughter curled up into a ball on my lap and fell asleep right away, but Marita was still in a rotten mood. I decided to take advantage of the situation to ask her a few things about my husband's past.

"I didn't know you and César were only half siblings on your father's side," I said.

"Who told you that?" Marita asked. "César?"

I shook my head. "He never tells me anything about his childhood. Your uncle told me."

"That old man's crazy. And nobody's interested in talking about the past."

"I'm interested." I took a sip of orange juice. "Now I understand so many things."

"What things?" Marita asked with a nasty look.

"Well, that César was a mistake. That he grew up without his parents' love."

My sister-in-law laughed bitterly. "All the love he lacked as a child he later made them pay for in spades."

"What do you mean?" I asked, trying to get her to keep talking.

But Marita was too sly to give in so easily to my curiosity. "Nothing. We shouldn't be talking about this. Stirring up shit just brings out more flies."

Seeing that I wasn't getting anywhere by being nice, I decided to change my strategy and poke at her the way bullfighters pester a bull to get it ready. I picked up a bottle of rum, mixed it with the orange juice, and offered her a glass.

"Why are you still afraid of your brother?" I asked.

My question really threw her, and for a split second before she turned defensive, there was a slight blush on her cheeks that told me I was right. "Don't be ridiculous."

"I'm afraid of him too," I said. "Very."

"I'm not afraid of my brother! Goddamn it!" Marita practically screamed. I thought she might have woken Daniela, but no, my daughter was still sound asleep.

"Liar. He puts you in a real panic. Anyone can see it all the way from China and even through the fog," I insisted. "You know how I know? You never take your eyes off him, just like you would never take your eyes off a tiger. When he's around, you're always quiet, and you never dare to contradict him. And it's not like you don't have a temper. With me, you're mad all the time, but with him, you keep all that fire to yourself."

"Hello? Everything you say I do, I do out of respect. César is a man, and he's my brother, and it's my duty to make him happy," she insisted.

I didn't believe a word of it. "I know the difference between respect and fear."

Marita swallowed hard. We both knew I was right, but my sister-in-law was too proud to admit it. I decided to give her a break and change the subject.

"Given what your uncle told me, César must have been a very resentful boy."

"On the contrary. As a boy, he was really sweet. One time, he saved a baby bird that had fallen out of its nest. He made a little cotton bed for it in a coffee can. That is, until our old man found it and threw it to the dogs."

"Your uncle also told me César is afraid of dogs."

"Yes, because of that Christmas Eve he had to spend with the German shepherds. Those dogs nipped at him all night long. But he got over it. I mean, he really got over it."

A blast of thunder jolted me. By then, Marita had drunk her first rum and orange juice and was going for a second. The liquor was doing its job—already, she was much less guarded and more talkative.

"I'm gonna tell you a story," she said. "When César turned fifteen, our father and his wife agreed to send him to Havana so he could work as an apprentice at an auto shop. César wasn't in the least bit interested in the trade, but he had no choice." Marita took a long swallow of her juice. "Do you know who Oswaldo 'the Bonebreaker' García is?" she asked me.

I nodded. Of course I knew. Oswaldo the Bonebreaker was a famous gangster and killer. Like Lucky Luciano and Meyer Lansky, he was one of the Cuban mafia's old kings. His cruelty was so infamous that when I was a little girl, the Bonebreaker was a kind of monster, a friend of the bogeyman and the witch on a broom, that many parents, including mine, would use as a threat to make us eat our vegetables or behave. *Either do your chores right now or I'll have Oswaldo the Bonebreaker come and squeeze the fat out of you*, the mothers of Havana would say.

"Well, Oswaldo was a customer at that auto shop, and he took César under his wing," my sister-in-law said.

That's when I realized the bogeyman had been my husband's mentor.

"You can't be serious," I said with a gasp.

"I'm serious. César started by washing and waxing his car, and in a very short time, he was his number two."

"How did he manage it?"

Marita went quiet again, trying to be mysterious.

Eventually she said, "It's better if I don't tell you. Nowadays it's pretty dangerous to know too much about the Bonebreaker. And, anyway, I don't know anything about anything. Except—"

"Except?" I repeated.

I served her more orange juice and rum and held my breath until she started her story again.

"César told me about the first big favor he did for Oswaldo. This was many years ago, when he was still a teenager who liked to brag. Later, he never talked about it again."

"C'mon, just tell me," I begged with my best little girl voice.

"Everything started when Oswaldo received a shipment of heroin from Colombia bound for the United States. I'm talking about millions of dollars in drugs. What Oswaldo didn't know was that among his men there was a traitor who had tipped off the cops." Marita had lowered her voice so much I had to press close to hear her. "One night," she whispered, "the cops came to one of the garages, knocked the door down, and went through everything. Oswaldo had just enough time to hide the drugs in a strongbox hidden in the floor. But what to do with the key? Well, he couldn't come up with a better idea other than to shove it into a sausage and then give it to his German shepherd to eat."

"You can't be serious."

"I swear by the Sacred Virgin. The thing is, the cops took Oswaldo and his men down to the police station. From there, the Bonebreaker sent a message to César, an insignificant apprentice the police hadn't considered important enough to arrest. Oswaldo knew the inspectors would search the place again and find the drugs, so he asked your husband to take the bags out of the strongbox and hide them in a more secure place. There was only one problem."

"The key was inside the dog?"

"And he couldn't wait for the dog to take a shit."

My mouth dropped open. "César killed the dog?"

Marita nodded. "He gutted that poor animal and pulled the key from its entrails. It wasn't easy. That was a big, bad, ferocious dog. César had to confront his greatest fear with his bare hands and a knife. He was never the same after that day. When Oswaldo got out of jail, he gave César his first pistol as a present, to show his appreciation."

I tried to imagine my husband as an adolescent, with the dead dog at his feet and his chest swollen with pride. He'd faced off with his demons and emerged victorious.

"But didn't Oswaldo die from a stroke a few years ago?" I said. "I think I remember something in the papers about it."

Marita nodded. "When he died, César became his heir. Now Lansky, Luciano, and César control the island."

"Why didn't you tell me anything about this before, Marita?"

"To protect you, stupid," she said. "Believe me, playing dumb is the best survival strategy."

That was certainly true. And it made me angry because all this time, and almost without realizing it, I'd been playing the fool. I tried to find out about my husband's life, yes, but only so I could sleep without losing my soul. I bit my tongue because I didn't want to tell Marita that thanks to Patricio, I'd learned survivors aren't just those who seem crazy or foolish but also those who may seem defeated yet continue the struggle in spite of the enormous challenges before them.

"Are your mother and father still alive?"

She shook her head. "My father died during the fires that razed half the province in 1935, and César's mother died in childbirth with her last son. The only family he has left are his half siblings and Uncle Aurelio. César has enough greenbacks to support all of us."

"It's odd that he takes care of you," I said. "I mean, in the end, you all had the love of your parents. It's strange he doesn't resent you."

"Oh, he does resent us! He treats us worse than the black people he's got working at his clubs. Besides, my brother doesn't just hand me dollars. Keeping you company is worse than harvesting sugarcane."

Marita stifled a yawn. After her confessions, all that rum was making her sleepy.

"Now you've managed to find out everything," she declared with her usual haughtiness. "Is there anything else my lady would like to know?"

"Just one more little thing. If you hate having to go everywhere with me, why do you continue living with us at our house?"

Marita looked at me with a profound sadness. Her eyes were glassy because of the rum and the memories. "What, I should stay in the countryside to be eaten alive by flies? I'm no fool. In Havana, I have a lovely house, a maid to wash my underwear, delicious things to eat, and many pretty dresses."

"Bought with dirty gangster money."

"Yes, but those are Coco Chanel dresses. What woman wouldn't sell her soul to the devil for a Chanel?" asked Marita, before she fell fast asleep and started snoring.

Who was I to judge her? The issue was not the life Marita was living, but rather, that everything that could be said about my sister-in-law could also be said about me.

CHAPTER 24

PATRICIO

Grescas wasn't ambushed in a dark alley, not when he was closing down the cantina alone, not in a dead end in the worst part of the city. No, the most terrifying thing is that they grabbed him on a Sunday morning right in the middle of the Prado, just as he was coming back from buying a couple of pork chops at the butcher shop. The Prado was jammed with people out for a Sunday stroll, including families and loads of tourists. A street musician was playing a Concha Piquer song. Two flower vendors rolled up their shirtsleeves to dance. A girl in high heels and a white dress with a frilly skirt strolled by with a matching white poodle that sashayed with the same charm as his owner. A bunch of kids stood in line before an ice cream cart selling mantecado, strawberry and chocolate ice cream, and fruit pops for only fifteen cents, while a group of bare-chested adolescents elbowed each other all the way to the beach.

Grescas's kidnapping happened in a matter of seconds. Two goons flanked him and in an instant pushed him into the back seat of a car. The pork chops, still wrapped in brown paper, were abandoned on the street.

Once he was in the car, he later told us, two other men covered his head with a cloth sack. They managed to tie his hands and feet but not before he got them with a fusillade of kicks and punches. A blow to the neck finally knocked him out.

He woke up when the car came to a screeching stop. They opened the door and threw him out. After coming to, he noticed there was grass under his knees although the place was paved. It smelled of countryside, of ash, of thyme and rabbit shit—and he could hear the murmur of water and the trill of birds. When they finally took the sack off his head, and his eyes got used to the light, he realized he was no longer in Havana. There were green hills and palm trees everywhere. A creek ran nearby.

It was an idyllic place except for the situation: Grescas was on his knees, his hands and feet tied. He was still flanked by the two goons. One of them was the man with the scar on his cheek, the supposed headwaiter at the Calypso who had come to see him at home. Grescas realized he was really in trouble when César himself calmly stepped out of the back of a car.

"So this is the stubborn little faggot," César said to the man with the scar. "He doesn't really look like he has any balls, does he?"

Grescas spat, aiming at César's white shoes.

"My name is Grescas. Or better yet, Mr. Grescas, if you have even a smidgen of manners."

César repaid him for spitting with a kick to the face.

"And to top it off, you're Asturian," he said when he heard the accent. "A bunch of hungry good-for-nothings coming to Cuba. Why can't the Spanish die of hunger in their own country and stop dicking around with the patience of us Cubans?"

"I would go back to Asturias, but then who would fuck your mother?" Grescas said with a laugh.

And that's when he got his first punch to the face.

"My men tell me you like to get beaten up," said César as he opened and closed his fist. "But when they went to see you, they left you whimpering like a baby."

"They beat the shit out of me, I won't lie. But it's also true they didn't get any state secrets."

"That's why I'm here," César said, smiling. "My men also tell me you share an apartment with two other good-for-nothings. Your boyfriends, I'm sure. Do the three of you get in the same bed to stem the rose?"

"Yes, and there's room for one more. You look like you could be a good lay." Grescas winked and blew him a kiss.

His words were cut off by yet another blow to the face. The second of many more to come. But my friend was determined. He knew the war was lost from the beginning, but as his father's son, he was going to go down fighting.

"Enough yakking," declared César. "I hear you're making a lot of money with that drink, and that can't happen. Give me the recipe."

"The recipe is dog piss and two of my ball hairs," responded Grescas with his usual elegance.

César pulled out a pistol and put it up to my friend's temple. "Tell me the ingredients, or I'm gonna blow your brains out."

"Blow my brains out, and you won't have a recipe."

César hesitated. Grescas enraged him so much, he nearly shot him right there, but his business instinct stopped his trigger finger at the last possible moment.

"You're right; you're right." The gangster put away his gun and shrugged. "No need to get ahead of myself. There are a lot of ways of getting information out of a man."

"You ought to beat the shit out of me again."

César smiled in a way that made Grescas's blood run cold. The gangster had regained control of the situation. "No, no, no. I see you don't care very much about getting beat up. And I'm more about getting things done, my friend."

Without the slightest urgency, César took off his jacket, folded it with extreme care, handed it to one of his lackeys, and rolled up his shirtsleeves. Then he walked over to the car and took something out of the trunk. Grescas completely lost his nerve when he saw him coming back with an apron and a pair of pliers. The gangster arranged the apron over his suit like a butcher who's about to quarter a calf and doesn't want to stain his clothes.

"Just so you see I'm not a bad guy, I'm gonna let you choose. Fingernails or teeth?"

Grescas froze with fear.

"Oh, you can't decide? Then I'll choose. Teeth. That way, it'll take us a little longer."

César cracked his knuckles and licked his lips.

"Before we begin, I'm gonna tell you a secret," he whispered. "Deep down, very deep down, I don't give three shits about the recipe for your stinky cocktail. But it's a question of respect, you understand? If I give an order, then a maggot like you has to obey. That's the way the world works. Respect is very important." He turned to his men. "Hold him."

Grescas's screams startled the birds, who shot out of the trees in a stampede.

César got what he needed after three teeth.

The pain Grescas felt was so inhumane, he confessed his secret and gave them the recipe for his creation. And, yes, the main ingredient was Bacardi rum, as I had suspected, but it also had unusual ingredients such as wild hibiscus flower and honey. Its complexity was the definitive proof that my friend was a master mixologist.

Grescas was convinced that, once César got the ingredients and the proportions, he'd kill him. Luckily, his screams had attracted about twenty peasants who had been collecting bananas.

There's no question César calculated whether it was worth it to him to kill with so many witnesses, but he must have decided Grescas wasn't worth the bother, or that he had more important things to do, because he tossed the pliers on the ground and left with his men. The peasants came to Grescas's aid and brought him home with the three teeth in his pocket.

Guzmán and I called the doctor so he could sew up his gums; then we put him to bed full of painkillers. His mouth was a mess, between the jagged teeth he had left and the gum boils starting to form; the poor man's cheeks were more swollen than a frog's.

"Are you stupid or what?" Guzmán scolded him. "Why didn't you just give it up from the beginning?"

Grescas's mouth was so swollen, we could barely understand when he spoke.

"Enough, enough!" he said after great effort. It was obvious every word caused him unspeakable agony. "Confess from the start? At least that bastard had to sweat to get the recipe."

"But you've lost three teeth, Grescas."

He smiled at us with his bloody mouth. "And I stained his shirt with my blood, even though he was wearing an apron!"

"That's little comfort to me."

"You can't just let dictators get away with it without putting up a fight. Listen, this is important. You have to do me a favor . . ."

That very night, all the waiters at the Calypso already knew how to make the new cocktail. Without a doubt, César had instructed them well. And customers fell under its spell like rats entranced by a pied piper. The drink sold like hotcakes. The second night, though, there were very few people at the club. There were even fewer the third night. On the fourth night, hardly anybody asked for the drink. What was happening? With his mouth still looking like scraps from the butcher shop, Grescas had told us the recipe and asked us to repeat it to anyone who would listen.

Neither dumb nor lazy, Guzmán and I went to every hotel, every bar, and every cantina in Havana as if we were priests on a mission to spread Grescas's word. By the time we had finished our rounds, every waiter, every bartender, and every rum fan in the city could make a more or less decent forajido. Grescas would rather give his secret to all of Cuba than let César make any money with it.

It was a Pyrrhic victory but a victory nonetheless.

CHAPTER 25

The whole episode with the forajido confirmed what I already knew: César was the most dangerous enemy a nobody like me could have. The gangster's status grew day by day, and just imagining what would have happened if he'd caught me kissing his wife gave me a stomach-churning infusion of panic and anguish that left my body aching.

I was tortured by my curiosity. How had a woman like Gloria married such a maniac? She'd told me once it wasn't her choice, but I was dying to know the whole story. Perhaps César had forced her to say "I do" at gunpoint? With a mafioso, anything was possible. What was certain was that our story couldn't end well. We were doomed to disaster. My common sense constantly drummed in my head that there was no point in winding up in the cemetery over a woman, but I remembered Gloria's lips against mine. Hesitant at first, then passionate. And the memory of that kiss and the promise of future kisses vanquished my fears and wiped away my prudence. I came to Havana hungry for adventures, and this one surpassed any I could have imagined. I had to keep rowing, harder now than ever. We were entering the rapids.

After his kidnapping, El Grescas went through a period of convalescence during which his smashed mouth only let him eat mush. Pronouncing a single syllable required a world of effort, so he didn't talk much, switching from swearing to giving us the finger left and right.

We were so terrified of retaliation by César when he found out we'd gone around giving away the forajido recipe that we decided to move. As an extra safeguard, El Grescas quit his job at the cantina in case the gangster's henchmen decided to look for him there. We hated to leave our watchtower, with its warm twilights and the view from the terrace of the beautiful woman next door, but nothing else mattered until that maniac forgot about my friend.

We moved to a house on Obispo Street, very close to the Hotel Ambos Mundos, Hemingway's preferred accommodation when he was in Havana. In fact, his room's balcony opened onto one of ours, so we saw him often as he sat in his underpants in front of his typewriter.

"I think I'm a reasonable guy," Guzmán used to joke. "Such a good guy, I could forgive César Valdés for being such a scary motherfucker. I could even forgive him for coming so close to killing us. But I can't forgive him for making us move and trading our view of naked Cachita for an old, fat bearded guy in his underpants, no matter how good he writes!"

Our new home was a small two-story house, old, with the facade painted egg-yolk yellow and balconies decorated with flower-shaped iron handrails. The exterior was quite lovely, even elegant, but inside, that house was a mess. The pipes howled every time we turned on a tap, the wooden floor creaked with every step and sounded like a ship in a storm, and there were so many drafts that doors would slam and make us jump every now and again.

Our landlord was a charming old gentleman who had worked the box office at the Teatro Chino on San Nicolás Street as a younger man. He was married to an Asian woman. They spent most of the year in Macao with her family, and since they knew their house in Havana was falling to pieces, they rented it to us for a laughable price as long as we took care of it.

The best part of the house was the big garden with an interior courtyard. It was a little plot of land full of trees, protected from the street by a tall wooden fence. Chinese paper lanterns hung from the branches, representing our hosts' youthful memories, but those weren't the only relics of their theatrical past. There were many remnants, like the huge golden lions that flanked the doors to the garden, puppets made of wood and fabric, and even a papier-mâché pagoda next to a fountain filled with carp.

El Grescas fell in love with the place as soon as he set foot in it. Shortly after we moved in, when he could talk again, he cleaned out the weeds, got tables and chairs, and invited some regular customers from King Kong for cocktails in the shade of the trees and the glow of the paper lanterns.

Soon, our courtyard became an underground cantina. They nick-named it La Pekinesa for its Asian decor. Thanks to our loyal and discreet customers, who could only enter with a secret password, El Grescas became the owner of a small, impromptu business. Nights at La Pekinesa were pure Havana. The lightning bugs swarmed, attracted by the lamps. The scent of fresh mint filled the night air while customers plucked leaves for their mojitos right off the plants. El Grescas served the drinks and, at the same time, tended a grill sizzling with steaks and sausages. The entertainment was provided by the regulars themselves, who were usually in the mood to sing mambos, boleros, and rumbas. On weekends, some friends of Guzmán's who had a small orchestra came too, and the trumpeter's girlfriend, Conchita, wowed us all with a version of "La Gloria Eres Tú," which she sung with as much feeling as Olga Guillot herself.

With the initial earnings from his little cantina, the first thing El Grescas did was pay the same dentist who'd sold us dentures for the bedbug sisters to reconstruct his mouth. But just the back teeth, of course. He kept the gap in the front forever.

"I knocked them out when I was thirteen, when I crashed head-on into a chestnut tree while running with a stolen chicken under my arm. It was a skinny little chicken, but my mother used it to make soup for the whole family for weeks. We even ate the feathers. I like to remember that every time I look in the mirror. I remember how lucky I've been in this country."

A few weeks after our move, we began to relax a little. Based on what some acquaintances who worked in his club told us, César had turned the page on the forajido. He had more important issues to deal with than searching for a shithead like El Grescas to knock out even more of his teeth. Just like on the night when I'd messed up his shoeshine, our status as poor devils unworthy of his attention had saved our lives again.

Since the profits from La Pekinesa were enough to cover our rent, Guzmán and I were in favor of El Grescas's cantina as long as the customers stayed in the garden and the upper floor was still just for the three of us. To be sure, we put "Do Not Enter" signs all over the staircase, although that didn't keep me from walking in on distracted and undressed couples in my room every now and then.

My compays and I were on a winning streak, but without Gloria by my side, I was incapable of enjoying life. The only thing that eased my suffering a little was buying myself a mariposa flower and placing it in the buttonhole of my uniform; the aroma consoled me. In La Rosa de Oro flower shop on Galiano Street, they got into the habit of setting one aside for me every morning. One day, when the usual shop clerk was home with a cold, I had to go without my flower.

That same day, Tomás Menéndez came up to me at the makeup counter in El Encanto. Mr. Menéndez was in charge of the store's advertising department, and I held him in high esteem. His genius slogans were well known, like the catchy "It's springtime now at El Encanto." The good feelings between us were mutual, and sometimes he used me as a guinea pig to try out his ideas.

"Good morning, Mr. Tomás."

"Hello, Patricio." Tomás pointed. "No flower today?"

"No, they didn't have one for me at the flower shop. You're very observant."

"It's my job to focus on the details." Tomás Menéndez smiled at me knowingly. "May I ask what secret you're hiding?"

I turned pale. Did he suspect something about my relationship with Gloria? It was totally impossible. When he saw my look of shock, Mr. Menéndez started laughing.

"I'm joking! I only ask because it was a tradition in the nineteenth century, during the war of independence, for women to use bunches of mariposa flowers to hide slips of paper with secret messages for the soldiers."

I exhaled in relief and decided to confide in him.

"I must confess, I do have a little secret," I said. "I wear the flower in my buttonhole because its scent reminds me of someone."

"A special lady, eh?"

"The most special of all," I agreed.

Tomás Menéndez looked thoughtful.

"Very interesting. It's a conditioned reflex, like with Pavlov's dog," he concluded.

"Whose dog?"

"Pavlov was a scientist who rang a little bell before feeding his dog. Eventually, he discovered the animal connected the two things: whenever he heard the bell, he started to salivate."

"The same thing happens to me!" I exclaimed, thinking Gloria would love the story about that scientist. "When I smell mariposas, I don't drool like a dog, but I feel like I'm with"—I was about to say "Gloria," and I stopped myself just in time—"her."

Mr. Menéndez stroked his chin, still deep in thought. "Wouldn't it be something if we could do the same thing with the store?"

At that, his face lit up, and he leaned over the counter to give me a hug.

"Patricio, you just gave me the best idea of my life!"

CHAPTER 26

GLORIA

Six months after our arrival in the countryside, the flies began to die. And if they were nightmarish while alive, they weren't much better dead. They piled up everywhere, even inside cupboards and furniture. The sensation of putting a bare foot into a shoe full of dead flies was as unpleasant as a cranky old lady.

But the dying flies were just making room for their cousins, the mosquitoes. Every night was a battle against their buzzing and bites. I must have had sweet blood, because the mosquito net over my bed posed no obstacle to them, and the little winged vampires almost ate me alive. There was a moment when I was so thoroughly consumed, the bite marks on my skin competed with my moles and freckles.

I tried everything to ward them off: rubbing vinegar on my skin, hanging bunches of catnip throughout the bedroom, burning incense, and leaving the light on all night. All for nothing. My blood was still their favorite food.

But what made me angriest of all was not the bites or scratching myself all day long: it was that Marita and Aurelio didn't suffer a single mosquito bite. Not one! Neither did César when he visited.

"Don't let it get to you, Mamita. They don't bite them because they have bad blood," Daniela told me. "The mosquitoes aren't stupid."

We were in the kitchen eating guacharita soup, which is made with a tiny freshwater fish whose only purpose is being turned into soup and choking you with its spines. My daughter's tone of voice reminded me so much of my grandmother that I froze, a half-chewed bone still in my mouth.

"Why do you say that?" I asked her.

"Bad blood?" Daniela shrugged. "Lala told me about that."

Ever since she was born, I had always tried to protect Daniela, keeping her away from César's dark universe. Of course, I had never told her what had happened at my parents' shop and never said a word against her father. But, thanks to the mosquitoes of Villa Valiente, I discovered Lala had told my daughter about César behind my back.

"You shouldn't speak ill of your father and his family," I told her, worried César might get angry with her.

"Don't worry, Mamita. I won't do it to his face."

"What else has your great-grandma told you?" I inquired.

"That Daddy is a cad, and he hurt you when you were little. That's why I always have to be careful around him."

I felt as if I were about to faint. The idea that César might do something to Daniela was too horrifying for me to bear.

"Your father—has he ever done anything to you?" I asked, my voice a thin whisper.

"No, Mamita. And he won't, don't worry. One afternoon he was a little tipsy, and he came very close to me, but I warned him that if he touched a hair on my head, I would throw such a tantrum, they would hear about it in China."

That's my girl, I thought. The same rebel I'd been, once upon a time, against the same monster. At that moment, imagining Daniela even talking to César was so repulsive, I felt I couldn't breathe, but I was also pleased to learn my daughter knew how to defend herself.

"And what did he say?"

"He said I was a little piece of shit, that my Lala had lied, and that you and he got married because you roped him into it. And besides, I was so disheveled and ugly, there were thousands of prettier urchins in Havana he could set his sights on before being an animal with me."

I burst into tears, a combination of disgust and relief. It was certain that if César wanted to continue abusing little girls, there were thousands in Havana he could torture before his own daughter. How could I know César wouldn't lose his mind and commit some savage act? Couldn't I do something to protect the victims from this raging lion?

"Don't worry, Mamita. Lala made me a little something to protect me. 'For faith, for hope, and for blessed charity.'"

My daughter put a piece of fish in her mouth, and I saw she had a mosquito bite on her arm.

"They're biting you too?"

Daniela nodded and showed me various bite marks with a look of pride, as if they were trophies.

"This means I don't have bad blood like the rest of the Valdéses," she said with a smile.

That afternoon, as always, I went to Uncle Aurelio's room. I had run out of eau de toilette, so I combed his hair with a comb soaked in chamomile tea and endured his impertinence and pinches.

"It's almost lunchtime, Aurelio. I'll tell the cook to make you tilapia and fried sweet potato."

"That black girl doesn't know the first thing about cooking," the old man grumbled.

Those were his last words.

Later, when Marita came back from spending the afternoon in town and went to give him a kiss, she got the fright of her life. Aurelio had died with a mouth full of fish and sweet potato.

The next day, César arrived from Havana. We buried his uncle on his own estate, after a lackluster funeral attended by no one but ourselves. As soon as the old man was in the ground, we packed our bags. After half a year of life in the country, we were finally returning to the capital. Before we left, the pillaging began. The servants took the furniture, and César and Marita kept Aurelio's few jewels. I chose a photo album as a souvenir.

In the car, while the chauffeur drove away from that desolation as fast as he could, I was surprised to open the album and discover its pages contained only two photographs. One was of Aurelio before he'd become a bitter old man. He was posing with another man, kissing as if they were husband and wife. The other was a black-and-white photo of a hen held in a woman's pretty hands.

When we got back to Havana, Marita and I escaped to El Encanto straight from the car, without even stopping by the house. César didn't complain; on the contrary, he was amused by our "pressing feminine need" to go shopping. He never suspected my pressing feminine need was to see Patricio again.

"Blessed Saint Barbara," whined Marita as we got out of the car, "I need a dab of Pond's cream more than I need food. All that sun has given me the face of a peasant."

"Go ahead and buy it. I have to go to the ladies' room first," I lied.

When I walked through the front door, I felt my legs shaking. At first sight, nothing had changed; the store was just as pretty and refined as ever. The surprise came when I breathed deeply, and my nose took in a familiar aroma: El Encanto smelled of mariposas.

The memory of my kiss with Patricio was so strongly connected to that scent, it was like experiencing it all over again. My face turned as red as a tomato, and I couldn't breathe. For a moment, I didn't know whether the scent was only in my head.

One of the elevator operators, a girl with freckles and bangs, passed by me, and I took the opportunity to ask her.

"Excuse me, do you smell mariposas too?"

I was afraid she would think I was crazy, but the girl smiled at me and giggled. She had a very musical laugh.

"What a refined sense of smell you have! It's mariposa, verbena, and some other secret ingredient," she replied in her happy little voice. "If you'd like, you can buy the scent."

"I don't understand."

The elevator operator led me to a display case before walking away. Piled on the counter were several bottles of perfume, crowned with a pretty sign: "Try the new El Encanto signature fragrance."

I stood there, shocked. Then I raised my eyes and saw Patricio. He had cut his hair, and he looked tanner. I could have sworn his blue eyes flashed even bluer when he saw me. He was so handsome, I could've eaten him up with a side of potatoes right then and there.

We looked at each other in silence for a minute that passed as fast as a second. It was like drinking cold water from a fountain after crossing the desert.

"That was the longest six months, four days, and six hours of my life," sighed Patricio.

"How did you get El Encanto to smell like us?" I asked.

"It was really all thanks to Pablo."

"Who?" I asked.

"Pablo, the scientist with the dog."

I thought for a moment, then laughed. "Pavlov?"

"That's the one! Since you left, I always put a mariposa flower in my lapel. One day, I was talking to Tomás Menéndez, the head of advertising, and he had the idea of making a perfume people would associate with El Encanto. The trick to make the scent spread through the whole building is mixing it in with the air conditioning."

"You couldn't be any sweeter, my love."

Patricio looked at me with so much desire that I felt warmth washing over me, from my fingers to my feet to the top of my head.

"Luckily, I was able to convince the perfumer to include mariposa flowers among the ingredients," Patricio said. "It was completely selfish. Every day I felt like you were by my side."

"From now on, I'll never use another perfume."

With the excuse of reaching for a bottle, I held out my hand and touched his. Just brushing against his fingertips gave me goose bumps.

"You can't imagine how badly I want to kiss you again," murmured Patricio.

"I feel the same way," I purred.

"When?"

"Soon," I promised.

CHAPTER 27

Soon.

But, unfortunately, "soon" was not soon at all.

Patricio couldn't come back to my house, and I couldn't go to his. My husband gave me relative freedom, but he had rigged it so he knew where I was every moment, thanks to Marita. Though we had actually gotten closer in Villa Valiente, once we were back in Havana our relationship returned to what it had always been. Besides playing dumb, my sister-in-law had only one task: to keep an eye on me.

In order to get some measure of intimacy, Patricio and I needed people to look away from us. And that wasn't easy on an island full of gossips. But life gave us a sudden gift. The unexpected arrival of a new invention entrapped the gaze of everyone in Cuba: television.

At first, television was just a rumor. Then one day the newspapers announced we would be the first country in Latin America to have it. Given my fascination with all things scientific, I searched until I found a book on the subject and learned all the secrets behind that incredible invention. I was fascinated to discover that one of the first television sets had been made with a bike axle, a coffee maker, and glass lenses attached with cords. I concluded that human ingenuity could come up with anything. Not everyone shared my admiration. My simpleton sister-in-law was annoyed by these tremendous advances in technology.

"They say it's like the radio, but you watch it. Little men inside a box. I think they're trying to fool us all. It's either that or witchcraft," concluded Marita.

"It's not witchcraft; television is possible thanks to cathodic rays," I explained.

"Well, what do you want me to say. Those Catholic rays strike me as black magic, and I don't like them one bit," she said.

"Then I suppose you won't want to watch television," I said, trying to get her going again.

"Of course I'll watch it. But if it's witchcraft, I'll avert my eyes before it can burn out my brain, and that television can just go to hell."

Just like my sister-in-law, Cuba was anxiously awaiting television, especially after the government confirmed they would soon begin broadcasting. But how would we see these programs if no one had a television? El Encanto provided the answer and announced they would be the first big store to sell the gadget.

On the predetermined day, they organized a party in the appliance section on the fifth floor. The employees set chairs in front of the new televisions and gave the kids balloons in blue and red, the colors of the Cuban flag. I went with César and Marita, neither of whom wanted to miss such an event. Before we dressed to go over, we all expressed our doubts. What was the proper protocol for watching television? Did we have to get dressed up, like when we went to the theater or the opera? Or could you watch television in more casual clothes or in your bathrobe, the way you listened to the radio at home?

Just in case, I decided to dress up for the ceremony. I wanted to wear a new strapless dress, or a "word of honor" dress, as Manet called them, with a small blue-flower print and long black gloves that went up to my elbows. I gathered my hair in a bun with a bejeweled tiara and chose a pair of gold earrings. César wore a dinner jacket, and Marita went with a black-and-gold jacket-and-skirt ensemble.

When we arrived on the fifth floor of the store, we realized we had made the right decision. The people had come in their finest. We were an incredibly well-dressed group sitting in front of a box.

We sat in reserved seats. The floor was jammed, and there was soon a circle of the curious around the television. We were all completely silent and full of expectation. The gadget seemed like some kind of mechanical genie right out of a science fiction novel.

"The broadcast is about to begin!" declared one of the clerks. "Ladies and gentlemen, I'm going to turn on the machine in a moment."

She approached the television and, as we all held our breath, pressed a button. As soon as she did, there was some sort of spark and then, suddenly, a white dot in the middle of the screen. The dot grew until it revealed an image. We all thought we would see the president, but the very first thing we saw was a box of cigarettes in bright black-and-white. We responded to the image of the cigarettes with applause and laughter.

"Turn it up!" ordered César.

The clerks turned the wheel, and we could hear a song from the television speaker.

"La competidora gaditana-tana! Cigarrillo inigualable-able!"

That thing was hypnotizing. We all just sat there like dummies in front of it. The pack of cigarettes was replaced by a bottle of Cristal beer and a new song.

"Cerveza cristal, cerveza cristal, bien sabrosa, bien fresquita, our national pride!"

Suddenly, something caught my attention and drew my eyes away from the television. Patricio had reached my side, making his way through the multitude. With a slight nod of his head, he indicated I should follow him. I had no trouble sneaking away. My husband, my sister-in-law, and—probably—all of Havana were watching television.

I followed Patricio to an employee stairway, and we went up to the roof. Once there, we opened the door and went outside. We were received by a torrent of sunlight and the screeching of seagulls. A delicious gust of wind refreshed my lungs with the smell of the sea and loosened my hair. The sky was splattered with spongy clouds that looked like marshmallows; it was as beautifully blue as Patricio's eyes. The sound of the cars on the streets below had been transformed into a murmur instead of an annoyance.

I looked down from the cornice. From this height, Havana seemed like a little town, with tile roofs and lines of laundry. I felt a wave of love for my city. Yes, I had suffered a great deal of misfortune here, but it was also where I had been born and where my daughter had been born.

For good or bad, Havana was my place in the world.

Patricio took my hand and pointed to a couple of metal rods up on the roof.

"Have you seen those? They're the television antennas," he told me.

Feeling the sun on my face was such a superb sensation, I stretched like a lazy cat and took my hair down so I could better enjoy the sea breeze.

"You brought me up here just so you could show me these antennas?" I asked slyly.

Patricio responded with his own sly smile.

"I thought they would interest you," he joked, "given how scientific you are."

"So I see we're not going to break the rules today."

"I didn't say that."

"Kiss me, you little fool."

With Havana at our feet, we tried all kinds of kisses. Short kisses, long kisses, on the cheek, on the lips, with our mouths open and closed, with and without our tongues . . . some were passionate, others affectionate; some were playful, others more daring. They were all as beautiful as the first one. We separated only when our mouths were raw, after hundreds of kisses.

"How long have we been up here?"

Patricio shrugged, as dazed as me.

"Five minutes?" I glanced at my wristwatch and almost had a stroke. "Almost a quarter of an hour!" I exclaimed.

"It's clear we have a problem with time whenever we're together," said Patricio.

We had no choice but to come back to reality, which, in our case, meant back to the fifth floor, back to the appliance section. After one more kiss, Patricio took off.

As stealthily as possible, I made my way back. To my great relief, I discovered that everyone was still paralyzed in front of the television. I returned to the seat next to my husband. A moment later, César turned to me angrily. "Fucking Christ!" I was scared but, fortunately, his fury wasn't directed at me but at the television. "This shitty thing makes you stupid; you lose all sense of time. Where were you?"

"In the bathroom, trying to fix a run in my stocking," I lied with ease. "Did I miss anything?"

"A speech by Grau and a bunch of commercials. Aren't they gonna play anything that's worth a shit?"

"Well, I like it," said Marita, her eyes still stuck on the screen. "I wanna buy one right now."

I smiled. They hadn't even noticed I'd been gone for fifteen minutes. All thanks to the magic of television.

CHAPTER 28

PATRICIO

Life in love with Gloria was torture and bliss all at once. In a matter of seconds, I could go from absolute exhilaration to the most crushing sorrow, and it all depended on minuscule, trivial details.

When Gloria walked through the department store's doors, a bubbling happiness rose up through my chest. But if, for some reason, another customer kept me from going to meet her, I sank into hell. That is, until Gloria smiled at me from a distance and euphoria swept over me again. It was like that all day, every day.

Living that way was exhausting, but I wouldn't have changed it for anything in the world. I felt more alive than ever. My feelings were mysterious, contradictory, and animalistic, with a hint of self-destructive madness but irresistible nonetheless. Sometimes I thought I was going to go into cardiac arrest. Can love provoke a heart attack?

El Grescas and Guzmán were also in sticky situations with their respective girlfriends. Specifically, they were in relationships with two employees at El Encanto, whom they had met thanks to me. Every weekend, the big department stores organized activities for their employees at Club Seyca, a social, cultural, and sporting organization.

I got used to stopping by for something to eat with the rest of the staff, and my two friends often joined me to talk to the girls.

There were activities of all kinds, including a baseball team, a theater group, and even a choir.

The choir at Club Seyca was so famous that even the Austrian orchestra conductor von Karajan had directed it with his skilled baton for a performance. Among its members were women from all the departments, but two of them in particular caught my friends' attention.

Guzmán started going out with Alma, an administrative secretary. Alma was shy and quiet as a mouse. She knew typing and languages, and you could tell from her good manners she was from a good family. Pepa, El Grescas's girlfriend, was the total opposite. She worked in the stockroom, where she was the only woman among all the boys, and she had the strength and manners of a mare. The two girls couldn't have been more different, but they had become close friends through singing in the choir, and they were both crazy about my two compays.

Alma and Pepa spent a lot of time at our house on their days off from the store, in La Pekinesa during the day and upstairs in the bedrooms at night. And since the mansion's inner walls were as thin as rolling paper, whenever the girls spent the night, I heard things that made me curse my luck.

One night I was awakened by a woman's voice on the other side of the wall.

"Mmm, you stud! Make me yours! Mount me like a filly! Put me on all fours!"

From the vulgarities coming out of her mouth, I figured it was Pepa, the girl from the stockroom, in bed with El Grescas.

With a combination of secondhand embarrassment and annoyance, I tried to go back to sleep with the pillow over my head so as not to hear Pepa's sweet nothings, but she was in the choir for a reason, and my feather pillow couldn't stifle her shrieks.

"C'mon, c'mon, give it to me till I can't walk for a week!"

The next night, the moans came from the other room.

"Blessed Saint Lazarus!" screamed another powerful voice, which I imagined belonged to Alma, the prim and proper secretary. "That's right, my darling, light of my life, baby love!"

That was the straw that broke the camel's back. Both of my friends' girlfriends were screamers. They both projected their voices with great skill—the only difference was that one was blasphemous while the other was sickly sweet. On nights when they both slept over, our place sounded like a henhouse, and the two women's screams combined into a sort of demented dialogue.

"Fill me up with cream, Daddy!" shrieked one of them.

"Blessed Saint Lazarus, what delicious kisses!" exclaimed the other.

"Give it to me hard!"

"Cuddle me!"

"Big boy!"

"Strawberry candy!"

The earplugs I bought at El Encanto put an end to the nocturnal concerts. But another surprise awaited me. One morning, I ran into the two couples at breakfast. We were talking about the weather and shooting the breeze when Alma, the timid secretary, burned her hand on the coffeepot.

"Fuck me!" the lady let slip.

Pepa, the girl from the stockroom, ran to help her friend.

"What happened, my sweet darling?" she asked delicately.

That's when I realized that Alma wasn't the one who screamed baby talk, and Pepa wasn't the one who spewed obscenities. It was the other way around. When they were making love with my friends, the proper young lady was the one who talked like a longshoreman, and the girl from the stockroom was cornier than a bow on a cabbage.

My friends' relationships with Alma and Pepa didn't last. When the choir took a weekend trip for a performance in Cabaiguán, the two friends traded my compays for two medical students they met on the train. El Grescas and Guzmán got over their lovesickness with a couple of dancers from the Buena Vista and soon forgot about the screamers, but the whole story taught me that in the bedroom, you can't judge a book by its cover.

If my friends' escapades made me jealous, it was only because they could actually touch the objects of their affection. In my case, with Gloria, our lips hadn't touched since our furtive kisses on the roof the day television arrived in Cuba. Such are the pitfalls of being in love behind closed doors.

Trapped in a sort of courtly love, I got used to milking every gesture and every glance with my imagination. And I completely understood the knights of bygone centuries, back when the mere sight of their beloved's knees could keep them hot and bothered for weeks. It drove me crazy to have Gloria so close and not be able to touch her. It was the same anguish as when you have an unbearable itch and can't scratch it or when you can't drink water to quench a hellish thirst. It was a chronic pain in my very bones.

Sometimes, when I showed her something on the counter and her sister-in-law was nearby, our hands would be just centimeters apart, yet in reality we could have been in different galaxies. Those forbidden spaces drove me wild, but not respecting her in public would have been suicide.

In lieu of anything else, I never tired of looking at her. I knew the constellations of her moles like the back of my hand. Her right arm, for example, had twelve moles, from the wrist to the forearm, all surrounded by galaxies of freckles. Like sailors navigating by the stars in the sky, I navigated by Gloria's moles. In my mind, I baptized them all with the names of kings and queens, and I kissed them and caressed them until I was sated. And those were just the ones I could see on her exposed skin: her face, neck, arms, and legs. Sometimes a miracle happened and the strap of her dress slipped down her shoulder or the hem of her skirt rose up her thigh to reveal a new mole to add to my mental collection. If I was obsessed with the ones I could see, I was even crazier about the ones I didn't know about. Just thinking about the marks hidden beneath her clothes was enough to make me need a cold shower.

To alleviate the distance that separated us, Gloria and I agreed on a secret hiding spot to leave each other messages. We decided on a female mannequin: the one in front of the second column in the accessories section, counting from the escalator. We got into the habit of pressing notes into the mannequin's closed hand, slipping them between her fingers. Little unsigned bits of paper on which we could write love letters.

How were we to know one of those messages would be our downfall?

CHAPTER 29

The message had only seven words: "I love you so much it hurts." But they were about to almost cost us our lives. I wrote it on a piece of paper I rolled up like a cigarette and placed inside the mannequin's hand.

Since it was early and the store hadn't opened yet, only the employees were there. I decided to go up to the office on the fifth floor to get my pay slips, and when I stepped toward the stairs, I heard a whistle behind my back.

"You going up in my elevator, Asturian?" Nely gestured for me to follow her.

"But of course. Fifth floor," I said as we entered the elevator on the left.

Nely pushed the button with her typical ease.

"Takeoff in three, two, one . . . and we're off! You're getting skinny, you know that?" I noticed a hint of resentment in her voice.

"Oh yeah?"

"Must be because of all the exercise you do. You never take the elevator anymore. You always go up the stairs."

She was right. I had been taking the stairs religiously for months.

"Are you avoiding me?" she asked, and she gave me such a piercing look, I was afraid she was reading my thoughts.

"No, that's not it, Nely—"

"We never kiss anymore."

I sighed. I knew the moment would come. It was only logical. Since the night I went to Gloria's house instead of the Hotel Nacional with Ava Gardner, my attitude toward the elevator operator had changed. That night, I had also chosen between Nely and Gloria.

After that day, I never kissed Nely again. We still went to the movies and had dinner together, but our companionship never went so far as it had before. We grew distant. The only strange part was that Nely had taken so long to demand an explanation.

I couldn't put it off any longer. It was time to be sincere with her and confess I was in love with another woman.

"The truth is, I have something to explain," I began.

The elevator stopped on the second floor and Don Gato walked in. For the first time in my life, I was happy to see him because with him there, we couldn't continue the conversation.

I walked out of the elevator feeling like the worst guy in the world. It's true I had never promised Nely anything, but it was obvious she'd had high hopes for me, and it was lousy of me not to clarify the situation. How could I be so brave with Gloria and so cowardly with Nely? Maybe because with the former I had done the right thing—I'd followed the voice in my heart—and with the latter, there was no voice. To ease my conscience, I decided to invite her for a drink that very afternoon to make it clear we could only be friends.

With that decided, my spirits improved, and I immersed myself in work. Finally, it was time to open the store, and El Encanto filled with customers. That morning I had to attend to the belt display in the accessories section.

Shortly after we opened, I saw Gloria walk in with César and Marita. César usually didn't come shopping with the girls, but that day he must have had nothing better to do. Her husband and sister-in-law examined some brooches, and Gloria took the opportunity to wink at me while they weren't looking. Then she walked toward our agreed-upon mannequin and touched its fingers absentmindedly to grab the piece of paper with my message. But in a flash of bad luck, a sudden apparition from behind the mannequin startled her.

"May I help you, madam?"

It was Don Gato, who had the bad habit of being one of those sticky clerks who latch onto customers to try and make more sales.

Between the fright and the anxiety caused by our clandestine communications, Gloria bumped into the mannequin and knocked it to the floor. The piece of paper slipped from its fingers. Gloria crouched and grabbed the paper from the floor, with the excuse of picking up the mannequin.

"Don't worry, madam," said Don Gato obsequiously. "I'll take care of it."

"It's no bother," insisted Gloria, trying not to call any further attention to herself.

Too late. All the commotion had attracted César, who returned to his wife's side.

"You're a clumsy girl, you know that?" her husband said, reprimanding her. "Go on, leave it; the employee has it," he added while Don Gato rushed to complete his orders.

While Don Gato set up the mannequin again, Gloria moved to put the message in her purse, but before she could do so, César grabbed her hand. I saw how the color drained out of Gloria's cheeks when César noticed the paper.

"What do you have there?" he asked.

César took the paper from her hand.

"I don't know. I found it on the floor," she gabbled.

"On the floor?"

"Yes," answered Gloria, her voice a whisper.

When César unrolled the paper and read the message, a shadow fell over his face. From my display, I could see how his nostrils flared with fury while my heart accelerated with fear.

"Don't lie to me, Gloria. Who the hell gave this to you?"

"I swear, it's not mine. I just found it."

The situation looked so bad, I had to act immediately. I walked away from the display as if unconcerned and ran toward the elevators. Luckily, Nely's elevator was stopped on the ground floor.

"You're right," I blurted out, point-blank.

The elevator operator looked at me with surprise. I had rushed up to her like a gust of wind.

"Huh? Right about what?" Nely asked.

"I've been acting strange around you. But there's a reason."

"What?"

"See that mannequin? The one in front of the second column from the escalators in the accessories department? I left you a hidden message in its hand."

I finished off the ploy by giving her a kiss on the lips and walked away before she could say anything.

Nely was used to my crazy behavior, so I was sure she would play along. Almost sure.

When I got back to the display, the argument between César and Gloria was still red-hot.

"You think I'm a dumbass? An idiot? Is that it?" César snarled at her.

"I swear, this isn't mine." Gloria talked as softly as possible so as not to make him any angrier. "What do I have to do to make you believe me?"

The couple fell silent, with Gloria staring at the floor and César flexing his fists and getting more furious by the second.

César looked like he was about to grab her by the neck, so I decided to intervene. But as I stepped out from behind the counter, about to jump forward to protect Gloria, Nely, knowing nothing about the situation, got to the mannequin and looked in its hand.

My plan had worked. I put on the brakes and returned to my post while mentally ordering Nely not to leave without finding the message.

"I'm gonna ask you one more time. Where did you get that piece of paper?" César said to Gloria.

"I already told you it was on the floor. I found it when I knocked over the mannequin."

Nely interrupted them. "Excuse me, ma'am. Did you say that paper was in the mannequin's hand?"

Gloria nodded, not understanding the source of her sudden salvation but embracing the possibility of escape.

"It's a message for me. Sorry for the inconvenience," Nely explained.

César was bewildered, and his rage transformed into annoyance at having been the victim of such a mix-up.

"There is no room, miss, for this sort of stupidity in the workplace," he scolded Nely.

"You're quite right, sir. Sorry for the inconvenience."

César balled up the message and tossed it on the floor. Gloria took the opportunity to pick up the wrinkled paper and handed it over to the elevator operator.

"Here. It's a love letter," she told her.

A smile of satisfaction broke out across Nely's face when she heard that. "Thank you. It's from someone very special."

When she heard I was "someone very special" to Nely, Gloria hid her surprise.

"A beau?" Gloria asked her.

"It was love at first sight." Nely nodded.

Still on the verge of falling to pieces because of the argument with her husband, Gloria shot me a look of confusion and jealousy.

"You're very fortunate. Goodbye."

Nely read the words—"I love you so much it hurts"—on the paper and rushed up to me.

"I love you too," she whispered while I watched with a heavy heart as Gloria walked out of the accessories section.

I had saved the day, but at the price of hurting Gloria's feelings and making Nely believe I was in love with her.

It was a fine mess. I had gone from wanting to clear things up with Nely to using her. If I wanted to clarify my feelings, it was clear I hadn't found the right way to go about it.

CHAPTER 30

GLORIA

César threw me a huge party at the Tropicana for my birthday. All our celebrations usually took place at the Calypso, but that month, the nightclub was being remodeled to install a crystal dome. César always said it was best to celebrate with family and friends, but since I didn't really have family of my own—my mother and grandmother were nothing to him—he invited his mafioso friends and their stupid wives.

The club was in the middle of a jungle on the outskirts of the city. Different stages were surrounded by royal palms, maples, pines, cornstalks, grapevines, climbing plants, and shrubs. Here and there, the jungle broke into clearings illuminated by little colored lights hanging from the lianas, as if they were bunches of stars. In each of the clearings, a freshwater fountain—each decorated with a different animal: dolphins, frogs, seals, and other aquatic creatures—provided relief from the night's heat.

Once past the entrance, visitors came through the casino, with its roulette tables, dice games, blackjack, and slot machines. The stage and dance floor were outdoors, and on the first stage, a black singer dressed in a nice emerald-green suit alternated boleros and rumbas while a keyboard player accompanied him on a piano hidden in the bushes. The pianist took turns with an orchestra whose members wore Cuban shirts with puff sleeves in all the colors of the rainbow.

But what gave the club its worldwide fame were the dancers: half-naked women in bikinis and bodices decorated with sequins or glass tears. With their skin covered in glitter so they'd sparkle under the spotlights, they looked gorgeous as they danced, wearing huge pieces with fruit or feathers atop their heads. The Tropicana dancers, along with the cancan girls at the Parisian Moulin Rouge, were the stuff of fantasy for men all over the world. They were flesh-and-blood goddesses who wiggled their hips so beautifully they could resurrect a dead man.

Any other girl in Havana would have felt lucky to celebrate her birthday there, but not me. It wasn't because of the place, which was a delight, or the guests, who—although they didn't know me at all—had brought me presents and tried to be nice. That night I was miserable because I was missing the most important thing: Patricio. I would've gladly exchanged my big party at the Tropicana for an evening under a bridge at his side.

I hadn't seen him since the day César found the secret note. Patricio must have intervened in some way to save the situation, but I didn't understand very well what had happened with the elevator operator with the bangs. Did she mean that Patricio was her lover? Was Patricio with her and hiding it from me? I hadn't had occasion to talk to him to clear up these doubts, but a dirty jealousy was eating me up inside. Which was crazy, considering I was married, but I couldn't help it.

Every love song reminded me of him. The black man in the green tuxedo sang "Contigo en la Distancia" with so much feeling, I had to make a tremendous effort to contain my tears. There I was, sitting at the best table in the whole club and in front of a giant chocolate cake, but I felt as inconsolable as the peasant in the song, when a cigar vendor—a young girl with a short dress and a tray of cigarettes and candies hanging from her neck—came up with something for me: a pretty bouquet of mariposas.

"A gift from an admirer, miss."

A ray of hope made my sadness evaporate, and I looked around. César was handing out Montecristo cigars to a group of his friends, and Marita was dancing, showing off a new dress. I didn't see Patricio anywhere, but I was sure the flowers were from him. I brought them to my nose to smell their scent, and the cigar vendor leaned close to my ear.

"Your admirer also said to tell you to meet him by the frog fountain," she whispered before taking off.

With my heart in my throat, I got up from the table. As I passed César, I made up some excuse.

"I'm going to say hi to a friend of Marita's."

César nodded without even looking at me as he cracked up laughing with his mobster buddies.

I went into the jungle in search of the frog fountain. I got lost a couple of times, but with directions from several employees, I managed to reach a dark part of the jungle, near the artist dressing rooms, where there was a small fountain decorated with a stone frog.

Patricio was waiting for me there. He wore a tuxedo and looked like a movie star. He looked so good, I feared my evening dress would melt from the heat of my skin.

I threw myself into his arms with a yelp of joy. We almost fell into the fountain from so much kissing and hugging. I was so turned on, I could've ripped his clothes off right there.

"Did you think I was gonna miss your birthday?" he whispered in my ear as he kissed my neck.

His hands slid inside my dress, and his caresses made me feel as if there were electric eels all over my body. I was dying to let myself go, but I needed to clarify something first.

"The elevator operator at El Encanto, she's your lover?" I asked him.

Patricio's blue gaze was so heartfelt, I knew he'd answer truthfully.

"Her name is Nely," he said. "We're good friends, that's all."

"But you've made out with her?"

"Yes."

"Well, then you're more than friends," I pointed out. "And do you like her?"

"I'd be lying if I said I didn't."

"And have you fucked?"

"No."

"What do you feel for her?"

Patricio was quiet for a while, thinking it through, before he answered.

"Nely's more than a friend, it's true," he confessed. "We have a good time. She's smart, fun, and beautiful, and she loves me. I would love to fall in love with her, to be honest. My life would be much simpler if I loved her. And I swear I've tried with all my might. I really have. But I can't."

His mouth hypnotized me. I heard him talk, but all I could do was think about his lips.

"Why?" I whispered.

"Because of you. Because falling in love with you has been like running with my eyes closed, like leaping without a net, Gloria. Our love is an uncontrollable madness. I love you, sweetheart, like I'll never love anyone else."

I kissed him so forcefully that the kiss became a bite, and I noticed the metallic taste of blood on my lips. *I don't care if the entire world goes to hell,* I thought, *so long as this kiss never ends.*

Suddenly, as if the universe had decided to grant my wish, all the lights in the city went out.

CHAPTER 31

On December 22, 1951, at 9:30 p.m., darkness fell over all of Havana. Later, we learned lightning had hit the power plant and left the capital without power. That moment, though, at the Tropicana, I thought Patricio and I had blown the fuses with our earth-shattering kiss.

The lack of light unsettled Havana. Around us, we could hear laughter; people singing, "Turn it on, turn on el mechón"; and even screams of panic. Patricio and I took each other's hands, and thanks to the moonlight, we were able to cross the jungle and arrive at a kind of barracks. The Tropicana's employees had lit candles so they could see in the dark.

"Does anyone know what happened?" Patricio asked.

"They say the whole city's blacked out. It'd be best for you to go home, if you can," responded a dancer with a headdress balanced dangerously on top of her head.

The girl handed us a candle, and we slipped back into the jungle with the help of its light.

"Will Daniela be all right?" Patricio asked me, worried.

I nodded. My little girl was in Vedado. "I left her with my mom and grandma. She's safe with my Lala, don't worry. I'm sure they're busy casting spells and haven't even noticed the blackout."

"What about you? Do you wanna go home?"

"That's the last thing I want right now."

It was that instant, while the candle's flame illuminated our faces, that Patricio and I fully understood the opportunity life had just handed us. Without electricity, the whole city was in the dark. While the black-out lasted, we were free.

"I want to spend the night with you," I whispered. "You're the best birthday present ever."

Patricio lifted me off the ground, just a little, before he kissed me.

"Where do you want me to take you?" he asked.

"Wherever you want."

With the help of the candle, we were able to reach Patricio's car and drive back to the city. There, with the rest of the residents, we witnessed a once-in-a-lifetime spectacle.

Without the sparkling lights of the street lamps and the houses, Havana had traveled back two centuries in time. The buildings were engulfed in shadows, and people were standing in clumps around roaring bonfires on the street corners. Little groups of neighbors had brought chairs out to the sidewalk to sit in circles, chattering about the blackout and cooling off with buckets of ice and bottles of beer. The howling dogs blended in with everyone's songs and laughter.

On the windowsills, beside the geraniums, candles uselessly con-fronted the darkness. People walked down the sidewalk carrying torches. For one night, the city had gone back to fire, to a more primitive, more beautiful time.

Patricio and I parked on the outskirts of town and walked into the city center.

In a park, a black woman cooled herself with a palm leaf fan next to a tin drum full of burning wood while her two kids played, toasting crickets on the embers. The lightless porticos were the perfect hiding place for furtive couples like us: shadows kissing in dim corners.

But the murk also fostered troublemakers and lunatics. The nar-row streets of Old Havana were full of drunk, rowdy city dwellers.

The most barbaric had decided to take advantage of the occasion to smash windows and loot shops. We saw two men throw a trash can through a jewelry store window, and a group of youngsters armed with knives surrounded a man to steal his wallet. A madman, wearing only underpants, bumped into us while cackling like a hyena, then set off in pursuit of two prostitutes who chased him away, swatting him with their handbags.

To protect me from such craziness, Patricio decided it would be safest to get off the streets.

"I know where we can take shelter," he said with a big smile.

Not long after, we were on the roof of the great department store, lying together on the tiles. It was an incomparable opportunity for stargazing, the sky closer than ever before. With Patricio at my side under the stars, I felt so happy, I could have climbed Pico Turquino with a broken leg.

"This is the most beautiful birthday present anyone's ever given me," I said.

Patricio curled up beside me and looked up at the starry sky. "Do you know the names of all the stars?"

I laughed. "Not all of them! But I can tell you a few."

I pointed at different parts of the sky, from right to left. "That's the constellation of Boötes. I know it because Arcturus is its brightest star. If we follow the arc, we reach Spica, the prettiest star in Virgo. There's Antares. Do you see how red it is? Many people confuse it with Mars. And if we look over there . . ."

I suddenly fell silent. There was something very strange going on.

"If we look over there?" repeated Patricio.

I counted the stars again, in case I'd made a mistake.

"It can't be," I murmured, growing more amazed by the second.

"What is it?"

"The constellation Sagittarius has eight stars. It has such a unique shape, they call it a teapot, but tonight there are nine, not eight."

I counted the stars again, but I'd made no mistake. Next to the teapot's handle, there was a tiny point of light I'd never seen before.

"Maybe it's an airplane," I ventured.

"If it was a plane, wouldn't it be moving?"

"Yes."

"And is it moving?"

"No. And besides, no plane could fly that high."

Patricio gave me a kiss on the tip of my nose. "Well, look at that. You've discovered a new star."

I shook my head. The very idea was crazy.

"It doesn't work like that. Astronomers are the ones who discover stars," I explained.

"You're a scientist."

"I mean real ones. People who have studied at the university."

"I might remind you that when we met, you told me anyone could be a scientist. And you have more right than anyone. You're the smartest person I know."

"And you're the best looking," I replied, flattered.

Patricio didn't know what to say. It was impossible to discover a new star with a simple glance. The possibilities of something like that happening were so small, they weren't worth considering. And still . . .

I decided not to lose sight of that little piece of sky and to buy myself a telescope as soon as I could.

When we got tired of looking at the stars, we took shelter in the building. With the moonlight shining through the shop windows, without a soul in sight and in complete silence, El Encanto looked like something out of a storybook. An enchanted palace where time had stopped. When we reached the home section, we lit all the candles we could find.

"Have you ever dreamed of spending a whole night locked up in one of these department stores?" Patricio asked with a glimmer of mischief in his voice.

"Of course," I answered, excited. "Who hasn't?"

"Well, I think tonight's our opportunity, and we should take advantage of it while we can."

And we certainly did. For the first hour, we turned into two little kids and transformed El Encanto into our own special amusement park. To start, we declared a grand pillow fight, jumping on the mattresses and running down the corridors.

Later, in the accessories department, we organized a competition to see how many hats we could pile on our heads—I managed six, Patricio four—and raced in high-heeled shoes. Patricio beat me but only because I fell over laughing when I saw him running like a fainting lizard.

Then, exhausted from all our shenanigans, we walked up to the English and French Rooms to try on outfits that would make each other laugh. Patricio dressed as a dandy and I as a princess. Then we swapped to make me the dandy and Patricio the princess.

Our adventures finally led us back to the home section, where we ended up in matching pajamas and collapsed on the nicest bed in the department, the one with a canopy and a feather mattress.

All around us, the candles from the gift section made the place even more magical. While I caught my breath as my head rested on Patricio's chest, I looked at our surroundings. The corner where we had ended up was decorated like a complete bedroom, with dressers, chests of drawers, and all the necessary furniture. There were even two glasses and an alarm clock on the nightstands.

I discovered I could ignore the posters reading "Enjoy Our Discounts at El Encanto" that hung from the ceiling and imagined I was home, and Patricio was my husband. He was thinking the same thing.

"Do you wanna play house?" he proposed.

"Sure," I said. "How was work today, dear?"

"Wonderful. In fact, today they promoted me to general director of El Encanto. How was your day?"

"Very nice. At the university, they congratulated me for my research into Einstein's theories."

"And Daniela? Did she walk the dog?"

"The dogs. She has two, remember? Mickey and Mouse."

"Of course, of course. What was I thinking? By the way, where should we go on vacation this year? New York or Paris?"

"To Asturias. I think it's time you showed me your village."

Suddenly, the game started to feel painful. It was sad to dream of things that would never happen. Patricio noticed immediately.

"Are you sad?"

"A little. But it'll pass. I'm used to holding it in; César doesn't like it when I cry. He says that with all the money we have, crying over nonsense is an offense to God."

I started to dry the tears on my cheeks, but Patricio stopped me. "You can be sad when you're with me. I like to see you laugh, but you can cry as well. You can feel however you want. I'm not your husband."

"I know that."

I gave him a kiss and continued crying freely.

"Can I ask you something?" he said.

"Go ahead."

"How did you end up married to him?"

"It's a long story," I sighed.

"I've got all night."

I took a deep breath to gird my loins. I had never talked to anyone about my first meeting with César, but Patricio deserved to know the truth. I realized I didn't just want to tell him everything, I needed to. I started with the first time I met César, the güije who ended up being more dangerous than the monster who lived in the walls.

"It happened one morning at the corner of Zanja and Galiano. I was a little girl collecting Susini postcards . . . ," I began.

I don't know how long I talked, but when I finished my story, my mouth was dry, and my soul felt lighter.

Patricio had tears in his eyes, and he stroked my face adoringly, as if I were an object of great value. "You're the bravest person I've ever met."

"I'm glad you know everything now," I said from the heart.

That's what I liked most about Patricio. He didn't judge me or look at me condescendingly. He simply saw the best in me.

"There are so many things in my life I hate," I said.

"You have the strength to change them. Even if you don't know it yet."

"I wish I could believe you."

"Can I do anything to make you feel better?"

"Kiss me."

Patricio obeyed and gave me such a fervent kiss, I was surprised my lips didn't melt and fuse with his. I held myself close to him, searching for comfort, and then my body took control. My legs wrapped around his waist, and I guided his hands to caress my breasts under the silk pajamas. I needed to feel my skin against his, the more of it the better. To be soaked in his sweat and his scent, to know I was his as much as I could be.

I stroked his face as our tongues met. I touched his firm chest, his tensed stomach. I continued running my fingertips over his body until they reached his hard and determined penis. By then, our breaths were keeping time, as were our moans, our gasps, our sighs.

I spread my legs and noticed I was wet. I led him so he could slip inside me. I wanted to feel him completely; I wanted him to fill me in every way. Patricio let me take the initiative until our hips began to move in rhythm. More sure of himself now, he grabbed my buttocks to penetrate me as deeply as I could take, while I bit my lip and let the pleasure overcome me.

Not long after, when we were both screaming with such force I was afraid El Encanto would collapse, I had an orgasm so intense, my whole body churned like the sea.

I felt it was the first time a man had made love to me.

The lights snapped back on at five thirty in the morning, illuminating El Encanto like a Christmas tree. It was an hour before dawn, and the return of electricity found us asleep, our naked bodies still intertwined. We woke up abruptly. At first I didn't know where I was. Why wasn't I in my bed? Where was César? But when Patricio looked at me with his blue eyes and whispered, "Good morning, my love," I felt like the luckiest woman in the universe.

"Your feet are freezing," I said.

"I always wake up with cold feet," Patricio said.

"How can that be?" I laughed a little. "It's hot as hell."

Patricio held his feet against mine. "I think it's because I was cold a lot as a kid, when I walked barefoot on snow. And my body will never forget that."

"I'll warm them up for you, my love."

I would have sold my soul to the devil to wake up like that, with Patricio's frozen feet against mine, every single morning.

"I have to go," I said with the same sadness Cinderella must have felt when she saw her carriage change back into a pumpkin.

"Can you imagine if the lights hadn't come back on?"

It would have been picture perfect: the two of us naked and asleep in the bed while the store filled up with customers.

"Should we make the bed and clean up?" I asked.

"Don't worry about it," Patricio told me. "I'll sort it out before the store opens."

"If only the lights went out every night."

"We'll find a way to be together. I promise."

"Even if only for stolen moments, for the rest of our lives?"

Patricio kissed me with his whole soul.

"I wouldn't mind, but . . ." He paused dramatically. "Who says we have to settle for stolen moments?"

I felt dizzy just thinking about the possibility of a future together with Daniela and Patricio.

Before going home, I passed by Vedado to pick up Daniela from Lala's house. As I had figured, neither great-grandmother nor great-granddaughter was aware of the blackout. They had been practicing spells and eating fufu—mashed plantain—by candlelight before falling asleep.

Back at the house, as soon as we crossed the threshold, a housekeeper pulled Daniela from my side and took her to the kitchen.

"Come on, mijita, your father told us you need to have breakfast."

"But I already ate with Grandma," Daniela protested.

"Well, then you'll have breakfast again because you need to grow strong," the housekeeper replied, whisking her away.

If my husband didn't want Daniela present, it couldn't be good. I walked into the living room, and César greeted me with a slap to the face. He caught me so much by surprise that at first I didn't feel anything. Then the pain spread over my cheek like waves lapping against the sand.

"Where were you?" César roared. "And don't lie to me!"

César was so infuriated, I was afraid he would slap me again—or worse. His hands were balled into fists, his knuckles white with rage. I was terrified, but my instinct to protect Patricio was greater than my fear.

"At my mom and grandma's house!" I lied with all the aplomb I could muster. "Where were you? I looked for you at the Tropicana for a whole hour."

"You slut! A waiter told me he saw you in the jungle, holding hands with some guy."

I secretly cursed that rat of a waiter and put on my best innocent puppy-dog eyes. "Me? That can't be. I was in the bathroom during the blackout. I was close to the jungle, yes. But I swear by blessed Saint Lazarus I wasn't with any man. That asshole waiter must have confused me with some whore."

César studied my face, looking for some sign that would give me away, but I lied with great feeling. His masculine pride and arrogance leaned in favor of my tall tales. The high esteem in which my husband held himself made him want to believe it was impossible I could be attracted to any man but him.

"How did you get back to the city, then?"

"After searching like crazy and not finding you, a very kind couple gave me a ride to Vedado. Mr. and Mrs. Castillejos, they live on Salud Street."

Of course, the Castillejos couple was a lie. But I knew my gamble had paid off when César relaxed his fists and held me against his chest.

"I'm sorry, Mami. If I get jealous, it's only because I love you."

"You get mad whenever you feel like it. You don't need a reason."

Calmer, César stroked my reddened cheek with affection. I made a tremendous effort not to look away from him. His caresses were more repulsive than his blows.

CHAPTER 32

PATRICIO

"There's another woman," Nely affirmed.

It was our day off, and we were at the movies, watching *The Lady from Shanghai*. At first, I assumed Nely was referring to the film.

"I think so too. Orson Welles isn't exactly a stand-up guy."

"I'm talking about you, Patricio. There's another woman in your life."

I'd invited her out to lunch and a movie to clear up our situation. We'd gone to the Cine Actualidades on Monserrate Street, between Neptuno and Ánimas. It was one of the oldest movie theaters in Havana, and the seats smelled like cigarettes and mothballs. I had picked the Actualidades because its concession stand sold Hershey's chocolate and Nao Capitana, a drink named after a ship and that tasted like a chocolate milkshake. Nely was crazy about chocolate, and the combination of eating a whole bar along with an equally chocolatey milkshake was unbeatable for her. I bought her both to put her in a good mood, but that afternoon, not even Milton Hershey personally handing over the keys to his factory would have been enough to keep her from biting my head off.

"Can't we talk about that later? When we get out of the movie?" I proposed, speaking softly.

But Nely was sick of my evasions. "No. We're talking right now. Can you tell me what the hell is going on? First you ignore me for months. Then, all of a sudden, you write me a note saying you love me. And then you go back to avoiding me like the plague. Have you no shame?"

She was quite right. But if I wanted to keep my relationship with Gloria secret, there was no reasonable explanation I could offer for my behavior.

"I'm a real son of a bitch. There's nothing else to it," I said.

"That's not true, and we both know it. The only thing I can think is that there's another woman. And depending on whether or not she'll have you, you pay more or less attention to me. Am I close? Is there someone else?" she asked, as direct as ever.

I was cornered, as much by the conversation as by the fact that I was trapped next to her in a narrow seat in a dark theater. "Yes, it's true."

"Who is she?"

"You don't know her," I said.

"Don't lie to me! You've fallen for another Cuban girl. Are you gonna tell me who she is or not?"

The usher shone his flashlight and hissed at us to be quiet.

I felt awful for being dishonest, but my priority, even over Nely's feelings, was protecting Gloria. It was vital César not find out about our relationship, and for that reason, the fewer people who knew, the better. "I can't tell you."

Nely crossed her arms angrily. "You know what I think? That if you're going to the movies with me instead of her, it's because she's married. Whatever, you know what you've gotten yourself into."

We watched the rest of the movie in silence. On the screen, the closing sequence took place in a labyrinth of mirrors in an amusement park. The protagonists shot at each other, shattering the mirrors into a thousand pieces. Just like the characters in the film, I had also ended a game of mirrors. I felt relieved.

Leaving the cinema, I tried to pick up the pieces of my relationship with Nely. "Can we still be friends?"

"I don't know," she answered, pained. "For now, I'd prefer we only see each other at work."

"Can I keep taking your elevator?"

"Of course. But don't expect me to laugh at your jokes."

We stood there, rooted in place, unsure of how to say goodbye. A kiss on the lips would have been all wrong, but shaking her hand struck me as ridiculous. I tried to give her a hug, but she anticipated my move and crossed her arms over her chest.

"Can I give you a kiss on the cheek?"

Nely shook her head. "I'll never give you another kiss, not even on the cheek. The next man who kisses me will have to swear he'll stay with me forever and never kiss anyone else."

"I'm sorry I can't be that man."

"I'm sorry too."

Finally, we said goodbye by turning and walking off in opposite directions.

At El Encanto, business was booming. Thanks to the goal I'd scored by giving Tomás Menéndez the idea of creating a perfume especially for the store, they promoted me to manager. On his express orders, I worked for a season by his side in the advertising department. I learned a lot under his wing, but my place was face-to-face with the public, where I could let my people skills shine.

There was just one thing that tarnished the triumph of my promotion: Carlos Duarte. Don Gato couldn't stand that we were now at the same level. What was disdain before had now become open warfare. He could no longer throw his weight around like when I was a cannonball or clerk, but he had more subtle and dangerous ways of making my life impossible.

In my new post as a manager, one of my main duties was attending to the most "special" of our famous customers, either because they had bad tempers or because they were very demanding. If selling a tube of lipstick to Ava Gardner had been an odyssey, it wasn't half as difficult as helping Kirk Douglas choose a pair of socks or Mario Moreno—the famous Cantinflas—buy sunglasses. Among our most demanding clients, the top prize went to Frank Sinatra.

On the street, it was no secret Frank Sinatra was the favorite singer of the Cosa Nostra's five families. It was also a well-known fact that, a few years before, in December 1946, the Hotel Nacional had served as the setting for one of the best-attended meetings of mafiosos in history and that Frank Sinatra had livened up the night with his songs. If the mob was Havana's mistress, Sinatra was her spoiled child. Every one of his shows was a major event, so he had to take care of every detail.

One of the star's peculiarities was the need to debut new clothes and shoes every time he stepped on stage. Sinatra liked to dressed smartly, and he was more than capable of throwing a whole suit in the garbage if he found the most minimal defect. Handling a sale to the Voice was like transporting a jar of nitroglycerine: it could all blow sky-high at any moment. No one was safe, especially a novice manager like me.

This time, Sinatra had opted for a Century suit, the Cuban suit par excellence, of pure linen. It was designed in person by Manet in the English Room to be as comfortable as a second skin. An Italian Borsalino hat and a Macao silk tie completed the ensemble. The shoes were made of calfskin and were so soft, it felt like you were putting on espadrilles.

That suit was worth its weight in gold, and I should have watched it like a hawk or left it in a secure closet under lock and key. But I was so exhausted after a long workday that I was dying to get back to my bed and decided to put my trust in one of our cannonballs. A fifteen-year-old kid answered my call for assistance. He was as skinny and long as a noodle. His hair was black and greasy, and his face was covered with spots. It was the first time I had seen him in the store.

"What's your name?" I asked.

"Silvestre, sir."

"Are you new?"

"Yes, sir."

"Silvestre, I need you to put away this suit. It should be ironed and perfect by tomorrow. It's for a special customer, so spare no effort."

The spotty youth took the clothes and the shoebox. "You can count on me."

I noticed something in his voice that put me on edge, an undertone of malice, but I thought it must have been my imagination. What's more, I had to give the cannonballs opportunities—I knew that from experience.

The next afternoon, Frank Sinatra arrived in the English Room to try on his new clothes. The Voice was a slender man with a wide forehead and sunken cheeks. He wasn't the typical hunk, but his magnetism and charisma made all the women swoon when he walked by. He greeted me with great courtesy, and I led him to a changing room. When he walked out of the stall with the suit on, I let out a sigh of relief. It couldn't have looked better.

"It's perfect," he commented in English. "It's just what I need for tonight."

"Are you performing?" I asked.

"Yes, at the Calypso. It's a private evening; the club will be closed to the public."

I didn't need to know any more. It was a mob meeting, without a doubt. And if it was happening at the Calypso, César was surely hosting.

Everything went smooth as silk until it was time for the shoes. Sinatra took his off, and I knelt down so he could try the right shoe on. When I took it out of the box, I went pale. The shiny chocolate-brown calfskin was stained with something that looked like a smear of grease. Frank noticed it too.

"Is that a stain?" he asked, horrified. "No, no, no! I can't wear dirty shoes!"

I put them back in the box as fast as lightning.

"Of course not, sir. I'm terribly sorry. I don't know what could have happened. I'll get you another pair tomorrow at no additional cost."

"Tomorrow will be too late," he said, annoyed. "I ordered them specifically for my show tonight."

This was serious. We had never missed a deadline, much less with a customer like Frank Sinatra. I spoke without thinking and a promise came out of my mouth.

"I understand. I'll have them tonight. I give you my word."

Sinatra nodded and decided to give me his vote of confidence. "Bring them to the club. At nine on the dot."

Until Sinatra left, I was unaware it would be impossible for me to keep my promise. The shoes were manufactured in Italy, and they couldn't send new shoes from Rome with such short notice. My consternation gave way to anger. How the hell had the shoes gotten stained? Furious, I took Nely's elevator down to look for Silvestre, the cannonball.

"Are you all right? You're white as paper," Nely said when she saw me.

"I thought you were still angry with me," I said, thankful for her concern.

"And I am. But if you're gonna have a fainting spell in my elevator, I'd prefer you to tell me in advance. What the hell is wrong with you?"

"Do you know a cannonball named Silvestre?"

"Carlos's son?"

My mouth dropped when I heard that.

"What?" I gasped.

Nely shrugged, not understanding why I was so flustered.

"A young guy, lanky, with black hair and a mangy look about him? He's Carlos Duarte's kid. He just started."

All the pieces suddenly fell into place: that stain wasn't an accident but an act of sabotage. Still, my priority wasn't proving it but fixing the mess. Just like with the porcelain zebra, I couldn't fall on the first hurdle—that could have been my life philosophy. Since it would be impossible for me to get new shoes in so little time, I had no other option but to remove the stain.

There was only one person I could turn to.

Guzmán was attending to a customer when I entered the shoe store with my tongue hanging out, thanks to the heat and the speed with which I had run over to seek his aid. The Garbo was a select but old-fashioned shoe store. The owner was an elderly widower, an admirer of the Imperio Argentina and its "reliquary" ("Pisa morena, pisa con garbo . . .") whose business had been stalled in a past era for years because it sold espadrilles for women and wickerwork shoes for men—that is, until Guzmán started working as a clerk and gave the place a breath of fresh air.

For starters, he'd bought cloth-lined chairs with soft seats so customers could be more comfortable when they took their shoes off and tried on a new pair. They were nothing like the old chairs, which had straw seats that creaked and caught on women's skirts. He decorated the walls with photos of Greta Garbo and updated the front window, placing shoes on presentation trays with jingling bells to attract the attention of the passersby. With an eye for current trends, Guzmán added the latest styles to the popular classic models. And so, the regular clients kept coming and buying, but Guzmán also managed to widen the market, drawing in their daughters as well.

"A thousand pardons," I said, apologizing to Guzmán's customer, "but I need my friend. It's an emergency." I pulled Guzmán over to a corner. Once we were alone, I didn't beat around the bush. "I need your help. You have to get a stain off these shoes."

"Are you kidding or what? Is this a joke for old times?"

My look of desperation made it clear I was serious. "This time my life isn't on the line, but my job is. The shoes are for Frank Sinatra. I don't have time to tell you the whole story."

"No problem. Let's see if we can find the crack in the coconut."

I took the shoes out of the box and showed them to him. Guzmán examined the stain meticulously. He opened a drawer under the counter and shuffled through various stain removers, but he couldn't find one he approved of.

"If the stain had happened just now, I could get it out easy. But now it's sunken in. You're pretty fucked, I'm not gonna lie," he added. "Maybe we could cover it with polish, but this tone is unusual, and no other color would look right. And the skin is so delicate that all the stain removers I have would damage the leather. There's just one thing that might work."

"What?" I asked, my voice an anxious whisper.

Guzmán waited a few seconds to answer.

"Lemon juice," he said with gravity.

I started laughing, relieved. "Lemon juice? That's it? I thought you were gonna say something impossible to find, like liquid gold. Let's get to it, then."

Guzmán answered me with a patience usually reserved for idiots. "Oh Lord, don't you know what's happening in the world? Or at least in Havana?"

"What?"

"When was the last time you ate an orange?"

It was a strange question, but when I thought about it, I realized it had been more than a few days. In fact, that morning I had passed a fruit stand and hadn't seen a single basket of oranges.

"Now that you mention it, it's been days."

"And you haven't considered why?"

I shrugged my shoulders.

"There's a plague of red mites on the plantations. The little buggers cause yellow leaves, which attack citrus plants. We haven't had oranges or lemons for weeks."

It sounded like a joke, and I thought my friend was exaggerating. "That's impossible! How could there not be a single lemon in all of Havana?"

Two hours later, after checking at every fruit stand on Galiano Street and the surrounding neighborhoods, I had to accept the evidence: indeed, there was not a single lemon in the whole city. The red mite was a devilish, extremely contagious insect that had affected all the crops. The farmers asked for patience and predicted the situation would improve within weeks, but for me, that was too late. Still, plagues be damned, I wasn't willing to give up. The fruit stands weren't the only place to find lemons. With a little luck, you could find one tucked away in your pantry. Desperate, I started to search the taverns and even knocked on people's doors.

"Good afternoon. Might you have a lemon you could sell me?" I asked, going door to door.

The folks who didn't assume I was a lemon-crazed madman sympathized with me. They had gone days without a lime to make a decent mojito. I was about to resign myself to my fate when I found a glimmer of hope where I least expected it. As I was walking down Porvenir Street, something caught my attention. In the little back garden of the Popular, several trees were growing, and one was a scraggly lemon tree.

With my heart in my throat, I entered the Asturian establishment. As always, Constantina was behind the bar, with her cheeks saggy and her gray hair pulled up in a bun.

"A sight for sore eyes! If it isn't the Marquis of Chorrapelada . . ."

"Bones tardes, Tina. How are you?"

"Still running, somehow. And you, Mr. Marquis? Have you finally convinced your princess to run away with you?"

"I'm working on it. But now I need another favor."

"Some more free tortilla?"

"A lemon."

"A lemon? What makes you think I have a lemon?"

"The tree in the back garden."

Tina rearranged the hairpins in her bun while she considered my request.

"I have one, it's true," she confessed. "But I can't give it to you. I'm keeping it as a remedy against a sore throat. With that plague, who knows when we'll have lemons again."

"I need it, please. It's extremely important."

"I know all about your extremely important. What do you want it for, eh?"

"To get a stain off Frank Sinatra's shoes!" I blurted out.

Tina was dumbstruck, her mouth wide open. Slowly, her smile began to blossom. Her laugh began as a soft chuckle, then grew into a hearty guffaw. "Oh, marquis! I don't know how you do it; you always know how to make me laugh. So now you know Frank Sinatra?"

"And he'll be furious if I don't clean his shoes."

Tina laughed again and bent over to get something from under the counter: a lemon as pretty as a diamond. "Here, take it before I stop laughing."

"You're the best, Tina."

"And you're the funniest liar I've ever met. Now get out of here!"

CHAPTER 33

I got to the Calypso five minutes before Frank Sinatra was due to go onstage, and I blew through the doors like a gust of wind. Two doormen with sour looks on their faces took up position in front of me.

"Entrance is by invitation only tonight," one of them spat at me.

"I have Mr. Sinatra's shoes."

With no further questions, they grabbed me by the shoulders, swept me through a labyrinth of hallways, and dumped me in the dressing room. There, the Voice was already wearing his new suit as he enjoyed a glass of champagne and peeked at the dancers changing clothes behind a skimpy folding screen.

"Hey, man! You made it," he said.

He was waiting for me in a pair of yellow socks. I knelt by his side and took the shoes out of the box. With a squirt of lemon juice and all his expertise, Guzmán had made the stain disappear completely. I showed him the shoes, and Sinatra nodded in satisfaction when he saw they were impeccable.

"To be honest, I thought you'd already be wearing different shoes," I told him in English.

"I knew you'd make it in time."

"Why?"

"You work at El Encanto. El Encanto isn't just any department store. It's an extraordinary place."

After tying his shoes, Sinatra stood up and checked his reflection in a full-length mirror. "Perfect. Thanks for everything."

"Thank you for having confidence in me."

Sinatra tipped his hat and walked out through a side door. From the applause and shrieks of joy, I deduced it opened directly onto the stage. I couldn't resist looking through the half-open door.

The Calypso was sensational. The place had a submarine ambience, simulating a seabed: anchors hanging off the walls, papier-mâché fish on the ceiling, and stone seahorses in the corners. In front of the stage, there were rows and rows of little tables lit with candles and attended by waiters dressed as sailors. The cigar girls were mermaids. They were wearing tube skirts with golden sequins to simulate scales and two white seashells on their breasts.

The walls and furniture were decorated in pastel colors: pinks and blues. There were tanks full of brightly colored tropical fish all over the place. There was even a fountain at the bar with dolphins that spat out champagne instead of water. The craziest part was the wall sconces, each shaped like an oyster with a luminous pearl as a lightbulb. That place was ostentatious, but its outmoded luxury made it a marvelous spectacle.

When Sinatra stepped on stage, the private party was hitting its peak, and the club was packed with smartly dressed mafiosos and their elegant wives. The singer greeted them respectfully. I saw his silhouette outlined by the spotlights. When he started singing, the force of his voice shook the crystal teardrops that hung from the crowns of the wooden mermaids.

When you heard him sing, it was hard to believe Frank Sinatra was just another man, like all of us. That guy was forged from stuff legends are made of. And, thanks to me, he wasn't singing barefoot.

I lingered in the doorway to watch his whole performance, and it was a memorable show. The Voice sang hits like "Oh, What a Beautiful Morning," "Dream," "My Melancholy Baby," and "Goodnight, Irene." The audience was enthralled, and it was no wonder. The last song, "I've Got a Crush on You," ended the show with such a bang that everyone in the room got on their feet. During the encore, I realized I should have left hours ago.

When I turned back to the changing rooms, I bumped into a flock of dancers changing to get onstage. They were all wearing flesh-colored leotards with peacock feathers stuck to their backs. I had never seen anything like it: I was in a room full of women in their underwear. When they saw me, the girls whistled and hurled insults until one of them grabbed me by the arm and dragged me out before her friends could lynch me.

It was Rita, the black girl who had seduced El Grescas so he would give her the forajido recipe. With her red lipstick and long legs, she was the prettiest peacock of them all.

She greeted me with a big smile. "Patricio, how nice to see you! What are you doing here, my man?"

"I came on a secret mission. To save Mr. Sinatra's show," I joked. "How are you? How are things going?"

Rita looked around to be sure no one was listening in. Just in case, we slipped into another dressing room and inside a stall, so we could talk alone.

"Good and bad. I'm in love," she confessed, unable to hide the excitement in her voice.

"I'm glad. Who's the lucky guy?"

"His name's Franklin; he plays trumpet at the club."

"Does he make you happy?"

"Happier than Christmas and my birthday put together. Being with him is like throwing a house party every day."

"Well, that's good news."

"Not while Franklin and I are still working at the Calypso. César will never let me be with him. I think he suspects something. The other dancers are a bunch of gossips. They spend all day spying on me."

"Can I help?"

Rita nodded, held a finger to her lips, and gestured for me to walk quietly with her. After going down a hallway, we entered a costume and prop storeroom, a huge space in almost total darkness. It was where they kept all the dresses, headdresses, and other accessories for the club's cabaret numbers. It was a mishmash of objects, full of large cases covered in sheets. Rita and I reached a papier-mâché statue of Neptune, the king of the seas, with a trident and all. To my amazement, the dancer pulled off the statue's head and extracted a suitcase from its hollow body.

"I need a favor," she begged me. "Franklin and I are gonna leave Havana together."

"When?"

"Soon. We've already started planning everything, but we can't leave the club until we get the money for our tickets. And that's where this suitcase comes in."

Rita opened the suitcase and showed me its contents. It was full of silver forks, knives, and spoons. Each had a little *C*, for Calypso, engraved on its handle.

"We've been collecting them for months, one piece every day, so as not to raise suspicion," said Rita. "If we sell them, we'll come away with enough to survive on for a while." The dancer offered me the suitcase. "I need you to get them out of here for me. They pat us girls down every time we leave the club."

"I'll stash it somewhere safe," I assured her. "El Grescas has an underground cantina. La Pekinesa, on Obispo Street. You can come pick it up whenever you want."

Rita handed me the suitcase and gave me a kiss on the cheek. "I'll never forget everything you and your friends have done for me. Now I should get going. My number starts in five minutes."

I walked out of the storeroom into a serpentine hallway. Left or right? I didn't have a damn clue how the doormen had brought me in. I turned right, not too concerned. At some point I would find an exit. Unfortunately, the hallway didn't open to the street but to an enormous dining room dominated by a huge round table with flower arrangements and porcelain plates. A banquet was about to kick off, and I wasn't invited, so I got out of there, whistling as I left.

I returned to the hallway. When I turned the corner, I saw something that shattered my good spirits. César was coming straight at me. There was no reason there should be a problem since my presence in his club was more than legitimate, but my instincts took over. What if he took the suitcase and discovered it was full of his cutlery? He would probably skin me alive just for stealing a teaspoon. I couldn't risk it. Before I could consider what the hell to do, I retreated and fell back into the dining room. That was a bad decision. Obviously, César was heading to the same place.

Then I made my second dumb move in under a minute and ran to the opposite end of the room, to a corner table weighed down with trays of fruit. Before I could think about it, I hid myself and the suitcase under the table, where the tablecloth hung down to the floor and concealed me completely.

A few seconds later, I heard footsteps and gruff laughs as a dozen mobsters filed in. I stealthily raised the tablecloth just in time to see the group, all male, take their seats, and I cursed myself for my cowardice and my stupid ideas. I was under a table at a meeting of mafiosos. It seemed like a joke, but I was trapped in a very dangerous situation. At least the table was isolated in a corner of the room, and no one had any reason to look under it.

The dinner was sumptuous and eternal. Two types of lobster for the first course, lamb and sea bass for the second, dessert, coffee, an after-dinner drink, and a cigar. By the time they went for the liquor, the three hours I had spent huddled on the ground were starting to take their toll. My joints hurt like hell, and I had started to cramp up. My throat itched from the smoke coming from their thick cigars, and I had to hold in a cough. Unaware of my presence, the men talked about things no outsider was meant to hear.

"What about the visas for Luciano and Lansky?"

"We've bought congressmen and senators. Grau won't dare lift a finger for now."

"Grau's not a bad guy, but we need to get Batista back in power. He's an expert at looking the other way in exchange for a little taste of the profits."

"If Luciano goes back to Italy, we'll have to think about the question of European heroin."

"We also need more girls for the clubs." I recognized César's voice. "Make a pass through the provinces, but make sure they're nice and young. Who wants beef when you can have veal?"

In the early hours of the morning, the mafiosos concluded their banquet. The scraping of the chairs on the floor was heavenly music to my ears. They bid each other farewell between laughs, as satisfied as drunk swine. But I went from relief to a heart attack when, as all his colleagues left the dining room, one of the gangsters stayed behind to talk to César.

"Mr. Valdés, could we chat for a moment?"

"But of course, Don Lorenzo. What can I do for you?"

I lifted the tablecloth a little and saw that Don Lorenzo must have been about seventy, with a face scarred by smallpox. He looked well fed, round as a barrel, his chubby fingers dripping with rings.

"It's about one of your girls," Don Lorenzo said. "Rita, a real babe, with tits and ass like you've never seen."

I stopped breathing.

"Rita's a pretty one," César agreed. "Tell me what you need."

"The problem is, I've taken a liking to her."

"I hope she feels the same way."

"Oh yes. Considering I pay her, of course. She's very affectionate with me. The issue is that I've heard she's keen on a trumpet player in the orchestra. A good-looking black guy named after a Yankee president. But the only flashy thing about him is the name. He must be poor as a street rat."

"Franklin?"

"That's the one. And you know how it goes. I don't want to get jealous, but I'm tenderhearted, and just imagining Rita with that black boy, the demons get the better of me."

"We'll take care of that at once. They're both working tonight. I'll call them in."

Run, Rita, I thought. *Don't let them get you. Get out of here*, I ordered her in my mind.

I felt a deep scorn for this Don Lorenzo, who surely kept the poor Rita as a pastime while his wife and children waited for him at home. If he had to buy her affection, why should he care if she had a lover in her free time?

A moment later, the pair entered the room. Rita still had on her peacock outfit. Franklin, in a modest and elegant suit, was very attractive indeed. They made a fine couple, both young and good-looking.

Not beating around the bush, César, his thugs in the background, started interrogating Rita.

"What is this I've been hearing about you messing around with this darkie? He's a monkey, and all he needs is a tail and a banana."

"It's not true. We just work together. That's all," she lied, trying to protect her boyfriend.

"Oh yeah?" said César, amused. "Then you won't mind watching him take some licks."

He gestured to two of his men to hold the trumpet player down, and then he gave him a brutal punch in the stomach. Rita screamed.

"Stop!"

César hit him again.

"Why do you care? You just work together—or no?" he asked playfully.

"Leave him alone! We love each other," Rita sobbed.

César's men let Franklin go, and he collapsed on the floor, gasping for breath.

"We're in love," Franklin confirmed as Rita helped him stand up.

César looked at him with all the condescension of someone trying to make two little kids, or two lunatics, see reason.

"The problem is that you can't be, cocksucker. Your girlfriend here is my friend Don Lorenzo's jebita. She's a gift I gave him, and if you take her away, it's like stealing, understand?"

"I'm nobody's property," Rita protested.

"That's a lie, my dear. You're mine until you finish paying your debt. And either you'll be an obliging little friend to Don Lorenzo, or we'll have a problem."

Rita crossed her arms and looked at Don Lorenzo with disdain. "Let the fat man's wife and mother put up with him."

"I'll pay her debt," Franklin said, "and I'll marry her tomorrow."

The marriage proposal was met by César's contemptuous smile. "These blacks still need civilizing! You're really gonna marry a whore? Your girlfriend has seen more dicks than a public toilet."

The trumpet player's punch hit César square in the jaw and made him stagger backward. Franklin had a hell of a right hook, but César had something he didn't: a pistol.

César gripped the gun tightly and, as if it were a summary execution, ordered Franklin to kneel in front of him. The scene was familiar to me. I'd also found myself staring down the barrel of the most quarrelsome mafioso in Havana. I had to do something. Guzmán had lent me a helping hand that day, and now it was my turn to help a friend.

There was no time to lose. After Franklin's punch, there was every reason to believe once César had run out of words—at that moment he was jabbering insults and curses—he would pull the trigger.

What could I do? By my side on the floor was a napkin I used to cover my face from the nose down—like the outlaws in Western movies—so César wouldn't recognize me. The only thing I had in my hands was the suitcase full of the Calypso's cutlery, and so without a second thought, I opened the clasps, stood up out of nowhere, and hurled it with all my might at César Valdés.

"Run, Rita!" I shouted with all my might.

Chaos broke out. Everything happened in just a few seconds. The gangsters looked at me in shock, and for a moment, with the silver cutlery flying at them, all they could do was instinctively protect themselves. César lost interest in Franklin and moved his right arm to point the gun at me instead.

Bang! This time it wasn't a bottle of champagne in the middle of the street. The shot was so easy and straight, it would have hit me if not for Franklin's action. The trumpet player had jumped on César just in time to throw off the pistol's aim, and now he had César trapped under the weight of his body.

"Get out of here, my love!" Franklin shouted at his girl. Then looked me square in the eyes. "Both of you, run!"

Rita was paralyzed, in shock. His words left no room for doubt. There could be no greater act of love, no more sincere and unconditional sacrifice. Franklin was telling us to get out of that death trap while he held the killers' attention. He was on a one-way street, and I had to do whatever I could to make sure his bravery wasn't in vain.

César growled, powerless on the floor, and his thugs opted to throw themselves on top of Franklin.

I ran to Rita, grabbed her hand, and pulled her away. Without looking back, we raced out of there as fast as we could. We were so determined, we leapt past the bouncers, not heeding their questions or giving them time to block our path. Inside, Franklin was giving his life to save ours.

CHAPTER 34

GLORIA

My books on astronomy made it plain. In that slice of sky, there should be no stars.

Ever since discovering that brilliant point in the heavens the night of the blackout, I hadn't been able to stop thinking about it. The mystery had rekindled my curiosity. Pondering the mysterious star kept me from thinking about my husband and helped me counteract boredom when I couldn't see Patricio at El Encanto. To study that fragment of the universe, I needed a telescope, and to get one, I would have to rely on my wits.

César thought I was overtaxing myself every time he saw me with books, like I was a puppy who tried to count when she should be limited to shaking hands. If I had asked him for a handout to buy a telescope, he would have forbidden me from owning one, and on top of that, he would have chewed me out for spending too much already on dresses.

Instead of being direct, I took advantage of a parents' meeting at Daniela's school to talk to a teacher, telling her my daughter was always asking about comets and meteor showers—an absolute lie.

"Is there any way the school could provide her with a little telescope to help with her lessons?" I asked.

Luck smiled on me, and I was astounded to hear one of the teachers had an old telescope she would be happy to give me. Very grateful, I took it home, happier than a little girl with a big piece of bread and guava paste. César spent most nights at the Calypso, so he wouldn't find out I was taking advantage of his absence to study the sky.

My love of astronomy became a little secret between our domestic employees and me: thanks to my generous tips, I convinced them not to say a word to the boss. What harm was I doing by amusing myself on the upstairs terrace? But, of course, there was an insufferable gossip in the house who thought she had the right to stick her nose into my business.

The evening when I debuted my telescope, I got out the hat Mr. Einstein had given me—salvaged from a chest I hadn't opened in years—and put it on so it might inspire my research. With the telescope mounted on its stand, I was waiting for twilight to turn to night when my sister-in-law appeared on the terrace and shot me a look of disgust.

"What an ugly contraption. What is that?" she demanded.

"It's a telescope, to look at the stars."

"Sure, shrivel up your brain with more fantasies," she scolded me angrily. "Things would go better for you if you kept your feet on the ground."

I wasn't in the mood for her little games, so I decided to cut to the chase. "You look unhappy, Marita."

"Does my brother know you have that thing?"

"No," I confessed. "But he doesn't tell me what he does away from the house every night either."

"It's not the same thing. A woman shouldn't keep secrets from her husband."

"This is a hobby. It doesn't matter! Should I also tell him I play dominoes? Or that I collect animal figurines?"

"Well, you should. And why are you suddenly so interested in the sky?"

"I think I've discovered a new star."

Marita laughed cruelly. "Holy Mother of God! And I'm Countess Merlin."

"Well, either way," I answered, hurt by her laughter, "if I'm just wasting my time, why do you care? Don't I deserve to be at least a little bit happy?"

"Keeping secrets is dangerous."

There was something in her voice—a hint of menace, a warning—that made me feel sick. God knows I should have pried further, but instead I decided to deny the importance of the whole issue.

"I'll make you a deal," I told her. "If you don't tell César about the telescope, I won't tell him you stuff yourself with chocolates every night. Or that you sometimes smoke his cigars to impress your friends."

Marita puffed up her cheeks like a toad, furious.

"That's bullshit!" she protested.

"C'mon, dear sister-in-law, do we have a deal?"

A few drops of rain interrupted our chat. A traitorous rain cloud had formed over our heads, suddenly cloaking the sky and obscuring the sunset.

"A big storm's coming," said Marita as she pulled her sweater over her dress. "You won't be seeing many stars tonight."

I rushed to cover the telescope. My sister-in-law was right. The sky was about to burst open. Suddenly, I had an idea, and a mischievous smile crept over my face.

"When you were a kid, didn't they tell you bathing in a rainstorm can give you a rush of energy and good health?" I asked.

In Cuba, getting soaked by rainstorms was a favorite childhood tradition. Older women always told us the first rainstorm in May was made of holy water, and its miraculous powers would protect us from illnesses, purify the soul, and fortify our hair. Anyone who didn't make use of it risked suffering the "bobo de mayo," a curse of terrible cramps and stomach pains. Kids liked the tradition because it gave us permission to act like fools and roll around in the mud without angering our families.

"That's an old wives' tale," answered Marita. "Only an idiot would get soaked in—"

She didn't finish the sentence because the rain started falling in sheets. Marita ran to get in the house, but I grabbed her by the wrist so she couldn't escape. The rain was falling so hard, our hair and clothes were soaked in seconds.

"Let me go. I'm getting wet!"

"You're already wet!" I replied, laughing.

The spectacle of Marita wetter than a dolphin, with her eyeliner staining her face and her hair disheveled, was the funniest thing I had seen in my life. I must not have looked my best either because my sister-in-law also started laughing.

"This is crazy!" she protested.

"You look like the crazy one!" I cackled.

"Come here. I'll slap the shit out of you!" said Marita, unable to hold back her laughter.

The downpour continued while Marita and I wrestled, jumped, played, and danced in the rain. Like teenagers, we let the storm soak through to our panties, and we jumped barefoot over puddles, splashed each other until we were both dumb with laughter, and ended up romping our way through a tickle fight. I had no sisters and no friends, but for an instant, I felt Marita was both.

It was a shame that the end of the rainstorm meant the end of our moment of complicity. The rain stopped, and just like after our conversations in Villa Valiente, the charm suddenly wore off, and Marita regained her composure.

"You're the stupidest girl I know. When this dress dries wrinkled, I'm taking one of yours!" she threatened before going back in the house.

Marita fulfilled her threat the next day and stole not one but two new dresses from my wardrobe.

But she didn't tell her brother about the telescope.

CHAPTER 35

PATRICIO

In the days following my getaway from the Calypso, I could hardly sleep or eat. On the street, life followed its course. Businesses bustled, cafés offered shade, and in the parks, kids dragged their parents to the candy stands full of licorice sticks and Peter-brand chewing gum. At the matinees, older women—well stocked with handkerchiefs to blow their noses at their leisure in the dark—lined up to see the Mexican melodramas featuring Pedro Infante and Jorge Negrete. At home, El Grescas and Guzmán had bought a record player and were spending their days listening to a new genre that promised to revolutionize the whole music scene: cool jazz.

But I couldn't enjoy any of it. In my mind, I was constantly reliving Franklin's act of heroism and the integrity and resolve Rita displayed on leaving the Calypso. Beautiful Rita was right: in life, there are moments that can completely change your fate. That night, her future had been shattered into pieces, and now she needed to find a way out of the debris. We survivors grow in extreme situations. So there was Rita, hiding out at her best friend's house while she prepared a swift exit from the country for herself and her family. It was clear her life was in danger, and perhaps mine as well. I couldn't be sure César hadn't recognized my blue eyes.

I could have taken the same boat to Florida, and if I didn't, it was because Gloria and her daughter were still held prisoner in Havana. I couldn't let them keep living with that murderer. Every day they spent with César was a chance he would harm them in some way.

And what had happened to Franklin that night was a warning for me too. Circumstances obliged me to act; I was determined to stand up to César Valdés. Above all, I had to save Gloria and Daniela.

I returned to El Encanto with the intention of speaking to Gloria as soon as possible. When we saw each other, I suggested she might be interested in our sofas. Choosing a new sofa is no small matter, so nobody was surprised when we spent more than an hour looking at the different models and—discreetly—conversing. I spoke plainly, and when I reached the moment in the story when César fired a gun at me, Gloria had to sit down on the nearest sofa out of shock.

"I'm sorry to scare you like this, but César is a monster," I whispered.

Gloria fanned herself with her hand, pulling herself together. "I know. I've always known."

"Every minute you and Daniela spend with him, you're in danger."

"But what can I do? We have nowhere to go."

"Come with me. Both of you."

"We can't. César owns Havana. He'd find us."

"Well, let's get out of Havana. We'll leave Cuba behind. We'll go somewhere he can't find us."

"What you're saying is impossible."

I drew my hand close to hers until they brushed together. "Gloria, do you love me?"

"More than anything in the world."

"Then trust me. I have a plan. It's still a secret, but Christian Dior is coming to Havana."

"The designer?" Gloria's jaw dropped.

"We've gotten an exclusive deal to sell his designs in the Americas. He wants to come in person to see the store, and we're organizing a big fashion show in his honor. We'll invite our best customers, including you and your husband, of course. It'll be the perfect opportunity."

"To do what?"

"To get out of here together. César will come to the show with Marita, I'm sure, because all the important people in the city will be invited, and he'll use the opportunity to do business. You'll have to make an excuse to stay home. While everyone's watching the show, Daniela, you, and I will go to the airport and take a flight somewhere far away."

Gloria looked me in the eyes, not knowing what to say. Doubts, desire, and fears seemed to swirl around inside her head. "I would have to leave my country, my mom, my grandma, my whole life . . ."

"You still have time to decide, my love. But don't think about what you'll leave behind; think about what you'll gain: a life away from César, where we would wake up together every morning."

Out of the corner of my eye, I saw Marita getting out of the elevator and walking decisively toward her sister-in-law. Our time was running out.

"Let's make a deal," I suggested. "If you accept my proposal, wear red tomorrow. If not, wear a black dress."

Gloria nodded seconds before Marita reached us and waved me away as if she were shooing off a pesky mosquito.

Marita asked, "Do you know which sofa you want yet?"

"This one here." With her head light years away, Gloria pointed to one at random, just to appease her sister-in-law.

"I love it!" Marita exclaimed. "It'll look lovely in the house; you'll see."

That night, I shared my plans with Guzmán and El Grescas while we ate a dinner of rice and beans in the garden. Before that, I had to bring them up to date on the secrets—there were more than a few—that had been building up for months: that Gloria and I were lovers, what had happened at the Calypso, and my intention of taking her far away. As soon as I spilled my guts, I was hit with a shower of angry questions.

"You little bastard, you bad friend, you rat!" bellowed El Grescas.

"You've got a hell of a nerve," Guzmán said.

"I know, I know. But I knew you guys would just tell me off for still being with her."

"And you'd have deserved it. You're a troublemaker who thinks he's Prince Charming."

El Grescas slammed his fist down on the table in anger. "Did you learn nothing from what happened with Rita, you fool? Holy shit, if he wasted her boyfriend just for breathing, imagine what he'll do to you for stealing his wife."

"Don't you realize you're risking your life?" insisted Guzmán.

"Life without Gloria is no life at all," I sighed.

El Grescas and Guzmán shared a look of resignation. It was true that both of them always watched out for my well-being, and they were horrified by the situation I had gotten myself into. At the same time, they were my best friends, they knew me as if we were brothers, and they could see clearly that I was deeply in love.

"That spoiled brat makes you happy, huh?" growled El Grescas.

"Well, if you love her, we love her too," affirmed Guzmán.

I was moved by my friends' loyalty, and all three of us hugged. El Grescas squeezed his gorilla arms around us until our ribs cracked.

"Everything will be settled tomorrow," I said.

I told them about our agreement. Gloria would wear a red dress if she was willing to escape with me or a black dress if she rejected my proposal. Seeing me trembling like jelly, they both decided to request the day off so they could go with me the next day and give me some support.

That night, we organized a little funeral for Franklin in our Chinese garden. Since we didn't know if he was a Catholic, a Santero, or a follower of some other religion, Guzmán thought it would be best to put on an innocuous ritual that wouldn't offend his memory. Inspired by the Oriental atmosphere that surrounded us at La Pekinesa, we lit four candles and hung them in four paper lanterns so that they would rise to the sky. One candle was for Franklin. We cried over his death and praised his courage and valor. The three other candles were for Rita, Gloria, and me in our new lives beyond the Cuban horizon.

The next morning dawned with a cloudy, drizzling sky. El Grescas, Guzmán, and I walked into El Encanto, and I decided to attend to the ground floor in order to see Gloria as soon as she walked in. My two squires stood nearby, lounging between the display counters, so they could be by my side when the moment arrived.

An hour passed. Then another. At eleven in the morning, I was a bundle of nerves. My hands were shaking so much, I almost couldn't wrap the customers' purchases. Finally, a little after midday, Gloria walked through the department store doors. And I almost had a heart attack when I saw that, thanks to the rain, she was wearing a fine brown raincoat.

Guzmán and El Grescas stood by my side like two soldiers protecting their comrade. The customers who had nicknamed us the Three Musketeers in our shoe-shining days weren't wrong.

"What do you think is underneath?" I asked them. "Red or black?"

"Whatever it is, we're with you."

Gloria looked around until she saw me. Without taking her eyes off mine, she unbuttoned the raincoat . . . and revealed a red dress, matching the flush that flooded her cheeks. In fact, I recognized it as the same red dress she had worn the day we met.

I had to keep myself from jumping for joy. Red! Gloria was willing to run away with me! Caught up in my excitement, El Grescas and Guzmán celebrated the moment with a cry that came straight from their souls.

"Compay, just know you two have two accomplices for your plan," Guzmán promised me.

CHAPTER 36

With the help of a wall calendar from La Imperial de Canadá insurance company, we began to plan our flight. The evening of the Dior show wasn't for a few days, but there were many things to figure out before that. First: our destination.

It was far from an easy decision, but I reached the conclusion we should go to Madrid. Although my body begged me to return to Santa Benxamina, we couldn't settle in my village. My return would draw too much attention, even more so if I was accompanied by a Cuban woman and a girl too old to be my daughter. We couldn't risk César finding out where we'd gone. As remote as the possibility seemed, it would be enough for one person to run their mouth in the village and the rumor would cross the sea, allowing César to reach us with his long tentacles. No, Madrid was a big city where we could hide and move around unseen. The money I'd saved from my work at El Encanto would help us get established. Then we would look for whatever work we could find.

Once the destination was decided, we needed a way to get there. I debated between ship and plane, but the latter won out. The shorter the trip, the fewer opportunities César would have to intercept us. What's more, we couldn't travel under our real names: the mafia had the police in their grip, and César would have no scruples about using them to find his wife and daughter. Luckily, my friends saved my skin once again.

Thanks to the friends he'd made among his customers at the cantina, El Grescas got the contact info for two document forgers who, using our photographs and inventing false names, created new passports for Daniela, Gloria, and yours truly. We took also advantage of Guzmán's friendship with a customs officer to whom he used to sell Italian shoes. The guy gave us three visas without asking too many questions.

Once the technical questions were resolved, I started wrestling with my emotional debts. Our getaway would be clandestine, so we would be there one day and gone the next, disappearing without a trace. But before that, we had people to say goodbye to. El Grescas and Guzmán lamented my leaving, but they both understood Gloria and I were fighting for our happiness, and they promised to write and come visit us in Spain.

The hardest goodbyes were the ones I couldn't say. And Nely was my biggest debt.

A few days before my departure, I approached her elevator to gauge whether she was still angry with me. To my surprise, she met me with a warm smile.

"Come on in; I don't bite. Can you tell I'm not cross with you anymore?" she asked.

"Why's that?"

"I'm still jealous and hurt, but I miss you."

"I miss you too. You're my best friend."

"You wanna go to the movies this Sunday? They're showing *Quo Vadis* at the Rex, and I hear it's a good one."

"Done deal," I told her, knowing I would have left Havana forever by then.

"You'll see; we'll have a hell of a time with those Romans."

I couldn't resist and gave her a hug. Squeezing her against my chest did me a world of good. It was my way of saying goodbye without saying a word. Oblivious to what I was thinking, Nely hugged me back.

"You're prettier than a doll," I whispered.

"You're not so bad yourself, but ease up. You're crushing me, you brute," she exclaimed between laughs.

Of course, I had to say goodbye to more than just people. There was one thing I was going to miss as much as my friends: El Encanto itself. The great department store had been my home. I had tried to explain it to El Grescas and Guzmán many times, but neither understood my devotion. Nely herself, despite loving her work, often quoted Karl Marx and said workers never owed anything to their bosses. But I was a more of a jackass than Mr. Marx, and all I knew was that, when I was hungry, El Encanto had given me shelter. And that was that. My mother always said, "To be well born is to be grateful." And no one was better born than me.

I would be lying if I said it didn't hurt a little to abandon my professional path. I was very proud of having climbed the ranks from cannonball to clerk to manager, and I knew that, with my flight, I was renouncing a bright future. However, I was sure there were lots of jobs in the world but only one woman like Gloria. I felt terrible about letting down the owners of El Encanto, running off when they least expected it.

Two days before Christian Dior's arrival, we were ready to receive him in style. The shop windows displayed only his perfumes and designs. The advertising department formed a special committee to organize the various festivities. The crowning moment would be the big fashion show. His visit was almost a state matter: the designer had a terrible fear of flying, and the fact that he was going to be cooped up for so long on a plane to come to the island was an unmatchable honor.

The fever for the French genius was so strong, lines formed on the street so people could admire the shop windows in all their splendor. Just like when television had captured the city's attention, Gloria and I took advantage of the dumbstruck crowds to put the finishing touches on our escape plans.

"César has already confirmed our attendance at the show," she whispered to me.

"Perfect. That evening, make up any excuse you can to stay home. Then, pick up Daniela at Lala's and take a taxi to the airport. We'll meet at the departures gate, right by the huge fish tank in the cantina. When the parade's over and César gets home, our plane will already be up in the air."

Gloria nodded, making mental note of my instructions.

"Do you realize the next time we see each other, at the airport, we'll be together? We'll be able to hold hands without hiding. And kiss each other in the street. And you can wake me up every morning with your frozen feet," she said, her voice trembling with excitement.

"I can't wait, my dear."

"Neither can I."

My last day in Havana was spent at the dress rehearsal for the fashion show. My job was to make things easier for Manet, who was in charge of planning the event. The dresses had been sent by plane, before Monsieur Dior's arrival, and unboxing them was a little ceremony in itself. The ironers removed them from their silk wrapping paper, and after flattening out their few wrinkles with consummate caution, they handed them over to us so we could arrange them on their stands and busts. Manet couldn't hide his enthusiasm.

"These dresses should be in a museum," he declared as he admired a vermilion design with an ermine-skin neckline as immaculate as snow.

"They sure are pretty," I said with all my ignorance.

"Pretty? Just pretty?" repeated Manet, indignant. "They're works of art! Oh Lord, Holy Virgin, forgive this heretic; he knows not what he says," he joked.

It was true that every dress was a jewel. Their upper parts were varied. They might have a smooth cut on the shoulders, short sleeves,

French sleeves, or long sleeves, but they all shared two special characteristics. The first: tight waistlines that hugged the feminine figure. And the second: huge, multilayered skirts shaped like a bell or a blooming flower. Meters and meters of fabric—some had more than fifty meters in the skirt alone—that gave them tremendous volume and transformed their wearers into real-life princesses.

"I like the skirts," I offered.

"The skirts are key," Manet agreed. "During the Second World War, fabric was rationed all over the world. Women wore those awful, dull dresses that looked like uniforms to waste as little material as possible."

"But this is the total opposite."

"Exactly. That's why they call it the New Look. With these designs, Dior means to say he's sick of austerity. The ignorant see it as a waste of fabric, but in reality, it's the opposite of that. These dresses are a hymn to life itself!" Manet exclaimed.

The night before my departure, with everything packed, I was so nervous I couldn't lie down and go to sleep. Guzmán and El Grescas proposed we take one last stroll down the Malecón, for old times' sake, but I wasn't in the mood for more goodbyes. Instead, I decided to settle an old debt.

A little while later, Tina almost turned to stone when I pressed a wad of bills down on the bar at the Popular.

"What's this, Mr. Marquis?"

"For the tortilla and the lemon. I hope it's enough."

"Are you nuts? This is more than a hundred pesos."

"And another thing. A gift."

I took out a framed photograph of Frank Sinatra. He was posing with me in El Encanto during one of his visits to the English Room. In one corner, above his unmistakable autograph, the Voice had written, "For Tina, my friend Patricio's friend." When Tina read her name next to mine in a living legend's handwriting, she was so amazed, I was afraid her eyes were going to pop out of their sockets and plop into the jar of olives by her side.

"You're fucking kidding me!" she blurted out.

Tina snatched the photo as desperately as a castaway grabbing a lifesaver.

I told her, "I came to pay my debt because tomorrow I'm going back to Spain."

"I can't believe it! I've spent all these years laughing at you, and now you tell me you're a real marquis after all!"

The poor woman was so confused, she didn't know what was real and what was fantasy.

"Have you convinced the princess to run away with you?" she asked without the slightest hint of irony.

I smiled, tickled by the fact that the story I had spun years before to get a free meal had become reality. It was incredible to think back on all that had happened since I'd first set foot in that dive.

"Yes, I got the princess," I answered from my heart. "But you have to keep my secret."

Tina nodded so eagerly, her bun fell out of place. "I swear! I'll take it to the grave."

"And I want you to know I never could've done it without that plate of tortilla."

She was moved: she dried her eyes on the kitchen rag hanging from the waistband of her skirt. "Oh, Chorrapelada . . . you'd better go; life waits for no one."

"Take care of yourself, Tina."

"You too, Mr. Marquis."

CHAPTER 37

"Attention, passengers for Cuba de Aviación's flight bound for Madrid, you may now begin boarding the *Estrella de Cuba*," a young woman announced over the loudspeaker.

It was twenty minutes before the flight, and Gloria and Daniela still hadn't shown up.

My hands were sweating so much, I had to dry them on my trousers. I was in the agreed-upon place at the agreed-upon time: in the airport, next to the big aquarium in the cantina, by the departures gate. To stop my head from buzzing, I watched the colorful fish swim in their little glass sea, and I flipped through the tickets with our seat numbers. Standing in front of the gate, the other passengers formed a line and started to board the plane. A mix of Spaniards and Cubans, happy to set off on a transatlantic journey.

Fifteen minutes.

My watch's minute hand advanced, and my head filled with bad thoughts. *Gloria and Daniela are in a traffic jam, or their car had a flat tire, or they had an accident.* The list of absurd possibilities gave way to more stabbing speculations. *César found out about everything and locked them up in the house.*

I breathed deeply until I managed to calm myself down.

Ten minutes.

Almost all the passengers had boarded, and the young woman at the counter looked at me with curiosity.

"Excuse me, sir . . . if this is your flight, you should board the plane as soon as possible."

"Yes, yes. I'm waiting for two people," I stuttered. "My wife and my daughter. My little daughter. And my wife, did I say that? They'll be here just in time, but they'll be here. I'm sure they'll be here because we're going to Madrid. I'm from Spain, you know?"

I was giving too many explanations, and she could tell. The young woman smiled condescendingly, as if to say, *You don't have to tell me your life story, mister.*

Five minutes.

"Final call for passengers traveling to Madrid."

Gloria and Daniela were still nowhere to be seen. At the edge of panic, I wrung my hat with such force that it hurt my hands. My stomach had shrunk to the size of a walnut. Another terrible thought snuck into my head: What if they got scared and decided to stay in Havana? I discarded the thought and clung like a fool to the image of Gloria in her red dress. Gloria telling me she loved me more than anything in the world. Our night in the department store. Our first kiss.

The young woman from the airline interrupted my memories.

"Sir, if you don't board immediately, the plane will leave without you."

In that instant, a scent reached my nose. Mariposas. Behind my back, I heard the hurried clicking of a pair of heels on the terminal tiles.

Gloria, at last!

I turned around with a smile too big for my face, but it wasn't Gloria. It was Mirta, Gloria's trusted maid who, dammit, must have also worn El Encanto's perfume. I was still recovering from my shock when Mirta handed me a letter.

"It's from Mrs. Valdés. If you'll excuse me, I have to go."

Before she left, the maid squeezed my shoulder affectionately, as if wishing me strength.

While the airport's employees closed the departures gate, I sat back down by the aquarium. I tore open the envelope with trembling hands and took out the note.

> *Patricio,*
>
> > *What we have cannot be. It's not just madness; it's truly absurd. I'm not getting on that plane because I don't love you. I've never loved you. Our adventure ends here. The game is over. I don't ask you to understand, and I don't expect you not to judge me. You can curse me if you like. You have every reason in the world to do so. My place is here, in Havana, with my husband, César Valdés.*
> >
> > *Goodbye and good luck,*
> > *Gloria*

I lifted my eyes from the letter. In the fish tank, a big fish ate a little fish, but the rest of the fish paid it no mind. I should have been sad, or furious, but instead I just sat there, still and numb. Even crumpling the letter and throwing it away seemed like too much effort.

I couldn't believe it.

What the note suggested was an even more resounding end: "My place is here, in Havana, with my husband, César Valdés." It didn't make any sense. It couldn't be. And I needed proof. I had to see with my own eyes that Gloria didn't love me and that she really wanted to stay with her gangster of a husband.

That thought pulled me out of my stupor, and I rushed out of the airport. I flagged a taxi and asked the driver to take me to El Encanto. From the car window, I saw an airplane cutting across the sky. It was probably the *Estrella de Cuba*, bound for Madrid.

At the store, the fashion show was in full swing. The models stalked down a raised catwalk while the guests admired their garments from their seats. But I had no interest in high fashion, just answers. I surveyed the great room until I spotted Marita, sitting in the first row. Gloria couldn't be too far away. Indeed, she was in the next row over . . . smiling and holding César's hand.

The sight was as painful as driving two pins into my eyes. I struggled to keep calm until Gloria looked up, and her gaze met my blue eyes watching her from a distance.

Just like every time we ever looked at each other, time stopped. I scrutinized her face in search of a sign of regret, of love, of sadness . . . any tiny slipup I could hang on to in order to prove Gloria didn't really feel what she had written in her letter. But it didn't come. Instead, Gloria raised her chin and coldly narrowed her eyes. Without taking her eyes off me, she kissed her husband on the lips.

I didn't stay until the end of the kiss. Unable to endure the sight any longer, I ran off and took shelter in the shadows of the perfume section.

I was still trying to digest Gloria's betrayal when I heard sobbing behind my back. A figure was crying in the darkness, crouched down behind a display desk.

"Patricio?"

It was Nely. For a moment, I thought her tears were related in some way to my wrongdoings.

"Are you all right, Nely? Why are you crying?"

"Haven't you heard? Batista has taken over."

"What?"

"The uprising worked. He got the Yankees' support."

I had been so submerged in my own problems, I hadn't the slightest idea of what had been going on in the country. "I'm so sorry, Nely."

"Ever since Eduardo Chibás died, this country has gone to shit. 'People of Cuba, wake up! Economic independence, political liberty, and social justice!'" Nely snorted loudly. "Cuba can't be fixed," she concluded.

Although it was for reasons very different from Nely's, I couldn't have agreed more.

"Maybe it's getting to be time to look for new directions," I whispered.

I dried the tears on her cheeks with the back of my hand and felt a burst of fondness for her brown eyes, her bangs, her too-bright smile. Loving Nely didn't hurt. Her kisses were the balm I needed just then. But when my lips were millimeters away from hers, Nely whispered a warning to me.

"You remember what I told you the night we went to see *The Lady from Shanghai*?"

"Yes, that you would never kiss another man," I answered.

"If you decide to kiss me, you'll have to stay with me forever."

The decision was too important to be made in an instant. But Gloria's betrayal had destroyed me, and I couldn't think clearly. The worst version of myself came to the fore.

"So be it," I agreed.

My need for comfort vanquished my prudence, and I pressed my lips against hers.

CHAPTER 38

GLORIA

The morning I decided I would run away to Spain with Patricio, I put on my red dress and felt like the most powerful woman in all of Cuba. From that moment on, my life became a secret countdown. Just ten more rotten kisses, I counted in my head when César gave me one of his slimy good-night kisses. Only nine more cups of coffee, I thought when the tiresome Marita invited me to Café Campoamor on Egido Street, just like every other afternoon.

Madrid was a vague idea in my head. I had never set foot off the island, and I could hardly imagine a city without the sea, where everyone spoke with a strange accent and wore heavy coats instead of cotton dresses.

Every time I tried to fantasize about it, one image came to mind: a small but pretty little room, with Patricio and me curled up on an armchair while Daniela played on the rug by our feet. Nothing more. It might not seem like much, but for me that was happiness itself. To make that image a reality, I would have gone with Patricio to Spain, to Mars, anywhere.

One night, while I tucked her into bed, I took a chance and decided to tell Daniela my plans.

"If I tell you a little secret, can you promise you won't say a word to anyone?"

Daniela nodded and crossed herself very seriously. "Yes, Mamita."

"You know I'm not happy with your father," I confessed. "Because of all the things your great-grandma Lala told you."

"Daddy is a bad man, right?"

The question gave me a chill.

"Yes, my darling," I answered. "That's right."

Daniela set her green eyes on me. "It scares me to have the same blood as him."

"Oh, darling, don't forget: you're also a little piece of me. The most important little piece."

"Lala and I did something to purify me. Great-grandma ground up a garlic clove and mixed it with lime juice, and I drank it so it would clean out the blood I got from my dad."

I squeezed Daniela in my arms with such strength, she writhed like a lizard. I pressed my nose to her head to smell her hair. As much as she had grown, the top of her head still smelled the same as it did when she was a baby.

"What would you think if we went far away?" I proposed.

"I'd like that. With Patricio?"

Again, I was blown away by her intuition. My little girl could read my mind as easily as her great-grandmother could. "Why do you say that, my little witch?"

"Because you really fancy him."

"Did Great-Grandma tell you that as well?"

"No, Mamita. I see that myself," she said with a wisdom that seemed impossible for such a young girl. "When you're with him, I can tell you're really happy. Did you know I keep playing with dolls like a little baby just so you can go see him at El Encanto?"

At that moment, I could've eaten her up with french fries. "Do you think anyone else knows?"

Daniela shook her head. "I know how to keep a secret."

"I think you're a good witch too, just like your Lala."

With Daniela's blessing, there was just one more impediment to leaving Cuba behind: my grandma and my mother. I was terrified to think of the savagery César might inflict on them in revenge for my escape. If I wasn't there to protect them, it was certain my husband would take away their house and my mother's nurse and dump them on the street without a second thought.

I decided to visit them and pour my heart out. A pleasant breeze had risen off the sea, so Lala and I went out to the patio and sat my mother down in a rocking chair by our side. I spoke without stopping until, when I was about to tell them our destination, Lala silenced me, placing her wrinkled hand over my lips.

"Shh! Don't tell us where you're going. It's better that way. César won't be able to get it out of me, no matter how hard he smacks me."

It hadn't occurred to me that César might torture my grandmother to find out my location, but the bastard was certainly capable of that. The idea of leaving them so defenseless struck me with the force of a punch to the gut.

"I can't leave you alone, Lala."

"Oh, mijita." Lala squeezed my hand between hers. "I hope you'll forgive me for waiting so long to tell you this."

My grandmother gulped and unbuttoned her blouse. She had a lump on her neck the size of a tamarind seed. "The doctor says it's cancer and that I should have been six feet under months ago. But every day for lunch, I have beet juice with the herbs that grow on your father's grave, to make a deal with Death so she won't take me yet."

I burst into tears. Lala cradled me in her lap and rocked me like when I was a little girl, afraid of the monster who lived in the walls.

"You should have told me!" I sobbed. "I'll take you to another doctor, to the best hospital—"

My grandmother interrupted my tears. "You won't do any of that. The only reason I've been putting up with this world is to see if you and your Patricio can finally give your asshole of a husband what's coming to him. But if you're getting away from Cuba, I can kick the bucket in peace."

I started to hiccup from emotion, and Lala rubbed my back harder to console me. "Shh . . . everything's all right, mijita. Everything will be fine."

I closed my eyes, and my grandmother kept stroking my hair. I must have dozed off for a moment because when I opened my eyes again, the sun was already setting. My grandmother had fallen asleep with my head resting on her lap.

"Hijita."

I jumped from shock on hearing that voice. My mother was still sitting in her rocking chair, but she was looking straight at me.

My mother, who had been still and quiet as a plant for nearly fifteen years, was smiling at me.

"Gloria," she said.

"Mamita?"

"Listen to me. Mind your grandma. Get off this island."

Tears blurred my vision, and I blinked to clear them away. When I could see clearly again, my mother's absent expression had returned. Her eyes looked at me without seeing, and her smile had vanished like a cloud evaporating on a summer afternoon. She had managed to escape from herself for an instant, but she was already back in the prison her body had become.

My mother's blessing was the last thing I needed. There was no turning back. It was strange to prepare for the most important trip of my life without packing a suitcase. Neither Daniela nor I could prepare a single bag without raising suspicions, so we would have to leave with only the clothes on our backs.

The day of our departure began like any other. I ate bread rolls with cream cheese with Marita at home, then accompanied her to a jewelry store so she could buy herself a necklace for the Dior show. At midday, César got out of bed, and we had lunch together on the terrace. After that, I took Daniela to Lala's house. The plan was to come by later and take her to the airport. We spent the entire afternoon getting ready for the show. My dress was stunning: from the new Christian Dior collection, of course.

The fabric was sea green, the color of the ocean on a stormy day. The French sleeves were designed to be rolled up and fastened at the elbow with a nacre button. The neckline was V-shaped and finished with emerald-green edging. But most divine of all was the lower part. It had a black silk bow that squeezed the dress around the waist and a skirt of overflowing fabric that ended just above the ankles.

If everything went according to plan, it would be the dress César would remember me in because he would never see me again.

An hour before the show was to begin, I feigned a stomachache. César and Marita looked at me, disgruntled.

"I'm bursting from the pain," I complained. "Maybe I should stay in bed."

"Dammit, girl, don't you realize you'll be missing a once-in-a-lifetime event?" my husband scolded me.

The real reason for César's annoyance was that he wouldn't be able to show me off. I wouldn't be hanging from his arm, his pretty young trophy with the exceedingly expensive dress he had ordered from Paris to dazzle his friends and their wives.

"You have to come. Make an effort," he ordered me.

"All right," I murmured.

I went to the entrance hall for a moment to get my shawl, but when I got back to the main room, I bent at the waist and, out of nowhere, vomited all over my shoes. In reality, it wasn't vomit but a mouthful of bread soaked in milk I had hidden in my mouth. Thanks to my little performance, César gagged and stopped insisting.

"If you're that sick, hurry up and get to bed, goddamn it," he said grudgingly.

I suppose he thought the only thing worse than not being able to show off his wife would be for me to vomit all over his friends. I ran to the bathroom and pretended to continue retching until I heard the front door slam shut. César and Marita were gone.

I jumped for pure joy. Making sure no servants saw me, I went running to change my clothes. I had just enough time to go and collect Daniela from Lala's house before getting a taxi to the airport.

I was enjoying my triumph when, as I undid the zipper on my Dior dress, I heard a voice behind my back.

"You think you're really clever, don't you?"

It was Marita. My sister-in-law watched me from the doorway, her face like a cruel cat with a ruthless smile. Marita was wearing another Dior dress, but since her legs were shorter than mine, her figure didn't do it justice, and her skirt dragged along the floor.

"You scared the hell out of me," I said, hiding my nerves. "I thought you had already left."

"César has gone to the show, but I told him one of my stockings ripped, and I would see him at El Encanto. My brother can be such an idiot sometimes."

I fought to hold back the panic beginning to pinch my insides. Had the bitch realized I wasn't ill? "I promise you, I don't feel well."

"Stop lying."

I decided to swap one lie for another. "All right, you caught me. The thing is, there's a meteor shower tonight, and I feel like staying home to watch it with my telescope."

"Shut up for once! You think I haven't realized what you're up to?"

"What am I up to?"

"I was the one who saw you two holding hands at the Tropicana."

I froze, like an animal trying to cross the highway but instead becoming dazed in the headlights of a car bearing down at top speed.

"César told you it was a waiter, but I was the one who told him," Marita said. "Of course, I decided not to let him know you were with that shop clerk scum."

The insult to Patricio forced me to react.

"Should I thank you for your silence?" I asked with disdain.

"You should. I just wanted César to give you a warning, to put some fear in you so you would see reason. I didn't realize my brother always believes you when you put on that puppy-dog face or that this clerk is no passing whim."

"No, he's not."

"I know. So I put two and two together and figured out why you were always looking for him every time we went shopping at El Encanto. And I'm sure that disgusting porcelain zoo of yours is just an excuse to keep seeking him out like a bitch in heat." Marita huffed through her nostrils with rage. "You probably have an illicit tryst planned right now. It's a shame. Because you're leaving him right this minute."

Marita's voice was as feverishly angry as César's got when he bossed me around. The two siblings shared the same arrogance, and I was sick and tired of them treating me as if I were their property.

"You can't order me around," I growled.

"Of course I can."

I faced Marita, prepared to push her aside and run if she didn't get out of the doorway. "What are you gonna do? Pull my hair?"

"Not me. But César will do much worse than that. We both know how savage he gets when something makes him angry."

I looked at my sister-in-law with deep scorn. "I don't care what either of you do to me. I'd rather die than keep sharing a bed with your brother every night."

"And you don't mind if he cuts Patricio's head off?"

I paused for a second, and Marita shot me a repulsive smile.

"I won't let him," I murmured.

"How are you gonna stop him?" My sister-in-law pierced me with her gaze like a lioness pierces her prey with her claws. "I know you. You're thinking about warning Patricio. But it's a shame because from now on you'll never be alone with him again."

Her fury frightened me. I knew Marita was as cruel as all the Valdéses, but somehow, I'd always hoped she wasn't as much of a bastard as her brother. On the terrace during the rainstorm, I thought I had glimpsed the true Marita, someone for whom I could even have felt fondness. But it had all been a lie.

"Do you know what hurts the most?" I asked. "That for a moment, under the rain, I thought we could be friends."

She looked away with a trace of shame.

"Traitorous slut. With the good life César has always given you," she snarled at me.

"A life I didn't choose."

"Ungrateful bitch."

"What do you want?"

"Nothing. I want things to go on as they are. I might remind you, you and my brother are united by the Holy Mother Church and that dirty laundry is always washed at home," she declared.

Her silence had a high price. But Patricio's life was at risk if I didn't comply.

"If things go on as always . . . you won't say anything to César?" I asked.

"My brother will never know about any of this. But under one condition: you won't see Patricio ever again."

"He'll never accept that."

"Well, make him accept it. If he doesn't, you won't even be able to identify his body once César's done with him."

My worst nightmare had come true. Marita had condemned me. Patricio and I would never be able to escape to Madrid. But our broken dreams were the least of my worries. If I didn't stop him, César would kill Patricio. The love of my life was in danger. There was only one way to save him: I had to break his heart.

Defeated, and under the watchful eye of my sister-in-law, I got out a pen and paper and sat down to write a letter.

CHAPTER 39

When Marita and I arrived at the Christian Dior show, you could feel the excitement in the air. At the doors of El Encanto, a massive crowd of curious habaneros were pressed up against the shop windows, trying to see what was happening inside. The building was prettier than ever, with multiple spotlights illuminating the facade like the premiere of a Hollywood movie. A red carpet led to the entrance. Our chauffeur drove through the crowd and stopped the car at the door.

It wasn't easy getting out of the car in our elaborate dresses, but we managed it and mingled with the rest of the guests. The curious onlookers watched us, and some started shouting flirtatious compliments. I heard two gentlemen asking each other if I was one of the models in the show, which would have made me feel quite flattered under normal circumstances.

Upon crossing the store's threshold, we entered another world. We had traveled to Paris, to a ready-to-wear fashion show. If El Encanto could make its customers sigh when they passed through its doors on a typical day, everything was that much prettier now.

Pennants in the colors of the French flag—blue, white, and red—hung from the ceiling in elaborate garlands. The entire ground floor was empty of display counters, and they had installed a raised catwalk to show off the designs. To accommodate the guests, they had laid out small tables facing the catwalk, each table crowned with a centerpiece of fresh mariposas tied with a silk ribbon. The little lamps on the tables gave off a warm light that shone off the women's jewelry and the men's slicked-back hair.

Marita and I met up with César at our table in the first row, and then the show began. The store's designer, Manet, gave the introductory welcome in person.

"Ladies and gentlemen!" announced Manet from a small stage under the spotlights. "It is an honor for El Encanto to present the new collection from the famous international fashionista Christian Dior. A genius who honors us with his presence, all the way from Paris. For all of you, without further ado . . . the *New Look*!"

The models began to walk out, drawing sighs of admiration and spontaneous applause from the crowd. Those dresses were magical: they transformed any woman who wore them into a powerful figure, completely sure of herself.

They were weapons for us women to conquer the world.

Although my mind was still somewhere far away, I couldn't help but admire Dior's genius. There was going to be a revolution in fashion. We were witnessing a historic event, but I would have given it up without a second thought to be in a taxi on the way to the airport.

The show was torture. I missed Patricio so much I could only think about what he might be doing at that moment. *Now he'll be wondering why I'm so late*, I thought. *Now he'll have realized I'm not coming. Is he getting on the plane? Is he damning me to hell? Does he hate me?* My thoughts were so painful, I was afraid I would die right then and there.

"Are you still sick, girl?" César asked when he saw me frowning.

I didn't have the strength to answer him. The audience burst into applause as a new design—a lovely sleeveless dress with a champagne-colored bodice and a skirt printed with royal palm leaves—appeared on the runway. That's when I saw him.

Patricio hadn't gotten on the plane. He was standing on the other side of the catwalk. His blue eyes, that gaze that was my whole world, fell upon me in search of answers. I was sure he had read my letter and hadn't believed a single word of my stupid lies. But he had to believe them.

My first impulse was to stand up and run to him, but that would have been a death sentence. At that instant, I could either save both our lives or doom them. I struggled with all my might, and going against everything in my heart, I looked at Patricio with intense coldness and kissed César on the lips.

The kiss repulsed me. My whole body wanted to pull away, but I prolonged the kiss as long as I could. When I separated from César and looked up again, Patricio was gone.

Thunderous applause announced the end of the fashion show, and Monsieur Dior himself got up on the catwalk to greet us. The designer was dressed in a gray suit and a blue silk tie. While he thanked the audience for its applause, lightly nodding his head, his eyes fell on me. He looked at me in perplexed surprise. That's when I realized I was the only person in the whole crowd not clapping.

A little later, the homage continued at a private dinner in the French Room with only around twenty special guests. While I swallowed my woes with the help of a glass of champagne, Dior approached me to talk privately.

"Excuse my boldness," he said in French-accented English. "Do I understand you didn't like the show?"

"Quite the contrary. I loved it."

"So why didn't you applaud, if you'll pardon the indiscretion?"

"I'm very sorry. Today I'm too sad to clap," I said.

The designer was very sweet, and he took my hand as if to wish me better spirits. "I hate to see a woman so sad wearing one of my designs. Is there anything I can do to cheer you up?"

"Do you know a cure for lovesickness?" I asked, after making sure César and Marita couldn't hear me.

"I'm afraid there's no cure for that. But in France we have a saying: 'Si on n'aime pas trop, on n'aime pas assez.' If we don't love too much, we don't love enough."

After the Christian Dior show, I went days without setting foot in El Encanto. It was the best option. Marita and I spent the afternoons in other stores or with her boring friends. My sister-in-law accompanied me even when I went to the bathroom, and in the rare moments she couldn't do it herself, a domestic employee served as my shadow.

I didn't see Patricio again until one afternoon when I decided to go to El Encanto with the excuse of buying Chanel mascara.

"You'll stay right by my side, my little sister-in-law," Marita warned me. "No sweet nothings to that clerk."

In spite of my drastic letter and rejection of Patricio, the threat was still in force: if I continued my "stupid, futureless romance," she would tell César everything.

We were being attended by a very nice female clerk when Patricio stopped at the next display desk over, not looking at us. When he took out a key to open a cabinet, I saw something that left me dumbstruck: he had a ring on his finger. Marita also noticed and, when Patricio walked away, she didn't hesitate to ask our assistant.

"That clerk . . ."

"Patricio? He's one of our managers."

"Manager, clerk, whatever. I didn't know he was married."

"Oh yes, ma'am," the innocent young woman answered. "The wedding was last week. With Nely, another of our employees. The elevator operator."

When she heard that, Marita looked so happy it could have been Christmas. Even more so when she saw my face heavy with regret.

"Please congratulate him on behalf of the Valdés family," she said, more venomous than a snake. "On our next visit, we'll leave him a tip."

"You'd better come back quickly then. Patricio and Nely are leaving Cuba."

"You don't say? Where are they going?"

"To Spain."

I thought I was about to faint. Marita noticed and took me by the arm to hold me up.

"Are you all right, miss?" the clerk asked when she saw I had gone pale.

"I need to get out of here."

On the street, my sister-in-law nearly crowed with triumph. "There you have it. You were so sure he loved you, but that pig has already married someone else."

When we returned to the house, I locked myself in the bathroom and cried until my tears left my cheeks red and raw. A stomach cramp mixed with profound nausea made me double over. *Just what I need*, I thought. *I have to get my period at this very moment.*

Suddenly, I realized it had been three months since I had last bled. Since before Patricio and I made love at El Encanto.

A visit to the doctor confirmed what my insides were already telling me: I was pregnant.

CHAPTER 40

PATRICIO

When we arrived in Madrid, I discovered I was poorly dressed for the Spanish climate. My linen trousers and my guayabera didn't protect me against the wind and cold. Nely, with her sleeveless floral dress, was freezing too.

We spent our first day in the new city going to Pontejos and buying wool clothing, sheepskin coats, and closed-toed shoes. After shopping, we tested out our new winter clothes by strolling down the snowy Gran Vía. It was Nely's first time seeing snow, and she walked a whole block, from Red de San Luis to Callao, sticking her tongue out to catch snowflakes like a little girl.

For me, the novelty of the snow didn't last long before giving way to a reality that was more dull gray than shining white. The stench of the coal yards assaulted my nostrils. The passersby were hazy figures all around us, sheltered behind their hats and scarves and illuminated by the weak lights of passing cars. The tall buildings flanked the street like hives of menacing insects. In Madrid, there was no music in the streets. I had wanted to see the Gran Vía my whole life, and now that I was there, I felt sad. It was strange to think that just two days before, I had been walking down the Malecón, wet with sweat and squinting because of the sun while the sea shone so blue that it fused with the blue of the sky.

Unaware of my unease, Nely stopped to give me a kiss that tasted like snow. "It's a beautiful city."

I tried to see Madrid through my wife's eyes. It was true, the place was beautiful. So why did it look so gray and sad to me? It was hard for me to acknowledge it, but I couldn't lie to myself. Madrid hurt because it was the city I would have gone to with Gloria. I had fantasized so much about walking down the Gran Vía with her that doing it with Nely was just a consolation prize. I embraced my new wife with all my might to make up for my guilt.

"Not as beautiful as you," I told her, feeling miserable.

Our wedding had been quick but rigged, much like our engagement. After we kissed at the Christian Dior show, I went home with Nely, holding hands all the way. El Grescas and Guzmán were flabbergasted. My friends thought I was already in Spain, running away with Gloria. Not only had I not left, but on top of that, I had come home with Nely on my arm.

That night, restless with unhappiness, I made love to Nely for the first time. Being inside a woman other than Gloria felt like a betrayal, but at the same time, it was just what I needed to ease the pain that had gripped me to my marrow. While Nely reached climax, I hung on to her hips and gave it to her hard, trying to reach an orgasm that would give me enough peace to be able to sleep that night. I couldn't. The memory of Gloria, her freckled skin, and her sweat made my body collapse. Resigned to my fate, I feigned ecstasy with a moan and sought refuge on the other side of the bed.

"Are you all right?" Nely asked while she curled up into a ball and pushed her warm body against my back. "Did you like it?"

"Yes," I lied.

"Your feet are freezing."

"As always."

"Give them to me. I'll warm them up."

She fell asleep, and I left the bed to hide in the garden. By candle-light, I read Gloria's letter again and again. When the light of dawn peeked over the horizon, I decided to stop torturing myself and burned the paper while crying like a little boy. I went back to bed beside Nely and managed to be half asleep for a couple of hours. Later, once we were up, as soon as the elevator operator got in the shower, my compays laid into me.

"Why the hell aren't you in Madrid?" asked Guzmán.

"Yeah, man, I have no idea what's going on," said El Grescas.

Though I burned Gloria's letter, I knew it by heart and repeated it to them word for word.

My friends hugged me, silent. There was nothing to say.

The weeks following that fateful evening were very hard, and Nely's presence was my only comfort. One night, naked and in each other's arms in bed, we got to talking under the cover of darkness.

"I know you're not over her," Nely said. I stayed quiet, not knowing what to say. "I mean that married lady. She left you."

It was very strange to be talking about this with Nely, but I was thankful to her. I needed to get it off my chest. "She never loved me, really. It was just a fling for her."

Nely kissed me on the lips. "Well, then, whoever she is, that girl is a bigger piece of shit than I thought. Because there's no better, more noble, more wonderful man in all of Cuba."

I felt an attack of love for Nely. My loyal and devoted Nely, so generous that she had always loved me without reservation. I returned her kiss with passion.

"I don't deserve for you to love me like this," I whispered.

"You deserve the best. And I'm the best because there's no woman in the world who could love you like I do," she said, laughing.

I felt as if her simple laughter could cure my wounded soul.

And I decided I needed that laughter by my side for the rest of my days.

To Nely's surprise, I jumped out of bed, turned on the light, and knelt at her feet.

"Marry me," I blurted out.

She burst out laughing again. Since she was looking at the image of a naked man kneeling at the foot of the bed asking for her hand in marriage, it was no wonder. "Are you serious?"

"I've never been more serious in my life. Let's get married and go far away from here. This country has gone to shit, you said it yourself. In the morning, we'll go to church and get married. You wanna do it?"

"No," answered Nely.

"No?"

I was dumbstruck, and she burst out laughing yet again. "What the hell makes you think I'm getting married in a church! I don't need any priest's permission to be your wife."

"Well, let's get married at the courthouse. I don't care if we're married by the Pope, a Buddhist monk, a Santera, or Lenin himself. I just know I wanna be with you."

"And I wanna be with you, dummy. Now come back to bed. Your ass is gonna get colder than your feet."

Our wedding was the next day in the garden, with a notary, in front of a framed photo of Eduardo Chibás. Since Nely had stopped talking to her family years before due to their disapproval of her militant devotion to the Orthodox Party, El Grescas and Guzmán were our witnesses and our only guests.

Nely was of the opinion that a honeymoon was a bourgeois, unnecessary waste, so she proposed we save that money to start a new life together. I proposed we do it in Spain.

"Patricio, baby, are you nuts? We're gonna leave Batista's dictatorship just to go live under that bastard Franco?"

I respected my new wife's opinion, but in truth, my desire to leave Cuba was deeper than any political belief. I only knew the prospect of still seeing Gloria at El Encanto was a torture I couldn't bear. Even the most minute possibility of crossing paths with her in the street was too painful. Havana was Gloria, and I needed an ocean between us to be able to move forward with my life.

"I need to go home, Nely. I really need to. And besides, the owners of El Encanto have opened new stores in Madrid."

"I don't know if I can live in a country under the yoke of a man with such a squeaky voice."

"But Madrid has its own life. You'll see."

"You know that if we go to Spain, I'm not gonna keep quiet, right? And I'm never gonna put on a mantilla like one of those obedient little ladies who go to Mass!"

"Does that mean we're moving?"

Once again, Nely showed me she loved me and made the greatest of sacrifices: she set her Communist beliefs aside to live in a dictatorship.

When Nely and I were settled in our new rented flat in the Las Ventas neighborhood in Madrid, the first thing I did was go and see two of the owners of El Encanto, Pepín Solís Fernández and Don Cesáreo Rodríguez, whom I'd met years ago in Havana. The two cousins welcomed me like an old friend and invited me to a restaurant called Botín to eat lamb.

"Patricio! The man who sold lipstick to Ava Gardner," Pepín greeted me.

"You heard about that?" I asked with a guffaw.

"Aquilino keeps us up to date. We were happy when he told us you wanted to come back to Spain."

"I needed a change in my life."

"He also told us you married Nely. Well done. You picked a real gem," César congratulated me.

"I know it, thanks. I called you guys because I need a job."

Fernández and Rodríguez shared a smile.

"First, let me give you the background," Pepín began. "My stores are called Galerías Preciados, and they're on the street of the same name."

"And I'm the president of El Corte Inglés, which is right in front," added César.

"You're competing with each other?" I asked, surprised.

"There are rumors we hate each other, but they're just that, rumors. We're business rivals, but that doesn't mean we can't break bread. We're both from God's country, after all."

Even though they both had gray hairs, the two cousins still grinned at each other like kids.

"And might there be a place for me in one of the stores?" I inquired.

The two cousins looked at each other out of the corners of their eyes.

"I'm afraid there's a problem with that," said César.

My soul dropped to my feet. I had taken it for granted that they would give me work. If there was no job for me, all my plans would fall apart. When they saw my distress, the cousins burst out laughing.

"The problem is, we both want you to be one of our managers!" laughed Pepín. "So you'll have to decide."

I passed from relief to consternation. It was just as impossible as picking between a father and a mother. "I can't choose."

"We suspected as much. We have no other option but to settle this like gentlemen." With a sly smile, Pepín took out a coin. "Heads or tails?"

Pepín showed us the peseta, with Franco's face on one side and the shield with the eaglet on the other.

"Tails, you work at El Corte Inglés. Heads, in Galerías Preciados. Everyone agree?"

The three of us nodded, and he tossed the coin. It fell and clattered on the table, showing the dictator's face.

"Dammit!" César lamented. "You won, cousin."

Suddenly, I had an idea. "If it would make up for it . . . could I offer you a new clerk? Nely?"

"It'd be a pleasure. But won't it be complicated for a married couple to work at rival stores?"

"If you both manage it, we can too," I answered, determined.

And so, my fate was sealed. Galerías Preciados became my second home for the next six years.

PART III

CHAPTER 41

Six years passed. Six Christmas church bells, and six July blow-out sales. Life with Nely was pleasant, although it didn't take long before it became routine. Every morning, we left for work at our respective department stores: Nely at the Corte Inglés and me at Galerías Preciados. We left home at the same time and came back on the same bus. On weekends, instead of going to see movies at the Payret or the Atlantic, we went to the Palacio de la Música or the Capitol. In the summers, we traveled to Asturias to spend a few days of vacation in Santa Benxamina and a few more in a guesthouse on the beach in Ribadesella. In those early summers, Nely got pregnant twice, but both times she lost the baby within the first few months.

Loyal to her word, my wife never put up with Francisco (Paquito Pantanos) Franco, and it didn't take long before she became an active participant in the opposition, contacting people who shared her ideology and attending clandestine meetings. Nely's activism often kept me up at night. On the one hand, I was worried my wife would be arrested—or, even worse, executed—by the regime. On the other, I was conscious of the fact that coming to Madrid had been my decision, and I couldn't force Nely to hang her head and act against her nature. Every time Nely went to one of her meetings, I waited up for her with bated breath.

Far from Havana, I entered a sort of hibernation state in which nothing affected me. At other times, I would've said that was no kind of life, but routine kept the pain at arm's length. I slept, I ate, and I worked and made love to Nely. From the outside, it looked like a good life, but I alone knew my heart had turned to ash. My romance with Gloria had been so intense that I had used up the ration of strong emotions meant to last me the rest of my life. I only noticed changes of seasons thanks to the attire of mannequins in shop windows. I started to get fat and lose my hair. The only thing that stayed the same was that my feet were always cold, winter and summer.

Although Nely and I lived on another continent, we kept track of everything happening in Cuba. Guzmán, El Grescas, and I talked on the phone on our birthdays, and thanks to them, I was more or less up to date on the big events in Havana. My friends didn't bring up the subject of Gloria often, but once, early on, Guzmán couldn't keep from telling me he had seen her from a distance at El Encanto and that she had "a stroller and a kid a few months old." That she'd had another child with her husband disturbed me for a while. I suffered, remembering Daniela, and it made me angry to think another child in the world had the soulless César Valdés for a father.

To the mafia's delight, Fulgencio Batista continued to govern with an iron fist in a silk glove. The new dictator reinstated the death penalty and eliminated the right to strike as well as freedom of the press. Nely was inconsolable. Her only hope was a young lawyer in the Orthodox Party named Fidel Castro who had jumped into the political arena a few years before by bringing the bell of Demajagua—a historic symbol from the war for independence—to the capital. But after his botched attack on the Moncada barracks, Castro seemed condemned to failure.

As for my own failures, Gloria was like a poorly scarred wound that would open again whenever I least expected it. Any detail that reminded me of her, whether as big as the death of Albert Einstein or as small as a porcelain figurine on a sideboard, forced me to relive the pain. Her very name was a curse because every time I heard a common expression ("God keep you in his glory," "No trouble, no glory," "Peace here and then glory"), it dragged me back to hell. Over the years, I resigned myself to my fate. Gloria was a chronic illness from which I would never be cured.

I awoke from my lethargy in the summer of 1958, on an afternoon when we went to the movies to see *Witness for the Prosecution*, in which Tyrone Power played a husband accused of murder. Nely left the cinema in high spirits.

"Mr. Power was amazing! You remember when that horrible lady yelled at him at El Encanto?"

"How could I forget? It was Marita Valdés," I said.

"Yeah! I saw she got married."

I was shocked when I heard that. "How do you know?"

"I read it in the paper."

When we got home, Nely brought me a copy of the most recent *Ecos de Sociedad*. Cuban gossip magazines were one of my wife's vices. Since it was impossible to buy them in Madrid, every couple of weeks a friend of hers sent them from Havana. I flipped through them as well, but only out of nostalgia. I liked the places I saw in the photos more than the celebrities.

But that issue left me dumbfounded. There were two whole pages dedicated to Marita Valdés's wedding. César's sister had married Nelson Suárez, a bald guy with a big gut. The caption said he was an important sugarcane impresario. There was no doubt he was the perfect puppet and would let his strings be pulled by his new family. In fact, in the photos he looked somewhat uncomfortable at his own wedding, especially whenever César had an arm around his shoulders.

But that wasn't what struck me most. In one of the photos of the guests, I saw Gloria. Not only that, she had a little boy on her knee. "Her son, little Gabriel," read the caption. Although she was smiling, Gloria looked into the camera with a deep sadness. I cut out the page and slipped it into my wallet. I was like a dummy for a whole hour, staring at the portrait, until Nely came in and told me off because I'd left the chicory-coffee pot on the fire.

The next day at work, my mind was still far away. I couldn't stop thinking about Gloria.

"Can I help you with the inventory?" I heard a friendly voice by my side.

"Hmm?" I turned around, distracted.

It was Felipe, the floor manager, a bright young boy.

"Sorry," I said with a yawn. "I couldn't sleep. I'm exhausted."

"No problem, man. If you need anything, let me know."

I took shelter behind a display counter to look at the photo of Gloria again, but a customer suddenly interrupted my nostalgia. "What a handsome little boy you have."

It was an old lady, a real chatterbox who sounded like she was from La Mancha. At first, I didn't understand what she meant.

"Excuse me?"

The lady pointed at the photo of Gloria and her son. "Your wife and the boy. They're so pretty."

I tried to correct the misunderstanding. "No, that's not my family."

The lady looked at me in disbelief.

"Well, if they're not yours, they must be your twin brother's," she insisted. "The child has your eyes."

I looked again. Gabriel had light eyes, that was true. But in the black-and-white photo, I couldn't tell if they were blue, like mine, or green, like César's. As if she could sense my doubts, the lady threw more fuel on the fire. "And not just the eyes. The chin, the chubby cheeks . . . you're exactly alike!"

I started to feel a little nervous, and I counted in my head. The boy must have been about six, so Gloria must have had him a few months after I left Cuba. The math added up, but a simple coincidence in timing didn't mean he was mine. How could I be a father? It was madness.

"He's really not mine, ma'am," I stated firmly.

"You must be joking!"

The stubborn lady stuck to her guns and called over Felipe, who was at a nearby cash register. "Hey, you, come here! We need a second opinion."

Felipe answered her call, and the lady pointed at the photo. "Does that little boy look like this gentleman or not?"

The floor manager studied the magazine page with great seriousness.

"It's true they're two peas in a pod," he confirmed.

Suddenly, I had to loosen my tie to breathe. It took all my willpower not to collapse on the floor right then and there. It was madness. And still . . .

When the lady left, I interrogated Felipe. "You really think Gabriel looks like me? Or did you just say that to please the customer?"

"At the risk of sticking my nose in where it's not wanted . . . if that woman was ever a girlfriend of yours, I think the two of you need to talk."

That conversation made me see things differently. The image of the kiss between Gloria and César started to lose its initial force, and I was assaulted by other possibilities the pain had kept me from seeing. In a deep place within myself, a new hope awoke. The eyes of that little boy, Gabriel, told me maybe the note I'd read at the airport wasn't entirely true, that there might be reasons I was unaware of for what happened and that what I had experienced with Gloria had been as real as the pain I felt due to her absence. Ours had been a story of true love, and according to Felipe and the customer, it seemed to have borne fruit.

CHAPTER 42

When lunchtime arrived, I left Galerías Preciados and walked across the street to collect Nely with the intention of getting a bite together at La Austriaca. My feelings swirled with such force that they threatened to become a tidal wave. I feared my wife would see my face and know something wasn't right. I practiced a mask of normalcy with my reflection in a shop window. But when I got to her section, I was met by an unpleasant surprise.

"Patricio! Bless my soul, we just sent a boy to tell you." Teresita, one of my wife's coworkers, had a look of distress on her face.

"What happened? Where's Nely?"

"The Political-Social Brigade took her away. She was arrested."

I ran to Puerta del Sol, to the offices of the General Directorate of Security. But no one was willing to tell me if Nely was there or not. Finally, after hours of insisting and begging, a young police officer took pity on me, and after checking the entry register, he confirmed my wife was there. My heart did a pirouette in my chest: this place was a well-known torture chamber.

"They arrested her after a raid on a printer where she and some of her little friends were stacking pamphlets praising La Pasionaria," the policeman told me. "It doesn't look good, my friend, not good at all."

Not knowing what else to do, I went back to Galerías Preciados to see Pepín Fernández. He welcomed me into his office, and after hearing about what had happened, he patted me on the shoulder, trying to calm me down.

"The main thing is to stay calm. We won't get anywhere by losing our composure."

I was thankful he used the plural to make it clear my problems mattered to him. "I'm sorry to show up like this, but I didn't know what else to do."

"You did the right thing. Don't worry, I think I have an idea about how to fix this."

Back at my house, it took me hours to get to sleep. My head was locked in a loop of curiosity and concern. On one hand, my doubt over whether Gabriel was my son ate away at me from inside like termites in wood. On the other hand, imagining Nely locked up in a cell almost killed me with anguish. I managed to sleep for a little while, and I dreamed I was in a jungle. Gloria and Nely were both drowning in quicksand, and I could only save one of them. I woke up soaked in sweat.

As soon as dawn broke, I put on my best jacket and headed to Puerta del Sol. Pepín Fernández had come up with a plan, but I was going to need all my courage to carry it out.

A police officer guarded the entrance to the GDS.

"Good morning," I said, clearing my throat to feign greater courage than I felt. "I've come to collect my wife. She was arrested yesterday."

"Well, then, she'll stay in jail until she learns her lesson," the guard spat.

"I know Commissioner Holguín, and I wanna speak with him," I said, following the instructions Pepín had given me.

The guard looked at me with a mixture of wariness and scorn and called out to a colleague. "Domínguez! This man is here to pick up his saint. Tell Holguín."

"There's nothing saintly about her," said Domínguez from the hall-way, "assuming it's one of those bitches we arrested yesterday at the printing house."

Domínguez was balding and plump, a few years away from being bald and fat. You could tell he was one of those guys who practically sleeps with his uniform on just to feel more important.

"What's the name of the gem in question?"

His tone of superiority annoyed me. In reality, everything annoyed me because this Domínguez reminded me of Don Gato and his airs of grandeur. I wondered if Don Gato had family in Spain, because they could've been brothers.

"Nely Yamary."

"And where does a weird name like that come from?"

"From Cuba."

"A Cuban! Well, let's get it over with. You can't trust them. All black and nasty. And traitors too. After the war in Cuba, my father told me, in the ports all you could hear was the toc-toc-toc of the wooden legs of our Spanish soldiers, coming off the boats incapacitated. That's why they beat us. They're traitors."

While I pretended to care about his history lesson, we walked back toward the cells in the building's depths. The place, just like all Francoist offices, looked like it was designed to rob you of your will to live. It was a huge gray block with soulless corridors, and the few windows that weren't mortared over offered views of a narrow interior courtyard. Not a single plant, not a single drop of color. I felt a stab of longing for Havana and its pleasing colors, its heat, and the flowers and planted pots everywhere imaginable.

We reached a small chamber with a table. A portrait of the dictator and his wife presided over the room. In short order, they brought out Nely. She was wearing the clothes she'd had on when she left the house the day before. Her hair was disheveled, and her eyes were baggy. She smelled of the mold and mildew of her cell. But her eyes were fierce and defiant. We ran into each other's arms.

"You can't take her until Holguín gives the go-ahead."

"We'll wait."

"And in the meantime, you apologize to your husband, squab."

"Why?"

"Why! For disrespecting and embarrassing him and running around like a red commie bitch, don't ya know. Not enough for you? Go on, apologize, I wanna hear it."

Nely pursed her lips and apologized. "Sorry."

"That's what I like to hear. And you, keep her under lock and key. The next time she gets out, we'll wear her out here between us, so she learns."

A fat man with gray hair and sweat stains on his uniform entered the room. He had white smears of saliva at the corners of his mouth that formed threads every time he spoke. A cigarette hung from his lips.

"Who might you be?" he bellowed.

"He told us he knew you," Domínguez explained to his boss.

I swallowed and girded my loins.

"We don't know each other, Mr. Holguín, but we have a mutual friend," I began.

"Who?"

I pointed to the portrait of Franco and his wife.

The commissioner burst into scornful laughter. "And how would a loser like you know Doña Carmen?"

He wasn't wrong. Carmen Polo was no friend of mine, but she was a friend of Pepín Fernández and was one of the best customers at Galerías Preciados. Mr. Fernández knew he could get away with asking her for a favor.

"I must warn you that, if you do not allow us to leave immediately, Doña Carmen will be quite displeased," I said.

Holguín was losing his patience. "Take this bitch back to her cell. And arrest her husband too, for wasting our time."

Domínguez approached to carry out his boss's orders. But all of a sudden, the office phone rang.

"Commissioner speaking," Holguín answered cockily.

When he heard the voice on the other end of the line, he turned as pale as a ghost. A vein in his forehead bulged out so far, I thought it was about to explode.

I didn't know until later, but Pepín Fernández, my guardian angel, had convinced Franco's wife, "La Collares" herself, to call the station.

The commissioner started sweating even more, if that was possible.

We all remained silent while Holguín nodded with the telephone pressed against his ear. "Yes, ma'am . . . of course, ma'am . . . at your service, ma'am . . ." Then he hung up the phone. Pulling himself together, he took a final puff on his cigarette and furiously put out the butt in the palm of his own hand. He was either going to let us go or blow my head off; there was no middle ground.

"Get out," the commissioner growled.

I took Nely by the hand and obeyed before he changed his mind.

"Thank you, Commissioner. It's been a pleasure doing business with you, a real honor," I said.

Holguín narrowed his eyes. He suspected we were laughing at him, but he wasn't sure.

Days later, having recovered from the fright, Nely and I went to Plaza Mayor to eat calamari sandwiches. My wife was telling me about an interview with an American journalist that proved Fidel Castro was still alive and leading guerillas in the Sierra Maestra when I suddenly interrupted her.

"Darling, do you wanna go back to Cuba?"

Nely was so taken aback, she stopped chewing her sandwich. "Are you bored with me, my love?"

"It's not that. I've just been missing Havana for a long time."

Since I couldn't tell her the real reason for my unease, I got as close as I could to the truth.

"I miss El Encanto," I sighed. "I know it might sound stupid, but I think about it every day."

"My head is back there too. They say Batista's government is about to fall, and it would be so nice to be there to see it."

"Let's go back, then. Right now, today," I blurted out.

"Right now? You're crazy, baby," said Nely, with a big smile on her face.

Nely kissed me hard, as excited as a little girl, and burst into a Communist song.

And so, with the excuse of aiding a revolution, we returned to Cuba. What we didn't imagine was that the true revolution in our lives was about to be unleashed within the walls of El Encanto.

CHAPTER 43

GLORIA

"Mamita, what's that?"

Gabriel pointed at my leg, just behind my knee. I bent down to look. I had a swollen, deep-purple varicose vein.

"Did you get a bruise while you were playing?" asked the little boy.

"It's a vein, my darling," I answered.

"A stain? Like on the carpet?"

"Vein. Sometimes little old ladies get them."

"Are you a little old lady?"

It took me a moment to answer. I had just turned thirty-four, but I felt seventy.

"Of course," I replied. "Come and give Mama a kiss."

"Well, I think you look pretty. You're prettier than a fire truck full of candy," Gabriel declared with all the wisdom of his six years.

My son was a treasure. A little boy with a big imagination who filled the house with happiness through his inventions and mischief.

"Can I play with the porcelain zoo?" he asked with his best manners.

"Only if you promise to be careful," I agreed.

"I'll be careful! I promise."

Since he was still too little to reach it by himself, I opened the cupboard and set several porcelain animals on the floor for him. But for all his promises, Gabriel was just a kid, and accidents were inevitable. Over the years, the figurines had suffered all sorts of mishaps. The little lion had no tail, the giraffe's neck was stuck to her body with glue, the penguins had lost their beaks . . . it was a zoo of broken little animals, but I loved it when Gabriel played with them. Although nobody knew it, every time he did so I felt a little closer to his real father.

When I first discovered I was pregnant, I felt like a plucked hen, naked and shaking.

My son's father, the man I loved, was on the other side of the world, married to another woman.

On a pregnant woman's impulse, I went so far as to secretly buy a ticket for a ship to Lisbon. I needed Patricio: to see him, talk to him, smell him, touch him. I needed him to know we had created a new life. But once I got hold of myself, I reflected on the situation and, with tremendous heartache, concluded it was better to stay in Havana. If Marita suspected I was going anywhere near Patricio, she wouldn't be so amenable the second time. My sacrifice was what kept him alive, so I tore my ticket into pieces and threw them in the sea.

That night, for the first time in our marriage, I was the one who sought out my husband in bed.

When I told him about my pregnancy a few weeks later, César was so happy, he didn't do the math. And when Gabriel was born three months premature (in reality, he was in my womb for nine and a half months) but very beautiful, César was so excited to have a boy, he suspected nothing. On the contrary, he took the opportunity to boast to his friends.

"The Valdés men come out like ship's masts. My son was born three months early, and he's built like a bull."

I remember Marita lowering her eyes when she heard that. I was sure she suspected Gabriel was not her brother's son, but she refrained from expressing her suspicion in order to keep up appearances. The house was on fire, but there was no smoke.

God knows it seemed strange to me César didn't realize the baby wasn't his. Gabriel looked more like Patricio with every passing day. As far as his blue eyes, I was saved by the fact that César's mother, the hen-holding lady from the photo, had eyes bluer than the Caribbean.

Mothers say the arrival of a baby is always cause for happiness, but the days after the birth were horrible. Lala died the day after she met her great-grandson. My grandmother hadn't been the same since my failed attempt to escape with Patricio. Her tumor got worse, growing so much that it kept her from swallowing her food properly. She suffered terrible pains, but she was so stubborn, she insisted on not dying until Gabriel was born.

"I just wanna see that little baby's face, and then I can kick the bucket," she would repeat to Daniela and me. "Mija, this is important . . . when I die, burn me and bury my ashes in the soil of my bitter melon plant. With the leaves and seeds that grow from the tree, make an infusion and give it to César."

Even on her deathbed, my grandmother was still plotting her vengeance against my husband.

Lala was a witch, but she was also a woman of her word. She gave newborn Gabriel a kiss, and hours later she died on the patio, looking out over her lovely garden. My mom also departed a few weeks later. Her nurse came in one morning to give her breakfast and saw she hadn't woken up. After years of a living death, she had finally learned to stop breathing.

Daniela and I fulfilled Lala's wishes. We planted her ashes in the soil of the bitter melon and picked the first fruits to make infusions. César started drinking it every morning—under the impression that it was a tasty tea—and he began growing warts and developed a nasty cough that never went away.

Now in her late teens, Daniela had become a beauty. Her hair was black and shiny, hanging down to her waist, and her father's green eyes were not cruel but lovely on her.

After Patricio's departure, I didn't rest until I convinced César we should send Daniela to study at a boarding school in Florida. I didn't want to risk my pretty girl becoming an attractive teenager, and her father proving himself a monster yet again. Just like with Patricio, I pushed her away in order to protect her. For those long years, I missed her with all my heart, since the days she spent at home, during Christmas holidays and summer vacations, could be counted on my fingers.

Daniela earned her diploma and returned to Cuba to enroll at the University of Havana. When she told me she was going to study chemistry, I thought my heart would burst with pride. She had such a wonderful future ahead that I panicked every time guys tried to flirt with her at the bus stop. My greatest fear was that a man would take a liking to her and steal her away from me. Of course, being the daughter of a mafioso worked in her favor in this case. Plus, Daniela was very bright, and she ignored the men's honeyed words.

No one ever tried to flirt with me anymore. My beauty had faded. The varicose vein was only one more reminder that I was on my way to becoming an old lady. Crow's feet surrounded my eyes. My buttocks and breasts weren't so firm anymore, and my waist never completely recovered its shape after I gave birth to Gabriel. César scolded me for not losing weight and not putting on antiwrinkle creams. He told me off for getting old. He was furious the little girl he had married was becoming a middle-aged woman.

My lack of interest in beauty products had one exception: the perfume from El Encanto. Putting it on was much more than a habit; it was a necessity. My skin had adopted its fragrance as the scent of my own body, and if I didn't wear it, I didn't feel entirely myself. That aroma was my shield. If I didn't have Patricio by my side, at least I could remember the sweet taste of his kisses every time I put a few drops of El Encanto on my neck or wrists.

Besides my children and the memory of Patricio, my reason for getting out of bed was the other love of my life: my star. My study of the shining point of light had kept me sane and occupied. I had only been able to study it in stolen moments with my little telescope, but over the years, I had arrived at interesting conclusions.

Thanks to the books and diagrams by Mr. Henry Norris Russell and my own observations, I realized my star was a white dwarf, which gives off bright light when it's about to explode under its own gravity.

God knows it was a wonderful sensation to think I was the only person in the whole world who knew that star existed.

CHAPTER 44

Daniela and I didn't talk about Patricio again for years. I was afraid to tell my daughter the reason we didn't go with him to Madrid. I thought it would be absolutely awful for her to know her own aunt had betrayed us. Before she went off to boarding school, all I told Daniela was that he had married another woman.

But when Daniela returned from Florida, I felt it was finally time to speak clearly and deliberately.

It was late, and César was at the Calypso. Taking advantage of his absence, I poured us a couple of glasses of rum in the living room. It still felt strange to drink with Daniela. It was so hard to believe the beautiful young woman at my side was no longer the little girl whose existence had kept me from throwing myself into the sea the day I visited the chapel of the Virgin of Regla.

"Mija, do you remember Patricio?" I asked hesitantly.

Daniela took a sip of her rum and smiled. "Of course, Mamita. Every day."

"Really?"

"Every time I look at Gabriel. His blue eyes didn't come from my grandmother, did they?"

I shook my head. My little witch had guessed the truth again.

"Does Gabriel know?" she asked me.

I shook my head again.

"And don't you think that, when he's grown, he'll have a right to know who his father is?"

She spoke so sensibly that I broke down. I began to cry and my daughter took me in her arms to comfort me. When had the little girl who used to take refuge in my arms become the person who would cradle me in hers?

"I realized I was pregnant after he had already left for Spain," I explained.

"You could write to him, you fool."

I began to hiccup from sobbing, and Daniela wiped my tears and my snot with a handkerchief. "What good would that do?"

"He could come back and get you. I never understood why he married that other woman."

"Knowing the truth would put him in danger."

I decided to be brave and tell her everything. I explained how Marita had threatened to tell César if I didn't stop seeing Patricio.

"Why didn't you tell me this back then?"

"You were just a kid, and I didn't want to turn you against your aunt."

"My aunt Marita has always had more venom than a viper."

I recognized my Lala in her words and smiled.

"Don't worry, Mamita. She'll get what's coming to her. In fact, it's already started."

"I don't understand."

"Just yesterday, my dad had a meeting with a man in the small living room, and I overheard them. The guy was a sugar baron, Nelson Suárez. They were talking about Marita. My dad told him he could marry her in exchange for a piece of his business."

I couldn't help but feel compassion toward my sister-in-law, even if she didn't deserve it. To be forced to marry someone you don't love is savage—I should know. Marita had been left without her Rubén, and

I was without Patricio. And now she would marry someone she didn't love. We were more alike all the time.

"You should've seen this guy," continued Daniela. "He had just four curly hairs on his head, big jowls, and a belly like a barrel."

"Marita could say no."

"She's a coward. She'd never go against anything her brother says. Anyway, if that big-bellied guy has any flair, maybe she could learn to love him," she declared.

I wanted to get back to the subject of Gabriel.

"You must keep Gabriel's secret," I said. "If César were to find out, he would . . ." A pair of images came to mind: César drowning Gabriel in a well as if he were a kitten, and César kicking him into a wall the way he had Canelo. The hair on my arms stood on end. "César would harm him. And he'd find Patricio and make him pay. We have to protect them by keeping the secret forever."

"Blood secrets can't be kept forever."

Daniela's words made me shiver.

"That's what Lala always said," she told me. "Blood calls blood. The day you least expect it, Patricio will realize he has a son. Life will find a way to bring them together."

"Let's hope that doesn't happen for a very long time, not until César is an old man and can't leave the old folks' home to take revenge," I said, laughter being the only way to combat my fear.

And yet, Daniela was right. Patricio returned to our lives. It happened abruptly, on a Sunday. As we had anticipated, Marita had to marry Nelson on César's advice—or order. At first, the marriage was one big drama. After the sacrifice she'd made in her youth of walking away from the heir of the chewing gum empire, Marita had imagined she'd at least go to the altar on the arm of a man who looked like a movie star. Nothing like Nelson's bald head, jowls, or belly had ever entered her fantasies.

"How can I possibly marry him?" she lamented. "He looks like a walrus! I'm even more unlucky than somebody who falls backward and breaks their nose!"

Luckily for Nelson, he was as rich as he was ugly, and his bulging wallet was more than willing to satisfy all her whims, which helped relieve much of my sister-in-law's disgust.

In addition, Nelson may not have looked like Cary Grant, but he was a hell of a good guy, and it didn't take long for Marita to discover she could maneuver him however she wanted. The combination of his money and sweetness produced a miracle in her. She was in a horrible mood the entire day of her wedding, but after a luxury honeymoon in Paris, everything changed. She went from not wanting to see him at all to being all over him.

"Oh, my precious little fatty . . . oh, my little walrus," she'd say, kissing his bald head.

We were all gathered in the living room at my house, with Marita and her husband just back from Paris and presenting the gifts they'd brought for everybody, when the phone rang.

It was sheer coincidence I answered it. Usually it would have been a housekeeper or César, but my husband was opening his gift from Paris, and the housekeeper was preparing a snack. I got up and went to get it in a really bad mood. My head pounded from having to listen to Marita go on and on about the stores in Paris.

"You should've seen those department stores: Bonmarché; La Samaritaine, which has a huge terrace up on the roof you would just die for; and Galeries Lafayette, which is the best. It has an amazing dome and box seats that completely outdo the opera!"

She was talking nonstop, interrupting her monologue only to screech with delight now and again, and all of it was making me want to kick her ass back to France.

"Hello?" I said flatly.

"Gloria?"

That voice was unforgettable. Patricio.

It had been years since I'd last heard it. I felt a wave of heat when I heard my name on his lips.

"This is she," I whispered.

"It's me," murmured Patricio.

My legs were shaking, and I swear to God I would've fallen to the floor if I hadn't leaned my back against the wall.

"Can you talk?" he asked me.

As if he'd heard, César looked over at me. Marita had brought him a tie with lilies on it. My husband raised an eyebrow angrily, as if asking, *What's going on?* I shrugged.

"No, today's not a good day," I said into the phone.

Upset that I was ignoring him, César asked, "Who's calling?"

"It's El Encanto. They want to bring over a dress I ordered," I lied, "but I don't want them to right now."

"I have to see you," Patricio said in my ear.

"I understand, but it's impossible right now."

Just to complicate things, Marita screamed at me from the sofa. "Gloria, come here, I have your gift!"

"I'm in Havana. I'm back at El Encanto," Patricio explained.

My heart skipped a beat.

"Gloria!" insisted Marita.

"It would be best for me to pick it up myself," I said into the phone. "But I don't know when that could be."

"I'll wait for you, then," Patricio promised before hanging up.

I went back to the couch with the rest of my family. Marita put my wrapped gift on my lap. "It's from Galeries Lafayette. Open it!"

I tried, but my trembling hands wouldn't cooperate.

"What's the matter with you, silly? Open it," insisted my sister-in-law.

"It's just that the wrapping paper is so pretty, I don't want to tear it," I said.

"Oh my God! Give it here."

Marita tore the paper for me. It was a beautiful bag. It was square and made of padded leather. The famous double *C* was stamped inside. Marita pointed to a little pocket on the side.

"Look at this cute little pocket. It's for lipstick."

"Chanel?"

"Yes, it's called matelassé," said Marita with a terrible French accent.

I noticed the handle was really strange. It was a long metal and leather chain. "The handle is so long."

"You don't carry it in your hand, you fool. You wear it on your shoulder! That way, your hands are free. Isn't that the most brilliant idea in the world?"

In that moment, I realized Coco Chanel had changed everything about handbags. It may not seem like a big deal to a man to have his hands free, but for women to not have to carry their bags in their hands meant a liberation of astounding proportions. I only hoped I could liberate myself from César and Marita long enough to go see Patricio.

Destiny determined that, when I saw Patricio again after so many years apart, he'd be working the perfume department.

"One bottle of El Encanto, please."

"I'm surprised you're still using that perfume," he said. His voice cracked.

Time had changed him. His hair was thinner, and he'd put on weight. His blue eyes seemed faded, but I could swear that, on seeing me, they recovered some of the intensity of his youth. In spite of the ravages of time, seeing his face again after so many years was like coming home after a long journey. Like cuddling in front of a fireplace after a snowstorm or diving into a cold pool of water after crossing the desert. His face was my home. When I realized he was looking back at me with the same fervor, I was embarrassed.

"I'm ugly," I said, blushing.

"You're beautiful," he whispered.

"I'm super ugly."

I'd spent years dreaming about a moment like this, of having Patricio in front of me, within reach. In my fantasies, I would wrap him in my arms and search for his mouth until we could melt together forever. It was a shame that, when that moment finally came, instead of throwing myself in his arms, I just babbled a bunch of stupid things.

"It's been so long," I said. "And now you're back in Havana."

"Yes, we've come back to Cuba."

Neither one of us missed that he'd used the plural. I had to ask. "So you and your wife are both back working at El Encanto?"

He nodded. "I'm a manager. And Nely is overseeing the clerks." Patricio changed the subject. "How is Daniela?"

"She's a woman now. She's in college."

"Does she remember me?"

"Of course! She's missed you very much."

"And you? Have you missed me very much?"

I couldn't answer.

We were silent. All around, life went on in spite of us. A woman was scolding her husband because he'd bought a horrible, orange-colored tie. Two little kids pulled on their dog's ears while their mother chose a hand lotion. But everyday life was like a distant rumor about a different galaxy as Patricio and I once more nodded at Einstein and stopped time, just like on every occasion when we were together.

Seeing I was speechless, Patricio decided to tell me a story.

"You know something? When I was little, there was a man in my village who lived with a bullet in his head. He'd had it since the war, when they tried to kill him. It was a metal bulge near the crown, and for five cents, he'd let you touch it. It was a miracle he could lead a normal life with that thing there. He always said his life was on loan. I want you to know your letter was a bullet in the head for me. And my life has been on loan since that cursed day when I saw you and César kissing.

You did me a lot of harm, Gloria. You hurt me terribly, but I haven't come back to reproach you or ask for explanations."

When Patricio paused, tears ran down my face.

"I've come back to ask you only one thing," he said. "Is Gabriel my son?"

CHAPTER 45

PATRICIO

"Yes," Gloria responded.

Yes.

I never imagined one word could change my life, but it did. By virtue of one word, I was now a father. The confirmation hit me so hard, I didn't know what to do. I felt a jumble of fear, luck, vertigo, euphoria, and melancholy. Soon, I discovered being a father meant feeling all those things at the same time.

Gloria's revelations didn't end there.

"I wrote that letter to protect you. Marita knew about us, and that letter was a condition so she wouldn't tell César. I've never forgotten about you, and I've never stopped using our perfume. I've missed you to death," she said in a rush, breathlessly, with the urgency with which we say things we've been waiting many years to say.

Her revelations set off another earthquake inside me. I wanted to ask her so many questions, but they got jammed, bottlenecked in my throat. This changed everything. Luckily, I managed one question, the most important one.

"Do you still love me?"

"Yes."

Another yes. The two most important yeses in my life had been pronounced by the same person in less than a minute. Two monosyllables that meant yes to life. An act of pure love without considering the consequences.

"Patricio?" said another familiar voice behind me.

Daniela had come to meet up with her mother. I was amazed to see her so much older, wearing heels instead of her school shoes.

"You're so much older that I don't know what to say. The last time we saw each other, you slept in a bed shaped like a ship, and you were crazy about pirates."

"Well, I outgrew the bed, and now it's my brother's. But I still like pirates a lot," she said with a sly shine in her beautiful green eyes.

We hugged tightly. The charming little girl who used to buy toys had turned into a marvelous young woman who'd come to buy textbooks.

By that time, a long line had formed in the perfume department, and a few people were giving us impatient looks. We had no choice but to say goodbye.

The rest of my workday was torture. My brain had turned into an endless loop that kept repeating Gloria's yeses over and over. When I left work, I took a long walk through Old Havana. Nely and I had rented an apartment on Egido Street, but I wasn't ready to face my wife yet.

I crossed Monserrate Street and went by the train station. Every time I blinked, Gloria's face would flash in front of me. Her image was permanently seared into my eyes, as if I'd been staring at the sun. My Gloria. The passage of time had given her a few lines around her eyes and mouth, which only made her more beautiful than ever. I couldn't get over the idea that we were parents. The thought that our two bodies had created a person struck me as nothing less than a miracle. Gabriel was the bond that united us and which could never be broken. And not just that, but Gloria still loved me. She'd never stopped loving me.

I felt incredibly guilty. I still loved her too. I'd spent years denying it, but I was tired of swimming against the current.

"I love Gloria," I said aloud with the seagulls as witnesses.

Admitting my feelings made me feel better, but that comfort didn't last long. Truth be told, the situation was just as impossible as it had been years before. César was more dangerous than ever, and the obstacles we faced were insurmountable. Plus, I couldn't forget that now there was someone else tangled up in all this: Nely.

Even though it would be very painful for her, it was unfair for my wife to live off the scraps of my love without knowing it. I was comfortable by her side, but I couldn't be selfish and continue misleading her. She deserved to know the truth. And although she would be furious and abandon me, she had a right to remake her life with a man who loved her as much as I loved Gloria.

I went back home determined to clear things up. I found Nely in the living room writing a slogan ("until victory") on a sign.

"I have to tell you something," I said before I lost my courage.

"Me too," she said, all giggly.

Her eyes were bright, like a pair of lanterns. If I'd spoken first, everything would have been different, but courtesy was my perdition.

"Well, you first," I said.

"I'm pregnant!" she exclaimed and followed it with her ringing laughter.

That was how Nely hitched her fate to mine and destroyed my plans.

CHAPTER 46

The whistling of fireworks filled the streets and drowned out the caw-
ing of the seagulls. The Caravan of Freedom was a sea of tanks, trucks,
horses, bikes, and people on foot. The entire city had been taken over by
this multitude of impassioned men, women, and children who waved
flags as if their very souls depended on it. Nobody wanted to miss the
arrival of the victorious revolutionaries, the heroes. They were soldiers
whose uniforms still reeked of mountain thyme, their fingernails black
with clay and their hair dusty from the roads. They had overgrown
beards, and rifles leaned on their shoulders with natural ease. When
they lined up on Missions Avenue all the way to the Presidential Palace,
people received them with applause. The march was progressing at a
turtle's pace because every few meters, soldiers would climb down from
the tanks to kiss the young women and to let themselves be kissed by the
older women. Bottles of rum were passed hand-to-hand, and complete
strangers would hug on street corners—everyone was a compañero,
compatriot, brother and sister. A swarm of photographers and television
and film crews surrounded the parade, anxious to capture every second,
drunk with importance because they knew they were caught up in a historic moment. Every few seconds, someone would scream "Viva Cuba
libre" and be rewarded with jubilant shouting. When Fidel Castro and

his entourage arrived at Camp Columbia, Movement women released a bunch of white doves, and one of them posed on Fidel's shoulder.

The people went mad.

As Cuba wrote a new page in its history, I was home, far from everything, with my baby sleeping against my chest. My son's heartbeat was more powerful than the echo of the fireworks.

Ernesto Eduardo Rubio Yamary was born on New Year's Eve in 1958, the same night Fulgencio Batista fled Havana. He was a big, beautiful, and healthy baby, with his mother's brown eyes. Nely used to joke that our child would arrive with the revolution under his arm, and she wasn't wrong.

Between pacifiers and diapers, Nely and I were witnesses to the revolutionaries' ascension to power. A Fidelista to the core, Nely was completely committed to the cause and would join the celebrations whenever possible. But I was more moved by staying at home and rocking Ernesto's cradle than by parading with my fist in the air. My son's face was all the revolution I needed. Confronted with my excitement as a new father, all of Castro's milestones faded in importance.

That's why I remembered January 2, 1959—the day Camilo Cienfuegos and Che entered Havana with numerous columns of men after a six-week march from Las Villas—as the day we came home with the baby in our arms.

While Manuel Urrutia began his presidency and Fidel Castro settled in to being commander-in-chief of the armed forces, Ernesto learned to laugh, chirp, sit up in his crib, and grip our fingers with the strength of a small titan.

The day the agrarian reform was declared—May 17th, 1959— peasants swarmed the city and took over the Plaza de la Revolución, climbing the lampposts as if they were palm trees, but Ernesto was teething and he was in so much pain, we could only get him to sleep by dipping his pacifiers in chamomile.

By the time the Cubans and the Russians had reestablished diplomatic relations, Ernesto had graduated from the bottle to baby food. His big favorite was watermelon with mango and banana. His least favorite, apple.

On my days off, I would take little Ernesto to La Pekinesa. He would fall happily asleep in his basket in the shade of the tamarind tree. The noise from the revelers never bothered him; to the contrary, laughter, music, and the clinking of glasses were better sedatives for him than any lullaby.

Reuniting with my friends had been one of the great joys of returning to the island. In the years we had been separated, their lives had changed drastically. For starters, the two owned their own businesses. El Grescas had continued running La Pekinesa, and Guzmán had bought the Garbo shoe store after its owner retired.

Both of my friends had also tied the knot. El Grescas had married María José Alvés, whom they called Ajo. She was a Cuban girl to be reckoned with, one who really lived up to that old saying: "Cuban with a delightful waist and a smooth and graceful gait." Long-legged and with dark hair parted on the side, she resembled Ava Gardner to a degree that was, at the very least, curious. In keeping with the harshness of her nickname—*Ajo* means *garlic*—she could be as thick and stubborn as her husband, and her pats on the back were as lethal as Grescas's, or even more. They were made for each other, and there was no greater proof than the fact that their union had already produced four children: Alba, Bartolomé, Cristina, and Dolores. The García Alvéses baptized their children in alphabetical order and aspired to get through the entire alphabet.

If Grescas had been lucky, Guzmán had also found—the phrase never so apt—his matching shoe to make a pair. His wife, Reina Miller, was as short as he was and just as well mannered and charming. With her blond hair, light eyes, and curvy body, she seemed like the typical

American. The daughter of a Cuban woman and an American man from Oregon, she worked as an English professor at an academy. In contrast to Grescas and Ajo, who showed their love by arguing at the top of their lungs, Guzmán and Reina were two quiet little creatures who, in spite of being married, continued to address each other with the more formal address: "usted."

Guzmán and Grescas told me that, when they first fell in love with their respective partners, they'd worried the two women wouldn't get along. But their concerns were in vain. Reina and Ajo were the best of friends from the moment they met. Ajo thought Reina was classy and was fascinated by her, and Reina admired Ajo's natural ease, which translated into hours and hours of confidences, laughter, and a good many sessions of putting their respective husbands in their places.

Among my colleagues at the store, Ernesto became the unofficial mascot. They had all been happy about our return to Cuba, and even more happy when they had learned we had a bun in the oven, a new little baby for the family. Although there was a notable exception to our welcome wagon: Don Gato.

I may have gotten older in my years away from Havana, but Carlos Duarte had mummified. He had lines from worry and bitterness on his brow and around his mouth. His mustache was still notable, but it was now completely white, and he didn't twist it with the same vigor when he found something disagreeable. Time had not diminished his antipathy toward me one bit, especially when he found out I'd be a store manager and, as a result, his immediate supervisor.

His son, Silvestre, had also continued working at the store. During the years Nely and I had been in Madrid, Silvestre had been promoted from cannonball to stock boy, and if he hadn't gotten any further, it was because of laziness and his argumentative personality. Given the generous disposition of the owners, to have only been promoted that far was quite a feat. It meant he had to be a complete zero. Physically, he was still the same clumsy kid who looked like a crow and had stained Frank Sinatra's shoes. In other words, a bird of ill omen.

Luckily, my job protected me from them. They couldn't be directly disrespectful, but they never ceased their hateful looks and their grumbling. Since it wasn't in my character to dwell on people who weren't important to me, I stopped thinking about them. Don Gato and his son were a necessary evil, but I never considered them dangerous. That was one of my many mistakes.

The store had a huge daycare for its employees' kids—an enormous and well-lit space on the building's top floor under the supervision of Mrs. Remedios, a very pretty fat woman—which is why Nely and I never had to take time off work to care for our son. I would frequently take five-minute breaks in the middle of the day just to watch him play or sleep or eat or simply breathe. He'd definitely put a spell on me. The only thing that would tarnish my happiness was the knowledge that Ernesto was not an only child; although he didn't know it, he had a half brother.

Gloria only stopped by the store every once in a while. We hadn't talked again since the day she told me Gabriel was my son. But now Marita was not the reason for our distance. After she got married, César's sister had loosened the fierce watch she'd kept over her sister-in-law. No, this time, I was responsible for our estrangement. Ernesto's birth had tossed my plans into disarray and created a close bond with him and his mother.

My conversation with Gloria after I found out Nely was pregnant was one of the most prickly I've had in my whole life. To make things even worse, it took place in the children's department, where Gloria had gone to buy Gabriel a new pair of pajamas.

"Congratulations," muttered Gloria when I told her. Her voice was choked with so many emotions—melancholy, sadness, joy, jealousy—that the word escaped her lips like a hard pebble.

"The truth is, I don't know how I should feel," I confessed. "Ever since Nely told me, I've been going crazy. Of course I'm happy. There are mornings I get up, and I just wanna hug the lampposts. But other mornings I'm filled with a tremendous fear. There are times when I feel such pressure in my chest, I think I'm having a stroke."

In spite of how strange and uncomfortable it was, Gloria chuckled.

"What you're feeling is called being a father," she said tenderly. "What, you think these nine months of pregnancy are just about the baby?"

Her brown eyes looked at me with such intensity that I had to make a great effort to respond.

"It's not just that. I feel like I'm deceiving Nely. I should have never married her. I love you. I should be with you," I stammered. "We were so close, Gloria!"

Because I couldn't contain myself, I touched her cheek with my hand. The feel of her skin was like a spark on my fingertips. My fingers traced her face from her cheek to her mouth. I circled her lips with my index finger . . . they were soft, thick, hot . . . and then Gloria pushed my hand away when another customer approached a nearby display of strollers.

"We can never be together, Patricio," whispered Gloria. "No matter how much we tell ourselves otherwise, this is something we've known from the start."

"And Gabriel? Don't you think having a child together changes things?" I protested.

"If you want to be a good father to Gabriel, you'll help me protect him from César."

"How? What do I have to do?"

"Nothing," she said. "That's the hardest part. Nothing. So long as César thinks Gabriel is his, he won't hurt him. Simply put, help me keep the secret. Do you promise?"

Gloria took my face in her hands, and I managed to nod. "Listen to me," she whispered. "Now you have to be happy. For your new baby. When you see his face, everything will be easier. You'll see."

Gloria was right, like always. Once Ernesto arrived, it helped mask the chronic pain of not being able to be with her, and it helped me to not think about it for months. But it couldn't last. It was like a bucket under a dripping faucet: sooner or later, it would overflow and flood the floor.

CHAPTER 47

I was in my office one afternoon, finishing up the weekly inventory, when I got an urgent call from Aquilino Entrialgo.

Aquilino hadn't had any problems negotiating my return to El Encanto. Like a good West Indian, Aquilino understood being homesick for Cuba, and he didn't ask the reasons for my return.

"Paisanu! How go the scarf sales?" he joked by way of greeting.

I looked out the window and laughed. The sun was beating down so hard, the pedestrians—the women with umbrellas and the men with wide-brimmed hats—crowded into what little shade was available.

"They're selling like hotcakes," I replied. "Thanks to El Encanto, not a single resident of Havana will catch a cold."

"Listen, I need you to keep the store open an extra hour tonight. There's a very important customer coming."

"Of course. May I ask who it is?"

"Che. Ernesto Guevara."

As soon as the last customer left that afternoon, El Encanto prepared for the arrival of the comandante.

The jittery clerks gossiped among themselves as if we were expecting a movie star. His most feverish supporters, like my Nely, were on the verge of keeling over. There were exceptions to the excitement, though. Don Gato and a little group of workers still nostalgic for Batista's government got together and declared that they wanted to go home. I gave them permission to do so. I didn't want to have a political debate, and I wasn't going to risk them attending to Che with ill humor.

"I'd rather cut off my hand than shake that butcher's," said Silvestre, trying to rile up his coworkers.

"The comandante is a hero," another clerk yelled out.

"A hero who executes the opposition!"

"They were war criminals!"

I cut off the discussion right there and then. "Enough! Outside of El Encanto, you can express your opinion however you want. Here, he is just a man whom we will treat with respect, the way we treat all our customers."

But as soon as he came through the door, it was clear Che was no ordinary man. He looked exactly like the hundreds of photographs that had appeared in the newspapers: he was dressed in a military uniform with a cigar in his mouth. His long hair and beard gave him a wild and leonine look. What was most impressive about him was his gaze. There was a ferocity and an energy in his eyes that exceeded his mere presence. The guy was boiling inside.

I stretched my hand to him as a matter of courtesy and noticed his hands were rough and calloused. Those hands had lived many lives.

"Welcome, Comandante. How can we be of assistance?" I said.

"I need a new coat."

"Of course. Come with me, please."

Che followed me toward the English Room. Behind him, men stood at attention, and women gazed at him with desire. The comandante responded by waving and shaking hands. It took us forever to get through the store. Everybody wanted a piece of him: a look, a word, a gesture . . . as is the case with every celebrity, what was pure routine for Che would, for those people, be a legendary meeting to tell their descendants about.

After his triumphant march through El Encanto, Che and I arrived in the English Room and were finally alone.

"What type of coat are you looking for?" I asked.

"Nothing too elaborate. I just need it to protect me from rain and wind, that's all."

Suddenly, I noticed something. A small detail. Tiny. But once I noticed, I couldn't help but stare. There was a little piece of lettuce in his teeth that made him seem as gap-toothed as El Grescas.

Ernesto "Che" Guevara had a paluego stuck in his teeth. I couldn't help it. I started to laugh, and the harder I tried to contain my laughter, the worse it got. Che looked at me with curiosity. I was afraid he'd think I was being disrespectful, but he was simply intrigued.

"What's going on?" he asked.

"I'm sorry, Comandante . . . ," I stammered. "Mr. Guevara . . . it's just . . ."

My nervous laughter just kept coming. The worst of it was that my laughter was contagious, and now Che was also smiling more and more. And the more he laughed, the more I could see his teeth, and the more I could see his teeth, the more I could see the lettuce, which made me laugh again.

"Tell me," he insisted.

"You have a piece of lettuce between your teeth," I managed to say.

Che looked in one of the mirrors and, to my infinite relief, burst out laughing once again.

"This is from my lunch! Can you believe nobody has said anything to me all afternoon? And I met with the entire cabinet. What blockheads!" he exclaimed, but he wasn't in the least bit angry.

"Don't be too hard on them. It can't be easy to tell a legend he has something in his teeth."

Che laughed again. "And what is your name?"

"Patricio."

"I'm no legend, Patricio! As you so kindly pointed out, I had a piece of lettuce in my teeth. I also sweat, burp, and fart. I'm just a shirtless guy who needs a coat."

It was obvious he was speaking from the heart. Just then, I had the closest thing to a presentiment that I've ever had in my life. I sensed that humility, that modesty, would be the ruin of this man. Some revolutionaries could exchange the jungle for a comfortable armchair, but not Che. That man would follow his destiny to victory or death. I shuddered and tried to close down those thoughts. My mission was not to philosophize about life but to make sure Che was satisfied with his purchase, which was no small thing.

"Let's find you the perfect coat," I said, returning his smile.

The perfect coat turned out to be a vinyl jacket that zipped all the way up to the neck, with black details around the collar and shoulders. Che was so happy, he left wearing it.

Some months later, the French freighter *La Coubre* blew up in the port of Havana. Castro and Guevara accused the CIA of sabotage and came up with the slogan, "Homeland or death." But for me, the day was historic for other reasons. At the time of the explosion, I was feeding Ernesto a snack out on the balcony. A column of smoke rose to the sky, and the boy pointed to it with his little hand. Then he reached for me.

"Papa," he said, for the very first time.

Later, when Ernesto was old enough to pee in the toilet instead of his diaper, the United States imposed an economic blockade, and the militias went into permanent alarm.

The revolution also caused infinite arguments in my marriage. When the blockade made it so I couldn't find powdered milk or my baby's favorite crackers, I was furious.

"Who cares about some crackers when we've managed to be free?" Nely would say, trying to be conciliatory.

"That's little comfort when the baby is throwing a tantrum," I would counter.

"Ernesto will learn not to sell out to the Americans just for a treat."

"He's just a boy who wants his crackers, Nely. He nourishes himself with milk and crackers, not political ideals."

"The blockade won't last forever."

"And what if one day he needs medicine?"

"Don't be such a downer."

The disagreements continued. One day, Nely cut out a photo of Che. In the image—a photo taken by Alberto Korda—Che is gazing out to infinity during the funeral for the victims of *La Coubre*. He's wearing the jacket he bought at El Encanto. However much he may not have considered himself a legend, history was determined to make him one.

CHAPTER 48

"They say they're gonna nationalize all the businesses," said Guzmán during one of our long sessions at La Pekinesa.

I'd also heard the rumor. In fact, trying to butter up the new government, El Encanto had taken out a huge ad with a photograph of Fidel Castro expressing "eternal gratitude to the heroes who liberated us."

"Well, that's all right by me, camarada," said El Grescas.

"Don't call me camarada," Guzmán replied. "That's what Fidel's people say."

"And proudly! I'm telling you, we could stand to have a Fidel in Spain to kick that bastard Franco's ass."

"Fascism and communism are almost the same thing, don't you know that?"

"Don't talk like that. How can you compare a dictatorship with the power of the people?"

"The people? The stores are gonna end up in the hands of Castro's people, just you watch. These liberators are a gang of opportunists."

"Man, you're really asking for a Cuban beating . . . it's just a matter of time!" threatened El Grescas.

But Guzmán's words came true October 13, 1960, when the new president, Osvaldo Dorticós, and the prime minister, Fidel Castro, signed a bill into law expropriating and nationalizing all industry and commercial enterprises on the island. Among these were Fin de Siglo, El Encanto, and thirteen other department stores.

The new regime brought many changes. The first was a duty to report all activities to a committee. Although we'd always treated all our customers equally, El Encanto's luxury products didn't really go well with the new revolutionary ideas about austerity. The US embargo also interfered with many things. Our loyal customers continued coming, but there were fewer and fewer exclusive products every day. It was just a question of time before we turned into another supply store.

For me, the beginning of the end came when Manet decided to leave the store and go live in New York so he could continue designing.

"Don't leave, maestro," I pleaded with him when I found out. "Don't you realize those New York women will never be able to show off your dresses with the same sexy charm as the Cubans?"

Manet gave me a sad smile. "Look around you, Patricio. The women in Havana no longer dress like peacocks but like sparrows."

When I left work that afternoon, I sat down on a bench to watch the people go by. I had no choice but to admit Manet was right. Havana's famous color had vanished. Ever since the revolution, whoever wasn't wearing a uniform had adopted new tones: browns, grays, cream.

The day Manet left for the United States, the orders for olive-green fabric went through the roof at El Encanto. In a blink, the army and its sympathizers went through our supply.

Fidel's ascent to power also brought with it a promise to get rid of the mafia. What little was left of the aristocracy on the island would get together at the Calypso, its last bastion, which, until then, had been left alone by the new order. And then one night, the two worlds collided. Guzmán and Reina had been having drinks at a nearby cantina and witnessed the whole thing.

The brawl began when some militia members made their way to the club door, and one of César's security guards denied them entrance.

"No bearded guys in the club."

"What's the problem, compañero? We're well groomed, our boots are shiny, and our coats are new."

"I don't like your looks; that's the problem."

"No need to get mad, compañero. We're just here to have a few daiquiris," said the militiaman.

"Well, you can drink them on whatever dirty block you live on." The doorman then spat in his face.

And that spit was the straw that broke the camel's back. The militia guys and the doormen ended up in a fistfight worthy of a saloon brawl in a wild American Western.

"I shit on your mother! And you're going with me to the station right now."

"Get your paws off me!"

There were many more Fidel supporters than there were doormen. The fight provoked panic among the clubgoers, and César himself had to go out to try and smooth things over.

"What's the problem?" asked César.

"Your workers are gonna spend a little time in jail," answered the militiaman.

"I wanna talk with your supervisor," demanded César, too angry to be submissive. "Call Commissioner Heredía."

"Heredía's been fired. We're the police now, and we answer only to the people."

César changed tactics and pulled a bill from his wallet.

"Surely there's some way to fix this," he insinuated.

"There is. As soon as people like you get it through their heads that things have changed."

"People like me?"

César was livid. Just a few months ago, he would have killed the man right there, without caring about the dozens of witnesses. But without corrupt cops or judges to protect him, he could no longer murder with impunity.

"You're just the little shits Batista let hang out by his side."

That militiaman had verbalized what the entire city already knew: César was no longer a god. The rumors about his diminished power ran like wildfire, and his enemies had begun to circle like vultures. César was a wounded animal. And it's important to remember that an animal is most dangerous when it's injured.

CHAPTER 49

March 5, 1961, marked the date of the final postwinter clearance sales—sales we all suspected would be the very last. If things were tense out in the street, El Encanto itself had become a battleground. Every employee had an opinion, and there was tremendous animosity between the groups that supported the revolution and those that didn't. Don Gato was among the most exalted of those nostalgic for Batista's regime.

"These shitty commies! They've fucked us, and they're gonna fuck us some more," he used to say, foaming at the mouth.

"You're against social justice, compañero? Because the store is now in the hands of working people." Nely would always get in the ring to hit back at him.

"What bothers me is that the government has us on a month-to-month employment contract. And that our pensions are going into the dirty pockets of that bearded gangster and his friends."

"The only gangster here is the little peasant from Banes who has fled the country with his tail between his legs," Nely said, taunting him by referring to ex-president Batista.

Don Gato didn't just voice his complaints. It was rumored his son, Silvestre, had become affiliated with the Movement to Save the People, a group of counterrevolutionaries opposed to Castro, controlled by the CIA, and led by President Eisenhower himself. Groups like this perpetrated violent acts all over Havana, and it was best to not joke around in their presence.

The other people who weren't into much joking around were the few bourgeois still left in Havana. They all came to the sales to acquire what few luxury products we had left.

Opening the doors on sales days had always been emotional. Customers would line up from the wee hours, and as soon as we opened, they'd rush into the store like little kids racing to hunt tadpoles in a creek. The store's nurse—Celia, a woman so sweet, more than one customer had faked heatstroke just so he could be under her loving care—always had extra work on sales days: twisted ankles, bruises from collisions with the counters, and all sorts of scrapes from the occasional malicious shove. Luckily for us, most people considered it all part of the fun.

But those last sales days were different. People were ill-humored, and irritation far outweighed understanding. Marita and Gloria were among the grouchiest customers. While Marita elbowed her way to the counter for the last silk handkerchiefs, Gloria came up to me. Behind us, a group was fighting over some handbags and managed to knock down a shelf with a loud bang.

"Our world is falling apart," I said.

"It's the end of an era," Gloria agreed, nodding.

"Are you worried?"

Gloria shrugged and looked at me with complicity. "Do you know what Albert Einstein said? That politics don't last long, but an equation is forever. I know it's selfish, but so long as they leave me alone with my books, I don't care who's in charge of the government."

Marita shot us a look. She didn't like it one bit that we were talking, but she didn't come over to interrupt because it would mean not getting one of the very last calfskin handbags on sale. I looked around.

"Where's César?" I asked.

"In New York," answered Gloria. "He's trying to get his American friends to help him find a way to keep the Calypso."

I nodded. The remaining hotels and the casinos were about to be nationalized. Lansky had even lost the Riviera Hotel.

"What did you come to buy?" I asked Gloria.

"My perfume. Every bottle you can find."

While I was getting her order ready, Daniela came to say hi to me.

"Patricio! You look good; give me a hug! Do you know the other day I taught Gabriel to make a shadow puppet of a dog on the wall?" she said, winking at me.

I hadn't realized it, but Gabriel was hiding behind his older sister's skirt. The little boy looked at me shyly. Seeing myself reflected in his blue eyes overwhelmed me with sadness and warmth. I noticed he had a little matchbox in his hand, and I knelt so I could talk to him at his level.

"What do you have there, Gabriel?"

"A beetle."

"Will you show it to me?"

The boy watched me for a minute and decided he could trust me because he opened the little box. There was a shiny green beetle inside, about the size of a button. Gabriel closed the matchbox quickly before it could get away.

"Do you know what beetles eat?" he asked me.

"Fruit?" I guessed. "The truth is, I don't know."

"Me either. Do you think they might like french fries?"

"I'm sure they do."

"Then I'll give him french fries so he can grow big, really big, like a horse. And I'll tame him, and I'll get a saddle so I can ride him," he said, getting excited.

His enthusiasm was contagious, and Gloria and Daniela and I all had a good laugh.

"He's certainly not lacking in imagination," I said proudly.

"He's always been a dreamer." And then she whispered in my ear, "Like his father. Let's hope fate smiles on him."

Seeing them there, the three of them together, a thought entered my head like a worm invading an apple. Gloria, Daniela, and Gabriel— they were my other family. God and society might say you could only have one, but for me, in my heart, I knew we shared a parallel universe every second of our lives.

Reality put my feet back on the ground when Nely and Ernesto, my official family, showed up. It was lunchtime, and we'd agreed to go eat together. My wife greeted me with a kiss and handed me the baby.

"This is Ernesto? He's huge!" said Gloria. "Can I hold him?" she asked, unable to contain herself.

"Of course."

I placed him in her arms, and Gloria snuggled him as if he were her own. "Look at those cheeks! You're a little man!"

Delighted, Ernesto responded to Gloria with a happy gurgle. Gloria kissed his little hands and squeezed his bare little feet.

"Your little feet are so cold, just like your papa's," she said without thinking.

It was such a casual comment, I hoped Nely wouldn't notice, but my wife furrowed her brow.

"It's true," said Nely, a little suspicious. "Patricio always has cold feet."

There was a silence that followed, even cooler than my feet, in which Gloria and I only made things worse by not offering any kind of explanation.

"How do you know that about my husband?" Nely asked.

Gloria gulped and looked to me for help. But my mind was blank. Luckily—or unfortunately—Daniela's scream interrupted our conversation. Gabriel had fainted in her arms.

We all crowded around him. Not knowing what to do, Daniela had cradled him in her lap and begun to fan him with her hand.

"He just fell all of a sudden. Mercifully, I caught him just before he hit the floor."

"Don't move him. It's probably just heatstroke. I'm gonna go get the nurse," Nely said.

Gloria and I knelt next to Gabriel. The boy was pale, his lips white and bloodless.

"He's been complaining about being dizzy for the last few days," said Gloria, worried. "But I didn't think it was anything."

"It isn't; you'll see."

The nurse, Celia, came right away and examined the boy. She took his pulse, checked his heartbeat, and tried, unsuccessfully, to bring him to.

"Don't worry, but I'm going to call an ambulance," she declared.

A bit later, the paramedics made their way through the store, cutting a path through the crowds of customers until they got to us. When they lifted the boy up to the stretcher, the matchbox slid from his hand and fell to the floor.

The beetle fled from his prison and disappeared under the tie counter.

CHAPTER 50

The ambulance transferred Gabriel to the hospital on Carlos III Avenue. We had hoped the doctors would only keep him for a bit, but it turned out his fainting spell was a symptom of something more serious. The doctors ran tests, but they couldn't figure out what was wrong. Two days later, Gabriel was still in the hospital. Gloria and Daniela were out of their minds with worry. Marita tried to call César, but when she reached his hotel in New York, they told her he had already checked out. After much insistence, she discovered he had gone to Las Vegas, probably to meet with the West Coast crime kings.

Luckily, before Marita could actually reach him, Gloria told me she convinced her to not say anything.

"Don't you think he deserves to know his son is in the hospital?" Marita asked.

"Why do you want to cause him unnecessary anguish? From the United States, he can't do anything but worry, and by the time he gets back to Havana, Gabriel will already have recuperated," argued Gloria, trying to be sensible.

"And what if he doesn't?"

"For the love of God, don't be such a vulture."

"Maybe what you really don't want is for me to tell him that fleabag of a clerk spends all day visiting the boy at the hospital."

That was a poison dart. Gloria knew that Marita had always suspected Gabriel's real parentage, but now her position was quite clear.

"You could tell him that, yes," answered Gloria without getting ruffled. "That is, if you want to hurt him. What I mean is, a scandal like that could seriously damage the reputation of the entire Valdés family, starting with César. And we all know just how understanding César can be when he's enraged, right, little sister-in-law?"

Marita bit her tongue. Gloria had turned the situation around and won the battle.

"Or," continued Gloria, "we could just stay quiet and keep up appearances as well as we can. Make it so no matter how hot it gets, there's no smoke to give us away, right?"

With a snort, Marita turned her head.

"If we're dealing in proverbs, let me offer you one: the goat that breaks the drum pays for it with his own skin." Every now and then, the peasant in Marita revealed itself. "I just hope we never have to regret any of this."

The upside to César's absence was that I could take my rightful place as Gabriel's father and be at the hospital the whole time. Gloria, Daniela, and I took turns so the boy was never alone or scared. Being sick was "deadly dull"—Gabriel's words—but the situation always got better when we used a little bit of imagination. And that wasn't something my son or I were ever lacking. When we were alone in his room, the syringes became dinosaur-sized mosquitoes, the bandages had once belonged to Egyptian mummies, and the cotton balls were camouflaged cotton candy. The man in the bed next to Gabriel, with both legs in plaster casts, was actually a centaur who'd had his horse parts removed. The nurses were divided between good and bad fairies, depending on how skillful they were at taking blood.

The doctor in charge of Gabriel's case finally told us he had a diagnosis. Dr. Juan Cruz was a middle-aged man with swinging jowls and droopy eyes that made him look like a basset hound. He was one of the best doctors in Cuba and had earned Gabriel's affection by letting him play with the stethoscope every time he came by. With his excellent bedside manner and dedication, he had won our trust completely.

Dr. Cruz took us into his office to talk. He didn't beat around the bush.

"Gabriel has a serious blood disorder," he said. "I've only seen one other case like it; they called it sea in the blood or Mediterranean anemia."

Gloria and I clutched each other's hands.

"What can we do?" I asked.

"Usually, I'd recommend a blood transfusion, but Gabriel's situation is much too serious. There's one other option, but I don't want to give you false hope. It's an experimental treatment that was recently developed by a French doctor named Georges Mathé, at a hospital in New York. It's called a bone marrow transplant."

"Please try it," pleaded Gloria.

"There's another problem. The bone marrow donor has to be a close relative. Male, if possible. In Gabriel's case, we think the ideal donor would be his father. But, from what I understand, his father is traveling out of the country."

Gloria and I glanced at each other. We had to choose between keeping our secret and saving Gabriel's life. But we didn't even need to discuss it; the decision was already made.

"I'm his real father," I confessed.

The doctor kept quiet for a few seconds. I was afraid he was judging us or about to say something hurtful. Instead, he nodded quietly.

"Then we're in luck. Gabriel has a chance," he said with a smile.

As soon as we stepped out of the doctor's office, Gloria and I hugged in despair. Our legs were trembling so much that if we hadn't each had the other to hold us up, we might both have fallen to the floor.

Dr. Cruz scheduled the operation for two days later. He would be in charge of the procedure himself. After we left his office, while Gloria went to rest, I went back down to Gabriel's room.

When I told him he was going to have surgery, he looked at me, his eyes wide open.

"Is it gonna hurt?" he asked, a little scared.

"You won't even know it's happening. And you know what? I'm gonna have surgery too. So we both have to be very brave."

"If you're brave, then I'm brave."

"That's what I like to hear. I brought you something."

I gave him his little matchbox. "There's something inside you're gonna like. But you can only open it after the operation."

The boy looked at me, excited. "Is it another beetle?"

"Maybe. Or maybe it's an elephant," I said, trying to sound mysterious.

"You can't fit an elephant in a matchbox!"

"You can if it's a magic elephant. But I think it's probably something else."

"Is it a dragon?"

"Maybe."

"A whale?"

"Maybe."

"Is it true you're my real father?"

Caught off guard, I didn't know how to respond at first. But I decided not to lie to him. "It's true. How did you know?"

"I heard when Mamita told Daniela. They thought I was asleep, but I just had my eyes closed. Is it a secret?"

I nodded. "Do you think it's all right that I'm your real dad?"

The boy thought about it for a few seconds. "Is my mom still my mom?"

"Of course."

"Is my sister still my sister?"

"Your mom and your sister will always be your mom and your sister."

My answer seemed to satisfy him.

"Then it's fine by me," he declared.

I gave him a kiss and tucked him in. Before he fell asleep, he shook the little matchbox and put it up to his ear.

"I hope it's a dragon," he said.

The night before the operation, Nely was waiting for me when I got home. Ever since Gabriel had been admitted to the hospital, we hadn't had a chance to talk. Nely was always asleep—or pretended to be—when I got home, and we avoided each other during the day. We both understood that what was waiting for us was the most difficult confrontation of our marriage.

As soon as I sat down, Nely began to talk.

"In the movies, the wives find out the husbands haven't been true to them because they find lipstick stains on shirt collars or suspicious dry-cleaning receipts. How did that woman know your feet are always cold?"

It was not, by any stretch, the best conversation for me to engage in the night before undergoing a risky procedure. But it was also the conversation we had to have. I couldn't help but think there was a chance I'd die on the operating table, and as a result, I could take the secret to my grave. But that wouldn't have been fair to Nely, so I spilled the beans, like the culprit confessing his sins to a priest so he'll get last rites.

"Gloria and I once spent the night together at El Encanto."

Nely's face couldn't hide the pain, as if she'd just bitten into a piece of ice.

"I don't need any details," she said with her usual directness. "Please, let's not make this harder than it has to be. Just answer with a simple yes or no. Were you lovers?"

"It was before we got married," I said, trying to explain.

"A simple yes or no," she said, interrupting me again.

"Yes."

"You do know she is César Valdés's wife?"

"Yes."

"That boy at the hospital, the one with the blue eyes, is he yours?"

"Yes."

It felt like I was slaughtering her. Every word out of my mouth was a bullet that hit its target.

"Do you love me?" asked Nely.

"Yes."

"And do you love her too?"

"Yes."

"More than you love me?"

I didn't answer. I knew the answer to that last question was yes as well and that it would be the bullet that shattered her heart. The one that killed her. I couldn't pull the trigger.

But it wasn't necessary because my eyes gave me away. Without a word, Nely shifted her gaze and didn't speak to me again.

I spent the rest of the night in Ernesto's room, holding my baby. The idea of making him an orphan tormented me, but the decision had been made. If it had been Ernesto who needed my bone marrow, I wouldn't have hesitated to do the same for him. At daybreak, I left him in his crib and went to the hospital.

The next few days were foggy for me. I was drowsy, and there were a lot of needles. There were needles in my arms and, especially, in my back. When they took me to the operating room, the face mask through which I got the anesthesia smelled like apple juice mixed with hydrogen peroxide. I inhaled and a few blood-colored spirals began to whirl in front of my eyes until I fainted.

When I woke up, it could have been minutes or years later. My mouth was sticky, and I couldn't talk or open my eyes. I concentrated on listening, trying to figure out if some sound might give me a clue as to whether it was day or night. I made out the sound of buses out on the streets and figured it must be daytime. I could also hear the laughter and clatter of kids playing ball. When I moaned, I felt a cold hand on my hot forehead.

"Easy . . . everything's okay . . . easy now."

I breathed in mariposa perfume and knew Gloria was with me.

"How's Gabriel?" I managed to say.

"He's resting. The operation went marvelously."

As soon as I heard this, I disappeared once again into the fog.

In the following days, Gloria became my connection to the world. She fed me and kissed me as I regained my strength. The fact that Gabriel was also getting well was my best medicine.

During my convalescence, Grescas and Guzmán came to see me and brought news. They told me they'd gone to see Nely to let her know my surgery had gone well, but she had refused to open the door.

When they saw my distress, they made an effort to talk about happier things. This included the news that El Grescas and Ajo were going to be parents again. Their fifth child, so the name would start with the letter *E*.

"Have you picked out a name?"

"Elena if it's a girl, Eduardo if it's a boy. Soon we'll get to Zacarias."

I looked over at Guzmán. "What about you and Reina? When are you gonna have a baby?"

"Babies will have to wait. There's something I need to tell you. Reina and I are leaving for the United States. We're going to Miami. And guess what? I managed to get a hold of Rita, the dancer from the Calypso, and she's waiting for us with open arms."

The news stunned us. El Grescas, no lover of surprises, responded by pinching Guzmán.

"Are you crazy? How can you desert the revolution?" he scolded. "Are you gonna go kiss Uncle Sam's ass?"

"This is the time to leave," Guzmán said in his defense. "Before things get really difficult."

"Difficult? Free education, housing for everyone, free transportation to get to work . . ." El Grescas was indignant with his friend's decision.

"I hope I'm wrong, but I don't think we'll be able to get ahead here."

"Don't be such a sellout."

"Here's the little Asturian come to give me lessons on patriotism. I'll remind you that I'm the one who was born in Cuba."

"Worm!"

"Commie!"

I interrupted the argument the way Grescas would have: by pinching both of my friends on the arm.

"Knock it off, assholes! Are you seriously gonna let this political shit come between us?" I looked at both my friends. "Us! We've shared fleas, hunger, long nights, and all sorts of successes, just like the Three Musketeers, right?"

Guzmán and El Grescas looked back at me like two repentant kids and shook hands to call a truce.

"Always," they said in chorus.

Awkwardly, because I could barely sit up in bed, we came together for a three-way hug.

I was released from the hospital the following day, and to celebrate, Gloria and I went to see Gabriel. The boy had to stay in the hospital a couple more days, but Dr. Cruz assured us he was out of danger. Thanks to my bone marrow, he was getting better. As soon as he saw me, my son pulled out the matchbox from the pocket of his pajamas.

"Can I open it now?" he asked, as happily as if it were Christmas.

"Yes."

I was expecting him to be disappointed. Obviously, there was nothing in the matchbox; it had been a ruse so his curiosity would keep him from thinking about the operation. I got ready for his disappointment, but the boy opened the matchbox and yelped with joy.

"It's a dragon! I knew it!"

And now it was my turn to be surprised. "But the box is empty."

"Because it's an invisible dragon!"

Gloria and I looked at each other and laughed.

"You're certainly a dreamer, just like your father," said Gloria, and then kissed each of us.

We didn't realize it yet, but the real dragon was about to arrive. César had returned to Cuba.

CHAPTER 51

GLORIA

The storms in Havana were the most beautiful in all the tropics. Like a natural opera, a Cuban storm was powerful and came in acts. The performance usually coincided with siesta time, in the early hours of the afternoon. The first signs were that the cicadas stopped singing and the earthworms wriggled to the surface, followed by the smell of wet earth that infused everything, even if the sky was still blue. The wind would gain force: it would start as a powerful breeze that shook the tree branches and rattled the dry leaves, becoming a gust that snatched men's hats and played with women's skirts. At that moment, both animals and vegetables prepared themselves for the onslaught. Canaries would stiffen in their little cages, flowers would grip their petals, and little kids would hold on to their ladybugs. The storm would then attack with a furious thunder that sounded like war drums. The sky went from gray to charred black, and the clouds would turn angry, desperate to throw off the reins. That was the last moment before the tempest, when women would look out their windows and call to the kids: "Hey, come in before you get drenched!" And in the animal world, mothers would grab their cubs by the neck and shelter them back in the dens.

And then, finally, it would rain. It would be a furious, savage, uncompromising rain. It would be a rain so thick, the peasants couldn't see a foot in front of their faces; the drops were as big as mango seeds. The sky would get so dark, it would turn to night in the middle of the day. Out on the streets, the cars would pull over, seeking refuge, and in homes everywhere, people would gather at the windows. The bravest among us—like Marita and I, that one time—would go out and play in the downpour. The storm's climax would last only ten minutes, but there would be so much lightning, it would feel like the end of the world. Until, as quickly as it began, it would end. It would suddenly stop raining, the clouds would evaporate, and the sky would turn a beautiful turquoise blue. Havana would be refreshed and cleansed, and only the puddles would serve as evidence that, an instant before, there had been a flood of biblical proportions.

Just like those afternoon rains, César's return was as abrupt as his departure. In fact, I found out he was back because of the staff, whom I saw unpacking his luggage.

"Where's my husband?" I asked.

"He said to tell you he was at the Calypso, miss. He'll come back for lunch," said one of the housekeepers.

Fear paralyzed me. Even though he had been in the United States, César had eyes and ears all over Havana, and Patricio and I hadn't been at all discreet during our hospital visits. Had he found out anything? I had no choice but to swallow my pride and ask Havana's biggest gossip: my sister-in-law.

Marita and her husband also lived in Miramar, in a California-style house with a great courtyard that led to the swimming pool. She received me wearing a white dress with matching cotton gloves. That caught my attention. It was incredibly hot, and I wondered how she could not be dying from wearing those gloves, but I told myself it was nothing. Marita was so crazy, she always favored fashion over common sense.

"César is back in Havana," I said.

"I know," she replied. "He came to see me, to ask me what's new since he's been gone."

"Did you tell him Patricio had surgery to save Gabriel?"

Marita shook her head. "He doesn't know anything."

I felt a tremendous relief. My sister-in-law had been loyal to her favorite refrain: appearances above all.

"The house is on fire, but it's a smokeless fire, right?" I said, getting a little sarcastic.

"I'm not in the mood for jokes. It's the last time I lie for you. You'll have to figure out what you're doing," she snapped. "Now go. I have no desire to see you."

When I got home, César was back from the Calypso, and he greeted me with a long kiss that turned my stomach.

"I hear Gabriel was sick."

"Yes, he was in the hospital, but the doctors cured him. We didn't tell you because we didn't want you to worry." I quickly closed down the subject. "How did it go in the United States?"

My husband twisted his face and lit a cigarette. "Bad. Luciano and Lansky are cut from the same cloth. All charm when things are going well, but when things take a turn, they toss you aside like horse shit."

"We'll be all right," I said, to say something. "Don't let it get to you."

"Thanks, Gloria."

That he called me Gloria instead of "love," "sweetheart," or any of his usual names for me should've given me a clue something wasn't right. But I was so relieved he hadn't interrogated me about my activities while he'd been out of the country, I didn't realize until it was too late.

That afternoon, Daniela took her brother on a trip to the beach at Kawama. I decided to take a long nap, but shortly after I closed my eyes, I woke up from a terrible nightmare. Patricio and I were on a snowy mountain, and we were dying, flattened by an avalanche. I decided to go down to the kitchen to get a healing cup of chamomile tea.

I was about to cross the living room when I saw César talking with two men. Both had their backs to me, so I couldn't see their faces. The three of them must have been down there for a long time because a dense cloud of cigar smoke hovered in the room. I turned so I could avoid the living room on the way to the kitchen, but something César said stopped me cold.

"I want it reduced to ashes."

I stayed hidden behind the door so I could figure out what the hell they were planning. I took another quick peek, and from what I could see of their backs, I could tell one was a younger man and the other was older. The younger man was sweating through his shirt, and the older had grayish hair.

"If I do it, I'm gonna have to leave the island immediately," said the younger man.

"My son is right," said the older man.

César growled and nodded. "You'll have a boat at your disposal."

"But I also want money so my family can leave Cuba too," demanded the younger man.

"Count on it," said my husband. "But there's one condition: Patricio Rubio has to be in the building."

I got goose bumps. For a moment, I wondered if my imagination was playing with me, but César had spoken with such hatred that, rather than pronouncing the name, he'd chewed it and spat it out. Hearing Patricio's name on my husband's lips was the worst nightmare of all.

When the older man got up to refill his cup, I snuck another look and recognized him. His mustache and anxious airs were painfully familiar: he was the guy from El Encanto that Patricio didn't like, the one he called Don Gato. His son, the younger man, also seemed familiar to me—probably from the store.

"I thought we were trying to hit Fidel supporters," said Don Gato after he cleared his throat, "not creating a smokescreen so you could commit murder."

César laughed with disdain. "It's not a hit if there aren't any victims. Surely Silvestre agrees with me that the insurrection has a price."

"A price in dollars that you'll pay with interest," said the son.

Silvestre and César clinked their cups to seal the agreement. César immediately pulled out a canvas bag he handed over to the younger man.

"Let us review, then," said my husband. "Inside, you'll find C-4, which is a hell of an explosive, so treat it with more care than you do your own dick. You'll activate the first case and hide it under two rolls of fabric. You'll do the same with the second case and put it on a shelf. Patricio is in charge of closing down the English Room, so you'll have to figure something out so you can be the last to leave."

"El Encanto is gonna burn hotter than hell."

I covered my mouth so I wouldn't scream. I had to warn Patricio. The police. Whomever I could, and I had to do it immediately. Stealthily, I crossed to the back door, pulled the spare car keys from a drawer, and went out to the garden. I was about to drive away, when, as I lowered my gaze to put the key in the ignition, someone opened the door brusquely and hit me over the head. I slumped forward over the wheel.

Dust danced in the air, illuminated by the sun's rays.

I came to, in my own bed. A wrenching pain shot through my head. I was dazed for a few seconds until I remembered my husband's conversation in the living room with those two men and then I came to, alert. Patricio's life was in danger.

"You're so clumsy, my love, falling down the stairs like that," said César, his voice filled with cruelty.

I tried to sit up and blinked several times to try to focus my eyes. There were two people in the room with me: my husband and my sister-in-law. César was sitting at the foot of the bed and Marita in the back of the room, on a chair next to the door. I tried again to move and panicked when I found myself tied to the bed.

"I know you heard us planning, so let's cut the bullshit," César said. "It's better; that way I don't have to go through the trouble of telling you about it."

I tried to feign ignorance. I was sure I hadn't made a sound. How had they discovered me?

"I don't know what you're talking about," I lied.

"Gloria, please. That perfume you wear gives you away every time. I smelled you as soon as you came downstairs."

His arrogance infuriated me, and for the first time since I was a little girl, I didn't bite my tongue.

"That's because you have a nose like a pig." César was stunned. He was used to a more submissive attitude from me. "And it's not just your nose. You're a pig from head to toe!"

My husband raised his hand and slapped me across the face. I felt no pain. I was so angry, he could have cut me into pieces, and my pieces would have continued hurling insults at him. But there was something that hurt more than César's slap: my sister-in-law's betrayal.

"You said you hadn't told him anything," I screamed at Marita.

My sister-in-law responded in a thin voice while staring at the floor. "He found out as soon as he got back. A nurse at the hospital told him Patricio is Gabriel's real father. With money, you can buy a snitch anywhere."

"Don't deny your own merits, little sister. She did indeed tell me the rest," said César. "That you've been in love with Patricio for years, that you were gonna run away with him . . . she sang like a bird."

I ignored César and addressed my sister-in-law again. "I thought you wanted to keep up appearances at all costs."

Marita opened her mouth to answer, but César got ahead of her. "And she did! Don't be so hard on her. She really didn't have a choice.

In fact, she put up so much resistance, I had to use pliers. I didn't realize you were such good friends."

Marita pulled off the glove on her left hand. She was missing two nails: he'd pulled them off. The poor woman was on the verge of tears and couldn't even look at her brother. I was so furious, I could have strangled César with my own hands. My sister-in-law had gone to bat for me, and that had been her reward.

"You're a monster," I said, trying to spit in his face.

"My wife turns me into a cuckold, protected by my goddamn sister, and I'm a monster? I'm the victim!"

But I was so angry, my fury overwhelmed by instinct for self-protection.

"Bastard, degenerate, son of a bitch!" I screamed at him.

"I'm gonna have to give you a few lashes on the ass. Like when you were a baby, do you remember? But before that, there's a lot I have to do."

"If you're such a man, kill me instead of Patricio," I pleaded.

"No, my love. That would be too easy. First, I have to take care of that scruffy clerk. Then I'll figure out what to do with the two of you."

"You're going to burn down El Encanto just to kill one man?"

"You can thank our new government for that because it's their fault I can't just go in and put a bullet in his head. Although, I prefer it this way. They're gonna blame the fire on anti-Castro elements and, in the process, your lover is gonna fry like a pork crackling."

"But other people will die too."

"I could give three shits about those assholes! They can all burn like rats."

"You little man! You dickless wonder! You jerk! You're disgusting!"

I kept throwing insults at him until I foamed at the mouth. The situation was completely fucked up. My hands and feet were tied, but I'd never felt more free. My life with César was over. I was no longer afraid of him, and I'd never keep my thoughts to myself again, even if it cost me my life.

"I swear by my grandparents and my parents, may they rest in peace, I'm never going to let you hurt anyone else again," I screamed at him.

"Oh yeah? And how are you gonna stop me when you're asleep?" he asked, his voice dripping with sarcasm.

César pulled out a bottle of sleeping pills. I tried to squirm away, but my hands and feet were tied very tightly with silk scarves to the corners of the bed. Ignoring my cries, César forcefully pinched my nose until I had to open my mouth to breathe, and then he stuck the pills down my throat with his fingers.

He wiped his fingers on his pants and addressed Marita. "If you wanna save your ass, you fucking traitor, you won't let her out of here. When I finish with Patricio, I'll decide what to do with her and her shitty son. I'll probably drown him, like he's one of those street cats."

I tried to scream, but everything went black.

I woke up because of the nausea. Feeling triumphant, I realized my body had rebelled and thrown up the pills. It took me a bit to come out of the fog, but once I did, I was as sharp as an owl.

El Encanto. I needed to get to the store before it went up in flames.

I began to scream and struggle against my ties. Marita got up from the chair by the door and came up to the bed. "Don't bother. He let the entire staff go for the day. We're alone. And, please, don't scream. My head is pounding."

"You have to untie me!"

"I can't."

"Quickly, there's no time to lose!"

"This is all your fault!" she shrieked. "If you hadn't fallen in love with that clerk, if you'd just behaved like you were supposed to—was your life really that bad? Now we're both paying the consequences for your stupidity!"

I had to get her to see the light. Patricio's life depended on it.

"Marita," I said softly, looking her in the eyes, "we have to do something. If we don't, we will be accomplices to murder."

"No, Gloria. If he can pull my nails out for lying, he'll pull my skin off if I let you go."

"But the answer can't be to hide, Marita. What will all your suffering have been for then?"

"You're not gonna talk me into untying you."

"Listen to me, please . . . Patricio will die. Help me one more time, please. I kept our agreement. I hadn't seen that clerk in all these years. But this was different. I needed him to save Gabriel."

"Shut up."

"If you won't do it for Patricio, think about Gabriel . . . he's innocent. He's not to blame for anything. For the love of God, he's just a boy!"

"Shut up!"

"Please . . . please . . . ," I pleaded with all my heart. "He's going to gut my baby, the way lions tear apart their prey. My Gabriel . . . please, I'm begging you to let me go."

I closed my eyes, exhausted. Angry tears were making my eyes itchy, and I couldn't rub them with my hands tied to the headboard. Suddenly, I noticed the pressure easing. Marita had freed me.

"César is gonna kill me," she said, sighing.

I untied my other hand and my feet, jumped from the bed, and wrapped Marita in the most heartfelt hug I'd ever given her in my whole life.

"Go back to your husband and disappear from the face of the earth," I ordered. "I'm going to turn César in to the police. He's not going to do anything to you. I promise."

I ran out of there as if I were possessed by the devil. It was almost closing time at El Encanto—the precise hour they were going to detonate the explosives.

CHAPTER 52

I jumped in the car and went straight to the center of the city. When I got to Galiano Street, I looked up at the sky and saw a column of smoke rising. People were gathering, blocking the street, so I abandoned the car right there and ran the last two blocks to the store.

What I saw was horrible. El Encanto had become an inferno. Coils of black smoke escaped from the windows, wrapping the building in a sinister fog. Through the open windows, you could see the orange radiance of the fire glimmer the way cats' eyes sometimes sparkle with malice from the corners of rooms. The facade had turned black, and the foundation creaked and clanked. The building howled with anguish as if it were a living thing.

I had to push my way through a multitude of the curious. Store employees were still running out of the building, and those standing out on the street had formed a circle on the sidewalk. I ran to them as fast as I could.

"What happened?" I asked.

"There was an explosion," one of the workers answered. Her face was smudged with soot.

"Is there anyone left inside?"

"I don't know; it's all filled with smoke."

I quickly looked over the group. Patricio wasn't among them. That meant he was still inside. Before I realized what I was doing, instinct took over, and I ran straight toward the burning building. I had to get him out of there.

"What's that woman doing?" I heard someone say behind my back.

"She's crazy. Stop her!" another voice ordered.

A couple of men tried to cut me off, but I shoved them with all my might and got through. I gathered my courage to go through the doors of El Encanto for the last time.

No sooner did I go in than smoke engulfed me, thick as molasses. I was blinded, and every breath made my throat and lungs burn. I still had the silk scarf around my wrist with which César had tied me to the bed so I grabbed it and put it over my nose and mouth. I tried taking short inhales instead of big gulps of air.

After so many years as a customer, I could intuit the way, even though I couldn't see more than a few meters in front of my nose. I crossed the perfume department. The counters and the displays had a phantasmagoric air about them, submerged in this ashy fog. I avoided the elevators and managed to get to the stairway.

When I got to the second floor, I burned my hand on the door-knob. I kicked the door open and saw the first flames. The fabric on the shelf was burning like hay, and the mannequins were on fire. It was a terrifying sight. It actually made me hesitate. Maybe I was being crazy. Maybe Patricio had gotten out through another door, and now I was unnecessarily putting myself in danger, not thinking about Daniela and Gabriel. I was still paralyzed by indecision and fear when I heard something. A voice asking for help.

Patricio.

Patricio's cry annihilated my common sense. I ran toward the fire, shouting his name over and over.

"I'm in the dressing room!" screamed Patricio.

I made my way there. I suddenly felt incredible pain in my legs. I looked down and saw the hem of my skirt had caught on fire. I tore it off without thinking and ran, half naked. I managed to get to the door of the dressing room and pounded on it. Patricio pounded from the other side. I protected my hands with the tail of my shirt and frantically tried to turn the doorknob. It was useless—the door was locked.

"It's locked!" I screamed.

"There are spare keys in the cashbox in the office!"

In spite of the searing heat around me, I felt a shiver of panic go up my spine. In order to get to the office, I had to cross the entire floor. It didn't look good, but I couldn't let fear stop me. I would walk through hell for Patricio, and more.

"I'm going to go get them!" I shouted. "Hold on, my love."

That was the moment Patricio realized it was me.

"Gloria?" he shouted, incredulous. "Is that you?"

"Yes, my love!"

"Get out of here right now! Do you hear me?"

"No way! We're leaving here together!"

It was so hot, every breath burned my chest. As I made my way to the office, I stopped in the bathroom, where the smoke was thinner, and took off the scarf. I had a coughing fit. My nose was black, as was my tongue. I blew my nose and spat as much as I could. I wet the scarf and put it back over my nose and mouth, then plunged back into the store.

As I made my way, avoiding the fire, a mannequin with a half-melted face, its clothes now just fiery rags, gave me a sardonic smile. The heat was so intense, I was afraid I would faint. When I got to the tiny office, I got so dizzy I feared I would lose consciousness. *Daniela and Gabriel. Who will protect them if you're not there?* I thought as I struggled with all my might to get myself together. I couldn't die in El Encanto; I refused to let César win. That thought gave me strength, and I held on to that fury and gritted my teeth as I looked through the drawers until I found the key.

With key in hand, I used the last of my strength to cross all the way back to the dressing room. The fire was now crawling up the walls, and the wallpaper was peeling, tossing ash and embers every which way. The sounds were receding, and my vision was turning black around the frames. I was fainting. Or worse, I was dying. I tried to breathe, but my lungs weren't accepting any more air. My strength had gone, and not even the memory of my children could save me. With my last breath, I managed to push the key under the door of the dressing room.

Then the fog wrapped itself around me, and the world disappeared.

CHAPTER 53

PATRICIO

I'd like to say I suspected something was wrong, but that would be a lie. It was an afternoon like any other, and we were just about to close. I was putting the tailor shop in order and preparing the orders for the next day. When Don Gato called me from the dressing room, I calmly went over. I noticed his mustache was dripping sweat, but I assumed it was because of the hot weather.

"I'm sorry," he stammered. "You don't deserve this, but I have to look out for my family."

I started to ask what he was talking about when his shove caught me by surprise. His son, Silvestre, was hiding behind the door of another dressing room and hit me brutally. I fell onto the floor.

"What are you doing?" I moaned.

"This is for César!" Silvestre howled.

He began to kick me with all his might while I processed what it meant to hear that name: this was the end. Since the night of the white shoes, our destinies had run parallel. Now at last, they'd crossed with a completely predictable violence.

I lost consciousness.

Sometime later, a sound like thunder brought me back. I got up, dazed. I was locked in the dressing room, the thick wooden door immune to my pounding. Trapped by my rage and my fear, I kept banging on it like a crazy person until I heard the second explosion.

I fell to the floor from fright, my ears ringing. Was that a bomb? *It's impossible; it can't have been a bomb*, I thought, trying not to panic. A third explosion, even more deafening than the ones before it, rid me of even the most minimal doubt. I had to get out of that dressing room. If I didn't, I'd be devoured by flames.

I pounded on the door again like a maniac until smoke began to come in from underneath. I understood then this had been the point of the explosions: to start a fire. I couldn't figure out why. But it wasn't the moment to think about that, what I had to do was save my skin. There was a shirt hanging in the dressing room and I wrapped it around my head to protect my nose and mouth.

Caught like a mouse in a trap, I screamed, I shouted, and I screeched and cried until I went hoarse. When my vocal cords gave up, I leaned against the wall and closed my eyes. My only comfort was that Nely had not come to work today and would be safe at home with Ernesto. But then an even more disturbing idea came into my head: Silvestre had said César was behind this. The fire was his revenge against me, which meant he knew about my relationship with his wife. The idea that Gloria and Gabriel could be in danger was more than I could bear. To die without knowing they were okay was horrifying. All of a sudden, when I had lost all hope, I heard a voice in the distance. A voice calling my name.

"I'm in the dressing room!" I screamed.

Somebody pounded the door, and I pounded back from the other side. The person tried to turn the doorknob.

"There are spare keys in the cashbox in the office!"

"I'm going to go get them!" she shouted. "Hold on, my love."

I suddenly recognized that voice. But it was impossible. My mind must be playing tricks on me. And yet . . .

"Gloria?" I screamed, incredulous. "Is that you?"

"Yes, my love!"

The euphoria of hearing her voice faded into a deep fear. What was she doing here? She had to save herself immediately.

"Get out of here right now! Do you hear me?"

"No way! We're leaving here together!"

I heard her steps as she walked away, and I began to pant because I was so nervous. The worst part was that all I could do was wait. After many minutes, an eternity, I heard a clink. Gloria had pushed the key under the door.

With a cry of joy, I grabbed it and unlocked the door. But what I saw when I came out of my tiny prison made my heart stop.

Gloria was on the floor. I tried to revive her, but she didn't respond to my words or my touch.

I gathered her in my arms and ran down the stairs. The flames had climbed ever higher and were devouring the roof, sending huge chunks down all around us. The creaking of the beams and columns let me know the building was about to collapse.

When I got to the first floor, the smoke was as thick as tar, and I couldn't see more than two steps in front of me. The heat was so intense, sweat poured off my forehead and into my eyes. The reality of the situation hit me with the force of a punch: if I wanted to get to the front door, I'd have to do it with my eyes closed.

There was no time to waste, so I entrusted my life and Gloria's to instinct. El Encanto was my home, the place where I had spent the best years of my young adulthood. Since that first day, when I had explored the rooms with the clumsiness of a dizzy duck, I'd come to know the perfection of every nook and cranny. I knew that first floor better than anybody. I took a deep breath, closed my eyes, and got going. My intuition could supply what my eyes could not see. Although Gloria couldn't hear me, I narrated our way. Talking to her helped calm my nerves.

"Look, love! Now we're by the hat display . . . three giant steps and now we're by socks and stockings. Do you remember when you came to buy lacy socks for Daniela's first day of school? To the left of us, handbags. Marita really liked this part of the store. She'd spend whole afternoons here . . . and five steps to the right, the display with the perfume bottles. I can almost smell it . . . and here's the mannequin where we used to leave those beautiful notes. Do you remember? We're almost there, my love. Hold on just a little bit more . . . from here on, it's straight ahead . . . and that's it. We should be at the door."

Before confirming it, I prayed to my parents, my grandparents, and all my dead loved ones for help. If my orientation had failed and we were lost, we would die like two fried little birds.

I opened my eyes and saw the glass doors in front of me. I couldn't repress a cry of joy. We had made it! I pushed the doors and left El Encanto with Gloria in my arms, not once looking back.

Out on the street, chaos reigned. People carried buckets of water to prevent the fire from spreading to nearby buildings. Firefighters, militiamen, and store employees fought together against the flames. My knees gave way, and I fell on the sidewalk. In my arms, Gloria wasn't breathing. Someone told me to hold on, that an ambulance was on its way. I buried my face in her hair and spoke in her ear.

"Life without you isn't life, Gloria. Don't leave me. If you can hear me, squeeze my hand."

Please, I pleaded, *I need you to make me a gesture. At least a pinch.* But Gloria's hand remained inert. Increasingly desperate, I tried to remember the first-aid course all employees got from Celia, the nurse, and I did mouth-to-mouth resuscitation. Her lips tasted like ash. I began to cry, and my tears left furrows on her blackened skin. Her long hair felt as rough as a scouring pad. I put my fingers on her neck. There was no pulse. My efforts had been useless. Gloria was dead.

At that moment, on the afternoon of April 13, 1961, something also died inside me. My soul went with my beloved, not to return. We had done the best we could, but we were unable to overcome misery and find happiness.

I was so devastated I almost didn't notice when the paramedics plucked Gloria's lifeless body from my arms and placed it onto a stretcher.

Without Gloria by my side, I sat on the ground, looking at the world through eyes no longer mine. Seconds later, El Encanto collapsed with a thunderous crack and a shower of burning debris. As if the entire building were an erupting volcano, a cloud of dust and black smoke rolled down the street, enveloping nearby buildings and people in an unhealthy darkness. Around me, people shouted and took cover, but I didn't flinch. My whole world had collapsed.

CHAPTER 54

I don't know how long I stayed on the ground. I would have stayed there for the rest of my life, but somebody forced me to get up: Daniela.

With her usual mettle and courage, the young woman took control of the situation, held out her hand, and pulled me off the ground. Together, we ran to get away from the pieces of building still falling, taking refuge in a nearby alley.

"What are you doing here?" I asked Daniela. "Where's Gabriel?"

"He's at home. I heard on the radio that El Encanto was on fire."

"Daniela, listen to me: don't let César come anywhere near your brother."

"I don't understand. Where's my mother? Aunt Marita called, and she said she was with you."

I didn't know what to say.

I was going to lie to her out of pity when I heard a voice, a voice like vermin growling, a voice that had always made my hair stand on end, and it answered for me.

"Your mother died."

César was in the alley. His green eyes shone as much as the fire that finished off the great store.

My rival was aiming a pistol at me.

"I saw everything," he snarled. "She died saving this asshole. And you know the best part? It doesn't matter one bit because I'm gonna blow his brains out anyway. I don't even care if I wind up in jail."

I should have been afraid. But Gloria had taken not just my heart with her but my fears as well. Instead of cowering, I turned to César, my chest out.

"You should have shot me years ago," I declared.

"What?" My audacity threw him off for an instant.

"Years ago, I worked as a shoeshine boy at the door of your club. I polished your shoes and stained them. You almost shot me then."

César smiled contemptuously, as if crushing an ant that had bitten him in the leg. "I'd tell you I remember, but it wouldn't be true. I've had countless men on the other side of my gun barrel. Do you think someone like me, the fucking king of Havana, could remember a simple clerk, a maggot like you?"

"I just hope you have better aim this time."

"What?" he asked again.

"I also threw the cutlery at you, remember, at the Calypso?"

"You son of a bitch."

"And I also made your wife and daughter happy. Much happier than you ever could."

César stared at me, furious. From the expression on his face—the red-hot glare in his eyes, the crooked mouth, the flush of shame on his cheeks—I could see my words had done him more harm than he could ever do me with his gun.

"You know?" he growled. "I was gonna shoot you in the head, but now I'll shoot you in the gut. So it'll take longer for you to die."

A brave, serene voice interrupted our duel.

"Daddy, don't shoot." César and I were so busy, we had momentarily forgotten about Daniela. We both stared at her. Wearing an intensely red strapless dress and high-heeled sandals, her hair loose over her shoulders, Daniela was the living image of a beautiful avenging angel. The young woman had pulled a gun from her purse and was pointing it at her father. Her face was a mask of determination.

"Don't shoot," Daniela ordered.

César's mouth dropped open, but he tried to regain control of the situation. "Daniela, don't be an idiot. Where did you get that?"

"At my great-grandmother Lala's house," the girl answered. "It belonged to my great-great-grandfather Justo, who fought in the battle of San Juan Hill. The day after my grandmother died, a butterfly came through the window and perched on top of the chest where it was stored. I'm sure it was a sign from heaven."

I didn't doubt Daniela was telling the truth. I've never understood guns, but the one she held in her hands had an antique look to it, with a square body and a very thin barrel. César didn't seem impressed.

"That old piece of junk can't shoot anymore," her father snapped.

"That's what I thought," Daniela replied. "That's why I took it to an antiquarian to be fixed."

I wondered if she was bluffing, but Daniela wasn't that kind of person. When she made a threat, she meant it. And apparently, she had inherited César's ruthless streak.

"Put that away and go home," César snarled.

"You can't order me around."

"I'm your father, and I can do whatever the fuck I please."

But Daniela wasn't intimidated and continued to hold her gun level. "I'll kill you before you can harm Patricio."

César spat on the ground, bitterly disappointed. "You're exactly like your whore of a mother. I'm ashamed to call you my daughter."

"That's rich, because the last thing I want is to be like you."

Sick of talking, César squeezed the trigger to blow my brains out.

The shot resounded through the alley like thunder.

I closed my eyes and prepared myself. I expected a painful impact when the bullet entered my skull, but the only pain I felt was from my nails pressing into the palms of my hands.

I opened my eyes. César was on the ground. He had fired at me, but he had missed because Daniela had shot him first. She was still holding the gun, a slight trail of smoke floating from the barrel.

Slowly, Daniela and I approached César, who was despondent. The gangster was dying. He had a fatal neck wound from which blood was gushing out. He was breathing his last.

"I know Lala will be waiting for you when you die, Daddy," Daniela announced. "She'll make sure you never set foot in heaven."

With his daughter's curse as a farewell, César died on the filthy ground of that alley. Daniela had become the instrument of her great-grandmother's revenge.

Daniela and I embraced. Now that she was tucked into my arms, her hard shell cracked, and the brave girl who had saved me was once more the girl I had taught to make wall shadows when she couldn't stop crying over her dead puppy. Daniela was tough, yes, but she wasn't a monster like her father.

When I saw the tears falling from her eyes, it didn't take but a second for me to make a decision. I wasn't willing to let the girl I loved like a daughter go to jail for murder. I quickly took the gun from her hands.

"What are you doing?" she protested.

I held her chin to get her attention. We didn't have much time. Police sirens could be heard in the distance.

"Listen to me. I'm the one who fired the gun."

Daniela shook her head. Her moment of weakness had passed, and she had regained her footing. "That's not true."

"Yes, it is. It's my word against yours," I said. "I pulled the trigger."

I put a finger to her lips so she wouldn't say anything else. "You didn't kill anyone, Daniela. And you aren't gonna lose a second of sleep because of this. You'll have a good life. A life in which you're gonna do what you want, without having to give explanations to anyone. You'll study and you'll travel and fall in love, and you'll be so happy, you'll want to explode."

Daniela nodded. She understood the gift I was giving her, and she accepted it.

"I promise," she whispered.

I kissed her head, inhaling the scent of her hair for the last time. "Take care of your brother. I love you, sweetheart."

By then, several people had arrived at the scene and spotted me with the gun in my hand. When the police questioned the witnesses, no one would hesitate to say I was the murderer. I started running; there was no turning back.

My first stop after becoming a fugitive was home. No doubt, it was the least intelligent thing I could do—the police would take little time to figure out who I was and would come after me—but I had to pick up Nely and Ernesto.

Luckily, I had kept the fake passport El Grescas had gotten me years ago for my aborted flight with Gloria. I was determined to use it to leave the island as soon as possible. Nely and Ernesto would have no choice but to accompany me. When I got home, my wife was mesmerized by the radio, listening to the news. The poor thing was stunned when she looked up and saw my clothes and face blackened by smoke and fire.

"It's true, then," she said. "El Encanto has burned down."

I quickly stripped off my charred clothes and put on a clean shirt and pants.

"We have to go," I warned her.

"I'll go with you to the hospital so they can check you out."

I grabbed a suitcase and began to fill it with the first things I saw. Clothes, toiletries, the little money I had at home . . . a hodgepodge.

"You don't get it. We have to leave Cuba. I can't explain it to you now, but the police are after me."

My wife looked at me with a mix of fear and apathy. "Can you tell me what you've done?"

There was no time to tell her about everything that had happened, so I kept packing. "What's done is done. I'll tell you everything, I promise, but we have to go now. Get the baby."

"I'm not going anywhere," Nely declared, crossing her arms.

"I can't leave without you."

"Well, you'll have to because Ernesto and I are staying here. My son will grow up in a free country, and you won't stop him."

Before Nely could stop me, I went to my son's crib and picked him up. With his white cotton pajamas, Ernesto was warm and smelled of cologne and talcum powder. He could feel my nervousness and began to cry. I rocked him on his belly, the way he liked best, until he calmed down and went from crying to laughter.

"Dammit, enough. Give him to me!" Nely demanded.

"Nely," I said with the child still in my arms, "we can start over wherever you want."

"Out!" she responded with all her fury.

"Please don't get like that."

"Give me the boy, or I call the police."

I couldn't believe it. How much had I hurt Nely? I felt sorry for Ernesto, for her, for me. Instinctively, I hugged our son. Now it was me who was crying, and after the saddest moments of my life, I heard my wife's voice.

"Officer, my husband is a fugitive. Come and get him. We live on Egido Street, number seventeen," she said, full of bitterness.

Ernesto grabbed my finger with his soft hands while Nely hung up the phone. I was very impressed with the cold-blooded way she'd turned me in.

"I didn't expect things to end like this. I'm sorry, Nely. I'm so sorry," I said.

"I loved you, Patricio, but you've never played fair. You've never been honest with me. Go now. I don't wanna see you anymore."

Defeated, I approached Nely and handed her the baby, who was scared and fussing, taking everything in.

"Ernesto, I'll come back for you," I promised. "Please don't forget about your dad."

The baby looked at me with his big brown eyes, not understanding my words but eager to please me.

"Can I kiss him?" I asked. "Please?"

"Do whatever you want. You're never gonna see him again," Nely snapped.

I ignored my wife and focused on the little one. I kissed his little face and little hands and whispered in his ear. "Don't forget me."

I stayed glued to my son until I heard the sirens. Then, without looking Nely in the eye, I left Ernesto in his mother's arms and ran out of my house for the last time.

CHAPTER 55

The life of a fugitive is not romantic and exciting like in the movies. On the contrary, it's sad and, above all, very boring. The night El Encanto burned down and I escaped from Cuba, I took a boat to the Dominican Republic, the first destination I was offered at the ticket window. After reaching port in Santo Domingo, I decided to get away from the big cities and take refuge in a village called Bonao. There, I got a job picking papayas at a plantation and hid from the world.

Working the land was backbreaking, but I needed to exhaust myself during the day in order to avoid thinking all night in the barracks. I needed to break my body so I could turn off my brain and not think about Ernesto, Nely, Gabriel, Daniela . . . and, above all, I needed to forget Gloria's death.

After four years, I ventured out of my hole and went to Miami. In Miami Beach, I met with Guzmán, who had settled there as planned. He and Reina had opened their own Garbo shoe store in the picturesque neighborhood of Little Havana, a redoubt for Cuban exiles. My friend received me with love and offered his help. He rented me a small apartment on Calle Ocho, gave me work in his shoe store, and held me up when I finally cried over everything I hadn't cried for in Santo Domingo.

One small joy was seeing Rita again, and she was as beautiful as ever. The ex-dancer had opened a clothing store and married a very blond and very nice American. She had a young son whom she'd named Franklin.

Settling in Little Havana gave me a strange feeling, a blend of familiarity and surprise. Its streets and squares were facsimiles of the original city, full of grocery stores in which to buy beans by the pound and small restaurants in which cooks sang and prepared finger-licking-good fried pork ribs. The streets were decorated with colorful murals with lanterns hanging from the streetlights, as if the inhabitants had wanted to re-create a cheery version of the Havana of their youth. Practically everyone was from Cuba, and to walk in the evenings, just as the heat faded, and watch the small groups of people on the corners and parks locked in domino games or other improvised gatherings was a delight. I could almost imagine I was in Havana again . . . until I reached Calle Veinte. The mirage vanished when, instead of leading to the Malecón and the sea, my steps took me to the Miami River.

At the Garbo shoe store, there was always a television tuned to Cuban news. A couple of years into my time there, the death of Che in Bolivia had caught Guzmán and me when we were at work.

"Poor wretch. They hunted him like a mouse," Guzmán said, his voice filled with regret.

I was surprised by the feeling in his voice. Guzmán had never been a fan of the revolution. "I never thought of you as a great admirer of Che."

"I'm not. But think: he could have gotten fat on his ass like Fidel did in a mansion in Havana, but he never traded the mountain for an office. That's admirable, at least."

That night I had a hard time sleeping because a morbid thought kept hovering in my head. I couldn't help but wonder if Ernesto Guevara had been wearing the jacket I'd sold him. If he had, I hoped that, at the very least, it protected him from the wind and the rain until the moment of his death.

The years went by with a sigh. Guzmán's shoe store was such a sound business that it eventually opened several branches in Florida, in Boca Raton, Orlando, and Tampa. Not bad for a boy whose golden dream was simply to make a living shining shoes. He and Reina had a daughter, Leslie, who inherited the business after her father retired.

Guzmán and El Grescas always stayed in touch, by letter and phone and through a few visits. El Grescas and Ajo didn't fulfill their dream of going through the alphabet, but they got to Hilario, and then Ajo told her husband she was tired of being a rabbit and if he wanted more kids, he was going to have to have them with his own damned mother. Their children grew up in a Cuba very different from the one we knew. To contribute to the family economy, all the children learned to cook at La Pekinesa and then opened private dining rooms in their homes. These primitive paladares owned by "the Asturian's children" became famous in Havana.

As for me, I managed to get ahead. My life had been shattered, but I did what I could with the pieces. Since I was condemned to live as a fugitive from justice, I had no choice but to keep using an assumed name. I stayed in my small apartment on Calle Ocho, and with what I saved from working in Guzmán's shoe store, I managed to set up a small business, a hardware store, La Ventajosa, which gained a loyal following, thanks to my charisma. My goal was not to get rich but to support myself by doing the only thing I knew how to do: selling and enjoying the process.

Over the years, I met other women. Some were one-night stands. Others were my girlfriends for weeks or months. One of them, Betty, a middle-aged mulato hairdresser with a sweet character and shapely legs, came to share my house for a couple of years. But all my relationships were doomed to failure. It was always my fault. I couldn't deliver. My body was present, but my mind always lived in the past, with Gloria.

The day Betty left me, I was reading the paper at the kitchen table when a story caught my attention. On a farm on the outskirts of Havana, workers had begun to build an apartment complex. The workers had found a skeleton. The news had made the front page because of a curious detail: the skull was separated from the body and had a trumpet embedded in its mouth.

When Betty came home from work at the salon, she found me crying at the kitchen table. I couldn't explain the reason for my tears, and from the sad way she sighed, I realized she'd grown tired of living with my secrets and enduring my silences. That night we dined on ropa vieja in front of the television, then made love in silence. When I fell asleep, she got up to pack her things and leave. Her farewell note left no room for doubt: "I hope one day you'll free yourself from your ghosts."

I thought about telling Rita the news about the trumpeter's body, but I didn't have the courage. It was bigger than me. My guts twisted when I thought about her warm gaze clouding over with pain. Franklin was a ghost in not only her life but also mine. One day, at his side, I had also been brave . . . between the two of us, we managed to save Rita. He paid for it with his life while I'd never learned from that rebellion against the powerful.

In Havana, it's well known that between the Malecón and San Lázaro Street, there's a statue of Antonio Maceo, known as the Bronze Titan, on horseback. Maceo was a black general who commanded the mambises, Cuban independence fighters, and fought to abolish slavery. A practitioner of Freemasonry, the owner of a nine-horse farm, and the brains behind the ill-fated Guerra Chiquita, Maceo was a key figure in Cuba's history and one of its national heroes. But in the eighties, after the Mariel exodus—the massive exit of Cubans through the port of Mariel—a curious legend spread through Havana. It was said that, years before, the statue looked toward the sea, but Fidel Castro, worried his compatriots might get ideas, had ordered the authorities to turn it around so it didn't look out at the United States. That was no more than a joke, but there was a terrible truth behind it: the bleeding of Cubans leaving the island was already unstoppable. And it was around then, when everyone was crazy to leave Havana to go to Miami, that I made the trip in reverse, from Miami to Havana.

It wasn't until 1981—twenty years after my flight—that I dared return to Cuba. But Havana was no longer the city I'd known. The buildings were falling apart. The cars were from my time, yes, but they circulated like acrobatic dinosaurs. The hotels were shells, with worn facades that housed empty, old rooms. The pools were dry. The soulless streets were fossils, with nothing of their former splendor. Havana was the ruins of my memories. Or maybe it was me who had become an old man.

The first thing I did was find Ernesto. He and Nely no longer lived in the apartment from twenty years ago, but with the help of a couple of gossipy neighbors, it didn't take me long to figure out his new address. With my heart pounding like a drum in my chest, I rang the bell at my son's house. The door was opened by a hairy young man dressed only in shorts and showing off a bare torso stained yellow. He carried a can of spray paint in one hand and a cigarette in the other.

"Ernesto Eduardo Rubio Yamary?" I asked in a thin voice.

The young man looked at me with a bewilderment I recognized from seeing it in the mirror. Like me, he unconsciously raised his right eyebrow when something upset him.

"I think you're confused. I'm Ernesto Bravo," he said.

I took a deep breath. "I'm Patricio, your father."

Ernesto was stunned. We stood still, like two pillars of salt, facing each other.

"Can I give you a hug?" I asked.

"Yes, yes, of course," he stammered.

We embraced in a somewhat clumsy way, and I could feel Ernesto keeping his distance. I wanted to believe it was because he was naked from the waist up and smeared with paint, but it was more likely that he didn't feel comfortable embracing a stranger, no matter how much kinship we shared.

Once over the initial surprise, my son invited me to come in. He lived with a very pretty young girl named Adela, who had paint stains on her clothes too and was making noodle soup. They told me they were graffiti artists who painted murals praising the revolution.

As much as he tried to conceal it, I noticed Ernesto was tense with me. Just like when he was a baby, he didn't understand what was happening, but he was so polite and tried so hard to please me. We talked for a couple of hours. I learned that, after my departure, Nely had fallen in love again with a carpenter named Raúl Bravo, and he raised Ernesto and gave him his last name. My ex-wife and her new husband lived in Cañoverde, a small town near Matanzas, where Nely headed the regional chapter of the Federation of Cuban Women. His mother had never told him the reason for my departure. She simply said I had gotten a job abroad, had taken advantage of the opening at the port of Camarioca to leave the island, and then, having betrayed my country, I couldn't come back. It was a story that didn't make much sense given that I was Spanish, not Cuban, but Ernesto had been so young when I left, he hadn't even considered questioning it. I wondered about telling him the whole truth, but he didn't seem very interested. For him, other people were his parents, and I was simply a loose end from his childhood.

My son said goodbye to me with a more affectionate hug than the one with which he had received me, and we promised to keep in touch. We kept it up for a few years: several Christmas greetings, calls on his birthdays, and little else. Nely had fulfilled her threat. With the help of time, she'd managed to take my son from me. Although, half a life later, I realized I didn't hold a grudge against her. Ernesto was a healthy and happy young man—everything I could wish for him. When it came to Nely, I simply felt too old to harbor the slightest resentment. I had pretty much screwed up both our lives by marrying her when I was in love with someone else. I was glad she had remade her life and hoped the carpenter loved her as much as I loved Gloria.

My next stop was to see El Grescas at La Pekinesa. The house and the cantina were still standing on Obispo Street, which was a feat in a Havana that was falling apart.

The building's exterior was no longer egg-yolk yellow but an insipid charcoal gray, but the wrought-iron balconies remained intact. In his letters, El Grescas had told me that, after the death of our landlord in Macao, the Chinese widow had given him the house on the condition that they let her keep the attic room so she could come to Havana a couple weeks a year. My friend had kept his promise, and at least once a year, the family shared food and shelter with the old Chinese woman— or Granny Mei Ling, as the children had nicknamed her.

In the courtyard, the smell of the garden revived my spirits, and the water from the fountain refreshed my face. I walked to the wooden bar and dropped down on a stool.

A girl who had inherited El Grescas's wide shoulders and her mother's mischievous smile greeted me. I figured it was Alba, the first-born.

"Good afternoon," she said. "What can I get you?"

"A forajido, please."

The girl looked at me, perplexed. "What kind of drink is that?"

"Ask your father. He'll know."

"Dad! There's someone here who says he wants a forajido," the girl called in the direction of the house.

El Grescas leaned out a window on the first floor. When he saw me, he smiled with his gap-toothed smile.

"Patricio! I shit on Christ the King!" He burst out laughing.

"Alza el rabu, marinín!" I exclaimed. "Alabí, alabá, alabí, bon, ban! Nobody can beat the Luanco Marines, and if that should happen . . ."

"What the hell!" When El Grescas completed the sentence, he ran outside and attacked me with one of his bear hugs.

Time had endowed my friend with a tremendous belly and a Cossack beard full of gray hair. If as a young man he was a mole, as an old man he threatened to become a full-fledged buffalo. I returned the hug as I struggled to breathe and prayed I wouldn't break a rib.

"What the hell are you doing here? Is everything all right in Miami?"

"Everything's fine. Don't worry."

"And Guzmán?"

"Same as always. He sends his regards and a gift I have in my suitcase, leather shoes 'the size of your hooves,' in his own words."

El Grescas let out another thunderous laugh and gave me another hug followed by a kiss on the nose. "You can't imagine how I miss that little guy! And you—you're a wretch! How could you not tell me you were coming back?"

"I've only come for a few days. I have to ask you a favor."

"Whatever you need."

"I need you to help me find Gloria's grave."

El Grescas and I spent the next few days scouring Colón Cemetery, which, unluckily for us, was the third largest in the world. Unfortunately, there was no one left to tell me if my Gloria was even buried there. Both Daniela and Gabriel must have left Cuba because, no matter how much I investigated, I couldn't find a trace of them. The only member of the family whose trail I could follow was Marita. Thanks to the society pages in the magazines, I knew that she and her millionaire husband had died in a plane crash off the island of Antigua and that their remains had never been found.

While El Grescas and I walked up and down from grave to mausoleum, I asked fate to give me some sort of sign. Maybe one of the stone angels could offer me a clue as to where the bones of the woman I loved might be. I questioned the gravediggers, the priests, and other denizens of that underworld. No one remembered Gloria Valdés among the ranks of the dead. To make matters worse, destiny seemed determined to spit in my eye when, on my last afternoon in the city, we found César Valdés's grave.

At first, it was difficult for us to accept it. The fearsome gangster who had terrorized all of Havana was buried in the shade of a tamarind tree in one of the worst areas of the cemetery. His grave consisted of a cheap and worn tombstone. There were no flowers.

After letting it sink in that this was truly the same César who had made our life impossible, El Grescas lowered his fly and peed on the tombstone without shame.

"Hello, motherfucker! Look what good all your power and all your money did for you," he said.

I didn't get any pleasure seeing his grave, but I was glad Gloria wasn't there. Wherever she was, knowing she wasn't buried with her husband was a great comfort. On the way to the exit, we passed by the tomb of La Milagrosa, where a group of people had lined up in front of a statue of the Virgin to touch the marble baby's butt.

Without a grave to visit, we finished our journey at Sin Corner. Where El Encanto had been, they'd built a park called Fe del Valle, in honor of an employee who'd died in the fire.

I bought a rose and left it on the sidewalk, in the approximate place where Gloria stopped breathing in my arms. I would have liked to say the park was a nice tribute to El Encanto and all its stories, but I'd be lying. Calling it a park was too much for that handful of dingy trees and back-pain-inducing benches. The place was full of beggars and hustlers who walked by dragging their feet and raising dust.

We stayed there, sitting on one of those infernal benches until it was dark, lost in our memories. I'm not ashamed to admit I got worked up a couple of times, and El Grescas had to squeeze my hand to comfort me. After all, in that little bit of the world, I had cried, laughed, and lived more than I ever thought possible. I had fallen in love there and made love with the woman of my dreams and begot a child. That was just my story, but that store had touched the lives of thousands of people. El Encanto was still present on that corner, although it was invisible to the eyes of the passersby.

EPILOGUE

PATRICIO

That morning in February 2005 promised to be just like all the other mornings. Like always, I was awakened by a mix of howling cats and aches in my bones. Just like every other morning, the first thing I saw when I opened my eyes was a palm tree framed in my bedroom window. That way, for an instant, I was back in Cuba before I returned to reality. I was in my apartment on the outskirts of Madrid, and I had planted that palm tree myself. Luckily, I lived on the second floor, and that lustrous palm tree had only taken a few months to reach my window. My neighbors thought it was a bit of eccentricity, something a crazy old man might do. What did they know.

After turning sixty-five, I had come back to Spain with the money I'd earned when I sold my hardware store. I spent a few years in Asturias, but home made me more nostalgic than happy. I'd finally settled in Madrid, which, being so big, had enough distractions to keep me from getting bogged down in my memories. Not long before, Guzmán and Reina had left the shoe stores to be managed by their daughter and had moved to Key West, to a little house right on the edge of the island. The closest geographic point to Cuba without being in Cuba. Guzmán liked to joke that if Grescas stood at the opening of the bay and looked at the sea from his porch, they could wave at each other. My two friends were as old and as wrinkled as I was, but it had been a real privilege to celebrate our seventieth birthdays with our feet on the ground and not under it, even if each of us was at different points on the planet.

After getting out of bed with a sigh, I went through my routine: shower, shave, breakfast, water the plants, scratch the cat's back, and leave the house to take the metro to the senior center. My plan was to spend the afternoon playing dominoes with the other center regulars: Paquito, Agustín, and Roque. Just another tiring and typical day. Life doesn't hold surprises for us old people anymore. That's reserved for youth.

But I was wrong. On the morning that seemed so much like all the others, my life took a sudden turn.

Everything started with a scent. A perfume like birds of paradise and so many other secret ingredients that a perfume maker had taken to the grave. As soon as it hit my nostrils, my memories transported me immediately to the Malecón. Even though I was in a subway car, I felt my hair tousled by the wind and smelled salt air. I heard the noises from the convertibles, the screeching of the seagulls, and I could almost feel the freshness in my throat and enjoy a really cold cocktail from La Pekinesa with Grescas and Guzmán. I breathed in, hoping it would never stop. The next aroma took me straight to the vestibule at El Encanto, with its inexhaustible parade of women in flowered dresses and elegant hats. And among those women, one in a red dress. The most handsome of all. The most important of all.

I got dizzy with emotion and closed my eyes. That's when I discovered the taste of the sea on my lips was really the salt of my tears. I hadn't realized it, but I'd started to cry, and big teardrops were sliding down my wrinkled cheeks. Those memories had sunk their fangs in my heart.

That was the scent. I thought it had disappeared decades ago. Somewhere on that subway, someone was wearing a perfume I hadn't smelled in decades. It was perfume from El Encanto. It had to be.

I quickly got up. I had to find the source of that scent. A woman and a man who looked like executives gave me strange looks. I suppose, at the very least, I must have seemed a curious sight: a seventy-seven-year-old man traversing a subway car with his nose in the air, sniffing as if he were a bloodhound.

My nose led me to a handsome young woman: an adolescent with dark hair, freckles on her face, her jeans split at the knees, and a nose ring. The girl was transfixed by her cell phone, typing a message into the screen. I sat down beside her and breathed in. There was no doubt; the perfume was coming from her neck and hair.

But who was this woman? How was she wearing a perfume whose last bottle had disappeared years before?

"Next station: Iglesia," announced the subway car speaker.

The girl stood up to get off, and on an impulse, I jumped off the train to go after her. "Hey!"

The girl turned around and looked at me. She had beautiful blue eyes. "Yes?"

"This is gonna sound as strange as anything, but you smell like butterflies."

She looked at me as if I were crazy. "Excuse me?"

"It's a flower—mariposa—that used to grow in Havana. They used it in a perfume at one of their great stores. I hadn't smelled anything like it in many years."

"It's from an old bottle my aunt had."

"You smell of another time. A time that doesn't exist anymore."

The two of us remained still, not knowing what to say next. The young woman took a quick glance at her watch. It was obvious she had things to do, but she didn't want to be rude.

"Don't leave just yet, please," I whimpered like a little boy. "If you leave, El Encanto will disappear with you."

A pair of tears slid off my white eyelashes. Touched, the girl lifted her wrist so I could smell it. I pressed my nose to her skin and closed my eyes. After all these years, Gloria was at my side again. We were kissing on the roof of the great store while everyone watched television several floors below. We were embracing next to the fountain of frogs in the jungle courtyard at the Tropicana. We were making love at El Encanto the night of the great blackout.

"The woman of my dreams wore this perfume," I told her. "Her name was Gloria Valdés, and she was from Havana. She had a lot of freckles, like you. She died in a fire."

When I opened my eyes again, the girl was smiling at me. "My name is Leire. Can I buy you a cup of coffee?"

We left the metro station via the exit that leads to Saint Isabel church and headed straight for Santa Engracia Street toward the little Alonso Martínez Plaza. The girl was patient with my slow old man's step, and she walked slower to go at my pace. As we crossed the Plaza de Chamberi, she offered me her arm when I stumbled on a loose paving stone. I was glad to hold on to her. The way she smelled and her excellent manners made me grow fond of her immediately.

"I need you to go somewhere with me," she said enigmatically. "But I can't tell you much more than that. I don't wanna get your hopes up."

"At my age, hope is a rare visitor."

We went down the street for a good ways until we were right in front of the monastery at Visitación. The building was atypical, with a square arch full of apartments that went into a small garden and from there led to a kind of terrace. The girl and I went inside and took the elevator to the fourth floor. She took a key from her bag, and we entered an apartment.

As soon as we stepped in, we were received by another cloud of perfume from El Encanto. It was an old and elegant apartment with very tall ceilings and visible beams, white walls, and creaky wooden floors. Two enormous banana plants flanked the door and gave the place a colonial feel. I could hear the trills of a little parakeet from a back room, which made it seem even more as if I'd just taken a journey to the tropics.

"Wait here one moment," Leire told me. "Let me get my aunt."

I waited in the vestibule. There was a framed photograph of the castle at El Morro and a little stamp of Cachita, the Virgin of Charity from Cobre. No question: a Cuban family must have lived there. I was received by two round little dogs that looked like meatballs, just mutts leaping all over me to get my attention. I was petting them when I heard a voice that, just like the perfume, stirred my entire being.

"Patricio!"

It was Daniela. She must've been about sixty-five years old, but in spite of her white hair, her serene green eyes were the same. We just stood there, looking at each other like a pair of fools. I don't know who took the first step, but suddenly we were embracing and crying, laughing and leaping—everything at once.

"What are you doing here?" exclaimed Daniela as she wiped her nose. "How is it possible?"

"We met by chance on the subway," said Leire. "When you mentioned the fire and Gloria Valdés, I thought you could be Patricio Rubio. You were a kind of legend in our family."

"Is this your daughter?" I asked Daniela.

"My niece. She's Gabriel's daughter."

My granddaughter. My heart wasn't ready for a jolt like this, and I got so weak, my legs began to tremble. Daniela and Leire must've seen the color leave my face because they each grabbed me by an arm to hold me up.

"It would be best if we sat down," said Leire with a smile.

Some time and a teapot later, I had recovered the color in my face. We sat in the living room, which was a small jungle filled with tropical trees and plants.

"My great-grandmother, Lala, had a beautiful garden," said Daniela, laughing. "I suppose this is my way of honoring her."

The two little dogs ran around our feet as Daniela and Leire each took one of my hands. Luckily, they'd turned on the overhead fan, and I was getting enough air so I wouldn't almost pass out again.

"I've known you're my grandfather since I was a little girl," said Leire. "My father and my aunt have told me the story many times."

"Where did you go after you escaped from Cuba?" Daniela asked me.

"I was in the Dominican Republic. And then Florida for many years, taken in by a friend of mine. Then I came to Madrid."

"Have you ever gone back to Havana?" inquired Leire.

"About twenty years later, after the statute of limitations was up on my crime."

I looked at Leire, not sure if I was revealing too much, but my granddaughter looked back at me with complicity.

"It's okay. I know my aunt shot César Valdés."

"I searched for you, but I didn't have any luck," I said.

"We also had to leave Cuba." Daniela sighed at the memory. "My father, César, still had a lot of friends, but he also had a lot of enemies who would've taken advantage of his death—and his kids. We grabbed all the money we could and fled to Argentina. Gabriel grew up there."

"What does he do?"

"He was an aeronautics engineer with the national Argentine airline," answered Leire. "He married my mother, Nadia, and they had me. When I was little, he got a job here in Madrid, so we moved."

I squeezed Leire's hand a little tighter, afraid my recently found granddaughter would disappear if I let her go.

"I have a granddaughter!" I murmured. "It's just that I still don't believe it." Leire kissed me on the cheek, her young, soft skin against mine, which was considerably more leathery thanks to the years. "This is incredible." I turned to Daniela. "And what about you? Did you ever get married?"

Daniela laughed and kissed my other cheek. "No. But I did everything you told me, and I've had a life in which I've studied, traveled, and enjoyed myself. After I retired, I started working in a shelter for abandoned animals. I've always preferred having dogs to children. That way, César's bloodline can die with me. I think that would complete my great-grandmother's vengeance."

I couldn't help but admire Daniela. She'd inherited her strong character from her father, but not his cruelty or malice. *Gloria would have been so proud*, I thought. Remembering her mother made me choke, and I let go of her hand and had to take a sip of tea so I could speak again.

"I spent half a lifetime asking myself where Gloria is buried. I searched Colón Cemetery in Havana from one end to the other, but I never managed to find her gravesite."

Daniela and Leire shared a look of astonishment.

"My God. Of course, you don't know . . . ," said Daniela.

"Know what?"

"That Gloria's alive."

As she said those words, time stopped for me. My fingers let go of the teacup, which fell to the wooden floor and scared the two little dogs.

The pain of Gloria's death had been so intense, I had tried to avoid thinking about her so I could survive. But now the dam broke, and all the feelings I'd experienced with her came back to me, alive and real: her hands clutching mine as our nude bodies exploded from pleasure, the delight of connecting a constellation of freckles on her back with my fingers, her breath on my neck, the softness of her hair caressing my skin, and our stolen kisses, each and every one of them.

"It's not possible," I stammered. "She died in the fire, in my arms."

"When they put her in the ambulance, she seemed dead. Yes. But at the hospital, they managed to bring her back. It was nothing less than a miracle. She was on the verge of death for days. Smoke inhalation almost killed her, but she survived. All three of us left for Argentina—my mother, Gabriel, and I. But, so César's enemies couldn't find her, she started using a family surname, Beiro."

"How is she?"

"She's got lung problems, arthritis, and diabetes, but you know the saying: delicate health, made of steel. Except for the usual things that come with age, she's like a rose. In fact, she still works as a consultant for the observatory when she feels strong enough."

"What?"

"Didn't you know? Gloria discovered a star. She'd been observing it half her life until we convinced her to send the Royal Astronomy Society and the International Astronomical Union her notes. It turned out the star hadn't been catalogued, so they gave it her name: Gloria."

"Where is she? Is she still in Argentina? Has she gone back to Cuba? Does she live far from here?" I asked breathlessly.

Each and every one of the cells in my body was clamoring to be with her. Now that I knew she was alive, every second I wasn't with Gloria burned my chest like a hot iron. I was afraid they were going to tell me she lived on the other side of the world, and I was getting ready to make plans to get a taxi that very instant and take a plane to China—tigers and all—so I could be with her as soon as possible. But Daniela and Leire were both smiling grandly.

"Gloria lives upstairs."

GLORIA

In my dreams, I'm not an old woman. My hands are not wrinkled; my freckles are not faded. My hair is so black, it has a blue sheen, just like crows' feathers. I am still wearing Christian Dior dresses cinched at my tiny waist instead of hiding my softer flesh under a loose robe. When I dream, I'm young and pretty, and Daniela and Gabriel are still children in my arms. My parents are alive and manage their sweet shop in Old Havana. Lala lives in a house with a tremendous garden full of all kinds of herbs and spices so she can practice her Santeria. We all live in an impossible Cuba, in which elements from many different periods mix and coincide. When you're old, time turns into a blend of sensations and memories in your head.

In the Havana of my dreams, El Encanto never burned down.

Patricio and I never separated. We live in a house with a bedroom just like the one in the home section at El Encanto where we made love for the first time. I've never dreamed about César. Not even once. I suspect this is Lala's work, that she uses her witchcraft from beyond to protect my dreams.

The clock on the wall plays a happy melody. It's midafternoon, and I'm taking a nap on the living room couch. In a little while, I'll get up and visit Daniela, like I do every afternoon. We'll probably take a stroll to the Plaza de Chamberi, and we'll sit on the porch at La Contenta and drink a Coca-Cola. After that, we'll go to the supermarket to buy some hake fillets and bread them for dinner. Maybe I'll even find ground corn and make us some tamales. If Leire is home, I'll take her a few. And the pan de gloria I made yesterday. That girl loves pan de gloria. If only she could've tasted the one my mother made. Later, when I come home for the night, I'll watch television for a while. I think tonight there's that program in which famous people dance. Then I'll go up to the roof with my telescope. The Gloria star has been shining more intensely than ever, and I'd like to know why.

I try to wake up, but my back is bothering me, and I want to nap for a little while longer. That's why, when I hear his voice, I'm sure I'm dreaming.

"Hello, my Gloria."

My name on his lips. I'm so sure I'm still dreaming, I don't even open my eyes. "Patricio, is that you?"

His hand takes mine, and I think my heart has stopped beating. My skin has its own memory, and it recognizes Patricio's skin. Maybe I'm not asleep. Maybe I'm dead, and I've suddenly arrived in heaven.

"The same as always, my love."

The sound of his voice makes the ache in my bones vanish. Everything that was wrong with me is suddenly cured as if by magic. I haven't felt this alive in years, in decades.

"It's impossible. I must be dreaming."

"It's no dream. Open your eyes."

"I can't. I don't want to. I don't dare. I'm afraid if I open them, you won't be there," I confess.

"I'll be here, my love. But I should warn you that I'm very old."

"Like me. Wrinkled up like a raisin."

"You're beautiful. Open your eyes, my sweetheart."

"Only if you promise me we'll be apart never again."

Patricio squeezes my hand so tightly, I'm afraid the bones of my fingers, as fragile as a bird's skeleton, will break. I hear him sit on the couch by my side, and I feel the warmth of his body near mine.

"Never again," he says. "It's taken us an entire lifetime, but we're finally together."

"Life has brought us this final gift as a reward for surviving everything without surrender."

"That's funny. That's precisely what you told me when we met, that I'm not the sort who gives up easily."

Patricio kisses me to silence me, and I feel the constellation of stars aligning above our heads to make everything possible. My destiny is to be kissing Patricio here and now. I'm at peace with the universe.

"But we're so old," I protest.

"There's still time," whispers Patricio. "Let's live every second of it. Be brave, my Gloria. Look at me."

I open my eyes.

Patricio, my Patricio, smiles at me.

ACKNOWLEDGMENTS

I would like to express my gratitude to Marcela Serras Guell and to Pepe López Jara. Without them, this book wouldn't exist. Thank you to Editorial Planeta and to Joaquín Álvarez de Toledo for having such faith in me.

A special thank-you goes to Josep Cister, for so much.

To Ana Rosa Semprun, Miryam Galaz, and the entire team at Espasa, who have made this dream come true.

Thank you to El Corte Inglés for the closeness and the magnificent welcome, especially to Jesus Nuño de la Rosa. It was an incredible privilege to receive his impressions and advice.

To Adrian Guerra and Nuria Valls for their help.

To my parents, my family, and my friends. You're all as beautiful as the sun for putting up with me.

And finally, a wink and a nod to all the men and women who worked at El Encanto, whose stories bring that great store back to life forever.

ABOUT THE AUTHOR

Photo © 2017 Asís Ayerbe

Susana López Rubio was born in Madrid, Spain, in 1978. She is a screenwriter who wrote the popular television adaptation of the novel *The Time In Between* by María Dueñas. She writes short stories for adults and children.

ABOUT THE TRANSLATOR

Achy Obejas is the author of *The Tower of the Antilles*, the critically acclaimed novels *Ruins* and *Days of Awe*, and three other books of fiction. Her poetry chapbook, *This Is What Happened in Our Other Life*, was both a critical favorite and a bestseller. As a translator, she has worked with Junot Díaz, Wendy Guerra, Rita Indiana, and many others. In 2014 she received the USA Ford Fellowship from USA Artists for both her writing and her translations. She's written for, among others, the *New York Times*, *Vanity Fair*, the *Village Voice*, *In These Times*, and the *Chicago Tribune*, where she was part of a 2001 Pulitzer Prize–winning team. Born in Havana, she currently resides in the San Francisco Bay Area.